A GLIMMER

THROUGH THE

BREACH

Juliet Ayres

Metal House Press

First published in Great Britain in 2022 by Metal House Press

This book is a work of fiction. Although certain institutions, businesses, locations, public figures or events may be real, the novel's story, characters and dialogue are purely fictitious. The opinions expressed are those of the characters and should not be confused with the author's. In relation to any facts included, every attempt has been made to verify them against reliable documentation.

A CIP catalogue record for this book is available from the British Library.

ISBN: 978-1-7391853-0-5 *(paperback)*
ISBN: 978-1-7391853-1-2 *(hardcover)*
ISBN: 978-1-7391853-2-9 *(eBook)*

Cover image used under license from Crystal Eye Studio/Shutterstock.com

Metal House Press, Manchester
metalhousepress@gmail.com
Author's website: www.julietayres.com

SCAN ME

CHAPTER 1

Friday, 14 March 2008

Trish and Tony Wilcox were on a mission of a lifetime to a holiday they could ill afford. They had spotted the heavily-discounted package offer in a tabloid newspaper and thought, *What the hell?*

"Ladies and gentlemen, this is your captain speaking, letting you know we'll be making preparations for our descent into Naples in approximately twenty minutes. We expect to have you on the ground around half past twelve local time. If you haven't already set your watches, this is a good time to do so. It is now 11:15 a.m. and considerably warmer in Naples than in Manchester today at twenty-six degrees Celsius. On behalf of myself and the cabin crew, we thank you for flying with us and hope to see you again soon."

Trish closed her eyes, trying to put a face to the captain's aphrodisiac voice. "Mmm, he sounds dreamy! Why can't you talk more like him?" she asked Tony, overlooking the fact her own Mancunian accent was thicker than his.

"And why can't you try zipping it for a change?" Tony retorted to his ever-complaining wife as he leafed through the duty-free magazine.

Trish stretched her legs and wriggled her ankles. "Bloody hell, look at my feet! I'll never get my sandals on now."

"Serves you right. Didn't I tell you to wear your flight socks and dump the heels? But would you listen?"

"Can't wait to see the hotel," Trish said, browsing through the Palazzo Napoli brochure. "It looks brilliant!" Raising her wrist, she glanced at her pink-strapped watch. "We'll be landing soon. Dying for a cig." Delving into her cavernous handbag, she pulled out a pair of red glass rosary beads. To ensure a safe landing, she thumbed the beads as she whispered the Hail Mary.

The holiday to Naples meant a lot to the couple, Tony especially. It had been his lifelong wish to find Fabio Bianchi – the Neapolitan father he had never known.

Trish and Tony lived on Manchester's Sharrinwood council estate. For them, Sharrinwood was a different world to how the media portrayed it.

"Nowt wrong with Sharry. Bloody reporters, they make half of it up!" Trish would snap.

Tony would echo her sentiments. At least this was one viewpoint on which they agreed. Sharrinwood was their life – where they worked, socialised, built relationships, raised their family, and buried loved ones. There may well have been some undesirables on the estate, as there are on any, but no one with whom Trish and Tony associated. They chose their friends carefully.

To Trish and Tony, Sharrinwood was vibrant with a warm community spirit, lush with pretty parks and woodland areas short bus rides away. Sharrinwood was designed to be a leafy suburb; not that it achieved that goal considering its leafiness was punctuated with poorly-designed high rise flats and it was flawed by crime.

Although Trish was happy enough living on the estate, she sometimes felt uncomfortable admitting where she lived to certain middle-class people. The reactions from most were of indifference, but from some came a sense of awkwardness with an urgency to change the subject. Much to Trish's disappointment in herself, she sometimes found herself saying she lived on a private estate over the border.

Tony would tick her off. "You should be proud of who you are and where you're from. If people look down on you 'cos you're from Sharry, they ain't worth knowing!"

And Trish would think how ironic coming from him.

Trish was an Adult Education classroom assistant. She sometimes philosophised about the differences between her basic communication to that of the higher echelons of the establishment. The accentless voices were like liquid gold to her; if only the content was as captivating. For her, middle-class conversation, particularly topics about world affairs and the weather, bored her senseless. She found them grey, icy and insincere, as if the focus was to impress rather than say what they truly believed. She noticed how meaningful topics such as divorce, abortion, addictions or terminal illness were swiftly avoided. Working-class conversation, on the other hand, was colourful, warm and transparent. Trish by far preferred conversing with people who were candid about their feelings – those who could tell anybody anything without the worry of saying the wrong thing. *My husband ran off with a slapper but I'm gonna get sloshed tonight and forget my troubles.* At least such folk were genuine, approachable and free from airs. Trish vowed if she ever won the lottery, she would forever remain working class and stick with Sharrinwood people.

* * *

Hannah and Saul Bernstein were also from Manchester. Their lifestyle in leafy Didsbury, however, was worlds apart from Trish and Tony's.

After disembarking the same flight as the Wilcoxes and settling into the same hotel, they boarded the Naples to Sorrento train to explore the town of lemons.

Two local boys with accordions draped around their necks boarded the train, headed for the gangway connection and began playing popular Neapolitan tunes. They were no older than twelve, yet going by their talent and wise brown eyes, they appeared much older.

"Sad, isn't it?" Hannah rummaged in her backpack for her purse. "The poor mites lack proper guidance on the importance of education. No wonder they look so sad."

Saul rolled his eyes. "Giving them money will encourage them to truant." Saul was not merely Conservative in politics; he was conservative in his attire. His grey linen jacket, colour-coordinated trousers and white shirt – always impeccably ironed – reflected his high standards. His skullcap publicly declared his Jewish faith.

"Maybe they have to," Hannah said pointedly. "Maybe they need to earn money for an ailing mother or sibling."

No sooner had the boys collected money from passengers and disembarked, than two new buskers boarded – one carrying a saxophone, the other with an accordion around his neck.

"Are you going to feel sorry for them as well, dear?" Saul quipped.

"Of course not. They're grown men."

From Stazione di Sorrento, the couple followed their map to Piazza Tasso. From the piazza, narrow, characterful streets drew them like magnets where their eyes met a blaze of sunshine colour. Myriad lemons greeted them in every shape, form and size, created into everything imaginable from lemon soaps, lemon tea towels, lemon crockery, lemon candy to lemon jewellery. Fresh whole lemons were especially in abundance, decoratively draped around doorways and windows and counters like works of art.

"How on earth do they survive when there's so much competition?" Hannah asked rhetorically.

"I guess there are enough tourists who are stupid enough to pay extortionate prices for lemons. What lemons!" Saul chuckled at his own joke, which went unnoticed.

Hannah was too preoccupied with an impressive ice cream parlour that offered gluten-free options. Such temptations to a coeliac were like candy to a child. "Oh, look! Gluten-free ice cream, and it says you can try before you buy. Let's go in!" Without further ado, she tugged Saul's jacket sleeve, guiding him to the counter.

Clearly labelled and appetisingly displayed were a wide range of options – classics as well as innovative flavours.

Wide eyed, Hannah marvelled at them. "Gosh, I'm spoilt for choice. I quite fancy the figs and ricotta. But look at the pistachio!"

"So have a scoop of each." Saul chose limoncello, keen to experience regional flavours.

Having heeded Saul's advice and licked every morsel clean, Hannah shamelessly hinted at buying another.

"C'mon, dear," Saul said. "You can always have another later. Let's head for the bus before we miss it."

And so, adhering to their cram-packed itinerary, they took a tour bus along the Amalfi Coast to experience the breathtaking clifftop views, stopping at Positano with its striking multi-coloured clifftop village.

"Looking forward to Pompeii tomorrow, aren't you, dear?" Saul asked.

"Absolutely," Hannah said enthusiastically. "Mount Vesuvius should be quite an experience too. Must remember to be appropriately attired and pack necessities. I'll make a list."

CHAPTER 2

The clickety-click of high heels on the marble foyer floor crescendoed, followed by a deafening squeal.

"Oh … my … God! This is a palace!"

Guests queuing to check in stifled giggles. A couple of British teenage girls, however, allowed theirs to unashamedly splutter out as they nudged each other, giggling even louder.

Tony hung his head, whispering through gritted teeth. "Shurrup, will ya'. You're showing me up."

"Don't be such a misery. Look at it, will you!"

"I can see it. I'm not blind. Just don't make such a bloody fuss." Taking two steps forward, they moved up the queue. "Anyone'd think you've never been in a hotel before."

"Well, none as posh as this, we haven't. I can't believe it!"

The five-star Palazzo Napoli, overlooking the Gulf of Naples and Mount Vesuvius, was a far cry from the two and three-star hotels they had frequented in the Costa del Sol. But this time was not about beach and poolside sunbathing: it was a cultural holiday with the additional intention of exploring Fabio Bianchi's hometown and possibly tracing him. Tony would have preferred to utilise *every* day searching for him. Trish, however, following the advice of their travel-agent daughter, was keen to pack Sorrento, the Amalfi Coast, Capri, Pompeii and Mount Vesuvius into their itinerary.

"It'll be good to see the places he visited. You want to learn about his life, don't you?" Trish urged.

After settling into their room, showering and changing into shorts and T-shirts, the couple embarked on their first day's adventure. Considering Tony's desperation to visit his father's hometown, Trish agreed on making it their first port of call.

Ponticelli, however, turned out to be a let-down, nondescript inner city. The most interesting aspect about it came from a conversation they overheard between a couple of English-speaking women. There had apparently been a feud between local Neapolitans and a large number of Roma gypsies who had formed numerous campsites in the district.

"Sounds rough." Tony pondered about the type of house and area in which Fabio lived. "Shame we couldn't get his address. For all we know he could live miles from Ponticelli by now, if he ever lived here at all. All my mam said was she thought he lived in a place in Naples that sounded like Ponticelli. Could be anywhere really."

And so, with a feeling of despondency, they caught the return bus to Naples. Shortly after arriving, they jumped on a Hop-on-Hop-off tour bus. Although numerous buildings were of historical value and cultural significance, they were in dire need of refurbishment. All Trish and Tony saw was the dilapidation, buildings defaced with graffiti and collarless dogs roaming freely, fouling streets.

Trish pointed to the colourful bunting of laundry hanging over balconies and across streets. "Look at that! It's like a slum!"

"I thought they said Naples was a UNESCO World Heritage site? They must've been having a laugh," Tony said, holding up his splayed hands.

"Yeah, like see Naples and die. Die from what? The shock of what a dump it is?" Trish shrugged her shoulders.

"Or getting killed by a Neapolitan driver!" Tony laughed.

"Or stabbed by the Mafia," added Trish, laughing even louder.

Tony, however, became distracted from their joviality. Nudging Trish, he whispered, "Have you noticed the poofs?"

"What've I told you about that? Shut it! What are you on about anyway?" Trish asked, looking from left to right to detect his source of irritation.

A couple of young Neapolitan men walked with their arms around each other. In Naples, displays of affection between young heterosexual males were not unusual, but it was new to Tony. At least he had been forewarned about Neapolitan road madness.

Paulo, the taxi driver, who had driven them to their hotel from the airport, afforded them their first taste of this by texting whilst driving, and driving at breakneck speed.

As Trish clung to the edge of her seat, Tony commented that such driving would be illegal in Britain.

Paulo laughed reassuringly. "Ahh, no you worry. I great a driver." Having taken the last drag of his cigarette, he tossed it through the window.

One less distraction, Trish thought as she fished out her own ciggies to calm her nerves. "Okay if I smoke?"

"Si, va bene."

Trish lit up and took a long drag of her Mayfair King Size. "There's loads of scooters and mopeds here."

"Ah, you must have the motorbike in Napoli. È necessario. I have a three."

In fairness to Naples, it held a certain charm that Trish and Tony were warming to. Like the Artful Dodger, despite being rough and ready, grimy and neglected, both were endearing and oozed character. The streets may well have been dilapidated and filled with chaotic madness, but they were vibrant, charming and authentic – real Italy without the polished commercialism.

On the tour bus, Tony listened studiously to a pre-recorded commentary via complimentary headphones. He was hungry to grasp flavours of his father's culture and especially relished snippets about Neapolitan superstitions. "Ha, you think you're superstitious," he said to Trish. "The Neapolitans have a saying about superstitions – *It's not true, but I believe it.* Oh, and did you hear that? It says Naples is a musical city. Funny that 'cos I've not seen a single busker. Have you?"

Naples, however, did not need buskers: the cacophony of frenzied traffic made its own music with melodic beeping of horns in a repertoire of rhythms and beats reflecting drivers' moods. Stravinsky might have composed the music as a choreographer might have choreographed the vehicles' dances – zigzagging, twisting, turning, stopping and starting. The ease at which motorcycles weaved in and out of miniscule spaces between large vehicles caused tourists to shut their eyes tight in dread.

Unsurprisingly, Fiats ruled the roost, especially Fiat 500s that buzzed around like busy ants. For Trish, the cherry on the cake was spotting a bride in a shiny red Fiat 500 convertible holding up a frilly white parasol as she waved to delighted onlookers.

And so, by the end of their city tour, Trish and Tony had fallen in love with charismatic Naples.

Later, they dined at an authentically Neapolitan restaurant with red gingham tablecloths and dark bentwood bistro chairs. At the recommendation of a waistcoated waiter, they ordered cannelloni with pesto and béchamel sauce which they devoured with relish. They had not, however, relished the idea of smoking their after-dinner ciggies in the restaurant alleyway. Ever since England's introduction of the smoking ban in public places almost a year earlier, they had lost interest in eating out. Little did they know that Italy was the first EU country to introduce the smoking ban.

"May as well cut this short if we can't have a smoke. It's like a bloody endurance test having a drink without one," Tony barked. "Let's go back to the hotel."

And so they enjoyed their ciggies whilst strolling through the narrow cobbled streets from which wafted the aromas of pizzas and espressos.

CHAPTER 3

Saturday morning, 15 March 2008

A queue formed in Palazzo Napoli's foyer for the Pompeii tour. The itinerary was to take a seventeen-mile guided coach tour to Pompeii and Mount Vesuvius, stopping en route to enjoy packed lunches the hotel had provided.

After stoking themselves up for the day with a hearty breakfast, Trish and Tony joined the queue to await their tour guide Rosaria.

A Neapolitan mandolin piece 'Core 'ngrato' played softly in the background.

"Oh, I love this! It's one of my mam's favourites. She loved Mario Lanza. Catarì, Catarì, daa, dee, daa, daa," came Trish's rendition recited in the voice of a crow.

"For God's sake woman, shurrup, will you. You're showing me up!" Lowering his head, Tony looked around to check if anyone had noticed.

"You're just jealous 'cos you can't sing as well," she cackled mischievously. "Catarì, Catarì, daa, dee, daa."

Many times Trish had tolerated Tony's singing as he strummed his guitar, but at least his singing voice was bearable. Although it was not as piercing as Trish's, he compensated with his loud attire, sporting a psychedelic pink and purple floral shirt with cringe-worthy, clashing orange shorts, white trainers and black ankle-socks. Trish had given up trying to teach him colour co-ordination. Waste of time. He would never get it. At least his questionable dress sense had not reached his hairstyle. Rather than conceal his bald patch with a dubious comb-over, Tony sported a trendy number one buzz cut. Shame he spoilt it with a fluorescent green baseball cap with 'Let's Rock' printed across the front. Tony considered himself the bees' knees, but Trish knew better.

A couple of young Italian men, arm in arm, minced passed them.

Tony shot them a look of contempt.

"Oi, don't start!" Trish hissed with a death stare.

Tony took heed, fully aware of the consequences of pushing the boundaries where homophobic comments were concerned.

"Oh no!" Trish gasped, clapping her hand to her forehead. "I've forgotten my sun specs! Better get 'em!"

"What? Where from?"

"Our room. I'm dying for a wee too. Won't be long," she said, teetering on her heels to the staircase.

"Be quick!" he called after her. "Coach leaves at half ten."

Their room was on the fifth floor and Trish winced at the idea of taking the stairs. She dashed toward the lift, but soon regretted her decision.

"Bloody lifts! C'mon! C'mon!" She crossed her legs, wiggling discreetly. "Argh, can't wait! Bloody typical!" Looking around, she spotted the ladies' room a few yards down the corridor and made a dash for them.

As she entered, a heady scent of lemons, orange blossom and jasmine hit her. She looked around to find the source of the fragrance wafting through two small, half opened, opaque windows from which peeped white-petalled orange blossom. Through the window openings, she caught sight of a landscaped garden with an array of ornamental trees, fragrant shrubs, lemon groves, and a large pond adorned with lily petals and a central fountain.

The garden's vibrant colours sharply contrasted with the room's white marble and gigantic glass chandelier suspended from the ceiling. A long, white marble countertop sat on gold tubular-legged frames. Set within it were ten oblong wash basins with gold taps. On the right of each stood luxurious liquid soaps and hand creams; on the left, crisp white towels rolled onto gilded trays.

Although Trish could not fail to miss the splendour that hit her, she was too desperate for the toilet to fully absorb it, and dashed into the first available cubicle.

As her cubicle door closed, the adjacent one swung open, from which Hannah rushed out, heading to the wash basins. Glancing in the mirror, she adjusted her short, dark hair before washing her hands with the sweet-smelling soap.

Presently, Trish followed, choosing a wash basin on Hannah's left.

There they stood side by side, both from Manchester, of similar age and short height, but poles apart in every other way possible. Hannah prided herself in having the same slim figure of her university days – testimony of her healthy diet and lifestyle. Trish's surplus weight, however, suggested a greater calorie intake than calories burned and endless hours of screen-viewing.

Hannah's greying hair was untouched by colourants whereas Trish's, going by her inch-length grey roots, was a brassy bottle-blonde with platinum ends brushing her shoulders. Trish strived to look younger than her fifty-five years, but failed miserably. The aftermath of sunbathing on Ibiza's beaches and countless sunbed top-ups was written all over her wrinkles; and her upper-lip smoker's lines, together with her deep, croaky voice was testimony to her years of heavy smoking.

Glancing in the mirror's reflection, the women exchanged tentative smiles. They had never met, yet their eyes indicated a flicker of recognition; unsurprising since they had shared the same flight and eaten in the same breakfast restaurant.

Fancy coming out like that on your hols! Trish thought. *Bloody walking boots, gardener's hat and shorts from the ark. She looks a right drip.*

At least feelings were mutual. Hannah inwardly grimaced at Trish's Chinese dragon tattoo on her forearm. *Dreadful enough, but at her age! Not even my offspring would dream of having a tattoo – well, apart from Sadie, but then she always was the rebel.* Hannah recalled how she and Saul vehemently objected to Sadie's suggestion of having a small butterfly tattoo on the back of her neck and how she defied them, arguing it was "body art" and "everyone has them".

Yes, everyone Sadie chose to associate with, Hannah thought.

Remembering the clickity-clack of heels, Hannah lowered her gaze to Trish's feet. *How on earth does she expect to get around Pompeii in those? You'd think she was attending a fashion show. That excess weight isn't going to help either.*

Hannah applied sun block to her face and arms. Apart from her platinum wedding ring and engagement ring, her hands and fingernails were as bare as her face.

Trish, having touched up her hot pink lipstick, pressed her lips together and widened her eyes to check her spikes of thick mascara had not run. Around her neck hung a gold crucifix and silver Saint Christopher medal. For luck, she rubbed them momentarily between her thumb and forefinger. Her long nail extensions with flowers printed on them, matched her equally adorned fingers that flashed yellow gold rings with various semi-precious stones.

Whereas Trish and Tony left school at fifteen without a qualification to their names, and now struggled on minimum wages, Hannah and Saul were high-income professionals. Hannah was a pharmacist with two degrees and postgraduate qualifications behind her name. Saul, equally qualified, was director of a leading pharmaceutical company.

Trish was a 'staunch' Labour supporter despite rarely, if ever, voting; Hannah a true-blue Conservative.

Trish was a Catholic and Hannah a Jew.

Although both Mancunians, they were socially and culturally worlds apart. Whereas Trish lived on the Sharrinwood council estate, Hannah lived in middle-class Didsbury. Being Manchester's most affluent suburb, it was considered to form a 'stockbroker belt'. Affluence, however, was not Didsbury's dominant factor: its cultural wealth and diversity dominated, proud to be the past and present hometown of notable people, including poet laureate Carol Ann Duffy; novelist and journalist Howard Spring; and promoter of the Manchester Ship Canal, Daniel Adamson. Didsbury, with its conservation areas, palatial mansions and listed buildings was a suburb that oozed character and soul. Didsbury was subtlety colourful with its red brick Victorian mansions; silver-grey turreted slate roofs; stunning stained-glass windows; lavender-blue wisteria adorning impressive porchways; and green summertime lanes bursting into stunning reds, oranges and yellows in autumn.

Colour also featured in Sharrinwood streets, green especially from the council-planted trees and privet hedging. Neighbourhood gardens, on which Trish modelled her own, were filled with multi-coloured, annual bedding plants with cute little garden gnomes that waved at passers-by.

Sharrinwood colours were not entirely horticultural in nature, but also sporty, patriotic and festive. During the football season, giant red and white England flags wafted proudly from the bedroom windows of loyal football fans. One patriotic family made their enthusiasm more permanent by painting the entire gable end of their house with a gigantic Union Jack.

It had to be said, however, that the season of goodwill was by far the most colourful time in Sharrinwood. Spectacular displays of giant-size flashing reindeer, twinkling Christmas trees and Santa legs popping out of chimney-tops illuminated the front gardens of Christmas enthusiasts. Rooftops, windows and door frames would be festooned with strings of flashing lights that must have taken an eternity to install. Some locals considered the displays cheap and vulgar, but the majority relished them as the next best thing to Blackpool Illuminations. Families would use them as an excuse for a drive out, touring the streets in search of the most impressive displays.

Many Sharrinwood tenants took pride in their estate's colourful vibrancy, and some took even greater pride in their homes. A small minority, however, did not. Abandoned car tyres, mattresses and rubbish littered their 'gardens', and their window panes were practically opaque with grime.

Tenants who took pride in their homes complained bitterly that such neighbours lowered the calibre of their streets. "What's the point of making an effort when the garden next door looks like a jungle?"

Regardless of such problem neighbours, pride in one's home was dampened when deprived of the autonomy to even choose the colour of one's front door. For some Sharrinwood tenants who wished to improve the aesthetics and calibre of their estate, they believed this was made possible by Margaret Thatcher's 'Right to Buy' scheme. The scheme enabled long-term tenants to buy their council homes at a fraction of the market value, and numerous discerning tenants pounced at the opportunity. Such former council houses thereafter could be spotted a mile off oozing with pride. No longer were front doors branded the council's uniform colour, but shone individuality. Alongside such newfound autonomy and pride sprung smart building extensions, garages and garden gates. Such qualities that improved the calibre of the estate were as contagious as the hitherto poisonous influences that dragged it down.

Ordinarily, Hannah and Trish's chalk and cheese socioeconomic backgrounds would never have brought them together in a month of Sundays, but today was different. Today they would begin to discover how they had more in common than they could ever have imagined, yet at the same time become acutely aware of their myriad social class differences.

"Nice here, intit?" Trish chirped.

"Yes, it certainly ..." Hannah's reply was cut short as their smiles morphed into contorted screams.

CHAPTER 4

As the room danced and groaned, terror stabbed their hearts; as the ground shook the foundations, they clung to the basins; as items flew in all directions, their minds worked triple speed. Towel trays, soap bottles and hand creams hurled, smashing to the ground as everything around them reeled and spun. In unison, they screamed in terror. But their screams were lost beneath rumbling roars.

"Oh my God! Get down!" Trish yelled.

In dazed haste, the women dropped to their knees, scrambled under the washstands and grabbed onto the tubular-legged frames for their lives. Flying debris shot from all directions. From above drooped a plasterboard ceiling with metal grids and air conditioning ducting, and electrical cables that powered the wall lights and chandelier. Like a hypnotist's pendulum, the spectacular chandelier swung to and fro, to and fro before playing tinkling tunes on its descent. Like the crescendo of crashing cymbals in Tchaikovsky's '1812 Overture', a dramatic finale ensued as it smashed to the ground. Small, heavy items flew with force. Larger, lightweight ones tumbled and collapsed in slow motion. Although the room had dimmed, miraculously, the wall and toilet cubicle lights continued to glow.

After scanning around for refuge, the women decided their current position was as good as any. To block out the horrors, they squatted into tight balls and squeezed their eyes shut. But there was no escape. Bereft of vision, other senses intensified the unfolding horrors around them: the sound of roars and crashes; the smell and taste of dust in the air raining down on them; the feeling of tightness in their lungs; grit on their skin and clothes; and debris tumbling towards them trapping the lower half of their bodies like quicksand. Although they were close enough to touch hands and hear each other, they were trapped in their own enclave. If they could free themselves, at least there would be head room, albeit in a crouching position as electrical cables hung precariously like live barbed-wire.

Titanic crossed Hannah's mind as the ground sloped like the deck of a sinking ship. Hand-cream bottles rolled across the floor, stopping and turning around obstructive shards of broken glass and other debris. Trish crossed herself, not caring whether the woman noticed.

At least the terror and shock overrode physical pain. Only later when their terror ebbed, would they feel it. As dust filled the room, their hair grew as ashen as Miss Havisham's and their eyes glistened with hot tears. As fits of coughing punctuated their screams, the washroom exhaled its last breath. Replacing the floral fragrances, a defiled stench of dust, debris and death erupted.

No sooner had the tremor struck, than silence fell upon them. Had it not been for the creaking walls and ceilings complaining of disturbance, for the women's wheezing and spluttering, and for rolling objects reaching their final destination – had it not been for these sombre sounds, the silence would have been deafening.

Before screaming once again for their lives, the women listened expectantly for any sign of hope. But their hope was in vain considering everyone else in the building was living the same nightmare – if they were lucky enough to be alive.

Time passed in silent baited breath, their minds buzzing. Presently, the women composed themselves and their breathing.

"My God! Are you okay? Can you hear me?" whimpered Trish as she covered her mouth and nose with her dusty hand.

"Yes, I'm okay, thanks," Hannah replied in her cut-glass English accent. "Are *you* okay?"

"Yeah, fine … I think. What was it? An earthquake? Or a bomb?"

"An earthquake. I'm trapped! Can you move at all?"

"Not much, and my legs hurt. And my chest. Oh my God, what do we do? We're gonna be buried alive!"

"No, we're not. Don't worry. Let things settle, then we'll decide what to do. Sure you're okay? Can you feel any blood?"

Probing gingerly, the hapless victims felt as much of their upper bodies as possible before confirming they had sustained nothing more than superficial cuts and bruises. Looking around in disbelief, their eyes darted everywhere for signs of imminent danger.

"Those two doors are shut." Trish's eyes stared at the toilet cubicles. "I wonder if anyone's in there. I didn't see anyone else, did you?"

"No, but someone could have entered before we did. Hello!" Hannah called, "Is anyone in there? Hello!"

"I think it's just the two of us."

"It looks like it. Who are you with?" Hannah asked as she brushed the dust from her face with her fingertips.

"My hubby Tony."

"Does he know where you are?"

"Oh, God, no! I left him in the foyer waiting for the tour bus. I said I was going to our room for my sun specs. So now he's gonna think I'm trapped up there. But I was desperate and noticed this toilet on the way. Who are you with? Do they know where you are?"

"I'm also with my husband. Saul. He knew I was going to the ladies', but I didn't specify which. He's waiting for me in the foyer as well. He nagged me to hurry so we could get good seats on the coach. Let's hope he's okay and can inform others of our whereabouts."

"Look at that toilet with the door ripped off." Trish nodded towards it. "That's the one I used. Oh my God, that could've smashed in my face!" The horror of it and the imminent danger hit her and she let out a pitiful whimper.

"It's okay," Hannah said, through a fit of coughing. "We're fine. Just sit tight and we'll work something out. We need to wait till things settle. In an hour or so, they'll be in a better position to organise a rescue team. No point wasting precious energy getting ourselves worked up. Just stay calm and keep your head protected under your arms. There might be falling debris. I'm Hannah by the way. What's your name?"

Hannah's soothing voice calmed Trish and her breathing slowed. "Patricia, but call me Trish." *What the hell am I gonna talk about with her? We've nowt in common*, she wondered before telling herself not to be stupid – like it mattered when she was at death's door.

CHAPTER 5

Trish rubbed her crucifix and Saint Christopher medal, praying with all her might they would work their miracles. Remembering her rosary beads, she fished them from her bag. Beginning with the sign of the cross and the Apostles' Creed, she continued with a repetitive litany of Hail Marys, Our Fathers and Glory Be's. The more rounds she recited, the greater her chance of survival.

Accepting it could take time before her prayers were answered, she scanned the room for potential exit points. The door from which she had entered was now hidden behind mounds of masonry and rubble. The only glimmer of hope came from one of the windows – now a mere breach. Blocked by blossom trees, shrubbery and masonry from the upper floors, Trish noticed small slithers of light shining through. "Hannah, maybe we could escape through that window."

"I wouldn't have thought so. The opening's much too small and it would be very risky. It would be like opening a can of worms. Besides, freeing ourselves is the priority right now."

"Well, yeah, I know that, but after we've freed ourselves, I mean," Trish said brusquely. She waited for a response, but Hannah offered none. "Are you okay?"

"I'm fine," Hannah replied. "Just a bit of grit in my eye. I need my tissues and wet wipes." On attempting to reach her backpack, she winced. But then she remembered a possible lifesaver and her discomfort vanished. "Our phones! Do you have one? Mine's in my bag, but I can't reach it."

Trish frantically pulled her Nokia from her bag. "No signal. Let's check yours."

"Can you reach my bag?"

Trish stretched as far as possible until her fingertips brushed the strap over Hannah's shoulder. "Can't reach. Move closer."

Hannah edged in a smidgen closer, enabling Trish to free her bag. "Thanks," she said as she urgently rummaged in it for her Motorola. "No signal. Better turn them off to preserve power. Hopefully, we'll get a signal later."

"I've got to reach my kids!" Trish exclaimed in desperation as she continued pressing her phone buttons.

"I'd leave it for now, Trish. Try later when it's more likely to respond."

Little did they know the cell towers had crumbled, deeming any attempts to access signals futile.

After the phone disappointment, Hannah wiped her eye with a wet wipe. "Let's be realistic – it could be days before we're found. If we stay calm and take care, we'll be fine. They'll find us, I'm sure. Do you have any provisions? Saul and I just had a hearty breakfast with the intention of stoking up for the Pompeii …" Hannah's voice trailed off when it occurred to her how close they were to Pompeii and how earthquakes sometimes trigger volcanic eruptions.

"For the Pompeii what?"

"Sorry, I was about to say for the Pompeii tour before realising just how close we are to Vesuvius. I'm sure we've nothing to worry about though."

Trish's eyes widened. "What? You mean an earthquake could start a volcanic eruption? Is that what you're thinking?"

"Don't worry. I'm sure the chances are extremely slim." After wiping her eyes, Hannah wiped her face and hands. "As I was saying, the hotel provided us with a packed lunch and bottled water. They're here in my bag. What about you? Have you had breakfast? Do you have any provisions with you?"

"Yeah. Yeah to both. We were going on the same tour and had the same idea as you – to stoke up for the day, and I've got the packed lunch too. So at least that'll keep us going till we're rescued. Hmm, let's see what we've got." She opened the plastic bag eagerly, peeping into the bread rolls to examine their contents. "Two rolls filled with what looks like ham, salami and roasted peppers. Then there's a boiled egg, an orange, two biscuits and a bottle of water – 500 ml. You've probably got the same 'cos the only difference I could see was for vegetarians."

"Actually, mine may look similar, but they're all gluten-free because I have coeliac disease. I don't require medication as I'm asymptomatic provided I follow a gluten-free diet. Are you on any meds?"

"Just blood pressure pills – Ramipril."

"So you're in reasonably good health apart from hypertension?"

"Yeah, just the high blood pressure. Are you a doctor?"

"I'm a pharmacist. What dosage?"

"Hmm, two milligrams I think, twice a day."

"Do you have them with you?"

"Think so. Hang on." Rummaging to find them caused a raucous clattering of the bag's contents. "Can't find a bloody thing in this bag. Here, see if you can find them." Unexpectedly, she tossed her bag towards Hannah.

The contents of women's handbags, it is said, are a mystery to men. Tony, however, was one of the privileged exceptions. He had, on a number of occasions, had the entire contents of Trish's handbag flaunted at him during her frequent outbursts when searching for mislaid items. And now it was Hannah's turn to witness the mysteries of Trish's mind. Fumbling in the cavernous bag, she felt a steel nail file, a small bottle of Jimmy Choo perfume, a Rimmel lipstick, a tube of lip gloss, a face powder compact with mirror, an empty packet of cigarettes, a string of rosary beads, two used scratch cards, a tube of hand cream, a red purse, a passport, a Nokia phone, a pink comb, reading glasses and a set of keys.

"No, I'm afraid they're not here," Hannah said, returning the bag to Trish.

"Must've left them in my room."

"You'll be fine. It isn't a high dose, so I guess your hypertension isn't too bad. Just try and stay calm otherwise it will be."

"Oh, I've got my watch too. Seems to be working. Twenty-five past ten."

"Good. At least we have a few things in our favour: the time, food and water, reasonably good health with no significant injuries, and each other's company. Also, we're expected on the coach now, so they'll know we're missing from the head count. Not that they'll be thinking of head counts right now, but maybe in an hour or so. Let's consider the worst-case scenario – that it could take as long as a week before we're rescued; in which case, we need to ration our provisions to last that long. We have to be very self-disciplined. How's your will-power?"

"Crap, especially at times like this. I eat like a horse when I'm stressed," Trish confessed.

"I'm the opposite. If you're unlikely to ration, maybe I should keep them safe for you. What do you think?"

"Hmmm, I dunno. How do I know I can trust you?"

"We're in it together and are going to have to trust each other. You have my word that I won't take any of your provisions. I'll merely keep them out of your reach until you *really* need them. Besides, I can't eat your sandwiches because they'll contain gluten. I have to stick with my gluten-free ones."

"Let's see what's in your bag, then," Trish demanded. "You might have a lot more in there that we could share if desperate."

"You clearly don't trust me, do you? I can assure you I have no more than you have. Look!" Hannah thrust her backpack at Trish in Trish-esque style. "Here, if it puts your mind at rest."

Unsurprisingly, Hannah's bag was bereft of cosmetics. There were tissues, wet wipes, a tube of sun block, a black comb, a purse, a small crossword puzzle booklet, a small pair of binoculars, a fold-up cagoule, a passport, a notepad and biro, an Italian dictionary and phrase book, a Pompeii tour pamphlet and the lunch pack.

"Satisfied?" Hannah held out her hand to receive Trish's food and water supply.

"If you insist," Trish replied reluctantly, handing over her packed lunch, drink and Hannah's bag.

"Now, let's see about moving," Hannah suggested. "At least it's only our lower halves that are trapped. Can you move anything? I know it's difficult when we're crouched like this."

"Can just about move my toes and that's a struggle. It kills."

"Do your best. Being in this crouching position isn't helping circulation. Still no bleeding? Just bruising?"

"Just bruising I think. Hurts like mad though."

"We need to prevent crush syndrome as it can be life-threatening."

"What?"

"Don't worry. It's only a risk factor after several hours of being crushed. It'll be fine for now. Let things settle first." Hannah's mind raced, mentally putting safeguards in place. "On second thoughts, more structures could collapse, in which case, better start now. Consider you're walking on eggshells and move items ever so gently, okay?"

Silence.

"Trish?"

Trish was mute, staring into nothing.

Delayed shock, no doubt. "Trish! Trish!" Hannah yelled.

In slow motion, Trish turned her head towards Hannah as if she had heard her for the first time. "Ehh?"

"Trish! Look, dear, you have to listen carefully as I'm trying to help you. Do you think you could do that?"

"Mmm, yeah. But I don't think we're gonna make it."

"Of course we're going to make it. It's going to be just fine. Okay?"

"Okay."

"Okay, so let's start freeing ourselves. But before we start, I want you to do a special type of breathing that will help relax you and keep your blood pressure under control. It's the seven-eleven technique. I want you to breathe in deeply for a count of seven, then exhale for a count of eleven. I'll do the counting so you can focus, okay? Generally, it's best done for five to ten minutes. You should do it whenever you feel panicky. For now, we'll just do it for a few minutes, okay? Ready?"

"Yeah, ready," Trish replied, looking unconvinced.

"Okay, breathe in, two, three, four, five, six, seven. Now breathe out, two, three, four, five, six, seven, eight, nine, ten, eleven. You're doing great. Again."

Despite Trish's scepticism, she followed Hannah's instructions to a T for a couple of minutes until Hannah drew the session to a close.

"You're looking so much better already. Good for you!"

"Wow! I actually enjoyed that. I thought it was gonna be boring but I actually felt it working. Thanks."

"Pleasure. Shall we start freeing ourselves now?"

"Course! Like I wanna be trapped in here forever."

"Look at those hanging cables. They're all over the place. When you're free, for goodness' sake, don't stand up. They could be live." Hannah began the meticulous task of removing rubble from below her waist. "Gently does it. Just one at a time. Place them as far away from you as you can reach."

Trish followed suit and in thirty minutes they had freed their legs and manoeuvred themselves into sitting positions, albeit onto uncomfortable rubble.

"Check your legs for injuries," Hannah said as she inspected her own. Any blood? Wounds?"

"I'm looking, I'm looking." Trish ran her hands and eyes meticulously over her legs and feet. "Ow, shit! 'Scuse my French."

"I think a few expletives are acceptable, all things considered."

"Can't see much blood. Just a bit that's dried up."

"Same here." Hannah fished some wet wipes from her bag and handed a couple to Trish. "Here, clean it up."

CHAPTER 6

A thought occurred to Trish. "The sinks!"

"What about them?" Hannah asked, bemused.

"Water!" Grabbing the edge of the basin, Trish pulled herself into a crouching position and eagerly turned on the cold tap.

Spluttering, it released dribbles of brown water. She tried the hot tap, with the same result.

"Hmm, doesn't look good. It's probably contaminated if the pipes have split."

"At least we can get to the loos now," Trish said.

"Yes, but better not flush unless vital. If we're trapped for long, we might have to rely on water from the cisterns. Remember – if it's yellow, let it mellow; if it's brown, flush it down. Have you heard the saying?"

"Trish laughed. Yeah, I've heard it. At least there's quite a few loos. Talking of loos, we should check if anyone's in there. Probably isn't, but best be safe than sorry."

"Yes, of course." Hannah said. "It's not going to be easy though considering the sharp debris, and it isn't as if we can walk across. We'd have to crouch walk."

The women debated possibilities. It was decided that Hannah should be the one to check the cubicles since she was the slimmest and fittest to negotiate her way to them.

"Look! That bit of stick'll help. Hang on, let me reach for it." Trish stretched to grasp the long piece of door frame. "Got it! You can use it to feel under the toilet doors."

Hannah accepted it with a smile. After considerable effort duck-walking whilst avoiding sharp debris, she reached the cubicles. Seven doors had collapsed and three remained intact. Before giving the first a push, she shut her eyes tight in anticipatory dread. On opening them, she found the cubicle empty. Exhaling in relief, she pressed her palm to her heart. Opening the other two doors was easier. Of the seven cubicles with collapsed doors, five enabled visibility, all of which were empty.

"The stick's come in useful," she said as she probed under a door that refused to open. The stick was long enough to feel as far as the toilet. "Thank goodness, they're all clear. So it's just the two of us, then."

Trish laughed. "Yeah, the dynamic duo."

"Ha! Yes, or the Manchester bees considering how hard we're going to have to work to get through this."

"Manchester bees?" Trish asked, her head tilted in bemusement.

"The worker bee has been a symbol of Manchester since the Industrial Revolution due to Manchester's hard-working past."

"Oh, I didn't know that."

"Yes, you'll find Manchester's bees in several places around Manchester – the town hall and the old Refuge building clock tower for a start." Hannah leaned against the vanity counter next to the first toilet cubicle. It seemed as solid as the wash basin countertops they had sheltered under – a replica design with gold tubular legged frames. A shatterproof mirrored wall remained intact above the counter. It previously reflected the windows on the opposite side. Now it only reflected rubble, anguish and shattered dreams. Evenly divided along the counter had been six gold cube tissue boxes with the top tissues pulled out decoratively. These had been hurled like missiles in all directions across the room and now lay despairingly in debris and dust.

"Come and settle over here," Hannah called. " It's just as safe for sheltering and closer to the loos."

"Don't you think we're better closer to the sinks where there's water?"

Hannah shook her head. "That brown poison? No thanks. We have our own water for now anyway, and there's water in the cisterns if we get desperate."

"I hope we don't have to resort to them," Trish said, wrinkling her nose.

"Don't worry. I doubt we will."

"Okay, I'll shift myself if you're sure. I hope you are 'cos it's gonna be harder for me to get over there than it was for you." With that, Trish flung her bag over her shoulder and across her chest, ready to make a move.

"Before you leave," Hannah said, "throw my bag over, please and some towels. As many as you can. We could use them for bedding."

"Oh yeah, good idea!" Trish checked for other items to bring. She popped a couple of hand creams into her bag which had fallen into a basin.

"My bag and towels, Trish?"

"Yeah, gimme a chance." Trish supported herself against each washbasin that she moved along, gathering towels from the ground beneath them. After returning to her original position, she threw Hannah's bag to her, followed by the dusty towels, one at a time. Out of twelve throws, nine reached their destination. She then made an ungainly effort at duck-walking towards Hannah. "Ow! Shit!"

"What's wrong?"

"Bloody pressed my hand into summat sharp!"

"Take more care! I'll have a look when you're here."

By the time Trish arrived, Hannah had made herself comfortable on a couple of newly acquired towels. Pushing away debris with her towel-covered hand, Trish placed two folded towels on the dusty, tiled floor next to Hannah. Sitting gingerly on it, she brought her knees up, clasping her hands around them over the hemline of her sundress.

"How's your hand?" Hannah asked as she folded the remaining towels and placed them beside her in a pile.

"It's okay, ta," Trish said as she examined it.

"Good. I've been thinking, considering we're going to restrict flushing to the barest minimum, we should use separate loos. So which one would you like? Luckily, these three closest to us seem the most serviceable."

"I'll have the one furthest away if you don't mind. Don't want you hearing me every time I have a wee, and definitely not the other!" Trish wrinkled her nose. "Bloody hell, there's gonna be no privacy around here, is there?"

"Privacy is the least of our worries, but I know what you mean." Hannah grinned. "I'll have the second one. The cisterns from the others can be reserved for drinking water if needs be. The towels will be useful for bedding. And there's plenty of toilet rolls to last us weeks. At least we have these resources."

Trish rummaged in her bag, pulling out the lemon scented hand creams, handing one to Hannah. "I grabbed some hand cream too. We could use them for cleansing cream as well as moisturiser."

"Thank you," Hannah said, smiling. "Good idea for when we run out of wet wipes."

"Ready for another scream?" Trish suggested. "They might hear us if we scream together."

"Absolutely. Ready?"

Yet again, they screamed with all their might. "Aieeeee! Help! Aieeeee! Help! Heeeeelp!" Over and over. They waited. Listened. Waited. Listened. They repeated the unison screaming, louder still until they felt their vocal cords would rip. After, it was quieter than ever. Eerily quiet.

"Never mind. It's obviously not the right time," Hannah said. "Nothing much we can do now except wait and keep trying at intervals."

"Yeah. Best stay positive. Listen, if you hear me whispering, I'm not going mad talking to myself – I'll be praying."

"Of course. Please feel free. I heard you praying earlier. Are you Christian?"

"I'm Catholic, but a rubbish one. I miss Mass more than I go. I only seem to go when I need help." Trish laughed through her nose. "Mind you, that's practically all the time. Haven't been to confession in ages either. Must be a year now," she said as she fished out her rosary beads.

"Hmm, the confessional," Hannah said meditatively. "I've sometimes wondered whether penitents confess *all* their sins or only the ones they dare admit. Do you confess *all* yours?"

"You must be joking! There's no way I'd confess the ones I'm ashamed of. Our priests – Father Walsh and Father Hughes – would recognise my voice right away. I wouldn't be able to show my face again. Besides, if I confessed all my sins, I'd be doing my penance for ever! The worse the sins, the more prayers you have to say before you get your absolution. I usually get summat like a decade of the Rosary. I was a good Catholic as a kid though. I mean I was top of the class in Catechism. Our school priest give us a pair of rosary beads for it. I had my first communion and confirmation too where we dressed like brides in long white dresses with veils. I chose Bernadette as my confirmation name 'cos I liked the story of Saint Bernadette of Lourdes."

"We had the religion drummed into us at home too," Trish continued. "We used to have a small holy water font on the wall in the hall next to the front door with Our Lady on it. We'd dip our finger in it, then make the sign of the cross with our wet finger. We did that before leaving the house and when we came home. Course, we did the same in church too. I did Irish dancing as well. Dead Irish we were. All that and the fact my name was O'Donnell was a dead giveaway. But I took my hubby's name Wilcox. What's yours?"

"Bernstein, so clearly not Irish," Hannah chuckled.

Trish missed the quip. "Our school assembly on Monday mornings used to be Mass at the church next door to our school. It was compulsory for us girls to wear something on our heads in church. I wore a black mantilla 'cos it didn't look as naff as our ugly school hat. God, it was horrible! Brown felt with a peak. I'd die before I looked ridiculous in front of the lads. Bad enough we had to wear an awful walking deckchair striped blazer. The girls sat on the pews on the left and the lads were on the right. But we could still see each other. Then the priest would say 'Dominus vobiscum' and we would say back, 'Et cum spiritu tuo'. We had no idea what it meant. Oh, I knew the meaning of *mea culpa, mea culpa, mea maxima culpa* which means through my fault, through my most grievous fault. Never forget that 'cos we said it a million times over the years. The school motto was in Latin too which I remember to this day."

"You went to school Mass on Monday mornings?" Hannah asked in surprise.

"Yeah, at secondary school. It's like they couldn't risk the idea of any of us committing the mortal sin of missing Sunday Mass, so made sure we went on Mondays to be on the safe side – to spare us from the eternal flames of damnation. Ha! Actually, we used to go to Sunday Mass sometimes with my mam. It was a drag 'cos it went on way too long. About an hour. Imagine an hour of bloody Latin when you don't understand a word?"

"It isn't that dissimilar to synagogue services which are mostly conducted in Hebrew, but they're not as long."

"Oh, right. Anyway, I'll be going to Mass Easter Sunday – if we get out of here alive. After that we're having Easter dinner with my kids and grandkids. We give 'em Easter eggs 'n' that. And before that on Good Friday we have hot-cross buns for breakfast. They say once a Catholic, always a Catholic, but I'm not so sure. Having it drummed into us put most of my class mates off for life, but I still believe. It gives me comfort and strength. Oh yeah, I was gonna say my prayers, wasn't I?"

"I know very little about Catholicism, so this is quite an education. Anyway, please go ahead if you wish to pray," Hannah said, before fishing out her Italian phrase book.

"Yeah, I will." Trish crossed herself with her rosary beads crucifix, placed the palms of her hands together and closed her eyes. After about ten minutes of thumbing her beads and praying, she said, "There! That'll bring us some luck. Hope it didn't bother you."

"Not at all. I found it quite relaxing."

"Are you religious?" Trish asked, tilting her head to the side.

"I'm Jewish, but agnostic."

"Agnostic?" Trish asked, stretching her legs out and covering them with her once white jacket, now a mottled dirt-grey.

"It means I neither believe in God, nor disbelieve. I prefer to keep an open mind, since I have no evidence to prove either way."

"Hmm, I like the sound of that. I suppose it's better than being an atheist."

"Exactly. I'm therefore only culturally Jewish. My husband is religious though."

"Does he have those long ringlets?" Trish asked, twirling her finger down the side of her face.

"Sidelocks? No, he's not that orthodox. He's religious to the extent he attends shul – that's the synagogue – at least once a week. He wears a kippah – the skullcap – much of the time, especially when he's praying, and he wears a prayer shawl at shul. Our family participate in religious holidays and observances one way or another. There are several fasting days each year, such as Yom Kippur, where we abstain from food and drink when Saul is home. When he works away, I personally don't fast."

"A bit like our lent I suppose," Trish intercepted, "though I'm rubbish at it. I should be doing it now for six weeks until Easter, but I stopped for this holiday. I was giving up chocolate."

"I wish Yom Kippur was that easy. Of course we all keep kosher and adhere to Shabbat, though not necessarily because we're religious."

"Shabbat?"

"Shabbat is our Sabbath which begins on Friday at sunset and ends the following evening after nightfall. It's our day of rest where we aren't allowed to perform any kind of work. It usually begins with a special Friday evening Shabbat dinner with candles and blessings. Only after Shabbat do we resume normal activities."

"You mean you can't go *out* to work?"

"That's right, but even in the home all kinds of work are prohibited including cooking, speaking on the phone, reading and answering emails, and even tearing toilet tissue from a roll."

Trish's eyes widened. "Bloody hell! That's a bit much, intit? You mean you can't even wipe your ..."

Haha, Hannah interjected. "Of course we can. We just need to ensure that squares of toilet tissue are torn off the roll in advance, or we use special Shabbat toilet tissue that is pre-cut."

"If you can't cook, do you have to order a take-away or summat?"

"No. We prepare and cook food just before the start of Shabbat and keep cooked dishes on a slow cooker or a warming tray until it's time to eat."

"So how do you keep a job if you're not allowed to work on Friday and Saturday?"

"I made my religious observances clear when I applied for the job. These were then stipulated in my contract of employment."

"What about your hubby's business?"

"Like many self-employed Jews, he has the autonomy to choose his own working hours, and therefore doesn't work during Shabbat."

"If you don't believe, why do you bother with all this?"

"To support Saul and because we believe it provides a sound moral grounding for the children. It's cultural and traditional; following these traditions helps embrace our Jewishness. But as I said, I do it mostly to support Saul. When he's away, I'm quite lax with the rules." Hannah sneezed and pulled the packet of tissues from her bag to blow her nose. "These aren't going to last two minutes with all this dust. I'll get some toilet roll." Hannah pushed herself into a duck-walk position, entered the toilet cubicle next to her and returned with a toilet roll. "If we get desperate, there's a few boxes of tissues scattered around as well. Where do you work, Trish?"

"The same place I live – in Sharrinwood." Trish had no hesitancy this time in admitting where she lived. The life-or-death situation expelled her pride, and besides, Hannah did not strike her as the snobbish type, despite her cut-glass accent.

"Ahh, Sharrinwood! I know it well from the days I worked at a pharmacy there."

"Oh, right. Anyway, I think it's great the way Jewish kids follow their religion. Most kids I know who were raised Catholic dump religion as soon as they're old enough. Were your parents religious?"

"Yes, they were. I was raised more strictly than I raise my children. Like any strict religion, I found it to be too narrow and limiting."

"I used to work with Jewish women when I was young," Trish said. "I really liked them. They were hard-working and had high standards in whatever they did. They were classy and wore expensive perfume too."

"Where did you work with them?" Hannah asked, turning towards Trish with interest.

"In a gown shop on Market Street – Joan Barry's. They sold wedding gowns too. Later, a toy shop I worked at bought some of its stock at a trade warehouse in Salford. The owners always took me with them to help. There were a lot of very religious Jews with the ringlets and big black hats. The women didn't seem interested in classy perfumes and clothes like the ones in the gown shop. They liked their wigs though."

"The wigs are part of the religion to cover their hair," Hannah clarified.

"Really? That's funny 'cos they could end up looking more gorgeous wearing a wig than without."

"It's nothing to do with looking attractive. Married women wear them as a statement to say they're taken and their hair is only for their husband's eyes."

"Ah, right. So they could wear an amazing long blonde wig to make them look drop dead gorgeous and that's okay, is it?" Trish laughed.

Hannah chuckled. "I know what you mean, but I can't say I've ever seen any Jewish women wearing long blonde wigs."

"Has anyone told you that you sound like a cross between Felicity Kendal from *The Good Life* and the queen?" That was Trish all over – saying whatever popped into her head – complimentary or otherwise.

Hannah's opinion on Trish's voice and accent, on the other hand, was best left unsaid.

CHAPTER 7

Trish closed her eyes. Visions of roast beef and Yorkshire pudding punctuated visions of loved ones wringing their hands in anguish over the earthquake news. "My stomach thinks my throat's been cut and I'm spitting feathers! Time we had summat to eat, eh?" she said, pressing her hands over her stomach ostentatiously.

"I'm sorry, Trish, but it's only been four hours since we had a huge breakfast. We're supposed to be on serious rations. Our provisions may need to last a week, if not more, remember?"

"This dust's making me really thirsty."

"Just think how much more thirsty you'll be when we run out of water."

"I'm even more starving!"

"Sorry, but it has to last. We'll eat when we really need to."

"I really need to now."

Exasperated, Hannah took a deep breath and slowly exhaled. Although she had been raised to choose her words carefully, this was not the time for niceties. "I'm sorry, Trish, but there's enough on you to last a week, and besides, you could do with losing some weight. You'll thank me for it."

Had Trish not been so taken aback by such directness, she might have retaliated. By the time she had taken it in, any potential anger had subsided. "It's okay for you. You're like a stick insect and don't need half as many calories as me."

"It's merely my professional opinion. I don't need to calculate your BMI to know you're overweight."

"Whatever. I'm still starving!"

"Let's talk about something else to take our minds off food, shall we? Is this your first time in Naples?"

"I'm too thirsty to talk, but you can if you want. Where do you live?"

"Didsbury, where I've …"

"Oh, I love Didsbury! I know it well," Trish interjected. "I used to go out with a lad who lived there. We used to do the Didsbury Dozen and that. Well, not really a dozen pubs. Mostly just to the Old Cock, The Didsbury, the Red Lion and the Fletcher Moss."

"Ah yes, the infamous Didsbury Dozen that attracts tourists from miles around. It should be renamed the Didsbury Score considering the number of new bars that have sprung up over the years – closer to twenty than a dozen."

Trish laughed. "I like that – the Didsbury Score. Like a place to cop off. Nice one!"

Hannah chuckled. "Unintentional pun, sorry. I meant score as in twenty. It's a shame Didsbury seems better known for its pubs than its treasures."

"Oh, I know it for other things as well. It's the home of Factory Records, intit?"

"I wouldn't know. I've never heard of them."

"You know – they made Joy Division famous. Not my thing but Tony loves them."

"I've never heard of Joy Division either. Sorry."

"Bet you've heard of Fletcher Moss Park." Trish chuckles. "I took my kids there a few times and from there we walked to the river through those rows of tall trees. Do you know where I mean?"

"Yes, of course – the poplar tree-lined avenue. We've had many family cycles through them to the river bank, then on to Chorlton Water Park for a picnic. Then there's Didsbury Park where the annual Didsbury Festival takes place. It makes for a pleasant afternoon out as there's so much going on with stalls, fancy dress, dancing displays, dog shows, a fairground and homemade local food."

"That sounds good. I might take my grandkids sometime. Ooh, I love the old Victorian houses too – they're like mansions, aren't they? What I'd give to live there."

"It is lovely, but not what it used to be. Didsbury's losing its soul and community spirit to a wave of trendy yuppies. Some of the much appreciated independent stores have been replaced with even more eateries and wine bars. For goodness' sake, how much can a person eat? Don't the new people of Didsbury cook in their designer kitchens anymore? We lost a jewellers, a dry cleaners and a deli, to name a few. The greatest loss for me personally was when they bulldozed the university's Capitol Theatre. We used to enjoy many excellent drama productions there. It's where Julie Walters and Steve Coogan were students, so you can imagine its standards. Prior to it being a theatre, it was a cinema; then ABC TV studios. They bulldozed an excellent hardware store in the village too. Then we lost Fletcher Moss Gardens' specialist gardeners. Such a shame considering all those beautiful, rare plants and trees are in dire need of their expertise. The council replaced them with contract gardeners and it's never been the same since. Thankfully, volunteers have been helping to maintain it. They do an excellent job. It's a labour of love for which locals, myself included, are very grateful, but it still isn't enough."

"Aww, that's a shame. Haven't been there in years, so wouldn't have known."

"Anyway," Hannah continued, "I've lived in Didsbury all my life. I've been married to Saul for thirty-four years and we have three children – Zach who's thirty-three, a criminal lawyer who also happens to be gay, then there's …"

"Gay? Aww, I love gay men, me!" Trish may well have been spitting feathers and not in a talkative mood, but she had no problem interrupting. "They're dead sensitive and much better to chat with than straight men. All straight men talk about is footy, cars and women, but gay men talk about things that matter. I used to work with a nice gay man. Matt he was called. We got on really well. My hubby's horrible about gays. He calls them poofs and says he's not watching that garbage if they're on the telly. I've played hell with him about it but it's a waste of time. Anyways, I love gay men. Does he live near you?"

"He lives in the city centre in Piccadilly Waterside."

"People actually live in Piccadilly?"

"Yes, it's a lovely town house set on the banks of the Ashton Canal within a beautiful enclosed communal garden area – just a short walk from Piccadilly Station and the Northern Quarter. Perfect for him."

"It sounds fantastic. He sounds likes he's got good taste. Has he got a boyfriend?"

"Yes, he's been with Robin for eighteen months now. A lovely chap. I'm hoping it lasts as I like him very much, besides the fact he's good for Zach. They've so much in common – both accomplished musicians and into the arts."

"Aww, be nice if they settled down, then. I bet they're both dead intelligent and lovely, aren't they?"

"Yes, they are. I'm sorry about your husband's views; sorry for my son and the gay community, since it's homophobia that contributes to mental health issues within it. Actually, Zach still carries the scar on his forehead from the time he was attacked by a bunch of homophobic monsters. That kind of persecution would make anyone depressed and suicidal, wouldn't it?"

"Yeah, and I'm dead sorry. Maybe I shouldn't have told you about my hubby, but that's my problem – say what I think." She points to her lips. "I should've kept it zipped."

"Not at all. I value your openness," Hannah said with sincerity.

"But bloody hell, he was attacked?" Where? When?"

"About a year ago. He was heading for the car park after an evening out at a bar in the Gay Village. It was raining, so he left Robin in the doorway whilst he dashed for the car to collect him. He heard the yobs behind him throwing homophobic insults. He made a dash for his car, but they caught him while he was struggling to open his door. One punched him so hard in the stomach he collapsed to the ground. While he was down, another kicked him in the head. Thankfully, someone witnessed the attack and blasted his car horn, scaring them off. Unfortunately, the perpetrators were never found."

Trish placed a comforting hand on Hannah's arm. "Oh my God, he must've been terrified, the poor lad. It must've broke your heart. I'd want to kill any bastard – excuse my French – who did that to any of my kids. Shame they never got caught. God, I hope you don't think Tony's like that! He's all talk and only says those things behind their backs. He wouldn't dream of saying anything to their faces – too much of a coward – and definitely would never attack. My God, no way!"

"To be honest, my husband can't deal with homosexuality either. He took Zach's coming out badly."

"Oh, God! When did Zach tell him?"

"He'd been seeing Robin for some months and was tired of hiding him from the family. He eventually decided to come out before mentioning Robin. Saul was extremely upset. He told Zach that it would have been bad enough if he'd married a non-Jew, but to be homosexual was too much for him to bear. Zach told him that he had no choice in being gay in the same way he had no choice being born Jewish. That was like a red rag to a bull and Saul nearly blew a fuse warning him never to dare compare Judaism with homosexuality again. Of course, Zach didn't mention Robin after that. If it hadn't been for the brutal attack on Zach later, I wonder if Saul would have ever come round. But he did because he felt guilty about it being a homophobic attack, and of course because he loves his son and wanted to support him."

"Poor Zach," Trish said, shaking her head.

"Only after the incident, when Saul slowly began to accept Zach's sexuality, did Zach finally tell him about Robin. I suppose he had to sooner or later since Zach and Robin had been practically living together at each other's homes. I'd known from the start when I unintentionally discovered Robin at Zach's early in their relationship. I took a liking to him immediately. We have a lot in common regarding our interest in music. He's a pianist and saxophonist – a Royal Northern College of Music graduate. Zach had eventually pointed out to Saul that at least Robin was Jewish. Saul would have preferred him to be Ashkenazi like ourselves rather than Sephardic, but at least he's Jewish."

"Ashkenazi? Sephardic? What are they?"

"Ashkenazi Jews originate from central and eastern Europe whereas Sephardic Jews originate mostly from Spain and Portugal."

"Ah, right. Do you have other kids?"

"We have a twenty-nine-year-old daughter – Miriam – who's a junior doctor at the MRI, and then there's Sadie who's twenty-one, doing Psychology at Lancaster."

"Wow! They've done well, haven't they. Bet you're dead proud."

"Yes, I am. However, the last time I saw Sadie, we'd argued about her lack of study commitment. Her father and I have been very concerned. Education is extremely important to us and Sadie seems to be throwing it in our faces. Maybe if she funded it herself, she'd hold more value for it. But I guess it's partly our fault for insisting she follows a degree in a subject that wasn't her first choice. She wanted to waste our hard-earned money on some degree that holds little value in the job market."

"What was the degree? Not that I know the slightest thing about degrees."

"Because it was so unimpressive, I've forgotten. Something related to art. We told her if she wished to waste three years on such a degree, she can fund it herself. So she reluctantly settled for Psychology. I wish our last words hadn't been so confrontational."

"I know what you mean. I'm worried about my son Ryan 'cos he's been really depressed about being unemployed. Like it wasn't bad enough when his girlfriend Shelly chucked him for another bloke with more money, the cow, then he lost his job. I'd told him earlier – don't bring any floozies back to my house, but would he listen?"

"I'm sorry. It must be such a worry for you all. How old is he?"

"Twenty-three. He's back with us now. And we got lumbered with his dog too – Rambo, a cross bull terrier. Do you have any pets?"

"Yes, we have a cat called Polly. At least Sadie's taking care of her otherwise I'd have Polly to worry about as well."

"Aww, that's good. Anyway, Ryan stopped out the night before we left and I didn't get chance to see him. Wanted to make sure he was okay, but couldn't reach him. I'm gonna try phoning again."

"Try if you wish, but remember your battery might have to last a week. Why not save it for emergencies?"

"What do you call this? This is an emergency!" Trish retorted as she tried her phone again – in vain.

CHAPTER 8

The rear of Zach's townhouse overlooked Ashton canal, along which frequently sailed colourful narrowboats. Zach often exchanged a friendly wave from his kitchen window or balcony. Like his Siamese cats Basil and Sybil, he enjoyed watching the world go by, especially the lazy narrowboats.

The waterways had attracted him to his property in the first place, and he fell in love with it at first sight. Friends were surprised on their first visit, having assumed a place in Piccadilly would be cramped amongst grey, industrial buildings. Instead, they found a chic townhouse set within a peaceful, idyllic canal-side setting with perfectly maintained semi-private gardens.

The interior was deceptively spacious with a white kitchen and separate breakfast area from which French windows opened onto his balcony. This was adorned with blooming pot plants hanging from a pretty wrought iron black railing. Through a door adjoining the kitchen and breakfast room was a lounge with Habitat furniture and an ivory three-seater sofa and matching armchair. Against the back wall, stood a high-gloss, black piano that Robin played on a daily basis. On the ground floor were the utility room, a toilet and spare bedroom, the two main bedrooms and bathroom being on the top floor.

Zach recalled how Sadie helped him furnish the house and it occurred to him that he had not heard from her in a while. He made a mental note to call her that day.

As he washed the lunchtime dishes, he glanced through the window periodically for any oncoming boats, only to see a young couple walking a golden Labrador along the canal bank. He could hear Robin's piano practice of Bach's 'Goldberg Variations' and wondered if he should write a cello accompaniment for them to play it together.

Robin was a part-time piano examiner at the Royal Northern College of Music. He also gave piano and saxophone lessons from home and performed the occasional gig for birthday parties, weddings, b'nai mitzvah and charity concerts, some of which Zach supported with cello.

"Down! Bad cat!" Robin yelled at Sybil who had jumped on his music sheets on the armchair. When Robin first met Zach, he could not tolerate cats, but over time, he grew increasingly more tolerant of them. On occasions, he had been caught talking affectionately to them, much to Zach's amusement.

"I thought you didn't like cats and look at you – smitten!"

"Rubbish! I'm just humouring them," Robin would retort.

* * *

On a spacious driveway in Didsbury, lazed three cars: Saul's navy Honda saloon, Hannah's bottle-green Audi and Sadie's red Volkswagen Polo, courtesy of Hannah and Saul for her eighteenth birthday. Polly, the family moggie, thus enjoyed the choice of three cars on which to sunbathe. She chose the Polo which was receiving the greatest belting of sunshine. Stretching out to her full length, her ginger fur glistened in the sunlight.

The mature garden, abundant with shrubs, bracken and rhododendrons, had a large, well-kept lawn on which crocuses pushed up from their beds. The branches of a cherry blossom cascaded over them in full bloom and the breeze shook the blossoms onto the lawn, creating a pink carpet.

At the end of the drive stood a double-fronted, Victorian mansion with stained-glass bay windows and a large, mock Tudor apex. Equally impressive was the ornate porch and large, teal-coloured front door with stunning stained-glass panels.

Surrounding the door were additional stained-glass sidelights and a fanlight that perfectly matched the door's glass panels.

A non-Jewish visitor arriving at this impressive doorway might easily fail to notice a significant clue to it being a Jewish household. If they look up to the top third of the right-hand doorframe, they would see the intriguing mezuzah. Tightly rolled inside every mezuzah is a scroll of parchment on which the Shema (a Hebrew prayer) is written. The Bernstein's mezuzah was stained-glass, set in a decorative silver frame about four inches in length. As characterful as the house and almost as old, it had been left by an earlier householder who also happened to have been Jewish. The following family to move in were non-Jewish. They felt the mezuzah added to the property's character and did not have the heart to remove it.

Inside, Sadie sprawled out on one of the pairs of smoke-blue three-seater sofas with her laptop resting precariously on her chest.

The elegant, high-ceilinged room was filled with tasteful antiques, contemporary table lamps and an eclectic mix of abstract and impressionist paintings graced the walls. A large Persian rug in rich purples and blues lay proudly on oak parquet flooring in front of a grand cast iron Victorian fireplace. In between the sofas was a large mahogany coffee table. Behind one of the sofas stood a mahogany Pembroke table, on which stood a Tiffany lamp. On the far right of the table hung a full-length gilded mirror facing a Victorian button-back armchair upholstered in a Laura Ashley smoke-blue print. Sunlight shining through the stained-glass bay windows highlighted the room's beauty, though it was most impressive in the evenings when dimly lit with atmospheric lighting. The ceiling light, an impressive crystal chandelier, was rarely, if ever used, unlike the matching one in the dining room. The contemporary and antiques mix worked perfectly and Hannah would sometimes quip that only a person with good taste could make such an eclectic look work so well.

Hannah's daughters only wished Hannah's dress sense was a fraction as tasteful. They marvelled at how she went to great lengths to find the most perfect paint colours – only Farrow and Ball would do – yet remain bereft of any colour co-ordinating dress sense – any dress sense for that matter. Since her marriage, Hannah had felt completely secure with Saul, having no desire whatsoever to impress men – Saul included.

Sadie had not relished the idea of remaining at her halls of residence during the Easter holidays when most of her peers had returned home. She therefore followed suit a couple of days before her parents' departure for Naples. Besides, she loved her home comforts, especially when she had the house to herself. She doubted she was welcome home considering her parents' constant nagging for her to do her studies, bring her laundry down, clean her bedroom, and turn the racket down. On and on and on.

Sadie was learning new guitar chords from YouTube to help broaden her repertoire. She fancied herself as another Amy Winehouse. She certainly resembled her with her long dark hair, her size eight dresses, her gap-toothed smile and her Winehouse style. With the iconic high bouffant and dramatic cat eyes, she was practically a Winehouse double. With hindsight, Hannah and Saul would never have bought her the guitar for her sixteenth birthday had they known the disproportionate amount of time she would spend jamming on it. They only wished she had been as motivated at practising her piano when younger. Had it not been for Hannah's encouragement, Sadie would never have achieved a grade four, let alone her grade eight with distinction. Only later did they realise the accomplishment was a double-edged sword. When Sadie proudly debuted her first piano composition to them, perhaps they should have shown less enthusiasm.

Sadie sat hugging her knees to her chest after pausing a guitar tutorial. She often viewed YouTube for studying anything other than her university coursework: song-writing, Amy Winehouse, guitar chords, makeup techniques, and fashion. Sadie procrastinated from her studies with any excuse – coffee being another favourite. It was now time for her second in three hours and she headed to the kitchen.

Whilst waiting for the coffee pod to brew, she turned on the television to chase away the silence. Unimpressed with the news channel, she was about to switch channels when the breaking news ticker tape grabbed her attention. As she turned up the volume, a sinking feeling hit her gut. In disbelief, she stared at the screen.

"At least a hundred and twenty people have lost their lives in an earthquake that rocked Naples at 10:10 a.m. local time today. It is believed at least five of the deceased are Britons. The grade 6.3 magnitude earthquake struck Vomero – a hilltop region popular with British tourists. Many victims are believed to be buried under the rubble, and the death toll is expected to rise. Despite several aftershocks, rescuers are working tirelessly to pull victims from the rubble. The British embassy is liaising with local authorities regarding British nationals in need of assistance. They urge Britons who have loved-ones in Naples to contact them. The UK government has offered assistance with the recovery effort, sending hundreds of rescue workers to join the rescue teams. Another concern is the proximity of Mount Vesuvius to the epicentre and the possibility that the earthquake could trigger an eruption."

Sadie stared at the screen, slack-jawed and ashen grey. With trembling hands, she tapped in her mother's number from her phone she happened to be holding.

No reply. She tried her father's. No reply.

"Please God, answer Mimi," she pleaded as she tapped in her sister's number. The line was busy.

"Jesus Christ!" she screamed as she finally tried Zach's number.

"Hey, Sadie!" Zach said cheerily, before hearing her voice. "I was about to call you," he added as he dried his hands on a kitchen towel, holding the phone between his ear and shoulder.

"Have you not heard the news?" Sadie asked in between sobs.

"Jesus, what's wrong, Sadie? What news?"

With deep, shuddering breaths, she let out another sob before telling him.

"Okay, I'm coming over. Don't worry. We'll decide what to do together. Be there in twenty, okay? Don't worry."

With a knotted stomach and puckered forehead she waited, manically checking the internet for updates, and noting relevant contact details.

Thirty minutes later Zach arrived. After giving Sadie a tight hug, he rushed to a power socket to charge his phone. "What's new since we last spoke? Anything?"

As the background news blared, Sadie updated him. "I phoned the emergency number to be told the hotel Mum and Dad are staying at has been hit. There's a chance they're trapped in there somewhere. They said much of the hotel's still intact and there are many survivors, so there's a good chance they're okay. But what if they're not? I've been ringing and ringing, but it sounds like their lines are dead. What if they went sightseeing after breakfast and were struck?"

"Try not to worry. The likelihood is they're okay. But Jesus, I can't believe this is happening!" Zach ran his fingers through his hair before searching for the airport number on Sadie's laptop. "We'll get the first available flight."

"No way! There could be aftershocks. Let's go when we're sure it's safe."

"Are you kidding? We need to see Mum and Dad. Let me get on with the arrangements, okay?"

Within fifteen minutes, he had made a series of phone calls as Sadie held her head in her palms.

"Okay, I've booked a flight for the morning – six thirty – to Rome Ciampino for the three of us. Naples is obviously out. We can assess the situation when we arrive and decide how close to Naples we're safe to stay."

"I'll never forgive myself if anything happens to them. I've been a terrible daughter. Mum and I fell out before she left. Did I tell you?"

"Of course you've not been a terrible daughter. Don't worry about it."

"She'd been on at me about my studies. I gave her a mouthful and we parted without even a goodbye, let alone a hug. I'll never forgive myself for giving her and Dad so much grief and parting on bad terms."

"Don't beat yourself up, Sadie. You have enough to worry about as it is."

CHAPTER 9

The sound of tremulous snoring resonated from Ryan's bedroom, punctuated by the ringing of his phone and Rambo's barking. Ryan grunted, turned over and tugged his grubby duvet over his outgrown buzz cut. Over the duvet, his outstretched arm flopped out revealing a large tattoo of a black guitar.

A musty smell of neglect and stale cigarette smoke lingered despite always leaning out of his window whenever he had a smoke. Trish and Tony objected to smoking indoors despite being smokers themselves. Occasionally, whiffs of cannabis lingered when home alone, but his current lack of funds spared that. On his bedside cabinet lay a packet of Rizla cigarette papers, a tin of tobacco and an overflowing ashtray. Mould grew from a half empty mug of instant coffee on the chest of drawers; and littering his badly stained carpet laid dirty clothes, empty beer cans, take-away trays and biscuit crumbs.

Although conscious of the need to clean his room, low priority chores such as this were the least of Ryan's worries. It was near impossible to contemplate housework when he lacked the motivation to even wake up in the mornings. Drowning his sorrows in drink had become the norm since losing his girlfriend Shelly to another man, followed soon after by losing his bartender job.

Trish and Tony's greatest concern, however, was when Ryan's guitar began to gather dust – a sure sign he had fallen into the pits of depression. Music had been his life. Over his bed hung two guitars and on other walls were posters of Amy Winehouse, Jimi

Hendrix and guitar chord charts. Since his losses, he found music too painful to listen to, let alone play. Music stirred his emotions, and his emotions were already shaken to the core. He kept reminding himself that his mam would kill him if she saw the mess. *Ah, sod it. Plenty of time before she gets back.*

The night before, he had drowned his sorrows in The Crown with a couple of mates. After returning home with curry and chips, he stayed up till the early hours watching WWE on the box. This merely rubbed salt into the wound considering he was now even more skint and depressed than before. It was a vicious circle, but at least it was gentler than his usual all-night benders.

His phone rang again for the fourth time.

"Christ's sake! Shurrup, will ya!" he yelled, exhaling stale morning breath.

The ringing persisted and Ryan continued ignoring it until it occurred to him that it might be urgent. With bloodshot eyes, he looked around to find its flashing screen on the littered carpet beside him. Stretching to reach it, he squinted to check the caller's name – Kelly.

"Yeah? What's so urgent, our kid?"

"Ryan, thank God!" Kelly said in between sobs. "It's Mam and Dad – there's been an earthquake. I think they're in it!"

"What? Fu – " He curbed the expletive, conscious of his priggish sister's distress. "Calm down, Kell. Don't cry. Are they okay?"

"We don't know. All we know is there was an earthquake this morning in Naples. It's all over the news. I tried ringing their hotel but the lines are dead.

"Ryan? Ryan, are you there?"

Ryan was numb. He had already been debilitated by life's cruel blows, and this final blow was more than he could bear.

"Ryan! Answer me."

Ryan exhaled deeply. "God, I can't friggin' believe it. They've been planning this holiday for bloody ages and this happens. I hope to God they're okay."

"I phoned the British Embassy. They're giving support to affected British nationals. They gave me a contact number, which I'll ring in a minute. I'll send it to you too."

"Ta. So what now?"

"I'm getting the first available flight. Work's chasing up flights for me. I'll hire a car and head for the closest B & B to Naples that hasn't been affected. Liam's going to take time off work to look after the kids."

Ryan swung his legs out of bed. "Are you mental? If anyone needs to go, it's me. You've got your family. I've no one. I'm skint though. I'd have to cadge the money off you – the money you would've used to go."

"Wish I could, but I've struggled to find the money for myself. If it wasn't for work, there'd be no way I could afford it. Don't worry – I'll tell Mam and Dad that you desperately wanted to come. They'll understand."

Can't even afford a flight to see my mam and dad – maybe for the last time, Ryan mused. *How shit is that?* At least his depression now morphed into determination. Now there were more pressing issues to worry about than his personal troubles, and he sorely wanted to take charge. For the first time in an age he had a goal. He urgently scanned the room for clothes to wear. "You shouldn't be going. It should be me. You need to be safe at home with the kids."

"I know, but that's how it is. Nothing we can do about it. Ryan, you've gone quiet. You okay?"

"Trying to find my keks. Got 'em. Hang on," he said, placing one foot into a pair of badly creased combats. "Like I said, the last thing we need is you in danger when you've mega loads to lose – two kids, a hubby, a gaff and a job. You'd be a much bigger loss than me if owt happened to you. I've nothing. Let me go, Kell! Phone work and see if it's possible – possible on compassionate grounds. See if they can get discounted tickets for me instead … though you'd still have to pay as I'm skint."

Ryan's suggestion made sense and Kelly needed little more convincing. Within minutes, she persuaded her manager to permit Ryan the discounted trip, and once agreed, Kelly transferred the travelling funds to Ryan's bank account.

"Nice one, Kell. You won't be sorry."

For the first time in months, Ryan moved like a rocket. After pulling on the first sweatshirt he could lay his hands on, he sprinted around the house, grabbing necessities for the trip.

"Shit, where the hell's my passport?" he asked himself, pressing his fingertips on his temple as his eyes scanned the living room. He had forgotten Trish kept important documents in her pine chest of drawers in the alcove next to her 1950s tiled fireplace.

She had made efforts to stylise her home with a mish-mash of mass produced prints to adorn her woodchip magnolia walls – J.H. Lynch's *Tina*, Munch's *The Scream* and Tretchikoff's *Chinese Girl*. Her pride and joy, however, was her Chinese paraphernalia – bamboo wall picture scrolls, red paper lanterns suspended from her living room and kitchen ceilings, and paper folding fans embellishing her fireplace.

Having remembered the location of family passports, Ryan eagerly pulled open the top drawer to find his passport tangled amongst three sets of rosary beads. One pair, made from sapphire blue glass with an ornate crucifix, was Trish's favourite. Untangling them from the others, he clasped them with his passport. *She'll be glad of these.*

Glancing up, he noticed the small print of the bay of Naples with Mount Vesuvius in the background. Trish had bought it from a charity shop for Tony, knowing how much he would appreciate it. For the first time, the effect it had on Ryan was ominously prophetic, and he shivered. He remembered the television, turned it on, and eagerly flipped channels for the news. While waiting for the earthquake news to come on, he looked around at the shambles surrounding him. *If Mam's home early, injured or not, she'll do her nut if she sees the place like this!* He shot upstairs to his room. Having ripped the grubby bedclothes from his bed, along with his malodorous clothes carpeting the floor, he flew downstairs to the kitchen to load them into the washing machine.

Rambo's sorrowful eyes looked up enquiringly, his chin slumped on the linoleum floor. It had been a couple of days since his last walk and his food and water bowls were empty.

"Aww, Ram, soz, mate!" Ryan reached to the wall cupboard for the dried dog food, only to discover the box was empty.

The hapless canine sprung up, wagging his tail as he thrust his nose into Ryan's hand. Eager for any morsel on offer, he closely followed Ryan's heels. Ryan foraged the cupboards for anything edible. The biscuit barrel contained a quarter pack of Garibaldi biscuits which he emptied into Rambo's dish.

"There you go, mate. That'll keep ya' going' till I get summat in."

Rambo wagged his tail ecstatically, wolfing them down with a couple of licks.

Meanwhile, Ryan attempted to fill Rambo's water bowl – a challenge considering the dirty dishes piling high in the sink. Whilst attempting to create space, he knocked over a drinking glass that smashed to the floor.

"Shit!" *That's it! This room next.*

However, his phone pinged, reminding him of his neglected messages and missed calls. Flinging a tea towel over his shoulder, he stopped to check them. Several were from Kelly and Zoe and others from various friends alerting him of the earthquake.

Family first, then a dog minder for Rambo. He tapped in Zoe's number, calmed her and updated her on his plans. His determination to focus on packing and cleaning the house was now paramount.

CHAPTER 10

"I'm sorry about your son," said Hannah. "Is it clinical or reactive depression?"

"I dunno. None of us do 'cos he won't go to the doctors about it. He said it'd make finding work even harder if it was on his records 'cos employers won't want anyone with mental health problems."

"That's such a shame because there's various help available in terms of medication and counselling. Depression seems to hit males harder because they're more likely to bottle things up. Unemployment is dreadful for self-esteem too, especially when one makes the effort to find work. What kind of work did he do?"

"You're dead right. Fellas don't open up, unless they're gay. He's done all sorts. His last job was as a barman. Before that he was a furniture remover. He's also been a fast food assistant. Oh yeah, and he worked for the council resurfacing roads for a bit."

"Does he have any interests?"

"He loved music – played guitar – and used to do a bit of boxing, but all that's stopped now."

"Training people to injure each other requires discipline, so there's that I suppose."

"Yeah, it was great discipline. He learned it at our local community centre when he was about fifteen. The centre offers kids activities like boxing and street dancing. Funny that street dancing keeps them off the streets," Trish said, chuckling. "Do you have any youth clubs in Didsbury?"

"Apart from the Scouts and Guides, I'm not aware of any. Is Ryan your only child?"

"No, we've got three. Ryan's the youngest and Zoe's the middle one. She's twenty-four. She works at a petrol station. She lives with her partner Dwayne and they've got three kids – Courtney, Brandon and Kylie. Actually, Dwayne isn't Courtney's dad. Zoe got pregnant at fifteen by a seventeen-year-old lad. Nightmare it was! Brought shame to our family. We brought her up proper and that's the thanks we got. Tony went ballistic, then he cried. It was like history repeating itself 'cos Tony's mam was only seventeen when she had him. He was determined our kids' lives would be a lot better. He said things would never be the same again, and he was right. We practically raised Courtney until Dwayne came along, then he and Zoe settled down and she had two more kids with him. He's a good man, Dwayne, and a great cook too. He's of mixed race, though prefers to call himself black. I don't know why 'cos you can hardly see any black in him. I wouldn't mind, but it was his white mam who raised him after his dad from Trinidad ran off with another woman. So it's not as if he was raised in the black culture. He cooks curried goat and plantain, loves reggae and used to have dreads. It's really good he's proud of his black heritage, but I don't get why he ignores the white in him, do you?"

"Yes, I totally understand. If I were estranged from a Jewish father, and my non-Jewish mother did nothing to encourage my Jewish culture, I would make it my business to embrace it, just as Dwayne embraces his West Indian culture. Good for him! Whites and non-Jews are the default in the Western world and he rightly wants to embrace and celebrate the side that needs protecting from discrimination. The default side doesn't need it. Or perhaps he simply finds the West Indian culture more interesting, which is understandable."

"Oh yeah, I see what you mean. Anyways, as I was saying – my eldest kid is twenty-six – Kelly. She's married to Liam and they've got two kids – Claire and Thomas. She works in a travel agent's.

We're dead proud of her. She's always worked hard and tries to better herself. Talks nice 'n' that and worked hard for her qualifications. Got a diploma in Travel and Tourism. Total opposite of Zoe and Ryan. She's the only one in the family without tattoos too. Thinks they're dead common. Tells us straight about mine. A right snob she is. She's a snob about dogs too – says you can always tell the class of people by the type of dog they own. She has a corgi 'cos she thinks if they're good enough for the queen, they're good enough for her," Trish laughed.

"She's right. Dog breeds say so much about their owners."

"You mean like ours?"

"I don't know about yours. I mean 'intimidation' dogs listed under the Dangerous Dogs Act. Self-assured men have no need for such *look how tough I am* dogs and can quite confidently walk down the street with a miniature toy poodle because they have nothing to prove. Actually, we used to have a cute little Yorkshire terrier that my six-foot-tall husband used to happily walk."

"Yeah, suppose you're right, considering my Ryan has a tough dog. He likes to dumb down in the way he dresses and talks. Drinks like a fish, smokes like a chimney, swears like a trooper and I'm sure he smokes weed too. I caught him red-handed once and chucked him out. He says he doesn't do it anymore, but I don't believe him. Being like that, he attracts the wrong sort. I told him if he wants to meet a nice girl, he should start going to nice places like church to find one. Course he doesn't listen to a word I say. Anyways, enough of me."

But Trish was on a roll, and could not stop. "As I said before, I really admire Jewish people. I think they have this amazing knack at being brilliant at everything. I mean, just think – Jews must only be a tiny percentage of the world's population, yet it seems that the best singers, the best actors and film directors are Jewish." She enumerated them on her decorated fingers. "There's Barbara Streisand, Stephen Spielberg … hmm … Amy Winehouse and Leonard Cohen. Hmm, can't think. Oh yeah, Ali

G and the actors – Woody Allen … hmm, sure there's loads more."

"Dustin Hoffman, Jerry Lewis, Kirk Douglas and Lauren Bacall to name a few," Hannah added.

"Wish I was Jewish to have that drive that makes them so successful."

Hannah grimaced. "Maybe you wouldn't if part of their motivation was driven by a long history of persecution."

"Oh God, sorry. I didn't think of that. Did any of your family suffer from the Holocaust?"

Hannah shot Trish a look before lowering her eyes and taking a moment to reflect. "My mother Ruth and her younger brother Natan were Polish refugees. They came to England from Warsaw on the Kindertransport when they were children, just before the outbreak of World War Two. Their parents were murdered by the Nazis in Treblinka extermination camp close to Warsaw. This was after being imprisoned for eighteen months in the Warsaw ghetto. It was a horrific high-walled ghetto, crammed with over four hundred thousand Jews into an unliveable small area. Thousands died of starvation and disease. Very painful to think of, but we must never forget."

The silence that followed was palpable until Trish whispered, "Oh God, that's so sad. The poor, poor kids. Your poor grandparents. I'm really sorry, Hannah. Let's just hope that was the last time as well as the first."

"The first? Mass extermination of Jews has been going on since antiquity. In fact, there hasn't been a century in which it hasn't taken place."

"Oh God! I had no idea. Sorry."

"Anyway, my Aunt Helena – my mother's elder sister – along with her husband and two-year-old son didn't stand a chance as they lived in Krakow where the vast majority of Jews were murdered. But first they suffered two years of hell imprisoned in the ghetto – over fifteen thousand of them. I say *imprisoned* because the ten-foot wall around them was impossible to escape.

Many books have been written about it and Spielberg's film *Shindler's List* was filmed in Krakow."

"I saw it. I cried my eyes out, I did. Evil bastards! Excuse my French."

"It's okay. It warrants it. You may remember, then, that Schindler was a factory owner and the list he created consisted of the names of twelve hundred of his workers he saved from execution by bribing SS officials. Unfortunately, my aunt, uncle and baby cousin weren't the lucky ones and perished."

"Oh God, that's so terrible. Your poor family. You wouldn't treat rats like that, let alone human beings. I think anyone against Jews are like that 'cos they're jealous sick 'cos Jews do so much better than them. And what those sickos are too stupid to realise is that Jewish people do so much better because they work so much harder and set themselves higher standards. So how old was your mam when she came to England?"

"Sixteen and her brother was twelve. They were two of the lucky ones as they were both fostered by a Jewish family in Didsbury after first being taken to a refugee hostel in Cheadle Hulme, supported by the Quakers. So at least they retained their religion and culture. Most went to non-Jewish families though."

"So did they go back to Poland after the war?"

"No. It was decided they should stay with their new family in England considering they had practically no family remaining in Poland. But at least Mum met new friends in England – Jewish friends who were very supportive. And then she met my father. They married and made a home for themselves in a poor part of the Jewish quarter in North Manchester called Red Bank.

"My father was a tailor – also a refugee, but from Germany," Hannah continued. "He started afresh, working all hours from home making men's suits until he had enough to set up in a small rented property. Thankfully, his business prospered over the years until he was eventually able to set up a tailor's shop in St Anne's Square in the city centre."

"Wow, it's posh there!"

"Yes, but he worked extremely hard to get there. A couple of years later, he opened up two others in Wilmslow and Chester. That's when we moved to Didsbury. I was eight at the time and my sister Rebecca was ten. Education was paramount to our family. Mum taught us the three Rs long before we started school, and when we were older, she prepped us every evening after school for grammar school entrance exams. We aimed to pass for Withington Girls', but took all the grammar school entrance exams to be on the safe side; that's Withington, Manchester High, Cheadle Hulme and Stockport. Thankfully, we passed them all and chose Withington where we stayed until we were eighteen. My daughter attended Withington too. My boys went to MGS."

"MGS? Is it private?"

"Sorry, that's Manchester Grammar, and yes, it's private."

"Weren't you lucky? Money can buy practically everything, can't it?"

Hannah shot Trish an icy glare. "It wasn't money that got any of us in. Children from all walks of life have an equal chance of entering grammar schools if the child works hard enough to pass and they have parental support. There are bursaries for families on low incomes. I worked very hard with my children to ensure they were of grammar school standard. And I don't mean merely supporting schoolwork. Besides teaching them the core subjects during their pre-school years, I later ensured they embraced sport opportunities and played a musical instrument. Zach chose cello, Miriam violin and Sadie the piano. I would've educated them at home before I sent them to a state school. Thanks to state education's obsession with child-centred teaching methods, with its lack of school discipline and *we mustn't hurt their self-esteem* nonsense, standards have plummeted. All this nonsense about the benefits of ignoring children's spelling mistakes because it might discourage the poor dears. I'd be damned before I allowed them to use my children as guinea pigs for trying out their newfangled educational theories, for the theories to be later added to their heap of mistakes at the detriment of the thousands of children who suffered the consequences. I'm for traditional, tried and tested old-school methods. If I wasn't able to afford prep school prior to them entering grammar school, I would have given up work and educated them at home. All that said, this is the thanks I get – a rebel who needs to be bribed into doing her studies."

"At least she's a girl and it won't matter as much 'cos she'll probably end up getting married and having kids."

Hannah pursed her lips before slowly enunciating, "And what if she chooses to remain single and have no children, or the opportunities never arise? Even if she does marry and have children, I'm sure she'll want more than motherhood and the kitchen sink. Like anyone, she'll want choices that offer a fulfilling profession. You only get such choices with a good degree and professional qualifications."

"Maybe she's rebelling. If you don't mind me saying, you sound like you were a bit pushy. I was never a pushy parent. I didn't have the time to even listen to their reading, let alone all you did. You were lucky you had the time."

"Had the time?" Hannah snapped. "Besides working as a pharmacist, I supported the admin side of my husband's demanding company as well as being mother and teacher to three children, housekeeper and cook. I made it my business to make time to the extent of often burning the midnight oil. I certainly never wasted precious time with TV or other time-wasting activities. Did you have time for TV?"

"That's besides the point."

"It's the main point. How much time did you spend watching TV when your children were growing up?"

"I dunno. About two or three hours a night on weekdays and about six hours a day weekends."

"That's nearly twenty-five hours a week of quality time you could have helped with school work or at least listened to them read. They could have gone to university with that amount of input – Oxbridge even."

"It'd make no difference 'cos none of my kids wanted uni. They couldn't wait to leave school at sixteen. But at least they never rebelled against doing their homework. Okay, they moaned, but they always did it."

"But they left school the minute they could without any qualifications. Did they achieve GCSE's?"

"Kelly did," Trish said proudly.

"What about your other two children?"

"No. So?"

"So they didn't have much of an education to rebel against."

"If they ever decide they want it, they can always go back to studying."

"That's true, though studying's far more challenging for adults. Most working-class adults struggle to simply pay the bills without losing earning time studying."

"But you're lucky being able to afford private education. Bet you have private healthcare too, do you?"

"We're with Bupa, yes, because we worked hard all our lives to afford these luxuries. I wish I had done more for my mother though. I felt bad putting her into a care home when her Alzheimer's required round-the-clock care. Saul and I discussed at length the possibility of her coming to live with us, but since we both had demanding jobs and realised how unreliable visiting daily care could be, we abandoned the idea. At least she spent her final years in an excellent Jewish care home close to us where we were able to keep an eye on her."

"Oh, I wonder if it's the same place I know of. Is it Morris summat?" Trish asked.

"Yes, Morris Feinmann."

"I know someone who did some electrical repairs there. He said it was the only old people's home he knew that didn't smell of wee. In fact he said it smelled like a posh hotel. I'm sure your mam wouldn't have minded ..." A feeling of being gently rocked interrupted Trish and she wondered if she was having a dizzy spell. "Oh, I feel weird."

The roaring sound of an aftershock clarified matters.

"Get under!" Hannah shouted.

"God, no! Not another!" Trish whimpered, crossing herself before switching her sitting position into a foetal ball under the counter with Hannah.

They desperately wanted to scream, but could barely produce a whimper. Rigid with terror, they squeezed themselves into the tightest of balls, then waited and prayed. The swaying room, falling debris and raucous rumblings were less dramatic than the first tremor's, but the fear was greater. They had since considered the possibility that sometimes big earthquakes start with smaller ones. The initial tremor had hit them like a bolt of lightning, allowing no time to increase fear of repercussions. This time was different: the dreaded anticipation of horrific scenarios lay imprinted in their minds in technicolour. As more debris crashed around them, the dust found its way into their lungs, punctuating their prayers and whimpers with coughs and spluttering.

Trish's whimpers morphed into wails as she pined for her loved ones. *Please God, let me see them again. Please God, make this stop.* She was the lucky one. Not only did she have her Catholic God to answer her prayers, she had Jesus, Mary and Joseph; not to mention the Holy Ghost, who is often forgotten by many confused Catholics due to their inability to understand who or what on earth it is. Trish also had her wealth of patron saints, though which one took care of earthquakes, she had no idea. Considering good old Saint Christopher, the patron saint of travellers, hung around her neck, and considering she had travelled to Naples to this nightmare, she reckoned he would have to do. Grasping his medal tightly, she promised to make the Saint Christopher medal everyone's Christmas present if only he would answer her prayers.

Poor Hannah only had one God, and in him she had little faith. In desperation, she prayed to him to be on the safe side. After all, she had not entirely ruled him out.

CHAPTER 11

Four months before the earthquake

Tony, a self-confessed technophobe, relied on Ryan to search for his Neapolitan father on the internet. When they found a Fabio Bianchi on Facebook, proprietor of a pizzeria in Naples, they felt sure it was him. He was about the right age, and the resemblance to Tony was undeniable – the same Roman nose, deep-set dark brown eyes, and a full bottom lip.

"Yeeeeees!" they whooped, giving a unison air punch.

"I'll write to him now," Tony said, excitedly. "You're gonna have to send him my message, Son. Just explain how I don't have a computer, let alone a Facebook account."

By luck, Kelly had dropped by for a dress alteration and offered to help. Collaboratively, the trio composed the letter at the kitchen table.

Tony claimed to be an old customer. "He's seventy. There's no way he'll remember every customer from the sixties," he said. "Definitely worth a try."

At the kitchen door, Rambo barked incessantly to go out. The writers, however, were so focused on their project that his demands fell upon deaf ears.

"Dad, you can't start with *Hiya mate*! It'll be hard for him to translate. Start with *Dear Fabio*," Kelly advised, looking up from the keyboard.

"Let's change *Cheers mate* at the end too; *many thanks* sounds better."

Tony squeezed Kelly's forearm appreciatively. "Whatever you say, love. You know best."

Presently, the distraction of Rambo's barking grated on Ryan's nerves. "For Christ's sake, Ram! Let him out will you, Dad."

Tony obliged, keen to see the letter completed.

Reading through it one more time, Kelly asked, "Okay with it, Dad? Shall we send?"

"Yep, go for it!" Tony replied, with a thumbs up.

Dear Fabio, my father asked me to send you his message (below) because he does not have a Facebook account. I hope that is ok. Regards, Ryan Wilcox

Dear Fabio,

I hope you are the same Fabio I knew around 1961 and that you remember me. The Fabio I knew worked at his uncle's Italian restaurant in Chorlton and lived with him above the restaurant. I often used to eat at the restaurant and we had a lot of laughs together when he served me and my friends his delicious pizzas.

I am hoping you are the same Fabio because you are the only Neapolitan person I know and I plan to visit Naples in a few months for the first time with my wife. I hope you might be able to suggest some good places for us to visit. Thanks very much.

Best wishes,

Tony Wilcox

Fabio's reply arrived in less than ten minutes.

"Woah! Dad! He's replied! Quick, come and see."

Tony had been reading the Mirror newspaper in the living room. Throwing it aside, he sprung out of his armchair, almost tripping over the fireplace rug. "Bloody hell, that was quick! Good or bad?" he asked as he shot to the laptop.

Ryan gestured to the screen. "See for yourself."

Kelly and Trish, having heard the excitement, dashed downstairs – Kelly wearing a dressing gown and Trish holding a pin cushion.

"What is it? Have we won the lottery?" Trish asked.

"Better than that. My father's replied!" Tony said excitedly. "Shh, let's read it."

Eager to see Tony's lottery prize, the family gathered around the screen.

Fabio's reply may not have been perfect English, but it was perfectly understandable. He had no hesitation confirming he was the same Fabio who worked at his uncle's restaurant in 1961. He remembered it well, but did not recall all the customers with whom he may have become friendly. He apologised, saying he would be glad to recommend places to visit in his beautiful city if Tony gave him some indication of his interests.

Tony was last to finish reading it – silent, still and dazed as he attempted to take it in. He read it over and over, reading between the lines for clues – any clues to his father's character. There was a lot to take in – the ramifications and implications, the emotions it stirred, the excitement, the wonder, the relief, but most of all – the anger. *Bloody hell, after all these decades. Can't believe I'm actually communicating with him. He seems friendly enough. Polite and helpful too. Maybe these were qualities Mam liked about him. A bastard who left her up the tub and ran off!* Hungry for further communication, he snapped out of his reverie and turned to Ryan. "Write this, quick." Without consideration to the consequences, he poured out his venom at the man who had deserted him and his mother.

"Christ, Dad, you can't write that," Ryan said, "unless you want to blow it."

Kelly nodded to affirm, and Trish slowly shook her head in dismay. Without giving Tony the opportunity to object, Ryan and Kelly set to work with a honeyed tone as Kelly moved her fingers deftly over the keyboard.

Dear Fabio,

Thanks very much for your quick reply. It is very kind of you to agree to recommend places to visit. However, I am sorry to say I have a confession to make. I was not entirely honest in my previous message. The truth is that I did not know you in 1961. It was my mother who knew you. Her name was Rosemary Galvin. She lived in Sharrinwood and she was short and slim with curly red hair. Do you remember her? When you returned to Naples, you left no forwarding address, otherwise she might have told you the news that she was pregnant with your child. That child is me. I am your son.

I am very sorry if this has come as a shock but I think you need to know because the one part of my letter that was true is that I will be visiting Naples soon. I am coming with my wife Trish on March 14 and I was hoping there might be a chance we could meet. I want nothing from you. All I want is to meet you. I am sure you must be a good man considering my mother fell for you and you do seem kind and helpful in your letter.

I look forward to hearing back from you.

Regards,

Tony (your son)

"There! Let's see what he has to say to that," Kelly said.

"He'll probably need a day or two for it to sink in and figure out how he's gonna tell his family," Ryan added, "but I'm sure he'll reply. He'll be desperate to know more."

"Yeah, course he will. It was a nice, friendly letter too. More than he deserves," said Tony.

However, despite the honeyed tone, they failed to sweeten Fabio. Far from it.

With a click of a button, Fabio Bianchi once again wiped Tony from his life, this time by blocking him from his Facebook page.

At least Ryan had the foresight to have screen-grabbed Fabio's profile photo.

CHAPTER 12

Saturday, 15 March 2008

When silence fell, the women waited like statues for the tremor of all tremors to end it all. Their eyes morphed into those of the insane: wide, staring, darting rapidly to every wall, crevice and draping ceiling for more to follow – any sign of the slightest movement. But the only movement that followed was the settling of debris and their thumping hearts.

As the afternoon passed and dusk fell with no signs of further aftershocks, their breathing grew deeper and even.

True to form, Trish raised the subject of food and drink.

"Look, I realise that now of all times, we need replenishing," Hannah said, "but remember it's got to last." Having no faith in Trish's willpower, she had pushed her bag out of Trish's reach. Stretching over to reach it, she tugged it over slithers of debris and fished out their lunch packs. After dividing an equally small portion of their bread rolls, she handed Trish's portion to her. That was the easy part. Not so easy was sharing the water, knowing Trish was likely to glug it down in one gulp.

"There you go. Savour it and please make it last. I'll give you some of your water when you're finished, okay?"

"Are you having a laugh? That wouldn't feed an ant!" Trish complained, and with that she devoured it in one mouthful. "I'm still starving!"

"For goodness' sake, did you not hear a word I said? Remember, it has to last," Hannah reiterated after savouring her first small mouthful.

Once they had consumed their morsels, they gingerly used their designated toilets.

"Remember not to flush!" Hannah called.

"Yeah, yeah, I know." On her return, Trish said, "Let's hope and pray for some good luck for a change."

"A little bit of luck is better than a ton of gold, according to my late mother," Hannah said. "Talking of luck, to think it was only a few weeks ago we escaped the UK earthquake. The epicentre was Market Rasen but it was felt over much of the country. Luckily, we were sleeping and didn't feel a thing. Did you?"

"Oh God, yeah, I remember it. I was just getting into bed and saw the dressing table rattle. I thought we had a bloody ghost! Tony was at work and Ryan was out, so I was brickin' it. I couldn't sleep a wink after that and was dead tired at work the next day. Which reminds me, I should get a decade of the rosary in to ward off another aftershock." With that, Trish fished her rosary beads from her bag.

After completing a decade, she asked, "Are you still working as a pharmacist?"

"Yes, I've worked at the Christie for six years now."

"The Christie?"

"Sorry. I expect you know it more by its former name, Christie's Hospital, don't you?"

"Yeah. In Withington, right?"

"Yes, one of the leading cancer hospitals in Europe, I'm proud to say."

"It must be dead rewarding helping cancer patients. And good money too."

"Yes, it is rewarding, though extremely sad for patients who don't make it. Do you still work?" Hannah asked.

"I'm a classroom assistant, that's in Adult Ed., not in a school. Crap wage, and I needed to work really hard to get this far. I did it voluntary at first. When I asked for a paid job, they made me go on a Basic Skills training course. Turns out I didn't have basic skills myself." Trish laughed. "But I knew that 'cos I was always taking the worksheets home to learn. I wasn't even sure when to use capital letters. When I was tested, my basic skills were only about Entry 3. I needed to be way higher than that, at Level 2 at least before I could work there."

"Entry 3? What level is that equivalent to in the school system?"

"About Year Four I think. I felt ashamed that nine-year-old kids had better English than me."

"But you did something about it, which is great."

"Yeah, suppose. I'm proud of myself for passing my exams and becoming a qualified classroom assistant."

"Well done you! It must be very rewarding work, and you can transfer those skills to your grandchildren. What did you do before you were a classroom assistant?"

"Oh, all sorts! You name it, I did …" Trish stopped to listen. "Shh! What was that?"

"What? I can't hear anything."

"Shh, listen! Thought I heard voices. Listen!"

They froze, holding their breath to hear the whisper of a sound. But nothing.

"Hmm, must've been wishful thinking. Anyway, where was I?"

"You were about to tell me about the different jobs you've had."

"Oh, yeah. How long have you got?" Trish chuckled. "When I left school at fifteen, I started in shops, then I did some office work, then I was an assistant hairdresser, then a window dresser. Ha, I remember once being in the window, dressing a model when a dirty old fella flashed at me through the window. In those days people just laughed at pervs like that and thought they were just dirty old gits. Everyone knew someone who'd been flashed at 'cos it happened that often."

"Thank goodness it's now considered a sex offence," said Hannah.

"Yeah, good. It should be."

"What about your family? You said you were with your husband?"

"Yeah, Tony. We'd been saving for this holiday for ages 'cos he's on a crap wage too."

"What does he do?"

"He's a baggage handler at Manchester Airport. Not by choice, mind. Just the best paid job he could find with no qualifications. And even then, the money's crap. He's on shifts and often has to work nights. He was keen to come to Naples to find his roots 'cos it's where his father came from. Not that he's ever met him. The swine scarpered back to Naples leaving his mam – rest her soul – six weeks pregnant. All she told Tony about him was his name and that he'd come to England for a few months to help his uncle set up an Italian restaurant. She said she'd gone out with him for a few months and they split when she found out he'd been cheating on her. When he went back to Naples, she found out she was pregnant. She never got to tell him 'cos she didn't know where he lived. The older Tony got, the more obsessed he got about finding him. Me and the kids don't get why he's mithered about a crap dad like that, but he is.

"Same thing happened to our Zoe," Trish continued. "She had her first kid when she was sixteen and the dad scarpered. Mind you, he was only seventeen himself. A terrible shock it was. She was still at school. Tony said things would never be the same again, and he was right. We practically raised Courtney. Not that we regret it. We love her like our own and she's worth it, bless. But we were hoping we'd soon be free of the kids and be able to start enjoying our freedom. Tony was hoping to start lessons in a guitar group and I – well, I'd be glad just to have the kids out of my hair. Instead, we had to start all over again with Courtney. It's a lot more of an effort when you're older. Don't have half the energy. Funny though, 'cos even though I've a lot less energy, I've more patience than I had as a young mother. I suppose it's 'cos we had more commitments back then. Raising kids was new to us, and our expectations were higher with our own, so there was a lot more pressure. At least now we've been there, done that, we know what to expect and we're more laid back. Courtney was the main reason I went to work in education so I'd be free during school holidays to look after her. Which reminds me, I'm gonna text Tony and the kids to say where we are."

"But there's no signal."

"I'm doing it anyway for when there is one – then the messages will send."

"But you'd need to keep your phone connected and waste the battery."

"I don't think trying to reach my family is a waste of battery," Trish snapped.

Hannah sighed in exasperation, knowing it was futile arguing with someone as obstinate as Trish. It was enough Hannah needed her wits about her to prevent Trish devouring the rations, without having to worry about Trish's battery life.

CHAPTER 13

How they managed to sleep that first night was not entirely miraculous: they slept from mental and physical exhaustion coupled with the lulling silence, the mild temperature and the hope they would soon be rescued.

Hannah had needed the toilet in the early hours and tried not to disturb Trish. At least the toilets were close by, and the dead of night served as a reminder to refrain from flushing.

At 6 a.m. the distant sound of competing church bells woke them.

"Can you hear that?" Trish asked excitedly.

"Yes, church bells. A good sign. Maybe the destruction out there isn't as bad as we thought. They're very faint though. They sound miles away. Not quite loud enough to detect the time, if indeed they ring at specific times. Still, we should listen out for them and try counting next time."

"Yeah, definitely, to check my watch is right," Trish replied as she glanced at it. "It's just turned six. Too early for breakfast, but I'm spitting feathers. Do you usually have breakfast?"

"I do – the most important meal of the day. Generally muesli followed by toast and marmalade with a coffee. What about you?"

"Not usually. A cuppa is all I need, then I might have a couple of slices of toast an hour or two later."

"Good. Then you won't mind hanging on for a drink and a bite to eat," Hannah quipped.

"It's night times I'm hungriest when I'm watching telly."

"Watch less television then," Hannah said. She ran her tongue over her teeth to be reminded they needed cleaning. Stretching the hemline of her blouse tightly over her finger, she rubbed her teeth vigorously. She could feel it doing its job and smiled at her ingenuity. She then wiped her face and neck with a wet-wipe before using the same wipe to freshen under her arms. Pulling a second one out, she offered it to Trish. "Have a wet-wipe. I'd offer two, but they have to last."

"Ta. You're a life saver." Having freshened up, Trish checked her phone again. "No! My text still hasn't gone. Still no signal."

"Your battery will be flat in no time at this rate," Hannah said.

And so, to preserve their batteries, they resisted the ritualistic checking of phones. However, as ritualistic as a cat washing after eating, they listened intently for any signs of rescue – as always in vain. The more of nothing they encountered, the more Trish craved food, and the more Hannah needed her wits about her to divert Trish's attention.

Fortunately, Trish enjoyed chatting, and Hannah capitalised on this.

"Do you like music, Trish?"

"Oh yeah, I love it, me," Trish replied enthusiastically.

"What do you like?"

"I like loads. Tamla, Soul, a lot of the 60s and 70s and a bit of HipHop. I got a taste for that from our Ryan and Zoe. Ha, funny 'cos I played hell when I first heard them playing it with all the bad language. I threatened to bin them if they dared play 'em again. Bloody sods took no notice and before I knew it, I loved it myself. Honest to God!" Trish burst into a contagious guffaw, causing Hannah to join her. "Oh yeah, I like Country too. Never did until I started going line dancing and since then it's grown on me. What do you …"

Hannah let out a short, high-pitched scream.

"Oh God, what is it?"

"Ugh, just some debris from the ceiling. It's okay." Hannah looked up to inspect the chaotic ceiling of dangling plasterboard, air conditioning ducting and electrical cables.

Trish followed Hannah's gaze. "Bloody hell, it looks like the lot could fall any minute!"

"It's fine. None of the objects are heavy. Just stay quiet and still for a while."

After a minute of quiet, the conversation resumed.

"Where were we?" Hannah asked. "Oh yes, music. My taste is quite eclectic too. I like most genres from opera to rap, and like you, I developed a liking for rap from my children when they were going through a somewhat rebellious stage. I mostly love classical though. I play cello in an amateur orchestra, which gives me plenty of practice playing classical music as well as listening to it."

"Can't say I know any classical music apart from some of the famous TV advert ones – not that I know what they're called. Hang on, let me think." Trish rolled her eyes to the side in concentration. "Oh, yeah, I know this one," which she unfortunately vocalised. "Daa daa dee daa daa, daa dee daa dee daa. What's that one? That's alright, I suppose."

"Ah, good choice. That's from Carmen – Bizet's 'Toreador Song'. I expect there are many more classical and operatic pieces you'd like which you haven't discovered yet."

"Just thinking of some others I know. Hmm, oh yeah, and I like da da da daaaaa, da da da daaaaa, da da da da, da da da da."

Fortunately for Hannah, she identified the tune immediately without the need to endure more of Trish's rendition. "Ah yes, Beethoven's 'Fifth Symphony'. Another good choice. I'm sure that's not the only Beethoven you know. What about this one?" Hannah gently hummed a few bars of 'Moonlight Sonata'.

"Oh, I like that! What is it?"

"'Moonlight Sonata'. A popular piano piece. Hmmm, let me think. Ah yes, I'll bet you know this one too."

And so the game of Spot the Tune killed some time before they tired of it and resumed conversation.

"Bet you weren't into classical music when you were young though, were you? What about pop music and discos?"

"I liked classical music when I was young too, but admittedly a lot more now I'm older. Of course I liked pop music when I was young, but I didn't frequent night clubs and discos very often. I tried a couple, one in the city centre called Beat City and another in Stockport called Bredbury Hall. But I was too conscientious about my studies to risk late nights. I played tennis at uni and the Northern Tennis Club. I'm still a member of the Northern but just for yoga and cardio fitness nowadays. Talking of tennis, wasn't it great that Federer won Wimbledon for the fifth consecutive year? Imagine playing for almost four hours! Did you see it?"

Trish yawned. "Naa, I'm not into tennis. The only tennis player I know of is McEnroe. He was a laugh. Oh, and the two coloured sisters. What are their names?"

"That'll be Venus and Serena Williams. Venus won the ladies title last year."

"Tennis never gets a mention in our house. It's all football – at least from Ryan. Man United. Tony's not into footie. If he wants to relax, he'll go down the pub, watch telly or practise his guitar. Ryan and his mates have been going on and on about whether United are gonna keep their Premier League title. I'm sick to death of hearing about it and Ronaldo. I hate football and all those bloody hooligans. There's a couple who live near us who've called their poor kid Cristiano, for God's sake. Fine if he's foreign, but the poor kid's a Manc from Sharrinwood. He's gonna have hell at school with a name like that. On the other hand, most Sharrinwood kids love footie, so they'll probably like it."

"I can tolerate football provided I don't have to watch it, hear it or read about it. At least rugby, cricket and tennis don't attract hooliganism as football does. Apart from tennis, I'm not into sport. Theatre's one of our loves. Saul and I grab any opportunity to attend, especially for good productions – the Royal Exchange being a favourite. We used to also enjoy the Capitol Theatre in Didsbury before it closed down. Coffee bars were another favourite during my late teens, especially a place called the Swinging Door on Barlow Moor Road in Didsbury. It was in the basement with dimmed atmospheric lighting. We went to a couple in town too – The Magambo on Mosley Street. The front was a coffee bar and the rear served Chinese food. There was also the Way Inn at Kendal's – part of the Way Inn boutique."

"Kendals was too expensive for my liking. I bought my clothes from Chelsea Girl or made them from fabric I bought from a shop in town called Bachers. Remember the departmental stores on Market Street – Lewis's and Paulden's? Lewis's is now Primark and Paulden's is Debenhams."

"Oh yes, how could we forget? How times have changed."

"Do you drink?" Trish asked.

"I enjoy a glass of red wine with certain meals, especially Italian, but that's about it I suppose. What about you?"

"The same really, but I prefer white. I went through a phase in my teens of getting drunk a lot when we went out, but I grew out of that. Used to get dolled up to the nines with false eyelashes and that. Loved my perfumes too. In those days I wore Coty L'aimant, but nowadays I like Elizabeth Arden's Blue Grass. Do you wear perfume?"

"Yes, I do for special occasions. I like Chanel 19 or Miss Dior."

"God, they must cost a month's wages! What about telly? Do you watch much?"

"Rarely. I like period dramas and the occasional documentary when I have time to spare – a rarity! I'd rather listen to the radio whilst I get on with chores or read at bedtime. What do you like to watch?"

"Always spoilt for choice, so we record a lot. Love Corrie, Casualty and The X Factor. But I better shut up since you won't know what I'm on about if you don't watch it. Ha-ha, you and me are like chalk and cheese, aren't we? Bet when you're having breakfast, you have milk in a jug, don't you, and serviettes with dinner, right?"

Hannah laughed, finding Trish's openness a breath of fresh air. "I admit I lay my table with napkins, but gone are the days we bother with milk jugs. My standards are slipping," she said, chuckling.

"Our standards are in the gutter, then, 'cos we eat our dinners from trays in front of the telly. Plates on trays that is!" she replied with more laughter. The laughter made her chest hurt, causing her to groan. "I like convenience food too – Iceland ready meals and that. Can't be doing with slaving in the kitchen. Making a brew and shoving a ready meal in the oven is my lot. I'll do the occasional roast on Sundays though as a treat. They love that. But generally I've got better things to do."

"Such as?"

"Telly, reading and the internet – Facebook and that. Joined about three months ago 'cos my kids are on it and I wanted to see what they're up to. It's addictive! I've got all my mates and family on it now. Ugh, my back and chest hurt when I laughed," Trish said, twisting herself into a more comfortable position. "That's better."

"I enjoy reading too," Hannah said. "Only at bedtime though as I'm far too busy any other time, and it helps me get off to sleep."

"Yeah, reading definitely helps you sleep, especially when it's boring. Better than sleeping pills!" Trish laughed. "What do you like?"

"Classics, especially Dickens and some Russian literature such as Chekov's short stories and Dostoyevsky."

"Bloody hell, I can't even pronounce that! What's she written?"

"She's a he. I enjoyed his *Crime and Punishment* and *Notes from Underground*."

"I've heard of *Crime and Punishment* but haven't a clue what it's about."

"It's one of Dostoyevsky's greatest works. It's about the mental torments of a young student who kills a mean old female pawnbroker and her sister for the greater good. He tries to hide his guilt and then eventually confesses."

"That sounds good. I think it's been on telly. I like Catherine Cookson. *Feathers in the Fire* was a good one. Have you read it?"

Hannah stifles a cough. "I can't say I have."

"I love biographies too. A great one was Doris Stokes *Voices in my Ear*. You should read it. Have you heard of her?"

"Is she a celebrity?"

"Kind of. She's a medium. I love stuff like that, me. I love celebrity stuff too. I've read Cilla Black's biography and Princess Diana's and Liz Taylor's. You should read 'em, they're …"

"I wonder what's happening outside?" Hannah said, swiftly changing the subject.

CHAPTER 14

"For God's sake," Trish whinged, "can we eat now?"

It was gone 6 p.m. and all they had eaten throughout the day was a small portion each of their bread rolls.

"I was hoping you could hang on a bit longer, but if you ins....."

Hannah's words were cut short by a thunderous roar as the room trembled yet again. Shards of debris flew from all directions. Their hair and nostrils magnetized the clouds of dust that filled the air – thick dust causing them to cough and splutter as they attempted to scream for their lives.

A heavy chunk of masonry hit the back of Trish's head causing her to yelp before losing consciousness.

"Trish! Are you okay? Trish! Trish!"

Trish slowly opened her eyes to meet only blackness.

"Trish, we've lost power. I can't see you. Are you okay? Are you in pain?"

With barely the strength to speak, Trish whispered, "What happened? My head …"

"Just a small after shock, but we've lost power. Something must've hit your head. I'd have a look but I can't see a thing. Have a feel. Is there any blood?"

Trish ran her hand over her head. "Can't feel any. There's a bump though. God, it's dark. What we gonna do?"

"We'll worry about that later. Let's get you sorted first. Put some pressure on it."

"How long was I out?" Trish asked, applying pressure to the bump with the palm of her hand.

"It seemed a long time, but was probably no more than a minute."

"Is that all? It seemed like days."

"Now we can't see the time, I guess we'll have to rely on the temperature as an indicator," Hannah said, "unless the crack in the window gives us some light."

"They say when you're about to kick the bucket your life flashes before you," Trish said, staring meditatively into the darkness. "God, that's so true! Mine did. It seemed to go on for hours – small snippets of it in no particular order. One minute I was grown up, the next a kid, then an adult again. It was like watching a film."

"Really? That's interesting," Hannah said encouragingly, mindful of the benefits of talk as well as a distraction for Trish from thoughts of food.

"First I was a kid when dogs roamed loose without collars and there was no such thing as dog poo bags. I remember that 'cos my mam was screaming at me for letting our Patch out earlier and for me being home late. She was upset 'cos Patch had come home without a tail. Some evil swine had cut it off and there was blood everywhere and Mam was screaming 'Jesus, Mary and Joseph' over and over, and she had to take him in to the RSPCA vet 'cos we couldn't afford a private one. Funny, the vision of her stood there screaming at the front door in her flowered apron dress and her rubber curlers; it was as clear as crystal, and it must've been a Bingo night 'cos that's the only time she put her hair curlers in, and I'd been playing Jax with my next-door-neighbour friend Maureen. Remember Jax with the tiny ball?"

Hannah nodded before remembering that Trish could not see her in the dark. "Yes, yes," she stressed encouragingly. "I used to play Jax too."

"Used to like that game, and when we had others with us, we played skipping where someone had to jump through the rope when it turns and we'd sing stuff like *Sausages in the pan, turn them over, turn them over, sausages in the pan,* and when you said *turn them over,* the girl skipping had to turn around to face the other way."

"Lovely memories," Hannah said, smiling. "We played skipping games like that too. You're bringing it all back. How's your head?"

"Not so bad, thanks. Anyway, next we ended up on Cookson Road fields. It was a gigantic field with big woods at the end of it, and on the way to the woods, we jumped over the stream and collected wild flowers while we sang the Beatle's 'She Loves You' at the top of our voices. Oops, I'd better stop before I bore you to death."

"You're not boring me at all. Carry on."

"Next, I was in labour with Kelly, screaming for gas and air and cursing Tony for putting me there, and Tony was holding my hand, reminding me to pant and I was telling him to sod off – what the frigging hell did he know about childbirth.

"Then I was at the Forum Cinema in Northenden with my sister Moira watching *Yellow Submarine.* We'd bought Coca-Cola and sugared almonds from a little shop over the road where they were cheaper. I miss those old cinemas.

"Then I got visions of the discos I went to in my teens: The Pop Inn over the Co-op on Platt Lane in Rusholme, Takis in town where a mynah bird would greet us when we reached the bottom of the stairs, and the Wheel all-nighter – that's the Twisted Wheel. I used to love Motown and Northern Soul that they played, and still do. Then I saw a lad I went out with at his flat on Clyde Road in Didsbury. Crystal clear it was."

"Ahh, Clyde Road! Everyone knows someone who lived on Clyde Road or thereabouts. In those days that area of West Didsbury was run-down bed-sit land, but nowadays it's a trendy, desirable place to live, full of excellent cosmopolitan restaurants."

"It was like yesterday," Trish continued. "I could hear the records he played – Marvin Gaye's and the Temptations. I saw his scooter and the parka he wore when he rode it – 'cos he was a mod. He's the lad my mam and dad wouldn't let me go out with 'cos he smoked weed and went to the Wheel.

"Then I was making myself a dress on my mam's old Singer sewing machine. I used to make my own clothes 'cos I couldn't afford the ones I liked. Good job I was a girl 'cos my mam almost forced my poor brother into being a priest. In the end, he told her straight that he'd sooner be a street sweeper, so she dropped it.

"Anyways, then I was a kid again – all dressed up in spanking new clothes for the Whit walks. Us kids used to go knocking on neighbours' doors to show off our new clothes and do a little twirl. And they'd say, 'Ooh, don't you look nice!' then give us sixpence or summat.

"Next, I had a vision of being in a Domestic Science class at school and getting sent to the Head by Sister Mary Ignacia – that's one of the nuns – for being caught with a dirty book *The Carpetbaggers*. I tried to explain to her that it got passed to me by Christine Flannigan and that I had no idea what it was about. It was true – I didn't, but she wouldn't have it and sent us both to the Head, and that was one of the times I got the strap. My mam was always on the teacher's side – said it served us right whenever I got it, and then she'd give us a clout for getting the strap. Some kids' parents used to come to school ranting and raving. Said it was abuse. Don't think my mam was clever enough to think that deeply about it, bless.

"They kept the boys and girls well separated everywhere at our school. Maybe they thought we'd have hanky panky in the middle of a lesson or summat. On the other hand, I never could concentrate if I saw a lad I fancied through a window when they were out playing sport. It's all I went to school for – to see whatever lad I fancied at the time. All I remember learning from school was that the Battle of Hastings was in 1066 and a bit of Latin. I'm obviously not academic and left school at fifteen without any O-levels. Ha! At least I learnt some Latin.

"Couldn't wait to start earning some money and neither could my mam. Had to give her most of my wages to pay my share of the rent and gas and lecky bills. My mam would have done better sending us to an all-girls convent school. I would've learned a lot more without lad and pop music distractions. But at least our school was one of the best in Sharrinwood. Kids used to come from as far as Rusholme. The top school in Sharrinwood in them days though was the grammar school of course – Mossways. A friend of mine used to go and said it was brilliant with a state of the arts gym, a library theatre and a debating theatre. They did Latin, lads played rugby and male teachers wore black gowns. A proper good grammar school. The best thing about it was that it was dead strict – like our Catholic school. Kids wouldn't have even dared walk home from school without their school hat. We need more schools like that. But then the government did a stupid thing and changed it to a comprehensive. Pillocks! Of course it went downhill fast. Everyone knew it would, and it did." A vision of the ice-cream van that used to park close to the school sprung to Trish's mind and she gasped, "Oh, we were gonna eat, remember? I'm starving."

I thought it was too good to be true, Hannah mused before sharing one of their boiled eggs.

Presently, they fell silent, lost in their reveries of loved ones, of regrets, of scenarios of being rescued, and of food. Trish visualised roast beef and Yorkshire pudding, sausage and mash, and eggs and bacon with dollops of tomato ketchup. Hannah dreamed of matzo ball soup with challah, cholent (Shabbat stew) crispy falafel and apple cake. As afterthoughts, the women remembered their husbands.

CHAPTER 15

Monday afternoon, 17 March 2008

Another day passed, much the same as the day before except for the darkened room, their darkened hopes and their darkened resolve. Any hope of rescue was diminishing, as was their physical and mental strength. All they had consumed throughout the day was half a boiled egg each and a few sips of water. Being down to their barest of morsels left them with a feeling of foreboding. They did their best, however, to stay positive.

"Thank God it's not as dark as we thought it'd be," Trish said after checking her watch for the umpteenth time. "It's half five."

The tiny breach in the hitherto window afforded them sufficient light to at least get by.

"It'll be dark soon. I guess we should do whatever's necessary before we're plunged into darkness again."

"How about eating?" Trish asked urgently.

"We only have one biscuit each and an orange between us. We could be here for days yet. Please stop pestering. They have to last."

"What?" Trish looked scandalised. "I'm starving. There's no way I'll sleep tonight being this hungry."

Reluctantly, Hannah pulled out the remaining provisions from her bag. "Okay, a couple of segments of orange or half a biscuit? Not both!"

Trish sighed dramatically. "The biscuit, then."

Hannah snapped their biscuits in half, handing Trish's share to her. "Savour it. And this is the last of the water. From tomorrow, we'll have to rely on the cisterns. In fact if we take our last sips now, I'll fill the bottles before it gets dark."

Trish swallowed her morsel of biscuit. "Eww! Do you think it'll be alright?"

"We don't have much choice, do we?"

After using the toilet, Hannah moved to another cubicle. Groping in the dark, she removed the cistern lid and plunged their water bottles in.

"So who's gonna be the guinea pig?" Trish asked.

"It'll be fine. Watch me." Gingerly, Hannah took a miniscule sip before taking a larger one. "Told you. It's fine. See for yourself," she said, handing Trish's bottle to her.

Trish gingerly took a sip, and smiled. "Yay! At least we won't die of thirst now. It's actually like normal water."

Hannah chuckled. "Well, it *is* normal water. Anyway, do you want another sip before we turn in? I know I said there's plenty more, but we don't know how long we're going to be trapped here, so let me take care of it again, okay?"

After her final swig, Trish obliged without question, feeling satisfied at having her thirst quenched, quenched enough to spring into chatter. "I'm chuffed for you, Hannah, being so successful with your work and kids and that. Wish I was doing as well though. But then you work a lot harder than most people to get where you are, so you more than deserve it. Don't get me wrong. We work hard too, but spend a lot of time playing hard as well."

"You're entitled to your pleasures after working hard. Nothing wrong with that."

After settling down on her bed of towels, Trish covered her legs with her jacket and her shoulders with another towel. "Better get our heads down since there's nowt else we can do in the pitch black."

Hannah followed suit, using her backpack covered by a towel as her pillow.

"At least we can chat," Trish enthused. "Nowadays it's hard to find jobs. When I was young, we easily walked into a job after leaving school but nowadays there aren't any. I blame the Tories!"

"You're a Labour supporter, then?"

"Course I am. Our family have always voted Labour 'cos they protect the working people from getting ripped off by greedy bosses," Trish replied proudly. "Thank God Labour help them with trade unions."

"Hmm, trade unions may *think* they're helping, but sometimes they cause businesses to go under with all their strikes; the consequences of course are job losses for the very people they claim to be helping. And picket lines that prevented workers earning their pay to feed their families were quite immoral. Thank goodness Thatcher had the sense to put a stop to it."

"Are you having a laugh?" Trish retorted.

"Of course not. Why do you say that?"

"Cos most people, like myself, can't stand the sight of her."

"I'm not saying I was a fan, but I admired her strength. Would you prefer we talked about your Labour party, then?"

"Yeah, if you want."

"Okay, well my children vote Labour. I've noticed how socialism seems to be especially fashionable with the younger generation – but I've never been a follower of fashion."

Ha, you can say that again, Trish mused as she considered Hannah's attire.

"If it's so great, why has it failed most countries that tried it? Look at Cuba's poverty for instance, and North Korea's. I agree an element of socialism is needed, but so is capitalism. It's necessary for democracy, for decent living standards and economic growth. And its competitive element raises standards of living. For the poor, it not merely creates employment but encourages self-employment."

"I can't argue with that. Without employment we'd starve. Actually, we already half starve as it is. We could never afford the posh foods you eat."

"I'm not surprised considering the amount of money you burn on smoking."

"I *am* trying to quit."

"Good on you. But look at all the highly processed foods you consume. They cost twice as much as fresh, wholesome produce."

"You must be joking. I don't have the time to faff around in the kitchen with fresh foods – not when I go out to work. I must admit though, a fat lot of good Labour's doing us at the moment. Ryan's been unemployed for eighteen months. He's been for dozens of job interviews and can't get work for love nor money."

"Could he not work for himself? Everyone who's able enough can do something."

"That's all very well to say with your education. We wouldn't know where to start with self-employment. Wouldn't have the skills. We're not thick, but I bet your IQs are way higher than ours 'cos of your private education."

"You're absolutely correct – you'd never succeed in anything with a defeatist attitude like that. Anyone, even people with disabilities, can succeed in self-employment if they put their minds to it. What about the billions of uneducated, self-employed people in developing countries? Many are often illiterate, yet manage self-employment. Look at the hawkers and rickshaw-pullers. In fact, having no benefits system gives them the incentive to strive to better themselves."

Trish pulled the towel higher around her neck. "Who wants hawkers and rickshaw-pullers in this country? What self-employment can I do? I can't do anything."

"Rubbish! If people with significant disabilities can succeed, anyone can. Look at Helen Keller – the first deaf and blind person to gain a degree; Stephen Hawking is quadriplegic, Stevie Wonder is blind, Beethoven was deaf, Richard Branson has dyslexia, not to mention the endless Paralympic medallists who …"

"Hang on," Trish interjected, "they're not the average run of the mill people like me. They're famous."

"Ah, but it was their incredible achievements that made them famous because they exceeded all expectations. Okay, if you want an example of a great achiever who isn't famous, let me tell you about Chris. Chris is a young man I know with Down's syndrome who has achieved a Gold Duke of Edinburgh award. He works in a supermarket, plays the trumpet well enough to perform in special needs orchestra concerts and ballroom dances far better than many able people. Do you think he whinged on and on with your woe-is-me attitude? Far from it. He – they all – focused on what they *can* do, rather than what they *can't* do. I think their barriers spurred them on. If they can succeed, there should be no reason why you, your son, or any unemployed able person can't succeed too. It's up to you to create self-employment if you can't find anyone who'll employ you. You can cook, iron, drive, clean, make and repair clothes and curtains too, can't you?"

"Of course I can do domestic work and yeah, I can sew too. I also do a bit of furniture restoration, doing up junk furniture."

"There you go! There's several skills you could turn into profitable businesses for a start. A repair and alteration service, or what about a cleaning business?"

"A cleaning business? Are you having a laugh? We'd need a team of cleaners in our house to fumigate my son's bedroom."

"You could combine a cleaning business with maybe an ironing service, an alteration and dressmaking service – an extra string to your bow. Or, you could upcycle junk furniture and sell them on the internet. If the furniture restoration took off, you could expand with your son and maybe set up an antique stall, maybe at the Antique Hypermarket in Levenshulme. What about your son? What can he do?"

"Nothing he could turn into a successful business."

"There you go again with your defeatist attitude. Tell me," Hannah demanded, before turning onto her side and straightening the towels under her. Four towels on a cold marble floor were a far cry from her pocket sprung, memory foam mattress. Her back was now paying the price.

Trish laughed. "You don't give up, do you? Okay, he can restore old furniture like me and he's good with computers – fixing and building them. He can create websites too. Oh, he's good with DIY, painting and decorating and has done basic construction in the building trade. Oh, and he plays guitar."

"Are you serious? He can do all that? He could have set up a variety of businesses by now and be well on his way to success. There's potential for an antique stall, a computer repair shop or web design company, or a painting and decorating service. Whatever he's best at, then he could possibly do a short college course to enhance his skills. He's practically spoilt for choice."

Trish rolled her eyes. "We can't afford to be setting up a business and renting premises. We can hardly afford to pay our rent and utility bills."

"You don't need capital to start a business. You could start most of those businesses from home by simply offering your services. Start small, then expand. What about his music to lift his spirits? If he's good, he could promote it on YouTube or even do amateur gigs. It's what my daughter Sadie does. She fancies herself as a singer-songwriter and does the occasional gig at a jazz club in the Northern Quarter called Jazz Fusion."

"Actually, we're worried, 'cos he's even stopped playing his guitar," Trish added, "and that's one of the reasons we think he must be proper depressed."

"Tell him about Jazz Fusion. They have an open mic every Thursday evening. It might encourage him to play again."

"I will if I remember what it's called," Trish replied. "I've got a memory like a sieve. But anyways, I wouldn't have thought he'd be good enough. He just messes around with it really. But yeah, he does need a goal."

"Actually, there are advantages to being self-employed: flexible working hours, the potential for increased earning, autonomy to do things your way and greater motivation to work harder since you reap the rewards. My father, and many more Jews like him who were successful in business, weren't necessarily well educated. His only accomplished skill was tailoring, so he capitalised on it, and look how successful he became. Many of his friends and relatives became equally successful in their various fields. I think Jews hold an extremely high value for skills and education because material gains can be ripped from us in a heartbeat, as it has for Jews over the ages, but knowledge and qualifications can't. Many Jewish parents have striven to give their children the best education possible to enable social mobility into the professions. Now, yourselves, not being Jewish, are free from such persecution. It doesn't matter quite so much that you're not academic because you can become self-employed. With a bit of hard work and determination, you could do quite well for yourselves."

"Yeah, in my dreams. I'd never be rich enough to afford private education and healthcare like you."

CHAPTER 16

"But surely you wouldn't have private education and healthcare if you could afford it, would you?" Hannah asked, bemused.

"Are you mental? Course I would! But at least we bought our council house."

"Ah yes," Hannah said, "Mrs Thatcher's 'Right to Buy'. So now you have the opportunity to eventually sell up and escape the council estate segregation trap. Good for you."

"Yeah, it was the only way we could get on the property ladder." Historically, the mere mention of the Tories turned the Wilcoxes vociferous. The Tory 'Right to Buy' scheme, however, did not stop Trish and Tony from jumping on its bandwagon.

"I think you're a Tory at heart."

"Don't be ridiculous. Why would you say that?"

"Because a true socialist wouldn't consider buying their council house, have private education and healthcare, and be in favour of grammar schools, but you're very much in favour of them all."

"What you on about? All my friends vote Labour and I'm sure they'd all pounce at the chance of all those things. Anyway, I never said I was a socialist. I said I voted Labour."

"It's the same thing. Labour has historically been known as a socialist party. Its red rose emblem is a common symbol of socialism and I believe the socialist song 'The Red Flag' is the Labour party's anthem. Yes, your ideas sound far more Conservative than socialist to me."

"You must be joking! I'd rather stick pins in my eyes than vote for a party that Thatcher ran! What about when the coal mines got closed down leaving all those poor miners unemployed."

"I agree it was extremely sad that the miners lost their livelihoods. Nobody's denying that. However, the coal mines were death traps. I wouldn't have sent a dog down there, let alone human beings. Coal pollutants don't merely cause silicosis and asbestosis, they can cause lung cancer, coronary diseases and asthma. That's not to mention the damage to the environment with air pollution."

"What about the disgusting way she treated the unions – unions that help working people."

Hannah exhaled frustration. "Working people. How I dislike that term considering employers and the self-employed who give their businesses their blood, sweat and tears – who take their business worries to bed, on holiday and to their death beds – aren't also referred to as *the working people*. So what are they? A bunch of layabouts?"

"What?" Trish retorted. "It's the workers who get ripped off by the bosses! Everyone knows that!"

"Have you ever employed staff?"

"No, but everyone knows they get ripped off by bosses. Thank God for trade unions."

"I accept trade unions can be helpful to workers, but have you forgotten the crippling Winter of Discontent caused by them in the late seventies?" Hannah asked, shaking her head on her makeshift pillow. "Thanks to them, we couldn't buy a loaf of bread, rubbish piled high in the streets, and we had to rely on candles because of the constant power cuts. Good Lord, we couldn't even bury the dead! Thanks to trade unions, my poor uncle's wholesale business, which had taken him years of extreme hard work to establish, folded causing over twenty job losses."

"I'm sorry about your uncle, but look at the other terrible things Thatcher did, like stopping kids' school milk."

"I'm not saying she didn't make mistakes, such as that one. All world leaders make some mistakes."

"Well, my family have always vote Labour and I would never vote for anyone else," Trish retorted, giving Hannah the V-sign with a look to kill. "Anyway, you should be thanking Labour for our NHS. I bet you're happy to use it, aren't you?" Trish said with a smug, tight-lipped grin.

"Of course, our NHS is a national treasure," Hannah replied. "However, some would argue that Labour merely inherited its initiation from the former coalition government, which consisted predominantly of Tories. It was Churchill who broadcast his NHS plan in 1943 and again in 1945. Around that time Willink, Minister of Health, another Tory, introduced the NHS in the White Paper. The video footage of that speech is there for anyone to see on the internet. When Labour came into power in 1945, they took the credit." Although indifferent to this argument, Hannah used it to wipe the smugness from Trish's face.

"I find that hard to believe. I'll look it up. Besides, I bet you followed what your parents voted," Trish said.

"Of course not. I vote for what I believe in, regardless of their political stance."

"Oh, so not that many Jewish people vote Conservative?" Trish asked.

"I'd hazard a guess that as many, if not more, vote for other parties. My parents always voted Labour because they believed, as you do, that it was for working-class people." Hannah turned over to her other side. "But politics is a bit heavy before sleep. Can't say I'm sleepy though. Are you?"

Trish wore her heart on her sleeve, loving nothing more than discussing matters most middle-class people would only divulge to their best friend. "Okay, so did you marry the love of your life?" she asked without any preamble.

Hannah's eyes widened before considering her response. "Well, of course." As she uttered this untruth, her thoughts returned to Andrew. She may well have moved on practically, but not emotionally: there had not been a week that passed when she had not thought of him – wondered how he was, where he was, what he was doing and whether he was happy – whether he still thought of her. She sometimes fantasied about him, conjuring up romantic scenarios of bumping into him in a coffee shop and them rekindling their relationship. She would then tell herself to stop behaving like a silly teenager. "There was another man I loved, but he wasn't Jewish and my parents would have been fiercely against me marrying him. I didn't dare tell them I was even seeing him. I managed to hide it from them for a year. I eventually ended the relationship because lying to them was too stressful and there could never have been a future in it anyway. It was for the best."

"Aww, what a shame. What was his name?"

"Andrew."

"Well, you should've followed your heart. Would your parents have accepted him if he'd converted to your religion?"

"I doubt it, and I would never have expected him to do so as he was an atheist."

"You should have followed your heart anyway. It's you who would've lived with him for the rest of your life, not your parents. What would you do if one of your kids wanted to marry someone who wasn't Jewish?"

"I would prefer they married a Jew, but if they chose to do otherwise, they would have my blessing. At least one advantage of marrying a non-Jew would be the reduced risk of their offspring suffering from antisemitism."

"I can understand parents moaning about us going out with bad lads," Trish said, "but just because he wasn't Jewish seems a bit harsh. But then mine were nearly as bad about Protestants. They wanted me to marry a Catholic like us. I took no notice and went out with whoever I fancied. Lucky for them I ended up with Tony who happens to be Catholic. It was his Italian looks I fell for. I was eight years older than him, but my mam and dad didn't really care, so long as he was Catholic. I remember them going berserk when I went out with a lad called Carl who took weed and went to the Wheel all-nighter."

"I knew a few Jewish people who used to go there," Hannah said. "The fact it didn't start until late Saturday evening enabled them to attend after Shabbat."

"I didn't know any Jewish people there. Anyway, this Carl took us a few times. It went on till morning. My mam and dad went ballistic when they found out. My mam gave me a right clouting. They thought I was stopping at his house with his mam and dad. Lucky for mine, he chucked me. To me, he was wonderful back then with his scooter and his parka. A proper mod. Now I realise he'd have been bad news. They say every cloud has a silver lining. I reckon this nightmare has one," said Trish.

"Oh, what's that?"

"Once we get out of here, we'll appreciate life more and do all the things we regret we haven't done."

"That's true. Are there many things you regret not having done?"

"Oh yeah, loads. I really wish I'd paid attention at school and made summat of myself. Wish I'd learned to play piano and guitar and to dance too."

"You can line dance, can't you?"

"Yeah, but it's not the same. I'd like to ballroom dance – the tango, quickstep and that. I'm sorry I did things that's aged and wrinkled me – smoking and sunbathing. I wish I'd left Manchester when I had kids and raised them in the country where there was less chance of bad influences and the temptation of drugs."

"You can't turn back the clock, but you can still learn piano, guitar and dancing. You can go back to learning and gain more qualifications. I wish I'd done better too. Wish I'd got the grades for medical school. I wanted to be a doctor. Wish I'd been a better mother too so Sadie didn't need to be nagged to do her studies."

"Don't be daft. You must be a great mam considering how well your kids have done."

"I'm sure you are too. We all want the best for our children – for them to be happy and healthy and enjoy the opportunities we didn't have."

"Yeah, that's true."

"Getting sleepy now. Goodnight," Hannah said, pulling her towel tightly up to her neck.

"Me too. Night."

* * *

Several hours later, Hannah woke bolt upright from a dream. In it, she had been in Morten's – a book shop nestled on a quaint cobbled side street in the village. Stepping out of the store, her high heel became stuck in between the cobbles, sending her tumbling forward. As she looked ahead, she saw Andrew running towards her, calling to her to watch out, holding out his arms to catch her. But it was too late. As she was about to crash face down onto the cobblestones, she awoke with a pounding heart. "Arrrrgh!"

"Oh my God, what is it?" Trish asked. "Are you okay?"

"I'm fine, thanks. Just an unpleasant dream."

"Since being here," Trish said, "every time I wake up, I think it's a nightmare, then I remember it's for real. I just wish to God it was a nightmare."

Once calmer, Hannah mused over her dream. *Funny I dreamt of Andrew. How are you, Andrew? Where are you? Who are you with? Do you still think of me like I think of you?* Whenever Hannah dreamt of him, the hurt returned for hours after waking, sometimes for days.

Trish struggled getting back to sleep. She grew concerned about a matter she desperately wanted to tell her children – something she had kept from them for years – something she realised could not be taken to the grave. She considered how she could let them know without a phone signal. She looked in Hannah's direction. *What if I tell Hannah? She could pass on the message if I don't make it. If I've got the guts to tell her, that is. It'd be dead embarrassing and she'd be as shocked as hell. Maybe I could leave a note for Ryan in my bag and hope Tony doesn't find it? But what if he does? No! That's out.* The more Trish considered her dilemma, the more she realised she had no alternative. She had to tell Hannah.

Her thoughts raced back to the day her life changed forever.

CHAPTER 17

Manchester, 1999

It was the time Britney Spears' hit single 'Baby One More Time' was in the charts. Ryan remembered it well because he had repeatedly complained that Trish sang it more times than his nerves could bear.

For Trish though, 1999 meant one thing: it was the year she became traumatised with a shocking revelation that changed her life forever.

She was working on the tills at Freshda supermarket when Matt, a workmate in Bakery, invited her and three others from the store to his fortieth birthday celebrations at Pulsation nightclub. It was Trish's first visit to the Gay Village and she had been looking forward to it. The Freshda party lived close to each other in Sharrinwood. Because they intended to do a fair bit of drinking, they shared a taxi to the venue. There was Trish, two young women and a lad in his late teens – all from Packing. Sue was an outsider who tagged along as Trish's best friend.

"Have you told Tony where you're going?" Sue asked with a chortle.

Trish guffawed. "Ha! Can you imagine his face? I think he'd have a heart attack!"

Matt and his partner Jake had made their way to the venue after arranging to meet an additional group of friends inside the club. They arrived at 8:30 p.m., shortly before the Freshda group's arrival. Above the throbbing dance beats, they attempted to make introductions by signing and yelling at the top of their voices, but it was futile. Once they had a few drinks inside them, they would have forgotten new names anyway.

By 10 p.m. and several litres of alcohol consumed by the party, the atmosphere was in full swing with everyone dancing to the rhythmic beats of electro and other dance floor music.

Sylvester's 'You Make Me Feel Mighty Real' was one of Trish's dance favourites. With a scream of delight, she yelled, "I love this!" and dragged Matt and Sue onto the dance floor. She was fond of Matt and it pleased her seeing him in an environment where he felt most at ease.

"Oi, you getting the drinks in?" Sue shouted to Trish, trying to be heard over the blaring music.

"What?" Trish called, cupping her hands around the back of her ears. "Can't hear!"

Shaking her drinking hand at her mouth, Sue mimed her question ostentatiously as she danced closer towards Trish before yelling into her ear, "Your turn to get the drinks in!"

Trish jumped back. "Bloody hell. You nearly burst my eardrum!" Having mentally noted the drinks order, she semi-danced to the bar.

A scantily clad petite oriental girl with small breasts pushed up to reveal a cleavage, looked Trish up and down and smiled provocatively. Trish politely returned a tight-lipped smile and quickly looked the other way.

"Yes?" a blonde transvestite barman asked.

Before Trish had the chance to respond, she caught sight of a familiar figure from the corner of her eye and did a double take. "Erm," she spluttered as she tried to process the confusion unfolding. She looked again to be sure, her mouth sagging open. "Ta, but never mind."

It can't be. I must be dreaming. What she saw was too ludicrous for words – a man who looked remarkably like Tony. However, Tony would never be caught dead near a gay nightclub, let alone inside one. The possibility was too incredulous to take in, especially as this man was wrapped in the arms of another – who he was about to kiss.

Trish laughed out loud at the ludicrous notion – Tony, a self-confessed homophobe in a gay nightclub about to kiss a man. To be sure she had not hallucinated, she took a longer look. The visibility was not great in dimmed lighting, especially as he was now hidden in a passionate embrace. But when he came up for air, reality hit her. It was Tony alright wearing his white T-shirt with 'Ibiza' printed across the front; Tony looking blissfully happy – happier than she had ever seen him in all their years together, laughing and kissing his … his what? Could it have been a woman after all? But what would be worse – him cheating with a woman or with a man?

Squinting for clearer visibility, she then saw an unmistakable thick dark moustache.

The room began to sway. She grabbed a chair top for balance. Blinking, she looked one more time. But there was no mistake. In an instant, her secure and reasonably content world collapsed into a heap. She stood motionless with her mouth still agog. Tears streamed down her cheeks and she looked around for Sue. Spotting her, she gestured her over.

"Bloody hell! Are you okay, chuck? You look like you've seen a ghost!"

"I need some air."

"C'mon, hun," Sue said as she escorted her outdoors.

A couple of burly bouncers in black policing the doorway asked if Trish needed assistance.

"Just get me a taxi. I need to go home." She always confided in Sue about everything, but at this moment all she wanted was to escape this nightmare and the risk of Tony spotting her. She needed the security of home to take it in. She would confide in Sue another time, once she knew what to do.

A friendly Asian taxi driver in his fifties began to strike up conversation. Trish's monosyllabic replies, however, told him she was not in the mood, and he soon gave up.

Her mind raced, wondering what tactics to take with Tony. At least he had not spotted her, and time was on her side before deciding if and when to have it out with him. She wondered how she could have been so blind in failing to notice he was gay and frequented gay nightclubs. But then he often worked nights which enabled him to lead this double life. She remembered his excuse for being out that night – overtime. *Liar!*

She remembered when he accepted his job offer at the airport. Shortly before this, he was offered an office-hour job that would have been ideal. Yet he had turned it down. Now she knew why. She flinched at how he always feigned hating gays. It had only been a couple of months ago he had cursed a new television programme called *Queer as Folk* about three gay men who lived in Manchester's Gay Village. Now she understood why: he was in denial, using the lie to hide his sexuality.

Maybe it's my fault. What if I'd been more loving? What if I hadn't nagged so much? Surely he wasn't always gay? He was straight when we got married. I would've known if he wasn't. I must've caused it – turned him off women. He couldn't have chosen to be gay like some who say they're queer by choice, not if he claims to hate gays, so maybe he's bi? Endless possible explanations whizzed around her head.

"Which house, Madam?" the driver repeated.

"Oh, sorry. Just at that white car, ta," Trish said, pointing out Tony's Astra. *Ahh, so that's why the bastard didn't take his car. Cos he's drinking. And he said his brakes were iffy. Lying bastard!*

As she trudged up her garden path and opened the front door, a dog whined pitifully in a neighbouring street. *Poor sod. He sounds how I bloody feel.*

Once inside, she made a beeline to the spare bedroom for an investigatory snoop. Tony had a chest of drawers that he used for his personal belongings – unwanted gifts, old watches, wallets and cuff links. What Trish expected to find, she was unsure. *Maybe women's clothes for cross-dressing? Do gay men cross-dress? Maybe makeup? Don't think he was wearing any at Pulsation though.*

She checked her watch. Ten thirty. *Christ, if he knows I've seen him, he might be home earlier.* She dashed downstairs to lock the front door. He would have to ring the doorbell, which would give her time to clear up before letting him in. She had been convinced she would find evidence of his other life, but after another fifteen minutes searching, to her astonishment, she found nothing. His old address book revealed only the contact details of neighbours, Tony's work and pub mates, and tradesmen. Still, at least she knew where it was should she later need it. An old school photo of Tony gave her an idea.

Returning downstairs to the chest of drawers where she kept her photo albums, she pulled out the most recent. Eagerly, she flipped through the cellophane-covered pages, extracting three recent photos of Tony: a full length shot, a head-on shot and a profile shot – all taken on holiday in Spain the previous year. She would ask Matt if he recognises him. As she placed the album back into the drawer, she spotted Tony's acoustic guitar propped up against the side of the fireplace. *His song lyrics! If there's gonna be clues anywhere, it'll be in his lyrics.*

She dashed back upstairs to locate them in his chest of drawers. There she found various guitar books – Simon and Garfunkel, Bob Dylan, Status Quo and a compendium of popular rock guitar music. Underneath them, a plastic wallet contained an assortment of sheets with Tony's hand-written chords and lyrics. Trish would recognise his handwriting anywhere – untidy, large and sloping to the right. Desperate for clues, she read through them eagerly. She found a song entitled 'Searching' about his father; one entitled 'Mam'; a couple about himself when younger; and a batch of his love songs. *Yes! There's bound to be something here!*

However, nothing hinted at the gender of these loves, nor revealed clues regarding his sexuality.

* * *

In work on Monday, Trish was fired up with anticipation, waiting for the opportunity to show Matt the photos. Since they had different tea breaks, she was unable to see him until lunchtime. When she spotted him enter the staff canteen, she eagerly dashed towards him.

Matt slowed his pace as he headed to the food counter. "Woah! What's up, Trish? You look fraught."

"I am fraught! Do you recognise this bloke?" she asked as she thrust the photos at him.

"Funny question," Matt replied as he inspected each photo. "Yeah, I know him. Why do you ask?"

"What's his name? How do you know him?"

"It's Anthony. I know him from Pulsation. He's in there sometimes with a bloke called Jarvis," he said, handing back the photos.

"Anthony? That's what he calls himself?"

"Yep, Anthony. How do you know him?"

Trish gulped. "It's Tony, my hubby."

"What? You're kidding me!" Matt replied, his hand motionless over the tuna and cucumber sandwich he was about to select.

"Do I look like I'm kidding?"

"I don't get it. You always said he was homophobic. So it can't be the same guy, surely?"

"Course it is. I got the photos from our family album."

"But you said he hates gays."

"Don't you think I'm as baffled as you?"

"Shit! You mean you didn't know he was gay?" Matt asked. "You've only just found out?"

"Yeah. After all these years, I discovered it on the night of your fortieth when I saw him snogging a fella. Until then I had no idea."

"Aww, Trish, I'm sorry, love. It must've been a helluva shock."

"Yeah, it was. Will you let us know if you see him in there again?"

"You're a mate, Trish, but so is he, and I can hardly grass on a mate, can I?"

"Yeah, course. I get it."

"Joining me for lunch?" Matt asked as he took hold of the sandwich pack.

"No ta. Got to get a bit of shopping in. Ta-ra."

"Don't let it get you down. Talk to him, Trish. See ya."

Suppose that's it, then. Gonna have to have it out with him. I'll do it tonight when he's back from work. I'll make a nice tea to butter him up, then pounce. Bastard! Ha, the bloody irony – me who's always loved gay men end up with my very own gay hubby!

CHAPTER 18

Trish geared herself up for the momentous showdown. Would he lie? Deny everything? Be relieved it was out in the open and agree to a divorce? Insist he was bisexual and that it would never happen again? Blame Trish for being a terrible wife who drove him to it?

Sticking to her plan, she kept her cool until after tea. Only later as they washed the dishes together did the soup hit the fan.

"Tony," she said sweetly, drying a dinner plate, "I need to ask you summat."

"Oh yeah? What?"

"Do you ever go into town when you're on a night shift?"

"Town? Why the hell would I do that? Why you asking?" He gulped, slowing down the dish brush rotation inside the stained coffee mug.

Trish placed the dried plate on the worktop. "So you never, for instance, go to the Gay Village?"

Colour drained from Tony's face as the brush rested motionless in the mug. "What the friggin' hell are you on about?"

Trish threw the dish towel on the worktop, placed her hands on her hips and gave him a power stare. "Bleeding liar! I saw you there snogging a fella! You lying bastard!"

Dread twisted in Tony's gut. "What the f . . .?"

Trish squared up to him, pointing her finger close to his face. "Don't lie, you bastard! Just admit it. I saw you."

Tony inched back. "You're mental. You must be seeing things or I have a lookalike. I'm no friggin' pansy!" he snarled.

Trish opened her mouth to reply, but before she uttered a word, Tony fired his next line of defence.

"See? You can't answer me, can you? Why? 'cos you know I'm right," he retorted, slamming the mug on the draining board.

"You're beyond belief. I caught you red-handed and you're still denying it. Besides, you don't need to be camp to be gay. Even I know that. Some of Matt's gay friends are really macho with six-packs. They look manlier than you ever could."

"Well, I'm no friggin' poof. What the hell were you doing in a gay bar anyway?"

"Don't dare turn the guilt around on me!" Spit shot out of her mouth as she screamed out the painful truth. "For your information, I was at Matt's fortieth. Remember Matt's gay? Well, he had the do at Pulsation where you were snogging a guy's face off. You bastard hypocrite. All these years you've slagged off gays when all along you're gay yourself. Christ, it beggars belief!"

"You're unhinged, woman! Go and see a shrink. Get it into your thick skull, it wasn't me."

"God, you're unbelievable! I saw it with my own eyes and you're still lying through your teeth. Okay, I'll tell you how I know. Matt had no idea you were related to me so when I showed him your photos, he recognised you straight away. Anthony he called you. Ha, bloody Anthony. He said you go to Pulsation often, sometimes with a Jarvis. Is he the one you were snogging? It was only after he told me all that did I admit who you were. So the secret's out. So what have you got to say about it?"

Tony's shoulders slumped in defeat as he stood mute. Slowly, he walked to the kitchen table. Sitting heavily on the nearest chair, he placed his head in his palms.

Trish pulled out a chair next to him. "I just want the truth. Is that too much to ask?"

Tony let out a long, mournful sigh. "How could I have told you? It would've been easier telling you I was having an affair with a woman than admit this and be seen as a hypocrite."

"So why were you a hypocrite when you're ashamed of being one?" Trish asked with upturned palms.

"I guess I pretended to hate gays so you wouldn't suspect and partly 'cos it's true – I can't be doing with camp gays who advertise being gay. No need for any of that in my book."

"So our marriage has been one big lie. You probably married me so no one would suspect you were gay. Is that it?"

"No, it's not. I did fancy – love – you, and still do. I'm bi, not gay."

"So you're saying you're greedy – you want a bit of both sexes?"

"It's not about greed. You can't help your feelings and who you fancy."

"Stop talking crap. You went out looking! You went to the gay bars looking. A faithful married man doesn't go looking anywhere, let alone to a pick-up joint like that."

"You'd never understand, so I won't even bother trying to explain."

"God, I don't know what the kids'll think about it. Are you gonna tell 'em or shall I?"

"You're joking, aren't you? Are you mad?" Tony's brown eyes turned owl-like.

"They need to know what a hypocrite you are. I don't want them thinking I threw you out for nothing."

"What do you mean, threw me out?" Tony spat. "I'm going nowhere!" He shot up, fetched himself a can of lager from the fridge and popped the top.

"Well, you're not coming in our bedroom, that's for sure. I don't know where you've been. You could have AIDs for all I know. You bastard! The kids need to know. Have you had an HIV test? A VD test?"

"Of course not. Now you're being ridiculous. Don't tell the kids, Trish. Please. Don't tell a soul. I don't know what I'd do if anyone knew."

"You should come out anyway for your own good. You can't live a lie," Trish said as she fetched a diet coke from the fridge.

"I agree if I was gay, but I'm not – I still love you and don't want to lose you. I'm sorry you found out this way. I've thought about telling you for years. Wondered whether the disadvantages of you knowing would outweigh the advantages and decided they would, so decided to keep it zipped. It wouldn't be half as bad being gay if we didn't live in Sharrinwood."

"What? What you on about?" Trish asked, bemused. "Gays are everywhere."

Tony took another swig of his lager. "My mates take the piss out of 'em."

"I don't know about that, but one thing I do know – my friends are decent people. I doubt any would be homophobic."

"It's different for fellas."

"You mean you have to be macho, like proper tough men?"

"Yeah, summat like that. It's probably not half as bad in places like Chorlton and Didsbury where people are more educated, but I'd be the laughing stock with my mates. Besides, I'm not gay." Tony stopped to listen to the sound of the front door opening. "Shh! Ryan's home. Don't breathe a word," he said, with pleading eyes.

"You better get some bedding together and sleep in the spare room," Trish said as she disposed of the empty cans in the pedal bin. "We'll talk about it tomorrow,"

However, they never did discuss it. Trish may have forgiven him, but she never forgot, and their marriage never recovered.

Seven years later she met Ian, fell in love and asked Tony for a divorce. Rather than comply, he threatened to kill himself. Too frightened to take the risk, Trish stayed with him and carried on with her clandestine affair with Ian. She had hoped Tony would have accepted that a dead marriage is worse than none and agree to a divorce. She assured him she would never tell a soul about his sexuality. Conversely, she tried to persuade him to come out. But despite her suggestions and pleas, nothing would change his mind. Despite his sexuality, he still loved her.

CHAPTER 19

Tuesday morning, 18 March 2008

After morning ablutions, after silence punctuated by forlorn sighs, after private thoughts about loved-ones, Trish cleared her throat.

"Hannah, I need to tell you summat – summat important," she said, wringing her hands. "A bit personal. Is that okay?"

"Yes, of course. What is it?"

"I've been seeing a fella called Ian who I met at line dancing a couple of years ago. Tony doesn't know. Least I don't think he does. I've been saving up for the day I can leave him. The thing is …" Trish hesitated to consider how she could admit her 'homophobic' husband was gay. *If I don't tell her, she'll think I'm a cow leaving him for no good reason. I can't lie and say summat else, like he had an affair. No, I'll tell her straight,* she concluded. "I found out Tony's gay. I caught him snogging a man in a gay nightclub and our marriage has never been the same since."

Had the room not been in darkness, Trish would have noticed Hannah's slack-jawed, saucer eyed expression.

"Tony? Gay? But you said he was homophobic."

"That's what I thought. The bloody hypocrite. Of all people to be gay. He told me it was his way of hiding he was gay. I mean no one would ever guess he was gay if he was married and pretended he hated gays, would they?"

"Good grief, what a surprise. Yes, it sounds like his feigned homophobia was a defence mechanism to hide his sexuality and maybe feelings of guilt, which is probably not uncommon amongst closeted gays."

"The weird thing is, even after it all came out in the open – at least with me – he still pretends to hate gays. It's like he's convinced himself. He did admit though that it's just the camp behaviour he can't tolerate. He doesn't look or act gay. No one would know. The only little give aways are that he hates football and loves Corrie."

"I assume most Coronation Street viewers are women and most football fans are men, but sport and TV programme preferences are hardly indicators of a person's sexuality," Hannah said.

"Exactly! Which goes to show that no one would guess he's gay considering those are the only two feminine things about him."

"So what happened?"

"I didn't hate him 'cos he's been a good dad and husband, except for living this lie. But I suppose I can understand why since he didn't have the guts to come out. Just wish he had come out and lived the life he wanted to live. He swears he's only bi, but either way, I could never trust him again – not when he actually went out looking in a gay nightclub. I would've left him sooner if I wasn't Catholic. But now I have no choice because I love Ian, and when you're in love you take leave of your senses. It was his London accent that did it. Well, Essex really, but he sounds like a Londoner to me."

Maybe Trish *had* taken leave of her senses. Ian had a reputation for being a grumpy old git and hardly the type women fell for with his hanging beer belly and a tattoo on his forearm of a former lover called Tracy. Although his occupation was honest work, he felt the need to glamourize his job description of warehouse security guard to senior security executive. His personalised number plate – IAN 323 – on his white BMW, added to his elevated ego. Such strategies worked wonders in impressing Trish. His piercing blue eyes reinforced her adoration of him.

"My mother used to say, 'A heavy heart talks a lot'. No wonder you talk so much considering all your troubles."

"Not heard that before," Trish said.

"It's a Yiddish proverb. Did you ever suspect your husband was gay before you caught him out?"

"Nope. I assumed that his feminine side of liking Corrie and hating football was 'cos he was raised with only women – his mam and his sister."

"Trish, is there a particular reason you're telling me all this?"

"Yeah, I'm coming to it. The thing is, if you make it and I don't …"

Hannah interrupted with a sharp, "We're *both* going to make it! It's only day four and quite possible for people to survive these conditions for much longer. Someone will find us. Trust me."

"I trust you, but you might be wrong. Maybe one of us might make it, but both of us making it is less likely."

"Look, if I thought for one minute we weren't going to make it, do you think I'd care about being glutened? Why do you think I'm still taking strides to avoid cross contamination from your provisions?"

"Because you don't want the symptoms, of course. Like you don't have enough to put up with."

"No, because I'm asymptomatic with or without gluten. The symptoms between one coeliac and another differ widely. Some just need a whiff of gluten and they're ill for days. For me, I could eat a whole gluten loaf and remain absolutely asymptomatic, except that the lining of my gut would become damaged – as happens with *all* coeliacs after consuming gluten. So, you see, I won't touch a crumb of your bread because I'm thinking of long-term damage, that is, when we get out of here. And we will get out of here."

"But what if I don't? If I don't, I want you to pass on messages to my kids."

"Not that it'll be necessary, but what are the messages, Trish?"

"I want you to tell my kids that I've hidden quite a bit of money under the floorboards in the under-stairs cupboard. Tell them it's for them; definitely not for their dad. Don't breathe a word about Ian. Tell them my will is with Weldon's Solicitors. Tell them I want a cheap funeral with a cardboard coffin and a cremation. Tell Ian I love him. Tell my kids too." She pulled her phone from her bag and turned it on. "Get yours out so I can at least give you Ryan's number. Bloody hell, there's only one percent battery left. Best be quick!"

Hannah complied, adding Ryan's phone number to her contact list. *This isn't such a bad idea*, she mused. "My battery's on its last legs too. Give me your phone, please. I'll give you Zach's number too."

Trish was not the only one with skeletons in her cupboard.

* * *

Hannah's reverie drifted back to 1972 when she was twenty-two – when Edward Heath was UK's Conservative Prime Minister and Rod Stewart was singing 'You Wear it Well'.

Hannah was in her fourth year of her Master's Degree in Pharmaceuticals at Manchester when she began dating Andrew from the same course. She had been attracted to him from the start. Although she knew he wasn't Jewish, she could not help herself. She had liked him for so long and was thrilled when he eventually asked her. Maybe if he had asked her on an official date, she might have thought twice. But it happened by chance. Pulling out of the university grounds one evening, her car suffered a flat tyre. Andrew spotted her, came to the rescue and gallantly changed it for her.

Three weeks later, they were officially an item with Elton John's 'Your Song' as *their* own.

Fully aware of the implications of dating a non-Jew, she chose only to worry about it if they grew serious about each other.

Unwittingly, however, they already had, despite the relationship being in vain.

It had been problematic enough when she had dated a Sephardic boy three years earlier. *For goodness' sake – he's Jewish – what do they want? Blood?* But he was a Sephardic and they were Ashkenazim, and her parents would not let her forget it. Hannah therefore never considered telling them about Andrew.

A year on, the deceit for Hannah was becoming too stressful. The last straw occurred one evening at the Red Lion in Withington. It was a pleasant spring evening when she and Andrew were enjoying a drink al fresco overlooking the bowling green. Although it was a relaxing environment, Hannah rarely relaxed at local places when out with Andrew for fear of being spotted. As she took a sip of wine, her fears became a reality when she caught sight of her father's friend David giving her a friendly wave. He was bound to mention to her father that he had seen her with a fair-haired young man who did not look remotely Jewish. The dread of upsetting them caused her sleepless nights, and the lack of sleep aggravated her anxiety.

A week later she informed Andrew it was over. Their goodbye kiss drowned in tears as Andrew's pleas proved futile. She could not continue living the lie.

* * *

Two months later she met Saul at her local pharmacy. Although the relationship lacked passion, she grew to love him – in a fashion. It never compared to the love she felt for Andrew, but at least Saul was Jewish, Ashkenazi to boot – anything to please her parents who had sacrificed so much for her.

Their wedding, six months later, was in typical Jewish style. After Hannah circled Saul seven times, the synagogue ceremony took place under a chuppah (a canopy of cloth supported by four poles), concluding with Saul crushing a wine glass under his foot. At the reception, the celebratory hora dance to 'Hava Nagila' highlighted the evening. With much jubilation, guests linked hands as they danced in circles around the newlyweds. Following tradition, the newlyweds, whilst seated on chairs, were lifted into the air as each of them held the edge of a handkerchief and laughed joyously.

* * *

The sound of Trish clearing dust from her throat brought Hannah back to the present.

"Trish, when you asked me to convey your wishes to your children, it got me thinking – maybe I need to do the same with you for my children. Well, one in particular – Zach."

"Yeah, course I will. What do you want me to tell him?"

"If, in the highly unlikely event I don't make it, I'd like you to tell him that ...." Hannah fell silent regretting she had begun her disclosure.

"What would you like me to tell him, Hannah?"

Possible repercussions of disclosing highly personal information to a stranger flooded Hannah's head. *What if Trish can't be trusted? What if she conveys the message incorrectly – to the wrong person even? How can I be sure she wouldn't consider blackmail? After all, she struggles financially. What if ...*

"Never mind, said Hannah. "Leave it for now. Maybe another time when there's no other choice."

"If you're sure. No problem. So back to me. I want Ryan to have my savings considering he's in a bad place. Then there's the gay issue too. I've always dreaded him being gay since I found out Tony was. Not that I have anything against gays of course, as you well know. I love gay men. They're better than straight men in my book. It's just that they're discriminated against and far more likely to suffer from mental breakdowns than straight people, as you've said yourself. I don't want my lad burdened with such terrible troubles. Anyways, I can't say I've seen any signs, but I still worry. Maybe my kids should be told about their dad's sexuality in case it's hereditary?"

"I wouldn't worry about that. Although it's more commonly believed that homosexuality is biologically determined than environmentally influenced, I'm somewhat doubtful and especially doubtful it's hereditary. I think nurture is as likely to play a part as nature."

"So you're saying that summat about the way you raised Zach could've made him gay? But if nurture, his sisters would be gay too 'cos they were raised the same, wouldn't they?"

"No, I'm not saying that at all. There could be a whole host of influential environmental factors; just as there are for all our personal preferences, such as how every offspring from the same parentage have different taste in food, in music, in anything for that matter. I think one's likes and dislikes, including sexual preferences, stem from a host of environmental factors from a very young age and also from the temperament of the child. There are endless factors that influence our various preferences regarding practically anything, for example birth order traits, familial ..."

"What do you mean? Give us examples."

"Okay, well some examples out of myriads could be for instance, whether a child suffered abandonment or whether a boy was raised without any male role models, or whether a father pressurised his son to be macho. Gender conditioning can backfire, especially with boys. There are myriads of environmental nuances. It's impossible to pinpoint one over another when it's more likely to be a combination of factors. What may be like water off a duck's back for one child, may be totally different for a sibling who is perhaps more sensitive. Of course I could be totally wrong as neither genetics nor psychology is my field. However, I've seen little or no evidence to suggest homosexuality is biologically determined, and whatever findings do exist are based on small-scale research which holds little weight. There is certainly no gay gene that I know of."

Trish pondered. "Hmm, maybe their sex genes have gone wrong."

"As far as I'm aware, there is no association between XYY, XXY or triple X syndrome and homosexuality, besides which, such syndromes can be diagnosed from blood tests. Now, I'm the last person to be wishing to support the nurture theory considering I have a son who is gay, so you could hardly say I'm biased – quite the contrary."

"I must say, it's dead interesting, the nature nurture thing. My mam was the only person I ever told about Tony 'cos I knew she'd keep it to herself. When I told her, she said he should see a doctor about getting cured. I suppose she was for nurture then. I think she thought it was an illness caused by summat in his childhood. But then she wasn't very bright, bless her."

"Your mother was clearly of the old school who believed in conversion therapy. After all, until the early seventies, homosexuality was wrongly categorised as a mental illness by the American Psychiatric Association. But thank goodness, after much campaigning by gay activists, the association was forced to remove this damaging label."

"Anyway, enough of all this. What've we got left to eat?" Trish asked.

"Half a biscuit each and one orange between us. But later!" Hannah asserted.

CHAPTER 20

Thursday, 20 March 2008

Two more days passed. The mutual support continued, as did the bickering over disagreements, forming opinions about each other, screaming for their lives at every false alarm, sharing their miniscule provisions and arguing about how much and when they should be consumed. The only difference between each passing day was their diminishing supplies. All that remained was the cistern water and glimmers of sunlight through the breach. By evening, as they lay in their beds of towels, even the slithers of light had left them.

When alone with their thoughts, they continued hoping and praying to be rescued, pining for their loved ones, pondering over regrets and possible resolutions, planning their first few days at home, creating mental bucket lists, and wondering if their husbands had survived.

Top of Hannah's bucket list was to visit Israel and the Taj Mahal, attend Sadie's graduation ceremony and her children's weddings, be around for the birth of her grandchildren and watch them grow. She especially felt an aching need to come clean to her family about Andrew, and to see him just one more time.

For Trish, after wishing for her family's health and happiness came her longing to leave Tony for her beloved Ian. *To think this could be it and what have I got to show for it? Apart from Ian, I've got nothing but a lying, hypocritical gay husband; a crappy education; a daughter who got pregnant at fifteen by a lad who scarpered; and a son who smokes weed, who's depressed as hell with no prospects of even a crummy job. All because I was a crap mam. Bloody hell, I'd be better off out of it than fighting for this crappy life.* But that was Trish's hunger and weakness speaking. In the next breath she was praying for her life to God, to Jesus, to the virgin Mary and Saint Christopher. *I promise I'll be a better person if you save us. I'll do some charity work – anything, just please let us be found soon.* From the strength of her prayers, came a thread of hope – hope enough to plan ahead. *By now they'll know who's missing. Tony would've told them I'm missing and they'll be looking for us. And they'll have checked our room and seen I'm not there, so they'll check other places, like the toilets. They're bound to find us soon.* Although Trish loved her offspring and grandchildren, her thoughts and plans focused on Ryan – the most vulnerable – and of course her darling Ian. *Ohh, to wake up together in the mornings, to go out together when the weather's nice, stay in together when it rains, go line dancing together holding hands. No need to hide anymore. The kids will love him and he'll … well … I know he hates kids, but I'm sure he'll at least tolerate mine. That's it, I'm gonna live with him ASAP rather than follow the plan and wait. Don't really need to save much more. We don't need our own house straight away. We've got Ian's. I'll move into his and Ryan can stay with his dad. If we're rescued before Easter, I'll go through the Easter Sunday motions: mass, family dinner, then give the grandkids their Easter eggs. Then on Monday I'll make my announcement to everyone. Bloody hell, the kids will never forgive us if I say I'm leaving for Ian. Sod it, I'll just tell 'em the truth about their swine dad. No, I'll make Tony admit it to them himself. If they know the truth, it'll help them understand why I have to leave. Then I'll explain how I met Ian later, which is the truth. It's not as if I'm lying. I'll leave soon after with important clothes and stuff, then go back for the rest once he's over the shock. Yeah, that's what I'll do. At least Ian lives nearby. I'll be able to visit my kids whenever I want. Every cloud has a silver lining, and this earthquake's mine. It'll push me to leave Tony sooner, and Ian will love me more than ever after being frantic with worry at the thought of losing me. And my kids will appreciate me more too, be more respectful, not treat me like a doormat. And Ryan worrying about me will help him forget his depression. So it's not so bad after all, is it? Provided we're rescued. Please Jesus, let us be rescued soon.*

Hannah, with no faith to draw upon, allowed her thoughts to drift back to the month leading up to her wedding, and now her dire need to come clean to her family about it.

* * *

For eight months whilst dating Saul back in 1974, she had listened to her head like a loyal daughter. However, she was only human: a month before her wedding, a temptation was thrown at her that she regretfully failed to resist.

"Hannah, it's me. Andrew." He knew which evening Hannah's parents attended their weekly arts appreciation group. He took a chance they would be out, and a bigger chance Hannah would be alone.

Hannah was researching a new drug for rheumatoid arthritis when the phone rang. Never had she dreamed he would attempt to contact her – not when he knew she was engaged to be married. She therefore nonchalantly picked up the cream receiver, stretching its spiral cord out of the way. On hearing his voice, her nonchalance morphed into shock as she took a sharp intake of breath. "My God! Is that you?"

"Glad to know you haven't forgotten me," Andrew replied.

"What the hell are you playing at? You must know I'm getting married. My parents or fiancé could've answered!"

"Yes, I know you're engaged, which is why I'm ringing. I need to see you urgently."

"Are you insane?"

"Hannah, please meet me. If only to understand what's so urgent about me needing to see you. If you don't, I'll come over to yours."

"You wouldn't dare!" Hannah said, springing out of her seat to check the window, nervous at the possibility of Saul turning up.

"Wouldn't I?"

At that, Hannah agreed to see him at his flat. *Less chance of being spotted at his than in a public place.*

He lived in Withington – a five-minute drive away.

"Okay. Ten minutes – not a second more. I'm free tomorrow evening. I can be there around eight."

* * *

Why she went to great lengths dressing and wearing her best perfume, she was unsure. Once she had made a commitment to Saul, she had convinced herself she no longer loved Andrew.

Yet it was so good to see his old familiar front door again. Not wishing to appear eager, she knocked gently. But her pounding heart screamed eagerness. When he appeared at the door, she felt sure he would hear it and see through her. It seemed like only yesterday they had last been together. Everything was the same, stronger even. But how could this be? She was now in love with Saul, wasn't she? Saul who she was about to marry.

As she entered the long, communal hallway to his one-bedroom flat, her estranged butterflies returned with a vengeance. "Okay, so what is it?" she asked as he ushered her into his flat, shutting the door behind them.

"Let me take your coat," he offered, holding his hands out to receive it.

"No need since I'm not staying. Say what needs to be said, and I'll go."

"It's simple really – I just need to know one thing. Look me in the eyes and tell me you no longer love me – that you're in love with your fiancé. I need to know in order to move on – for closure. Tell me!"

Silence.

Hannah stood mute as she looked everywhere but at his face.

"I think that answers my question. You can't say it because you still love me, don't you?"

Hannah was far from the type to cheat, but she still loved Andrew deeply. Much to her later shame and regret, she succumbed to the temptation.

CHAPTER 21

Lost in her reverie, Hannah gently hummed Elton John's 'Your Song'.

"Penny for 'em?" Trish asked.

"Huh?"

"I said penny for them."

This time Hannah had no hesitation. "You're not the only one with a secret that can't be taken to the grave. I have one too. Okay, I'm going to tell you, but first I need your absolute word that you'll keep this strictly to yourself if I survive."

"Yeah, course I will. So what is it?"

"As I said yesterday, if I don't make it, I would appreciate if you could let Zach know …" Hannah paused to consider her words.

"Let Zach know what?" Trish asked eagerly. She only wished she could see Hannah's face to read her expressions.

"This is very difficult for me. Promise that if we both survive – and we will, I'm sure – what I'm about to tell you is forgotten and you never breathe a word about it to a soul."

"Yes, of course I promise. So what is it?"

Hannah swallowed the lump in her throat. "Saul is not Zach's father. His biological father is Andrew Redmond – the chap I was with before I met Saul. Remember, I told you about Andrew yesterday? Please explain to Zach that Andrew pleaded with me to marry him a month before I married Saul, and that's when I conceived with Zach. I made that mistake, but I was forever loyal to Saul from then on. I've had no contact whatsoever with

Andrew since and have certainly never cheated with anyone else. In fact I have no idea if Andrew is dead or alive. Saul has naturally always assumed he was the father. I can't take that to grave. Zach needs to know the truth about his biological father. Maybe you could also mention that Andrew isn't Jewish."

Trish's mouth dropped open, agog. "Oh my God! And I thought I had troubles! Of course I'd tell him if I had to, but you will make it, so there'll be no need. Yes, I'll tell him if it came to that, but don't you think it might be a bit much for him to deal with if he's just lost his mother? Don't you think it'd be best if I waited a year or so before telling him – give him time to get over losing you first? Not that he's gonna lose you, of course!"

"Oh yes, of course. Silly of me. I never thought of that."

"Did you love him? Andrew I mean."

"Of course. Very much."

"You should have followed your heart. You were wrong to marry someone else just because he was Jewish to please your parents."

"Maybe. Who knows how it would have turned out."

"He'll still be Jewish though, won't he? Zach I mean, 'cos you are?"

"Yes. A person's status as a Jew is dependent upon the mother."

"Hey, what a coincidence that both of us have a man in the family who is not only gay, but both don't know their real fathers!" Her eyes widened. "Wow! I wonder if that's summat to do with them being gay? Maybe it affected them?"

"It is a coincidence, yes, but I'm sure that's all it is," Hannah said.

"Oh, I'll need your email address," Trish added. "You've got a pen and paper, haven't you?"

"Yes, hang on." Hannah delved into her bag. Tearing off a sheet from her notepad, she handed it to Trish, along with her biro. "Write yours here," she said, before writing hers in her notepad and exchanging sheets with Trish. "As a child, I used to read under the bedcovers with a torch when I should've been sleeping, but writing in pitch darkness is so much harder and certainly a first. I hope you'll be able to decipher my writing. Have you managed okay?"

"Yeah, fine. I've written in big capital letters. That teacher I used to support would go mad," Trish quipped. "Don't lose it! Push it deep in your bag so it can't fall out. You'll see it includes Tony's name 'cos we share the same email, but don't worry about that 'cos he's a computer dinosaur."

"That's rather awkward, isn't it, if you want to discuss private matters?"

"Me and my mates don't chat in email anyway. We text and Facebook."

"What if you want to email Ian?"

"Oh, he doesn't know a thing about computers either. We only text."

"That's risky. What if Tony sees them?"

"Ahh, I'm not just a pretty face, you know," Trish grinned mischievously. "I've got a cheating phone just for Ian. By the way, what are your favourite flowers?"

Hannah chortled. "How are my favourite flowers related to your secret phone?"

"They're not. I was just thinking – when we get home, I want to send you a bunch as a thank you for helping me get through this, and for stopping me from scoffing all my rations in one go. I'd never have managed that without you."

"That's sweet of you. Thank you, but it's a two way street. It's helped me having your company too."

"You know what? You're not a typical posh person. Most posh people I've met don't want to know me when I ask about them – you know, what they do for a living, where they live, have they got any kids. Some have rambled on with their answers, loving to talk about themselves, but never ask the same questions to me, or any questions for that matter. That's a terrible insult. It's like they don't want to know a thing about me – don't want to know me. But you're different. At least you show some interest in my life."

"That's because I'm genuinely interested. After all, we're practically living together," Hannah chuckled. "Fancy a game to help pass the time? Shame we don't have a pack of cards. If we did, we could play bridge. Since there's only two of us, it would need to be a variant. I've played at the Manchester Bridge Club for years. We take it quite seriously with tournaments and such. Do you play?"

"Never. I bet you play chess too, don't you? Hard games for intelligent people, so obviously not my thing. I'm more into Snap," Trish laughed. "Just kidding. I can play Rummy though. Don't think I've ever noticed a bridge club anywhere in my life. Where is it?"

"On Palatine Road – a five-minute walk from where I live. It's been there since the thirties, though used to be called the Country Club until the eighties. Anyway, we don't have cards, so let's think of something else. Hmm, let's see." Hannah pondered. "I know. If you were to write a book about this experience, what would you call it?"

"Funny you should ask that 'cos I was thinking of that song earlier about the three old ladies locked in the lavatory. Maybe I could call my book *A Catholic and a Jew Locked in the Loo*," Trish said with a loud guffaw. "Bloody hell, it hurts when I laugh."

Hannah chuckled. "Very good. Or *A Catholic, a Jew and a Quake*. Do you see?"

"See what?"

"The play on words with *quake*. With the title starting with two religions, readers would then connect quake with the Quaker religion, but really it's earth*quake*."

"Oh yeah! That's good! Or *Manchester's Queen Bees* – that's me and you. Na, never mind. Right, book titles done, how's about a game we play in Basic Literacy where you have to think of famous people whose first and second names start with the same letter?"

"Yes, that sounds good. You start."

"Okay. Adam Ant."

"Boris Becker."

"God, I can't believe Andrew is Zach's dad!"

"I know. Neither could I. Charlie Chaplin."

"Diana Dors."

"Elvis … Edward … hmmm, I'm stuck," Trish said. "I'm sick of this anyway. How's about Alliteration? We play this in class too. You try and make the sentences as long as you can with all words beginning with the same letter. Amy always … asks … about awful Andy, hmmm … and Andrea … asks about Adam's … adorable … ants."

"Haha, that's fun. I guess it's my turn with B, huh? Hmmm," Hannah paused to think. "Boring, bashful Boris Beddows believes … beautiful, bubbly, bountiful … Betty Blackburn blamed big, blubbering, boastful Billy Benjamin Bateman because being big …."

"Give up on that?"

"I guess so."

"Sod C. I'm going for T this time," Trish said before reciting a well-practised alliterated sentence.

And so the game continued until they drifted off to sleep.

CHAPTER 22

Friday morning, 21 March 2008

"Shhh! Listen! Did you hear that?" Trish rubbed the night's sleep from her eyes. "I can hear someone! Listen!"

"Ugh?" Hannah said, still half asleep. "I didn't hear …"

"Shhh, quiet! Listen!" Trish demanded sharply, holding up her palm to silence Hannah.

Straining their ears, they heard distant voices and machines humming faintly – sounds so far away, they sounded surreal.

"My God, it must be rescue workers. Scream with me! Together now!" Trish demanded urgently.

In unison they screamed and screamed and screamed until their throats grew raw. Not daring to breathe, they listened intently.

"Ciao! C'è qualcuno qui? Ciao! Ciao!?" came a disembodied voice over a megaphone.

The women did not understand a word, but no matter. They were about to be rescued, provided they made themselves heard. Up to this point, duck-walking took huge effort, but on hearing a human voice, they could not get to the exterior wall fast enough. If only the mounds of hazardous debris piled below the aperture was not deterring their access to it. As close as possible, and as loud as their vocal chords could muster, they screamed and screamed relentlessly. With baited breath, they waited and listened.

The Italian beckoned others for support. "Qui! Alcuni inglesi. Presto! Presto!"

A scurry of movement proceeded towards him and soon there were five jabbering voices talking urgently – three Italians and two English.

The women listened desperately, but the voices were too muffled to decipher. They screamed and listened, screamed and listened – but in vain. To add insult to injury, the glimmer of precious light – their lifeline – snuffed out in a flash. As the room returned to blackness, their hopes dampened. However, just as they were about to scream again, they heard an English-speaking voice.

"Hello! Can you hear me? Please make some noise so we can identify your location."

"Oh, thank God! Thank God! We're in the ladies' room. Please get us out!" Hannah yelled.

"Hello there! You're very faint. Can you shout louder, please?"

Hannah tapped Trish's shoulder. "Scream with me."

In true teamwork, they cupped their hands around their mouths and screamed with all their might.

"We're in the ladies' room," Hannah yelled. "What's happened? It's gone pitch black in here!"

"Don't worry. We'll soon have you out." He moved aside to allow light back through the breach and requested his team to follow suit. "Is that better? Can you see now?"

The women breathed a sigh of relief as chinks of light shone through.

"Yes, better. Thank you, but please get us out!" Hannah yelled.

"It'll go dark from time to time whenever we unintentionally block the openings, but don't worry. We'll soon have you out. How many of you are in there?"

"Just the two of us," Trish called. "Hurry up! Please!"

"I'm Steve. What are your names?" Steve hushed his team with the wave of his arm in order to listen.

"Hello Steve. I'm Hannah Bernstein. And I have Patricia Wilcox with me."

Trish craned her neck closer to the breach. "I'm Trish. Please get us out!"

"Hello, Hannah. Sorry, I didn't catch the other person's name."

"Her name's Trish." Hannah called.

"Thank you, Hannah and Trish. Are either of you injured?"

"Just a few cuts and bruises," Hannah replied.

"That's good to hear. Hang on in there. It won't be long now."

"Hail Mary, full of grace," Trish prayed quietly and urgently before switching to an Our Father to be on the safe side. "Oh my God! Do you realise what day it is?"

"No. What day is it?" Hannah asked.

"It's Maundy Thursday – Holy Thursday! So my praying worked, and this is a sign – the fact it's happened on this holy day."

"It's good you have your faith. Good for you."

The women held their breath and listened, not daring to utter a word. From the direction of the breach, the sound of digging and scraping grew louder, sounds from various tools and from dogs' claws digging ferociously. It reminded Trish of Rambo digging to retrieve his buried bone in the back garden.

Slowly and steadily, the breach widened until rays of light shone through as if they were coming from the heavens.

Transfixed, the women stared, not daring to blink, like an audience watching a magician about to cut his assistant in half.

"Ladies, we're nearly there. We now need you to stand clear due to the possibility of flying debris. Can you do that?"

"Yes. One minute, please." Hannah called before she and Trish returned to the vanity counter, their duck-walking speed beating all records.

"Okay, we're a safe eight metres away now." Hannah surveyed the ground, ensuring no contents of her backpack had escaped. Reaching for it, she positioned it securely over her shoulders.

"Okay, ladies. Not long now."

With a chink, chink, chink, the aperture widened until eventually, the moment arrived.

"Ahh, Steve. Thank God!" Hannah gasped.

"Oh my God, I can see you!" Trish screeched at Steve. Overwhelmed with a mixture of emotions, she reached to hold Hannah's hand before remembering Hannah was not the tactile type. "Yeah, I think I'd call my book *The Queen Bees of Manchester*. We did it, Hannah! We did it!" Trish said joyously.

"Are we safe to move towards you now?" Hannah asked Steve.

"Absolutely, but mind how you go, ladies. Take your time."

Grabbing a few towels, Trish said, "Remember, we've got to get up that pile of rubble to reach the ... hey, we can call it a window again! Better take some of these to save our hands and knees."

"Good idea!" Hannah smiled as she grabbed a few. "And don't forget your bag."

For the final time, the women duck-walked to the opening, slower this time since they were laden with bags and towels, and because they were comforted by the knowledge they had been rescued.

"Well done, ladies!" Steve said, looking down in their direction. "All set to go now?"

"Yeah," Trish replied eagerly. "I'm bringing these towels to help us crawl over the rubble. It's covered in glass 'n' stuff."

Steve leaned over the opening to take a closer look. "Ahh, in that case, let's hold fire for a moment while I call for some protection. You have more than enough cuts and bruises as it is."

Presently, after making the request to his team, a pile of large, thick woollen blankets arrived. Slowly, Steve threw each one down, stretching them out wide over the mound below him. "There, that should make it gentler on your knees."

However, as Trish struggled duck-walking towards the mound, Steve noticed her excess weight. He gave a stifled cough and said, "Ladies, on second thoughts, I think we should widen the opening a tad more before you attempt to squeeze through it."

"I could easily get through that!" Hannah blurted, throwing Trish an apologetic glance.

"If you're sure," Steve replied.

Before crawling up the mound, Hannah turned to Trish with a smile. "See you soon. Good luck."

* * *

Stunned from the week's trauma and the wreckage around her, euphoric over her rescue, fearful for Saul's safety and the unknown, and feeling emotionally drained, Hannah lay dazed and speechless as she was carried over the wreckage on a green canvas stretcher. Although her eyes drooped with fatigue and squinted from the unaccustomed sunlight, she was at least well enough to take in her surroundings as she hungrily inhaled fresh air into her lungs.

Surrounding her, teams of rescue workers wearing high-visibility jackets continued working feverishly. Ambulances, paramedics and stretchers waited on standby. Holding cameras at arm's length, cameramen craned their necks, eager for the first shot of the rescued taking in their first glimpse of sunlight.

"Stand back!" rescuers shouted in Italian to onlookers. "Give them space!"

Most complied apart from a Mancunian family who thrust their way through the crowd. With open arms, Hannah's offspring yelled, "It's Mum! Mum! Mum!" The relief on their faces through their tears and outstretched arms was palpable.

Sadie was the first to reach Hannah. "Mum! Thank God you're okay!"

Zach and Miriam stepped back, conscious that the two women needed a moment together.

As mother and daughter cried and embraced, their previous harsh words were forgotten.

"Oh, Mum! We've been out of our minds with worry. But you're going to be just fine. You're in great hands and the hospital isn't far. And Mum, I'm so sorry about being a brat before you left. Love you loads," Sadie said before turning to give Zach and Miriam a nod. "But listen, I'm being selfish. Zach and Mimi are desperate to see you too," and with that she stepped back, making way for her siblings.

Fifteen minutes after Hannah's rescue, Trish followed. Attempting to prop herself up to observe the devastated surroundings, she blinked and shaded her eyes with her hand. "Oh my God! Where's Tony? Where's my family?" she called, turning her head from left to right in search of them.

"Calm, Signora." Nando, an Italian paramedic, attempted to take her blood pressure. "First, attend you."

Trish heard British reporters questioning rescuers. An English-speaking rescuer recounted how he had heard Trish and Hannah's screams via their audio detection equipment. It had taken them almost an hour of digging to reach them. "Considering they've been trapped for six days, they appear to be in reasonably good health and spirits. It was a blessing they had each other for support."

"Wait!" Trish shouted as Nando and his assistant were about to transport her to the ambulance. "I think someone's calling me – calling Mam. Can you hear? Wait!"

"The ambulance wait, Signora. We go," Nando said impatiently.

"No! I can hear my son. Wait!" she demanded as she craned her neck in the direction of the voice.

Ryan scrambled frantically over the rubble. "Mam! Mam!" On reaching her, he bent to hold her tight and kissed her cheek. "Thank God you're alright. How are you?"

"I'm fine, love. Just dead happy to see you," Trish said, unable to take her eyes off him. "Starving though."

"Soz, Man, I never thought to bring owt. But I bet the rescue team and paramedics will have something. Where's my dad?"

"I don't know, love. Not seen him since I got trapped 'cos I was in the toilets. Don't worry, he'll be okay. We'll probably see him at the hospital."

* * *

Several hours after arriving at Ospedale di San Leucius, Trish and Ryan were informed of Tony's death.

Trish was propped up in bed in a Casualty ward and Ryan was advised to take a seat beside her.

"Rest assured," the young female doctor said softly, "he was killed instantly and would not have suffered."

Rescuers found Tony's body in the hotel foyer under the remains of a giant pillar. Like a house of cards, it collapsed onto him and others in the Pompeii tour queue – Saul included.

With tear-filled eyes, Ryan pleaded, "How do you know it's him? It could be someone else!"

"I'm very sorry but there is no mistake. Your father was identified by his European health insurance card which was found on his person. I have his personal effects here," the doctor informed them, handing Trish a clear plastic bag.

Tony's wedding ring, his wristwatch and wallet were clearly visible through the plastic. A photograph of Fabio Bianchi, which Ryan had screen-grabbed from Fabio's Facebook profile, rested in the wallet – a reminder of Tony's lifelong wish to find the Neapolitan father he never knew.

Ryan laid his head over Trish's bed into her arms. Trish could barely muster a word. Although she was stunned, her primary concern was for her kids and grandkids. At least being with her beloved Ian should be simpler once the kids recover from their loss.

For Hannah, although the news of Saul's death was more painful, the consequences were not as straightforward. She had already decided, when trapped, that she would finally admit to Zach about his biological father, but now he would need a period of recovery before receiving this second blow. Some serious thinking was needed, especially as Andrew also needed to be informed ... once she had traced him.

Four days later on Easter Monday, the women were discharged from hospital. It might have been earlier, but discharges did not take place over the weekend, especially not over Easter – a major holiday in Italy.

Before leaving with Ryan, Trish asked a nurse if Hannah had been treated at the hospital. It was Trish's last opportunity before returning home of seeing Hannah, and she was keen to see her. The nurse had no recollection until Trish mentioned that Hannah was Jewish.

"Ah, the lady with the – what you say? Ahh si, a kosher menu. She go this morning. Gone 'ome with her family to Inghilterra."

CHAPTER 23

Late March 2008

The week of closure finally arrived for Tony Wilcox and Saul Bernstein when their bodies were released from the mortuary and flown home in the hold of a Boeing 737.

Still numb with shock, the Wilcoxes and Bernsteins had flown home days earlier to make funeral preparations. Remarkably, there had been no contact between the two families – not during the rescue, at the hospital, at the mortuary, or during their flights home. Or was it so remarkable? After all, aside from sharing the same nightmare, what else would they have in common?

Tony and Saul may well have been socially worlds' apart, but in death they shared the same resting place as artist L. S. Lowry, philanthropist John Rylands and Manchester United manager Matt Busby – at Manchester's Southern Cemetery.

* * *

On a grey Monday morning, a large congregation of mourners gathered at the Jewish section of the cemetery. Within Jewish tradition, burials generally take place within twenty-four hours after death. Not for Saul Bernstein, however – with or without his rabbi's consent. Deeper into the graveyard laid the Sephardic graves, whereas the Ashkenazim and Manchester Reform synagogue graves were closer to the entrance gates and prayer chapel. Saul's mourners gathered there – close to the hum of Barlow Moor Road's passing traffic that accompanied the sound of tears and tribulation.

A black hearse carrying Saul's body rolled slowly through the Victorian wrought-iron gates. Closely following, came a dark limousine carrying Hannah, Zach, Miriam, Sadie and Saul's brothers Seth and Natan. Respectfully, mourners stepped back to allow them ample space. Their woeful eyes, however, still disbelieving, remained fixed on Saul's coffin. There were at least fifty mourners as Saul was a popular member of his community.

Jane, an elderly non-Jewish mourner, brought a bouquet of lilies – perfect for a funeral she thought. If only someone had forewarned her about Jewish funeral etiquette. Even graves were bereft of flowers, lovingly adorned instead with stones and pebbles. A kind soul wishing to spare Jane the embarrassment, whispered in her ear that flowers were not customary. With that, Jane swiftly returned the lilies to the boot of her car, hoping her faux pas went unnoticed.

It was a brief, simple funeral with mourners dressed respectfully in black and dark formal attire and males' heads crowned with kippahs. As a symbol of grief and loss, close family members and friends performed Keriah, that is arriving with a visibly ripped part of their lapel or collar. Others chose black ribbons, provided by the funeral director, pinned to a lapel and ripped during the service.

Following Jewish tradition, the family chose a basic pine coffin, free from metal to ensure it was completely biodegradable. The coffin was embellished with a deep blue velvet cover with a gold menorah design. Hannah had planned for six male pallbearers: Zach, Seth, Natan, Saul's two cousins and Saul's good friend Daniel. Miriam and Sadie, however, asked to be included in the honour – their mitzvah – their good deed. It was not as if they needed to help carry the coffin: the coffin merely needed to be guided on a gurney to the graveside.

And so, to the rhythm of Rabbi Rosen's recital of Psalm 91, the sisters joined the men in guiding their father to his resting place. Before reaching the graveside, they made seven ritualistic pauses to indicate they wished to stay with Saul just that little bit longer.

Presently, the procession reached the graveside. As Saul's coffin was lowered into the grave, Rabbi Rosen delivered prayers, Psalm 23 and a brief, but stirring eulogy. After reciting, "May Saul go to his place in peace," he gestured to Zach to take the small spade which stood erect in a mound of soil beside Saul's grave.

Thus far, Zach had appeared strong and composed. However, this final act rendered him motionless. He stared down blankly, dropping his tears onto his father's coffin.

"It's okay, darling," Hannah whispered as she gently placed her hand on his forearm. "You don't have to if it's too much."

Zach took a deep breath. "No, I want to," and with that, he picked up the spade and shovelled three spadefuls of soil into the grave. On doing so, others followed with their mitzvah of filling the grave, either with the spade or by throwing in a handful of soil.

Rabbi Rosen looked around at the solemn, tear-stained faces and asked if anyone would like to say a few words.

Sadie, guilt-ridden from the years of grief she had given her parents, especially from her audacious last words, was determined to make her peace – nothing from a script as she wanted it to come straight from the heart. Standing between her mother and Zach, she stepped forward with handkerchief in hand and coughed to clear her throat.

"Dad was my hero, a man loved by everyone who knew him – for his kindness, his wisdom, his principles and his intelligence. He was such a hard-working man, yet despite the demands of his business, he always found the time for anyone in need, especially … " She paused in a failed attempt to compose herself before letting out a faint, whimpering sob.

Alarmed, Hannah and Zach rushed to her, placing comforting arms around her shoulder.

With this, Sadie's strength resumed and she continued after dabbing her eyes with her handkerchief-covered finger.

"Dad was such a good, charitable man who always found the time for people in need. He was the most wonderful father to Zach, Miriam and me, and a loving husband to Mum. His family always came first. I wish I had thanked him more when he was alive and told him how much I loved him, so I want to say it loud and clear now – thank you for everything, Dad. We all love you very much and will miss you desperately. Rest in peace, Dad." Having bared her soul to all, she exhaled and noticed faces within her peripheral vision smiling empathetically. On stepping back, Hannah and Zach offered comforting words of praise.

A significant pause ensued after Sadie's eulogy, after which Rabbi Rosen initiated the recital of the Mourner's Kaddish at a minyan of ten male Jews, Zach included, all of whom proceeded to the foot of the grave. Participating in the Kaddish was their mitzvah, amongst others, for one's presence at the funeral alone was a great mitzvah in itself.

Thus far, mourners had refrained from extending their condolences until the customary time. When that time arrived, they arranged themselves into two parallel lines for the Bernsteins to walk through.

Finally, the bereaved family received their condolences as they walked slowly back to their limousine between the two lines of comforters. Zach, taking the lead, offered an arm to his mother, while Miriam and Sadie, also arm in arm, followed. Before returning to their vehicle, they honoured the final funeral custom of washing their hands in the chapel's washing area.

* * *

Within Jewish tradition, there is a seven-day mourning period called Shiva for first-degree relatives which commences immediately after the burial. Hannah limited the extent to which she followed Shiva: rather than taking a week off work, she took three days' absence; rather than confining herself to her home, she popped out for necessities; rather than wear ripped clothing, she wore her black torn ribbon; and rather than cover up mirrors, she kept her bathroom mirror free for oral hygiene. Avoiding bathing and cooking was where she drew the line.

*　*　*

Four days later, on a wet Friday afternoon, a requiem Mass was held at Saint Mary Magdalene Catholic Church. Public notices stipulated a colourful funeral in keeping with Tony's character. Mourners honoured this, arriving in vivid-coloured attire. Instead of Trish's usual black church mantilla, she wore a red grande fedora to match her red boots and trouser suit.

In terms of high church ostentation, the Mass was equally colourful. The priest, wearing a violet and white robe, swung a gold smoking censer, filling the church with a spicy fragrance of frankincense and myrrh. Its smoke encircled colourful Stations of the Cross statues and rose in clouds towards the elaborate multi-coloured stained-glass windows. Despite the rich colours, the Mass was cold and grey with greater emphasis on pomp, ceremony and Jesus than on Tony. Had the congregation failed to notice the scant mention of Tony's name, the Mass might well have been in honour of anyone.

Had it not been for Ryan's insistence on delivering a 'eulogy', against Father Dolan's wishes, the personal touch for Tony might never have happened. It was not that Ryan relished the idea of speaking publicly; far from it – it would be his first and he was a bag of nerves. He simply felt the need.

"It pains me to refuse you, Ryan, but eulogies are not customary, especially not delivered by members of the congregation," Father Dolan asserted.

"Members of the congregation?" Ryan snapped. "I'm his only son!"

"Okay, Ryan, don't upset yourself, now," Father Dolan said softly. "Let's see what we can do. Now, what if we forget the word *eulogy* and say you wish to say *a few words,* and you make it short? How does that sound?"

And so, with clammy hands and a pounding heart, Ryan gulped before standing to make his way to the pulpit. He had been seated in the front pew with Trish, Kelly and Zoe; the remaining family were seated directly behind them.

Trish patted his hand encouragingly, whispering, "You'll do your dad proud, love. I know you will."

As the congregation waited, silence fell upon the church.

Ryan's legs, leaden with trepidation, climbed the thirty steps to the pulpit. At least he had the pulpit to steady himself once he stood in it before the congregation. Looking down at Trish's encouraging face, he focused on her words about doing his father proud. His words then tumbled out.

"My dad died in Naples looking for his Italian father who he never knew. It was his dying wish to meet him. Me and my family all had the pleasure and honour of knowing my dad, knowing what a top bloke he was, learning from him, laughing and joking with him. He had a great sense of humour. If it's the last thing I do, I'm going to trace his Italian father, my grandfather, because he needs to know what a top bloke my dad, his son was. He was a loving husband to my mam, a fantastic dad to us kids and a doting grandad. Tracing his father is the least I can do for him to say thanks for all he did for us. He worked hard, raised us well, helped me with my school work – even though he struggled with it himself – and taught me to play guitar. I'll be forever grateful to you, Dad. Love you loads. Sleep tight."

As Ryan stepped down from the pulpit, he discreetly dashed a tear from his eye. His father had raised him to believe that men should never cry, and this was the last place to be letting him down. At least Ryan's words allowed others to weep.

The hymns triggered even more tears. Because Trish was unsure of Tony's favourites, she chose her own: 'Here I am Lord', 'You Raise Me Up' and 'Morning Has Broken'. A wave of guilt swept over her for her lack of sorrow. Tony's passing was no loss to her. It was her gain. She would finally have her freedom, a new life with Ian and escape living a lie.

Still, guests were not to know this and enveloped her in hugs, offering condolences for her apparent loss. Trish could not wait for it to be over. She hated the ostentatious head tilts of sympathy when asked *How are you?* and the *Sorry for your loss* cliché seemed so cheap. On the other hand, the genuine faces forlorn with sympathy were worse as she hated feeling pitied.

As expected, several guests were unknown to the immediate family. Unexpected, however, was the body language of a couple of middle-aged men seated alone at the back of the church.

Hmm, funny – it's like they're trying not to be noticed. Wonder if they're Tony's gay friends. They're sitting a bit close to each other to be straight. Keen for her assumption to be confirmed, she sauntered over to them. "Hiya. I'm Tony's wife Trish. Are you friends of Tony or relatives?"

The shorter one shot a glance at his partner before scratching the back of his neck, allowing his partner to answer.

"We're very sorry for your loss, Trish" the taller one said. "We're friends of Tony. This is Hughie," he said, gesturing to his partner, "and I'm Ray."

"Pleased to meet you. So how do you know Tony?"

"The pub," Ray said as Hughie spluttered, "Yes, the pub."

Trish's suspicions, by now, became adequately confirmed to whisper, "Look, it's okay – I know about his other life."

"I'm sorry?" Ray said, shifting his weight from side to side while Hughie shifted his glances around the room.

"I know about Tony being gay and his other life, so it's okay for you to say how you knew him."

Ray placed a hand over his chest in relief. "Ahh, I see. Yes, we knew Anthony from the gay village. He was a great guy and we wanted to pay our respects."

"Thanks. When did you last see him?" Trish queried, expecting it to be years.

Hughie paused to consider. "Hmm, it must've been around Valentine's Day. I remember 'cos Ray bought me a box of Valentine chocolates and I gave a couple to Anthony."

So he'd not left that life behind after all. Bastard! Trish mused. "Look, although I know all about his other life, his kids know nowt, so do us a favour and keep it to yourself, will you?"

"We perfectly understand. Don't worry. Our lips are sealed," Hughie said.

Ray reiterated. "Yes, don't worry about us. We just wanted to pay our respects. And don't worry – we'll keep a safe distance at the burial … that's if you don't mind us tagging along. We could follow the entourage if that's okay."

"Yeah, course. Tony would be chuffed if he knew. I'll look out for you," Trish said.

After a slow, thirty-minute drive to Southern Cemetery, Tony's funeral entourage rolled through the majestic, cast iron gates. A floral tribute of 'Dad' adorned the back window onto which gentle raindrops fell.

At Tony's graveside, under a colourful rainbow umbrella, Trish spotted Hughie and Ray observing from a distance. As they smiled with a nod, a wave of relief flooded over her. She took a last drag of her ciggy, dropped it onto the gravel and crushed it under her red boot.

Following the burial, mourners made their way to the wake held at the 1950s-built White Swan pub. Whilst exchanging memories and anecdotes of Tony, they tucked into a buffet of cheese and ham sandwiches, pork pies, sausages on sticks and chicken drumsticks. Mini trifles were the only desserts on offer. To compensate, glass dishes filled with Quality Street chocolates embellished the bars and table-tops.

Tony's immediate family struggled to eat a thing. Ryan drowned his sorrows in one beer too many while Trish, with each relished cigarette and glass of white wine, counted the hours until she could be with her darling Ian again.

CHAPTER 24

Early April 2008

In a neighbouring garden, a young woman sprayed her soapy dog with a hose pipe as the disgruntled mongrel barked incessantly. Meanwhile, a group of children played boisterously close to Trish's front garden whilst a black BMW blared hip-hop from its sound system on the roadside.

"God, I can't hear myself bloody think!" Trish complained to herself, clicking her tongue in annoyance. Her head throbbed and her patience was running thin. As if coping with the loss of her children's father was not enough, she could not even be allowed some peace to deal with pressing matters, including planning her future with Ian. She had never wished Tony harm and certainly not dead, but admittedly had wanted him out of her life. So this had turned out to be the easy way out for her and Ian to be together. Or had it?

Now she had to worry about her children's loss. Ryan especially was taking it particularly badly and Trish was concerned his loss might push him over the edge. Fraught with worry, she gave him her utmost attention and encouragement. With this added responsibility, there was even less time for Ian than before.

Earlier in the day she had drafted an email to Hannah. Before sending it, she proofread it for errors (albeit, meagrely), ensuring she had covered the important points.

From: trishtonywilcox@ulon.co.uk
To: hannahbernstein@vnet.com
Subject: Very sorry
Sent: 04/04/2008, 14:25

Hiya Hannah

I'm very sorry that Saul didn't make it, I saw his name on the news as one of the Brits who died. I suppose you must of had the funeral by now and I hope it went well and I hope you and your kids are coping all right. You might of heard that my Tony didn't make it either, they said they found him in the foyer and that a large pillar fell on him. It must be hell for you it's not as bad for me cos I have Ian. I hope you and the kids are bearing up, it's my kids I feel sorry for cos it hit them a lot, especialy Ryan. Thank you as well for looking after me when we were trapped, if it wasn't for you I would of scoffed all my packed lunch on the first day and starved to death or gone mad from lonliness. I want to say thanks as well for giving me some business ideas, I'm defenitely going to look into them cos Ryan is really down and I want to find him something to take his mind of things.

Let me know how you are.

Love Trish xx

From Ryan's bedroom came stifled sobbing. A Bruce Springsteen song 'Born to Run' played on the radio. It reminded Ryan of the times Tony taught him the guitar chords to it and how they often sang the song together. Ryan was in a dark place and failing to respond to his friends' pleas to join them at the pub.

"C'mon, mate, it'll do you good," Loz said in a phone call. "It's not the same without you. The lads miss you and I miss your ugly mush too."

But nothing pulled Ryan out of his depression, not even his sister Kelly who was usually good at cheering him up. All she got out of him were outbursts of anger towards Fabio Bianchi.

"I'd like to kill the bastard. If it wasn't for him, Dad would be alive now."

"I know. I know," Kelly replied softly.

"If it's the last thing I do, I'm gonna make the bastard acknowledge my dad as his son. Just wish I had the friggin' money to return to Naples to do it. Then I could tell Dad that he can rest in peace. I could tell him that his father turned out to be a top bloke after all who's sorry for letting him down. I need to hear the bastard say that so our dad can rest in peace."

"I know," Kelly said sympathetically. "Maybe that can be your goal – find a job and earn enough money to go."

* * *

Hannah shared similar concerns for Zach. It was late morning as she worked at her laptop in the breakfast room, unable to focus because of concerns for him.

Sadie had not long been up from her lie-in and was making cheese on toast in the adjoining kitchen. "Want some, Mum?"

"No, thanks, love. I had breakfast earlier."

"Busy?" Sadie fetched her plate and placed a napkin and cutlery next to Hannah's place.

"Not particularly – just catching up on neglected emails. About to reply to Trish for starters." Hannah glanced at the unopened emails. "Did you need me for something?"

"No, just wondered what you're up to. Trish is the woman you were trapped with, right?"

"Yes. She emailed me news about her husband. Sadly, he didn't make it either; most likely because he was waiting in the same queue as your father in the hotel foyer. Sorry you've been reminded of it, love."

The mood darkened momentarily as Sadie lowered her gaze to the ground and replied solemnly, "So sad." She remained pensive until the smell of burning snapped her out of her reverie. Grabbing the pan from the grill, she examined the cheese whilst wafting away the smoke. "That was close. I wonder if they spoke to each other."

"I guess we'll never know, darling."

"Are you going to be good friends now you've shared a life-threatening experience?"

"I doubt it."

"That's a shame. Didn't you get on?"

"She was pleasant enough but we're like chalk and cheese, besides the fact she was such hard work."

"Oh?"

"I mean she was totally bereft of self-discipline," Hannah said as she glanced at another unanswered email.

"Self-discipline from what? Is she into drugs?"

"Oh, nothing like that. I mean she lacked the self-discipline for food-rationing. I needed to supervise her like a child, else she would have devoured the rations on day one. As a matter of fact, she's just admitted it in her email. It was good we had each other for company and support though, and she does have many qualities."

"Well, it's good you've kept in touch this far."

"I expect there'll be a few more emails before they peter out. There's only so much one can say about a traumatic experience without it becoming a bore. I prefer to move on. We have nothing else in common," she said, taking hold of the mouse to make a start on the email.

From: hannahbernstein@vnet.com
To: trishtonywilcox@ulon.co.uk
Subject: Sorry
Sent: 06/04/2008, 11:42

Dear Trish,

Thank you for your email. My deepest condolences to you and your family for your loss. I'm sorry to hear Ryan is taking it particularly badly and do hope his spirits lift very soon.

No thanks are needed. Keeping each other company was a two-way street.

I'm very pleased to hear you're going to consider the business ideas I suggested. I'm sure a business venture will do Ryan a power of good. Let me know how you get on.

All the very best.

Hannah

CHAPTER 25

July 2008

Ian lived a five-minute drive from Trish in a one-bedroom council cottage flat.

Trish generally took her car to his, but took the bus this time as her car was being serviced. At the bus stop, a youth sporting a pair of blue rosary beads around his neck caught her attention.

"Nice rosary beads. Are you Catholic?"

"Nope. What makes you think I am?" he asked, irritated at being interrupted from his exchange of text messages on his phone.

"The rosary beads," Trish said, pointing to them.

"Oh, right. My brover give 'em us."

"Aww, so is he trying to convert you?"

Shooting her an irritated glance, he mumbled, "Nah, he hates religion," before pulling out his bus pass from his hoody pocket.

A blue double-decker slowed to a halt and the lad hopped on without a backward glance.

A young woman in the bus shelter chuckled. "It was hard keeping a straight face there."

"Oh? Why's that?" Trish asked, bemused.

"His rosary beads. They're nothing to do with religion. The colour of them show the street gang he belongs to," she said, laughing through her nose.

"You're joking!"

"Not joke. It's true."

Trish let out a guffaw. "Oh my God, I can't believe I was so stupid."

Arriving at Ian's, Trish suggested a change of plan. "Fancy a chippy tea?" She felt tired after sleepless nights worrying about Ryan, and the idea of making the planned spaghetti Bolognese no longer appealed.

"Again? We'll be bloody growing fins at this rate." On noticing Trish's icy glare, and not wishing to face another one of her moods, he muttered, "Okay, let's go."

The chippy, being two short streets away, allowed them to take a leisurely stroll to it.

"Anyway, it's a nice evening for a walk," Trish said, feeling guilty about the spaghetti Bolognese.

"What's nice about it?"

Ignore it. He's in one of his moods. "It was dead funny at the bus stop before," she began, hoping to give him a laugh, but Ian's attention was elsewhere.

On the street approaching the chippy, a youth wearing a hoody hopped into a Ford Fiesta; as he pulled away, a yapping mongrel chased after it.

"Bleeding dogs! They should be banned from roaming loose," Ian mumbled.

The chippy stood in the middle of a row of eight shops. The shop on the left, boarded up, was previously a newsagent's; the one on the right conveniently an off-licence. The chippy queue was short and they were served quickly, the food being placed into a plastic carrier bag that Trish carried.

"Need some fags," Ian said, guiding Trish into the off-licence with him. Besides his twenty Bensons, he purchased an eight-pack of his usual Stella Artois. He needed some Dutch courage to have it out with her.

Outside the chippy, a girl in her late teens with a mobile phone pinned between her ear and shoulder, blew at a steaming chip before handing it to her screaming three-year-old. As she continued her monologue, the child grabbed it, put it straight to his mouth to lick before biting into it. As he did so, he had the misfortune of bumping into Ian – Ian who found children intolerable at the best of times, having had little or no experience of them, nor ever wishing to.

Ian stepped around the child, pushing him aside, disregarding the fact the poor mite was still in the process of finding his equilibrium after the collision.

"Frigging kids. If she didn't have that bleeding phone glued to her earhole, she might find the time to teach the brat some manners."

"For God's sake," Trish protested, rolling her eyes, "he's just a baby and it was an accident. Good job his mam didn't see that. Honest to God, you're worse than Victor Meldrew!" Victor Meldrew was an elderly grumpy character from a 1990s television sitcom. Oddly, Trish found him attractive, so maybe Ian's grumpiness was part of the attraction.

Ian kicked rebelliously at an empty beer can. "You'd be grumpy if you were in limbo!"

Trish slowed, falling out of step with him as she pursed her lips. "What's that supposed to mean?"

"Forget it," he said, leaving her tagging behind.

Quickening her pace, she fell back into step with him. "Forget a comment like that? You must be joking!"

"You might be up for having a public domestic, but I'd rather wait till we get home," Ian retorted.

"A domestic? I just want to know what you mean by *being in limbo*!" Trish demanded.

"I'll tell you when we're home. Just wait your sweat."

Minutes later, Ian snapped on his living room ceiling light, illuminating the tired décor and the room drooped in despair.

"Need the bog. Get a couple of trays, will you," he said as he placed the food on the chipped mahogany coffee table before heading upstairs.

After putting the kettle on, Trish brought in a couple of plastic serving trays, onto which she placed the wrapped food. A chippy dinner tasted so much better when eaten from the paper they came in, just as a cuppa was obligatory with fish and chips in front of the telly. She fetched two mugs of tea from the kitchen and placed them onto the coffee table.

On returning from the loo, Ian sank into his dated three-seater settee and the smell of fish and chips filled his nostrils. Generally, he would have turned the telly on by now. Not this time though.

Trish bit into a steaming chip. "So, go on."

Ian blew a bite-size piece of fish that sat on his fork in mid air. "I shouldn't have to tell you. You should already know why I feel I'm in limbo," he said before popping the fish into his mouth.

"I don't know. Just tell me!"

Ian swallowed his food. "I'd been counting the days when I'd be welcome at yours for a change and I could sleep over. Better still, move in. But you're still hiding me like I'm a bloody leper. I don't appreciate being hid like you're ashamed of me. I hate having to drag ourselves out of bed at night as we're about to nod off, to then get dressed, see you to the door, then get back into an empty bed wide awake, unable to get back to sleep again. I'm sick of it. It's been over four months since Tony passed. Don't you think it's time we thought about living together? You've been dying for it for ages and now you keep putting it off. I know we couldn't shack up straight away, but …"

"You what?" Trish interjected as she returned her mug of tea to the coffee table with a slam. "You think it's okay for us to live together after just four months? Imagine how my kids'd feel – what they'd think! What everyone'd think!"

"It isn't as if you loved him. You couldn't wait to escape. You were fine about leaving him when he was alive. Now he's gone, now it's more respectable to be with someone else, you're making excuses."

"It's fine for you with no kids. You could never understand how mothers put their kids first unless you've had them yourself. Bloody hell, you can't even stand kids."

"Kids? They're grown adults! Eat your chips. They're getting cold."

Trish obliged, more out of hunger than compliance. "Adults or not – they loved their dad and it'd be like rubbing salt in the wound if we lived together so soon. Bloody hell, they don't even know you exist yet! I've got to tell 'em I've met someone before I even hint that I plan to live with you. Like lying isn't bad enough. How do I explain that we're gonna live together when they think we've only just met? I don't think you've thought it through. I don't think you even care."

"Course I care, otherwise I wouldn't wanna commit to being with you, would I?"

"Yeah, you care for me, but you don't seem to care about their feelings."

"Course I do 'cos if they're hurt, so are you," Ian returned.

"Good. So you get it that I'd be upset at them being upset about you moving in so soon."

Ian screwed up his face and scratched his head. "What? Ah, whatever. Let's change the subject, shall we? Eat up. I'll make another brew," he said, taking another bite of his food before standing up with his mug, ready for the kitchen.

"No, you're alright."

"Aww, c'mon, girl. I'll drop it, okay?"

Trish handed him her mug. "Okay, we'll cross that bridge nearer the time."

Later in the evening when Trish's mood lifted, they agreed to give it another eight months before living together – a year after Tony's death.

Of course Trish wanted to live with Ian – desperately – but her kids and her reputation mattered equally. She had previously assumed she would move into Ian's when she left Tony, but now Tony was gone, she owned her ex-council house outright. It therefore made more sense for Ian to move in with her, especially as her place was considerably more substantial than his; hers being a three-bedroom semi, whereas his was only a one-bedroom flat.

"I don't care where we live so long as we're together." Ian twisted his gold sovereign ring around his finger.

"Oh, I forgot to tell you," Trish said. "I've been googling for ideas for a cleaning business for me and Ryan. You did say it sounded like a good idea, didn't you?"

"Yeah, I did and still do, provided you can drag Ryan off his arse to put in a fraction of the effort you'd make."

"Don't start. You know he's depressed."

"Well, sitting on his arse aint gonna help, is it?"

"Exactly, which is why I need a business to give him a reason to get out of bed in the mornings."

"The afternoons you mean. When has Ryan ever got up in the morning?" Ian took a luxurious drag of his cigarette.

"Shurrup, will you and give him a chance. I'm sure he'd get up in the mornings if he had a job. He always used to. Anyway, gimme a ciggie. Mine are in the kitchen, but remember when we live together, there's no smoking in the house."

Ian obliged, lighting her cigarette with his Zippo lighter. "Yeah, as you keep saying."

"Anyway, as I was saying, I googled and got loads of ideas. There's loads of cleaning businesses that do everything – cleaning, laundry, ironing and clothes alterations. I could do all that. I'm good at sewing. The great thing is, there were pages and pages of these businesses which makes me think there must be a big demand. Then I put Sharrinwood in the search and there seemed to be loads there too. Then I thought, hmm, maybe there's too much competition?"

"Who knows till you've tried it?" Ian said.

"Ahh! Well, I have. I mean, I phoned a few asking if they could fit us in. And guess what?"

"I hate guessing. Just tell me."

"They were all fully booked. Well, all except one. They said I'd need to wait a week before they could fit us in. That's a great sign, intit? I mean, there must be a demand if they're fully booked."

"What about the one that wasn't? Wonder why they're not so popular?"

"That's what I thought, so I went back to the link where I found its number to check if it had a website, and they didn't." Trish paused for effect. "All the others did. The others were more professional, so that's probably the thing. Do it professionally with a good website."

Ian squeezed her hand. "You're not just a pretty face, are you, girl? And Ryan can create the website, can't he?"

"Definitely! So I'm gonna tell him. See what he thinks. Be really good if he's interested. Having a goal will pull him out of this depression. Gonna wait till he's a bit better though. He's way too down right now to see any good in anything."

CHAPTER 26

August 2008

A reproduction brass clock ticked loudly on the mantelpiece, but louder still was the candy pink floral wallpaper it stood against. Much to Ryan's protests, Trish had insisted it would add contrast to her magnolia woodchip walls. As she gazed at the clock, she considered the best time for catching him in a good mood. Sunday evening when they planned to watch a DVD together would be perfect, she decided.

When the evening arrived, Trish chose James Dean's *Rebel Without a Cause* from their DVD collection. "They don't make 'em like this anymore. I love the oldies and you love James Dean, so it's a win-win, intit?"

"Yeah. Let's hope we've forgotten most of it from the last two times we watched it," Ryan quipped.

Trish had bought a giant packet of crisps and some salted peanuts to enjoy with the film, determined the evening would go well.

After clearing away the dishes, she returned to the living room with two mugs of tea to find Ryan stretched out on the sofa, staring at the paused movie. "There you go, love. Shove up, will you," she said as she placed the mugs on the coffee table next to the nibbles.

"Ta, Mam." Ryan reached for a handful of peanuts and inched up the settee to make room for Trish. "I've paused it on the intro."

"Good. Just keep it there for a minute, will you. I've summat I want to tell you." In an attempt to look nonchalant, she reached for a handful of crisps.

"Oh?" Ryan replied suspiciously, wondering if she was about to nag him about finding a job again.

"The thing is, I've been thinking about us going into business together."

"Oh yeah?" Ryan said, turning to look at her with interest. "What kind of business?"

Trish coughed nervously. "A cleaning business."

It was clearly not the best timing for Ryan to have taken a mouthful of peanuts. Gobsmacked, he coughed, causing them to shoot out like hailstones over Trish's baby pink T-shirt.

"Bloody hell!" she snapped, brushing them away. "Don't be such a drama queen!"

Ryan looked at her in disbelief. "You want me to be a bloody cleaner? Are you having a laugh?"

"Just hear me out, will you, you daft 'apeth. I could hire the staff and you could do the man's work; set up the web site, do the admin and take charge of the equipment and anything else you can do better than me. We'd make a good team."

"I can't believe it even crossed your mind," Ryan said, shaking his head, "let alone settled there! Go on, then. But you're wasting your time."

"Look, I'm just trying to help. If you can't find a job, you could be self-employed. You've got lots of skills. Or, if you don't fancy a cleaning business, you could start a computer repair shop. I could help you with it; answer the phone, man the shop. We have no money to set up shop, but we could start from home. We've got Zoe's old bedroom. You could use that to start with. Then when you build up enough customers …"

"Mam, I'm not good enough to do it as a business."

"You could go on a college course to improve."

"No way. People who do it for a living have degrees, not crappy college certificates. Besides, I'd lose my Jobseeker's Allowance if I went on a proper training course."

"Okay, what about web design? You're good at that."

"Nah. There's way too much competition out there. I'd be competing with the geeks who've got degrees 'n' that. I've got nowt. Besides, people use Facebook for their business websites nowadays; they don't need proper websites. Those that need a website can get free templates that even chimpanzees can set up."

Trish was on a roll and nothing was going to stop her. "Then there's buying and selling junk furniture to do up and sell on eBay or that other place. What's it called? Oh yeah, Gumtree. We could try bits of all these to see where there's a greater demand, then go for that."

"Not interested. Too much hassle for little return."

"Okay, back to the cleaning business. There's loads of men doing it. I've been googling. We could include an ironing service too. Do whatever we get work for. Then when we get established, we can be picky."

"A bloody cleaning job! I'd be the laughing stock with my mates." He pulled himself up from the sofa and headed for the kitchen. "Making a brew. Want one?"

Trish followed him. "Blow the brew. It's not what you think. Just give us a chance. Give you a chance. At least look at the website links I give you. I've looked into it a lot. I think it could work. All I ask is you look at my ideas."

"Mam, stop peckin' my head!"

"Well, at least think about it, will you?"

"Okay, okay, okaaaay. Just stop mitherin'."

* * *

The following day Trish emailed Hannah.

From: trishtonywilcox@ulon.co.uk
To: hannahbernstein@vnet.com
Subject: Business ideas
Sent: 09/08/2008, 17:28

Hiya Hannah
I hope you and your family are well and your all feeling a bit better after your loss it is definetely getting better for me but the kids are still really sad especially Ryan. Guess what. Remember when you encouraged me to start a business with Ryan, well I've been googling about cleaning businesses and I think your right, there seems to be a demand and I am definetely thinking of giving it a go with Ryan once I've pursuaded him. I think a project like this will help pull him out of his depression and give him something to get up for. I was thinking that to keep overheads low we could start in my house using our own appliences and materials then if it gets bigger we could rent a cheap room somewhere. I chatted with Ryan last night about it he thought I was joking cos he said he'd be the laughing stock with his mates if they knew he was a cleaner but I told him you won't be a cleaner, you'll be boss of a cleaning business. Then I suggested all the other things he could do like computer repairs or doing up furniture like you said but he said there would be no money in them and was'nt interested so I'm going to have to pursuade him into a cleaning business and I want to thank you for the ideas. I will let you know how we get on.
Love Trish xx

Three days later, Hannah's reply arrived.

From: hannahbernstein@vnet.com
To: trishtonywilcox@ulon.co.uk
Subject: Business ideas
Sent: 12/08/2008, 09:13

Dear Trish,

I'm delighted you are considering some of the business ideas I suggested and I wish you well with whichever one you go for.

We are as well as can be expected, all things considered, thank you. Thankfully, it is getting easier, albeit, slowly.

Let me know how you get on.

Best wishes,

Hannah

On opening the email, Trish's pupils dilated. *Is that it? No questions? No how are you? God, I must be boring if she can't think of a single buggering question to ask me to show she's interested. And there was I – idiot – thinking we'd be good friends.*

CHAPTER 27

Early December 2008

During orchestra break, Hannah joined Margot for coffee. Margot played clarinet, Hannah the cello. Ordinarily, this difference might have separated them as much in the café as it did in orchestra. The women, however, shared other common interests besides orchestra – both were Jewish and also neighbours.

Margot opened her mini pack of digestive biscuits after stirring her coffee. "Would you like one?"

Hannah held up her palm. "I'm fine, thanks."

"That was a good session, but I struggle with the Bach. How is it for cello?"

"A few challenging bars for me too. We'll just have to practise them repeatedly until we drive our families mad, won't we?" Hannah said with a chuckle.

Margot laughed. "Ha! You are wicked! Anyway, how are you and the family? I must say, you're looking more like your old self again, which is good to see."

"We're all well, thanks. And yes, I'm feeling a lot better, thanks to Sadie. Did I tell you about her turnaround? I can't remember who I have and haven't told," Hannah said, before taking a sip of her coffee.

"I can't say you did. Gosh, it must be good for you to be this pleased!"

"Exactly! It's practically a miracle. For a girl who generally needed a rocket behind her to push her to study, one would have expected that losing her father would have been the final straw, but it seems to have been the catalyst for her buckling down. She's been working flat out and has been commended at uni for her dramatic turnaround."

"Good for her! I'm very pleased to hear it. It must've been hard for her though."

"Yes, she was devastated, naturally. She was given compassionate leave at uni. Then, a couple of months later, like a miracle, she suddenly picked herself up. We chatted about it and she said she felt guilt-ridden and wanted to put things right. It isn't that she believes in the after-life; she doesn't really. But she felt if she could do something positive to make up for the worry she caused Saul, it would be worth it if there was a miniscule chance he might look down on her, be proud and finally rest in peace. Well, that's my understanding of her explanation. This is the advantage of daughters over sons, isn't it? Opening up about worries I mean – being more communicative."

Sadie, however, had not entirely opened up, not about wishing to make up for the grief she had also caused Hannah. Hannah rarely smiled since losing Saul, and this caused Sadie additional sadness. It was not that Hannah had lost her love; she had lost her companion and she felt desperately lonely without him. Although she made huge efforts to remain positive for her family's sake, they could see through the pretence: her eyes lacked their usual lustre; her movements became sluggish, without purpose; and she lost interest in activities that previously gave her pleasure. For Sadie, making up to her parents was a far greater motivation to study than being bribed with a new car or guitar. This drive helped her feelings of guilt and self-hatred – helped her sleep better at night.

* * *

Although Sadie's loss was the catalyst for her dramatic turnaround, for Zach it was the cause of his downward spiral. Minor issues became mammoth and he interpreted people's innocent comments as personal affronts.

Robin received the brunt of Zach's mood swings, despite his efforts to be understanding and supportive. Being snapped at for the smallest thing was becoming the norm.

The final straw came one Friday evening. There had been a delicate matter Robin needed to discuss with Zach. Regardless of how sensitively Robin put it, he accepted it was likely to result in a scene, and he was right. They had finished their evening meal by 6:45 p.m., earlier than usual because Robin was giving three back-to-back piano lessons from 7 p.m.

When the last student left at 8:30 p.m., Robin headed to the kitchen. "Coffee?" he asked, waving the coffee jar. "Need a chat with you anyway, so maybe you should have one."

"Sounds ominous. Something wrong, darling?" Zach asked.

"No, everything's fine. Back in a tick."

In the lounge, they entwined on the sofa.

Robin took a deep breath before broaching the subject. "Remember the promise we made about always being totally honest, no matter what?"

"Yes, and?"

"Look, you know how much I love you, and what I'm about to ask is necessary, so please don't think I'm having a go."

Zach dropped his arm from Robin's shoulder. "Ah, so you're about to have a go! Can't wait!"

"Stop it!" Robin said, taking hold of Zach's hand. "I'm not having a go and this isn't easy. Just hear me out. The thing is, a colleague told me he'd seen you with a guy at Sam's Chop House on Friday. That would've been the night I was doing the charity concert. He said you were behaving like you were an item over a candle-lit meal."

Zach gaped in disbelief, snatching his hand away from Robin's. "What? Are you serious?"

"Do you think I'd joke about a thing like this?"

"The arsehole is either making it up or needs to get back to Specsavers! Who is this malicious slanderer? Does he realise he's defaming a lawyer?"

"I know. I would've taken it with a pinch of salt – considered it mistaken identity or something – but he seemed certain it was you."

"I was nowhere near Sam's Chop House on Friday or any Friday. The last time – the only time – I've ever set foot in the place was with you last year."

"It isn't as if he said he'd seen someone who looked like you; he was adamant it was you," Robin said.

At this, Zach shot up from the sofa. Planting his hands on his hips, he retorted, "So you choose to believe him over me? Is he gay? Maybe he has the hots for you and is hoping to split us up? Maybe you should be with him if you trust him more!"

"Now you're being ridiculous. I'm just asking if you know anything about it – if you can offer an explanation to show it's a misunderstanding. I dunno, maybe you went over to the guy at the table to speak to him and Ben spotted you just at the wrong moment? Maybe it was a client? Maybe …"

"No maybes. I'm telling you – the only time I ever set foot in the place was with you. Give me his number. I want to hear it from the horse's mouth," Zach demanded.

Robin shook his head. "Sorry. I gave him my word I wouldn't say who told me."

"But you just did. Ben. I can't think who this Ben is, but I can easily find out. Get back to him and explain it most categorically wasn't me. If he continues to be an arsehole, tell him I want to see him. I want him to tell me to my face. And you may wish to remind him I'm a lawyer. In the meantime, I think you should sleep on the sofa. I'm hardly going to be sharing a bed with someone who believes an arsehole over his partner."

Panic swept over Robin at the dread of losing Zach, especially as Zach's claims of innocence seemed valid. Might there have been a misunderstanding? He tried to remember Ben's exact words about Robin's apparent relationship break-up. Robin had been bemused, asking Ben to clarify because he had not split with his partner, not that it was any of Ben's business. Ben had been reluctant to explain until Robin insisted. That was when it came out about seeing Zach in Sam's Chop House.

Robin patted his trouser pocket to locate his phone, pulled it out and texted Ben. Turning to Zach, he announced, "Right, I've arranged to meet him tomorrow lunchtime in the Brodsky. Hopefully, we can clear up the confusion."

With an icy stare, Zach replied, "The greatest confusion is that you actually believed him over me. I'm not sure how we can resolve that."

CHAPTER 28

"Five, six, seven, eight, right kick, shuffle back," Cath called.

Trish and Ian were enjoying their weekly line dancing at Saint Thomas's church hall. It was where they first met over two years earlier and had continued to be known there as 'just friends'.

Cath and Pete, a middle-aged couple, ran the group. They always made a point of looking the part in their line dancing boots, hillbilly check shirts, turn-up blue jeans and Stetson hats. On stage, Pete operated the music, which consisted predominantly of Country. Cath, with the aid of her radio mic attached to a headband, demonstrated the dance steps at the front of the dance floor.

It was a close-knit community. Cath and Pete never failed to give a special mention for members' celebratory days, and every first week in September the group enjoyed weekend breaks to Blackpool together.

Trish and Ian pounced at the opportunity. Legitimate excuses were rarities. By day they would stroll along the promenade taking in the sea air and the sounds of crying seagulls. The Pleasure Beach came next where they would subject themselves to the terrors of thrilling rides that made them scream, curse and feel nauseous. Despite the nausea, they would then gravitate towards the waft of pink fluffy candy floss … followed by hotdogs … followed by sticky toffee apples … followed by more nausea.

Ian, however, drew a line at the Gypsy Rose fortune reading. "Load of bollocks! Go if you want to be ripped off, but I'm no mug. I'll wait outside."

And so Trish would cross Gypsy Rose's palm with silver and a twenty-pound note, and wait with a fluttering heart to learn when she and her beloved Ian would live together. The fact she was given a different future each year did not deter her in the least, despite Ian's ridicule about her gullibility.

"You're a right mug. They saw you coming alright!" His mood would lighten, however, with the waft of fish and chips which they would order with mushy peas and lashings of salt and vinegar. After finding a promenade bench, they would eat them with their fingers before jumping on the tour bus to enjoy the spectacular Blackpool Illuminations.

Later, they would head to the Crown Hotel that hosted a line dancing evening. In an attempt to keep their affair clandestine, they would attend, as always, under the ruse of 'just friends'. They fooled no one, however, especially as it was common knowledge they shared the same bedroom.

Luckily, Tony had no interest in line dancing, which had kept him well away; hence he never suspected a thing.

Lacy J. Dalton's 'Black Coffee' came on and Trish, tugging at Ian's sleeve, shouted, "God, I love this! C'mon!" as she pulled him onto the dance floor.

Into the microphone, Cath called, "Kick, ball, change and shimmy!" as she demonstrated an exaggerated shimmy, shaking her shoulders for the benefit of the front-row newbies, whilst experienced dancers improvised their own dance moves at the back of the hall.

In between dances, Trish raised the subject with Ian of them living together.

Ian was miles away, his eyes fixed into nothingness.

"Did you not hear a word I said? Are you not interested?"

"Course I am, girl. Yeah, we will."

"When?" Trish asked, her eyes narrowing over the rim of her glass of spritzer. "Tony's been gone nine months now."

"I thought you wanted to wait till it was respectable," he said, taking a long gulp of his Stella and avoiding eye contact. "We agreed on a year, remember?"

"What?" Trish exclaimed, crestfallen. "But we need to plan."

"You were going on about planning Christmas yesterday – having the kids and grandkids round. Don't you think you need to get that over with first?"

Spoiling the grandkids at Christmas was important to Trish. She wanted them to have more than the cheap *Snakes and Ladders* and plastic dolls she was given as a child. Christmas was important to her, but at this time her priority was securing her future with Ian. Before she had the chance to sway the subject back to it, Fiona returned from the dance floor.

Fiona was new to Saint Thomas's, though hardly new to line-dancing. Trish was in awe of the way she floated around the dance floor as if her steps were second nature, but then she was twelve years younger than Trish and a couple of stones lighter. She also happened to be an attractive green-eyed blonde. She had previously worked for the NHS as an auxiliary nurse in Sheffield. After an acrimonious divorce, she relocated to a Manchester NHS hospital where a better-paid position came up. Trish welcomed her to join her and Ian, and this seating position became the default. Besides, Trish hoped to pick up new dance techniques, and Fiona was always happy to support fellow line dancers.

CHAPTER 29

December 2008

Robin's eyes darted to every corner of the café as he mentally chanted *come on Ben, come on Ben!* After several repetitions, Ben appeared through the swing doors and headed to the cash desk. By the time Robin reached him, Ben had purchased his coffee.

"Thanks for coming. Appreciated," Robin said, removing his shoulder bag and duffle coat. He beckoned to the nearest sofa. "This okay?"

"Yeah, sure." Ben leaned over to place his mug on the coffee table before flopping onto the sofa. "Is this regarding what we discussed Friday?"

"Yep. Zach wasn't too pleased. He says the only time he's ever been near Sam's Chop House was with me last year and he's adamant he isn't seeing anyone else. He reckons it must be a case of mistaken identity and asked me to clear up the confusion with you."

"I really wish I could, Robin, but as I already said, I have no doubt it was your partner ..." He paused before continuing with the cruel blow, "with another man. I've seen him here with you enough times to have recognised him. Granted, I've not seen him for at least eighteen months while I've been away, but I'd recognise him anywhere considering his distinctive looks."

"Hang on a sec." Robin held up his index finger. "Eighteen months? Distinctive looks? My partner may well be good looking, but there's nothing particularly distinctive about him. What did this guy look like?"

"As I said, he looked exactly like your partner – tall, slim, black hair with a beard. That's him, isn't it?"

Robin's eyes lit up. "Yes!" he whooped, giving an air punch. "I mean no, that's not my *current* partner. The guy you saw is my ex – Daniel!" Joining his hands, as if in prayer, he looked up to the ceiling and whispered, "Thank you, God!"

Ben tilted his head quizzically. "Why didn't you say you'd changed partners in the first place? We would've …"

"Never mind. It's all good. Gotta go!" Robin said, grabbing his coat and bag. "Thanks again!" With that, he turned on his heels and hurried to the foyer to phone Zach.

Zach answered in hands-free mode. He needed free hands to eat his egg and cress sandwich and type at his desktop computer. Rarely did he take lunch breaks when there was an opportunity to work.

"Come closer to the phone, babe. This is important," Robin said.

Zach took a bite of his sandwich. "It better be. I'm busy."

"Hun, I'm sorry. I should never have doubted you," Robin returned in a hushed tone as he drew closer to the wall for privacy.

"So, what's with the change of mind? You've come to your senses and now realise I'd never lie to you? Or have you just discovered Bovine Ben bollocksed up?"

"Aww, come on, I believed you anyway, but yes, Ben and I finally worked out that the guy he saw wasn't you after all. It was Daniel. Ben's been away for a while and wasn't aware I was with someone new."

"Yabba-dabba! So you reckon everything should be okay now?"

"Well, yes, of course. Why shouldn't it be, babe?"

"Wrong answer! What you should've said was how sorry you are for having doubted me, for accusing me of a crime I hadn't committed, and acknowledge it'll take huge efforts to repair the damage, and you'll do whatever it takes to make up for it. Anyway, I'm busy. Have to go," he said, without waiting for Robin's response.

That evening, after a bitter row, Zach announced, "I think you'd better start looking for alternative accommodation."

After futile pleas, after reminding Zach how perfect they were together, of the fun they would have during Hanukkah and Christmas, Robin was forced to pack his necessities and move into his sister's semi in Cheadle. Naomi had a spare bedroom and insisted Robin stay until he was able to return to his flat.

When Robin moved in with Zach, he had let his flat out on a six-monthly contract. Another month and the contract would expire. How he wished that option was not open because having his own place only made the chance of reconciliation less likely.

* * *

For the bereaved, red-letter days are painful reminders. This was certainly the case for the Wilcoxes and the Bernsteins during December's festive period – Christmas for the Wilcoxes and Hanukkah for the Bernsteins. Given the choice, both families would have preferred to ignore celebrations, but for the sake of younger family members, they painfully trudged through the motions.

Throughout the eight-day period of these celebrations, good food is enjoyed, candles are lit, hymns are sung, charitable deeds are made, and gifts exchanged. Hanukkah is therefore often seen as the Jewish Christmas, especially because of its close proximity to it. The two celebrations, however, are very different: whereas Christmas celebrates the birth of Christ, Hanukkah celebrates the Jewish triumph over religious persecution by the Roman Empire. Although Christmas dates are fixed, Hanukkah dates are determined by the lunar calendar, resulting in Hanukkah falling any time from late November to late December. For the year 2008, it began December twenty-first and ended on the twenty-ninth.

Although Hanukkah was not as important to the Bernsteins as Christmas was to the Wilcoxes, the reminder of previous years' celebrations was more painful. Not merely were they grieving the loss of Saul, they were missing Robin. Much to their disappointment, there had been no communication between Zach and Robin due to a silly matter of pride.

CHAPTER 30

Late March 2009

On a private housing estate in Woolington stood a row of lock-up garages. A woman with two young children passed by, heading for the nearby primary school; an early bird considering it was only 8:20 a.m.

"Watch the road!" she yelled to her eldest, who skipped too close to the kerb.

Close to the end garage, a sad old Ford estate with rusty panels pulled up. Sellotaped on the interior rear window was a laminated sign in large black print: *P & R PRO CLEANING | Domestic & Office Cleaning | Laundry | Ironing | Alterations & Repairs. Competitive prices.* Set in larger, bolder print screamed a telephone number, website and email address.

With a squeak, the driver's door swung open. Looking strangely unfamiliar, Ryan stepped out wearing navy cargo pants with a matching button-up polo shirt. The shirt's left breast pocket sported a white logo with the business name *P & R Pro Cleaning.* After placing two large cardboard boxes on the pavement, Ryan unlocked and pulled up the blue metal door.

Inside, makeshift shelves, cupboards and utility hooks, from which hung various tools and cleaning equipment, utilised every inch of the whitewashed brick walls. Hanging against the far wall were two large ironing boards, two steam irons and two white laundry baskets. An array of empty clothes hangers hung from two steel clothes rails positioned against the side wall. Next to them, a makeshift desk made from a flush door, rested on two badly scratched Formica bedside cupboards. Although it managed to accommodate Ryan's laptop and printer, a clutter of paperwork spilled over the edge. Under the desk lay Ryan's guitar, which, to Trish's delight, he had taken up again. A worktop sink unit stood along the opposite wall. Adjoining it stood two washing machines with tumble dryers precariously perched on top. Next to them on the terracotta-painted concrete floor sat three red Henry cylinder vacuum cleaners.

Ryan dumped the boxes onto the worktop and let out a sigh of discontentment. *How the hell have I ended up with a friggin' cleaning business?* He crouched to switch on a small convector heater and remained on his haunches to warm up and brood over his predicament.

He had been vehemently against Trish's idea, but her art of persuasion was more tenacious than his stubbornness. "What part of no don't you understand?" he had often said, but it always fell upon deaf ears, until one morning, shortly after waking – too groggy to protest – he relented, if only to shut Trish up.

"Ohh, thank God! Thanks, love. You won't regret it. I promise," Trish had squealed with excitement, as she hugged him, kissing his cheek.

"Okay, Mam! Gerroff before I change my mind."

After many hours of online research into the business idea, Trish grew increasingly more confident it stood a chance, and equally confident the project would help lift Ryan's depression. Although she put considerably more effort into it than him, she felt no resentment for his lack of effort, not considering she had pressurised him into it. There were certain jobs he refused to do, but she accepted this, provided he helped with whatever he was willing and able to do. Handling a duster, a dishcloth, a mop or broom was where he drew the line. Vacuuming and yard jet-spraying were exceptions due to the machine element which guarded his masculinity. He also drew the line at marketing the business. It was embarrassing enough admitting he was a professional cleaner without flaunting the fact by circulating flyers.

"It's your baby, Mam, so it's only fair you do the pushing."

At least he agreed to create the flyers and business cards that Trish was happy to distribute. She had plenty of opportunities: via family and friends, her line dancing club, the school gates, and newsagents' windows. Once Ryan had taught Trish how to push the business on Facebook, there was no stopping her. Remembering Hannah's words of encouragement about utilising all skills and seeing which generate the greatest demand motivated Trish all the more. *If anyone should know, Hannah should with her education and brains,* Trish mused. And so, aside from cleaning, laundry and ironing, Trish also offered a repair and alteration service.

By October 2008, P & R Pro Cleaning had secured its first regular domestic cleaning customer, and by late November it had a total of twelve regulars – eight for domestic cleaning and four for laundry and ironing. Alongside this regular work, came a steady demand for alterations and repairs. By this stage Trish was forced to give up her teaching-assistant job. Apart from Trish and Ryan's under-eye shadows and short tempers from lack of sleep, business was looking good. Besides utilising their kitchen washing machine and tumble dryer, they had considered converting the spare bedroom into a second laundry room, but thought better of it in consideration of their next-door neighbours.

As luck would have it, the lock-up garage became available, complete with an electric power supply for only £15 per week. It was just as well considering the workload continued to expand. Although the demand was greater than Trish and Ryan had dreamed, they agreed to keep their overheads to the barest minimum until there was greater certainty of the business's long-term success.

Ryan's phone had been ringing intermittently. He told himself the caller would call back if important. Feeling nonchalant about potential customers worked wonders on his self-esteem despite the cleaning business stain on his street cred. Whilst stacking away the cleaning materials, he switched on the radio and sang along to Amy Winehouse's 'Back to Black'. Coffee was his next priority. Once made, he pulled out a plastic fold-up garden chair from under the desk and gingerly lowered himself into it. It had given way once before and he was not taking any chances. Glugging his coffee, he checked his phone for the last caller. It was an unknown number; probably another potential customer. Business was looking so good that he sometimes felt the need to slap his face to check he was not dreaming.

From his peripheral vision, a large black blur flashed past. "What the f –?"

"Only me!" Trish called as she followed the black laundry bag she had tossed in. Accompanying her was a blonde woman wearing the same uniform as Trish and Ryan.

"Been here long?" Trish chirped.

"Hiya Mam, Pauline. About ten minutes. Kettle's just boiled if you want a brew."

Pauline was one of five helpers Ryan and Trish had taken on as casuals. Trish knew Pauline from church. She was a practising Catholic, and therefore, according to Trish, a trustworthy woman.

Another female they had taken on – the sister of Ryan's friend Loz – had served six months of a ten-month sentence at Styal Prison for drug possession with intent to supply. Trish had been reluctant to take her on. Ryan argued, however, that if Trish considered herself a good Catholic, she should be forgiving and give Chelsea a chance. How else would the poor girl turn herself around if no one was willing to give her a break? On this basis, and because Trish had taken a liking to Chelsea (she reminded her of her middle daughter Zoe), she agreed to give her a two-week trial. And the weeks became months.

Trish and Pauline's day was planned working as a team: two ninety-minute domestic cleaning sessions, one in Northenden and the other in Sale. They had arrived at the garage to drop off the bag of ironing and to collect their gear.

Minutes later, Sarah arrived, a twenty-one-year-old university student who grabbed whatever hours she could to support her tuition fees.

Trish handed Sarah a bag of ironing she had collected from a busy working mother. "It's for the Cooksons. Don't forget, the husband likes starched collars and cuffs, chuck."

Driving to their first job, Trish's mind was fixed on Ian – eager for the day they could finally be together. She was happier than she had been in years, looking forward to the day she could tell her family about him – tell the world about him. She would discuss it with Ian at the first opportunity.

CHAPTER 31

April 2009

Although many Facebook profiles bore the name Andrew Redmond, none looked remotely like Hannah's Andrew. Hannah wondered if she needed a Facebook account to delve deeper, but she had her standards. She tried LinkedIn, again with no luck. She was unaware of any other social media sites. Besides, she doubted she would find him on any. Andrew and Hannah had been alike in so many ways and she felt sure he would dislike social media as much as she did. That left Google. After ten minutes of trying a variety of keyword combinations unsuccessfully, she began to despair.

As she pondered more search combinations, Polly jumped onto her lap. Hannah stroked the moggy's silky coat who purred appreciatively. The more she stroked her, the louder Polly's purring became, and Hannah imagined Polly to be smiling like a Cheshire cat. Then it hit her – Cheshire. Andrew had always preferred Cheshire to Manchester.

Quickly, she changed 'Manchester' to 'Cheshire' in the search field, and there he was.

Hannah's eyes turned to saucers as her heart thumped fiercely. "Down, Polly, down!" Hungry for details, there was no time for Polly now.

Andrew was profiled on a pharmacist website as 'pharmacist' and 'owner', situated in Alderley Edge – just ten miles from

Hannah. His small circular photograph showed the same blue eyes and infectious smile. He had aged well – now more distinguished and still dashingly handsome.

"Oh, my lord! It's really him!" she whispered, eagerly scanning the page to find his contact details. On spotting his address, telephone number and email address, she gasped. Pressing her fingertips against each cheek, she pondered her options. *I can't ring or email – anyone could answer. No, I have no choice – it has to be a letter.* Immediately, she set about writing one. Not an easy task. Had it been with pen and paper, the waste paper basket would have overflowed in no time. But she typed at her computer, erasing every line over and over until she eventually thought, *to hell with it – just type and see what materialises.*

14 Elmtree Road
West Didsbury
M20 3PP
12th April, 2009

Dear Andrew,

I hope this letter finds you well. Apologies if hearing from me after all this time comes as a shock. I found your address on your website after googling your name.

I'm writing regarding a personal matter – something that affects you. I need to speak with you urgently about it, preferably face to face.

Please let me know if you're agreeable to this. You can reach me at hannahbernstein@vnet.com and 07950 321 01.

All the very best to you and your family (it would be lovely to hear you have children).

Hannah Bernstein (née Cohen)

Writing the letter may well have been tough, especially in attempting nonchalance when inquiring if he had children, but posting it was far harder. Clutching the envelope with a clammy hand, she grabbed her house keys, slipped into her jacket and slammed the door behind her. The nearest post box was two minutes' walk away, but she procrastinated, giving herself time to reflect – maybe change her mind.

On reaching the post box, she lingered, staring at the envelope with Andrew's name and address written in her hand – handwriting he might recognise. Standing motionless, she mused over the possible consequences. *What if his wife opens it? What if it turns out to be a huge mistake causing heartache to everyone involved? Was it too familiar asking if he had children? Maybe I should rewrite it, excluding that part? What if …*

An elderly, bespectacled woman holding an envelope intercepted Hannah's thoughts. "Excuse me, are you posting that?"

"Sorry, just checking the time of the next collection," Hannah lied, before pushing her doubts into the red post box without another thought. Ambling home, she estimated that he should receive the letter by Tuesday – in two days' time.

However, two days passed without a word. Her disappointment was palpable as she checked her email and texts fanatically. She was sure he would have replied promptly. He was like that – dependable, efficient and so lovely, she mused.

By Thursday she had almost given up hope. Next time she would email. Give it a week first though. While searching online for books to suggest at the book club, she glanced nonchalantly at her email box before doing a double take. There sat an email from Andrew. Too overwhelmed to open it, she blinked before staring at it. She wanted to savour the moment she first had contact from her love in thirty years. After such musings, she opened it with relish, like a chocaholic opens a box of luxury Belgian chocolates for the first time.

From: andrewredmond2000@cmedia.com
To: hannahbernstein@vnet.com
Subject: Lovely surprise!
Sent: 16/04/2009, 13:31

Hannah,

How lovely to hear from you after all these years! I hope you are well and the matter you wish to discuss isn't too concerning.

Naturally, I'm keen to know what it's about. In fact the suspense is killing me so I'm hoping we can meet asap. Most evenings are fine for me except Thursdays. I'm also available most weekends. Do you have anywhere in mind? Here's my number in case you prefer to text: 07142 58579

Yes, I have children, two daughters – Phoebe aged 28 and Harriet 25. Sadly, I lost my wife Jill to cancer in 2004. We are all otherwise fine.

I look forward to hearing from you.

Fondest regards,

Andrew

Hannah read the email over and over to analyse each word – for any hint he still cared. Not wishing to appear eager, she replied in text later in the day when she had time alone and could choose her words carefully.

Hello Andrew. Lovely to hear from you.

> I'm so very sorry for your loss, but delighted to hear you
> have two daughters.
> How does a week Sunday midday suit you? We could meet
> halfway, but if you don't mind the drive, Didsbury is great
> for pubs and eateries. Your call. Best wishes, Hannah

She chose text because she wanted to hear his reply ping into her phone. Silly, wasn't it? Or was it? After all, she had romanticised such a scenario for decades. This time she had no parents to influence her life choices. This time she could follow her heart as Trish had suggested. Some relatives might have something to say about it if she and Andrew got back together, but at Hannah's age, she could not care less. How she wished she could meet him sooner, but Zach needed to hear the truth first.

Much to Hannah's elation, Andrew replied immediately, agreeing to Sunday, the 25th at 12:30 p.m.

> The Metropolitan do good food. Let's meet for lunch, then
> you'll have time to explain what's on your mind.
> I'll wait near the fireplace, ok? The one at the far end
> beyond the tall bookcase.
> Andrew :)

Lord, is this actually happening? Hannah's reveries were in overdrive considering the possibility of them becoming an item again, and of Andrew and Zach securing a good father-son relationship. *Oh, for goodness' sake, woman, stop it! You might not be attracted to him anymore. He may be a totally different person now. Besides, he may be with someone.*

CHAPTER 32

Business had been looking exceptionally good. However, there had been a sudden, noticeable drop in incomings. This prompted Trish to tackle the badly neglected bookkeeping, where suspicions were confirmed. Profits had dropped by almost twenty percent and they had lost three regular customers. Another discrepancy was that usage of laundry and cleaning materials had not reduced, despite the workload reduction.

"Stupid I am!" Trish spat. "The cow's not only been nicking our customers, but our materials as well. After giving her a chance too!" Dashing to the bottom of the stairs, she yelled up to Ryan. "Ryan, where are you? Get down here now!"

Ryan flew down, two stairs at a time, with a bath towel slung around his neck. "Bloody hell, Mam. What's up?"

"I told you we should never have taken that madam on, but would you listen?" she barked.

"Taken who on? Who you on about?" Ryan asked, rubbing the bath towel over his wet hair.

"Chelsea, of course. She's been robbing us right, left and centre. I've just done the books and the takings are way down. On top of that, so are our materials. And what's more, remember how three of our customers went AWOL? That's customers who had always been happy with our work. Funny that, intit? It's that Chelsea. She's pinched them. I could bloody swing for her."

Ryan held his palms up, fingers splayed. "Woah! That's a bit harsh, Mam. Where's your evidence?"

"Don't need it. It's obvious!" Trish retorted, looking away from his glare. "After all, most workers nick a bit from bosses, so if anyone's gonna nick more than average, it's gonna be an ex-con, intit?"

"Don't you be saying owt unless you've got proof!" Ryan ordered.

It later transpired, however, that the perpetrator was not Chelsea after all, but Pauline – Pauline who Trish had praised to the skies for being such a devout Catholic. Trish had heard from a woman at line dancing that Pauline cleaned her neighbour's house – a house from which Trish had recently lost work.

Although Trish considered herself a reasonably good Catholic, the Christian doctrine of forgiveness was where she drew the line. "Get your bloody coat and clear off, you thieving cow! And don't think of coming back for your wages – not until you've paid back what you robbed from us. You're lucky we've not called the police."

"How can I trust staff again after that?" she asked Ryan. "I mean if you can't trust a devout Catholic, who can you bloody trust?"

Ryan's phone rang. He could see from the screen it was Bob, the garage owner. "Hi, Bob. Everything okay?"

"Erm, not quite, mate. Afraid it's a bit awkward. I've been told, not mentioning names, that you've been using the garage as a business. I just wanted to ask if there was any truth in it."

"No, course not. Well, not the type of business you're thinking of. We definitely don't have customers coming and going, if that's what you mean."

"I mean any type of business, whether customers visit or not. Do you?"

"The only work we do in here is related to my cleaning business, but customers never set foot in it. The garage is just for doing their laundry, ironing and repairing clothes. We could just as well be doing the jobs for ourselves, so what's the difference?"

"Ahh, so that would explain your excessive electricity usage too. Did you not read the contract? It clearly states no businesses to be conducted on the premises. Makes no difference if customers set foot in there or not. You're carrying out business services that require excessive use of electricity. Actually ironing is a fire hazard and goes against fire regs."

"Aww, come on, mate, we don't mention it as a business address and the bulk of the cleaning is done in the customers' own homes."

"What's up?" Trish mouthed as she flapped a freshly laundered shirt at Ryan.

Ryan waved her question away. "Shh!"

"It doesn't matter, Ryan. It contravenes my insurance terms. Sorry but you're gonna have to cease trading. I'll give you two weeks to vacate the premises."

Ryan hung up slowly, trying to take in the implications.

Trish looked at him expectantly, before pouncing with a flurry of questions.

"It's not good, Mam. We've got two weeks to vacate the premises. Apparently we're contravening Bob's terms."

"You're joking, aren't you? I mean it's not as if we're using it for a cannabis farm or a brothel or summat. God, I can't believe it. It never bloody rains, but pours!"

Alongside business troubles, Trish was feeling increasingly insecure about Ian. She tried to assure herself that it was all in her head, but the more she observed his behaviour, the more paranoid she became. No longer did he leave his phone lying around, and often kept it switched off when they were together. He had never been secretive with his phone before; far from it – she would often answer it for him. They had always spent Saturday evenings together, but for the second time in a month he claimed he was needed at work.

"Sorry, girl, but there's no way I can get out of it," he had said, unable to meet her questioning eyes.

CHAPTER 33

Hannah's book club had made a pact to support their treasured independent village bookstore. Despite the temptation, members refrained from buying books online. It was unsurprising, then, when Hannah ran into her book club friend Diane in the store on her day off.

Almost fifty years in business, Morten's was a well-respected booksellers. Philip, a devoted employee of many years, wrapped Hannah's book *The Girl with the Dragon Tattoo*. Having added it to the re-order list, into a Morten's paper bag it went, carefully sellotaped at both corners. True to form, Philip took as much pride and attention in this wrapping and re-ordering procedure as he did in caring for the thousands of books he fondly shepherded into their floor-to-ceiling shelves each day.

Diane placed another copy of the same book on the counter. "Hi, Hannah."

"Ha! Great minds, eh?" Hannah replied.

"Well, it is the next read for the book club, isn't it? Looking forward to reading it," Diane said as she paid for her copy.

Outside on the cobbled pavement, Hannah suggested coffee. The women initially considered Café Rouge, but decided on Saints and Scholars across the road from it – a quaint little ivy-covered cottage restaurant that oozed charm. After all, they wanted to support independents wherever possible, and so made their way to it.

As the weather was fine, they chatted and people-watched al fresco.

"It's so good to see you looking more like your old self again, Hannah," Diane said, beaming, as she stirred her latte. "We were worried about you, wondering how you'd cope with your loss, especially after such a traumatic experience."

"Thank you, Diane," Hannah replied, sitting back in the white slatted chair. "I admit I've been feeling much better recently, especially since Sadie turned a new leaf with her studies. And it isn't just a flash in the pan reaction to losing her father. She's kept up her studies and continues to make excellent progress, which is nothing short of a miracle, all things considered. We talk about her father now in a more positive way, remembering the happy times. It helps us both. I wish Zach could be as open. It's difficult to know how he's doing, though he does seem to be getting through it, despite his split with Robin."

"That was such a shame. They seemed such a perfect match, and you and Robin got along very well too, didn't you? How long has it been now?"

"Yes, I was very fond of Robin and was almost as upset about the split as Zach. It's been about four months now. Thankfully Zach seems to be moving on. At least he's able to laugh again. So there's another reason I'm feeling so much better."

"I'm very happy to hear it. Soooo," Diane asked, "fancy coming to the Hay Festival next month?"

"I'd love to, provided I'm not working and provided it doesn't clash with Shabbat or anything major at the bridge club," Hannah replied, pulling out her Filofax to check her diary. "When exactly?"

"Sunday, the twenty-fourth seems a good day. If we set off Saturday evening and check in to the nearest B and B, that should accommodate your Shabbat, and Ruth's, as I'm sure she'd love to come too. We could suggest it at the next meeting. What do you think?"

"Sounds like a plan! I'll pencil it in and check with work."

Hannah was bursting to tell Diane about Andrew, but she first needed to have a serious conversation with Zach. Until then, she could tell no one.

* * *

Hannah mentally rehearsed ways of telling Zach, and how she might deal with the possibility of him taking it badly. It was planned to a T. She was to invite him for dinner and break it to him with after-dinner coffee and amaretti biscuits. She had baked them especially, knowing how much he loved them. She had made herself sick with worry. *How would he take it? Would he hate her? Would he demand to know the whereabouts of his biological father?* Whatever his response, the decision was made – he had the right to know – and soon considering thirteen months had passed since Saul's death.

"*C'mon, woman, do it!*" And with that, she tapped in his number.

"Ah, Zach, darling! Glad I caught you. How are you? Everything okay at work?"

"Hi, Mum. I'm well, thanks. What's … ow!" Zach yelled, as Sybil took a leap onto his knee, misjudged and dug her claws in to hang on. Zach repositioned her comfortably before continuing. "Sorry, Sybil dug her claws into me as she was jumping up. Everything okay?"

"Yes, fine. I was wondering if you'd like to have dinner here tomorrow? Around six?"

"Sounds good. What's the occasion? Who's coming?"

"Just the two of us. Thought it'd be nice to have some quality time. I'll do the same with Mimi and Sadie another time."

Zach agreed, hung up and tilted his head quizzically. *Weird! Wonder what that's about?*

CHAPTER 34

With suspicions in overdrive, Trish cooked up a plan for the upcoming Saturday evening. Anticipating it could be a long wait, she filled a plastic carrier bag with a flask of coffee, ham sandwiches, a milk chocolate bar, a camera and a pair of binoculars. She may not have possessed a doctorate in surveillance, but she was far from stupid: Ian was less likely to recognise Ryan's car, so she took his rather than her own; she would park discreetly, in a position that enabled her to follow Ian's car without having to make a U-turn; and she wore Ryan's black hoodie to conceal her face. She may well have been jealous about the possibility of Ian cheating on her, and fearful of the possible confirmation, but at least the thought of spying on him gave her a buzz of excitement. *Maybe I should look into being a private detective for women with cheating fellas. Quite fancy myself as a Miss Marple. Can't be much to it, surely?*

Shortly after seven, her musings were interrupted by Ian's front door opening. Thankful for remembering her binoculars, she peered into them. *Hmm, only jeans, so not out to make much of an impression. And what's with the sports bag? He's not been to the gym in ages.*

Slamming the door, he locked it with his mortice key before heading to his BMW parked a couple of doors away.

Trish was thankful it was white, enabling maximum night-time visibility. After flinging her binoculars onto the passenger seat, she wiped her sweaty hands on her jeans. "Pull yourself together, woman," she berated herself as she nervously started the engine. "If you fancy yourself as a private eye, you need to be cool." Slipping into first gear, she prayed he would not do a U-turn. Luckily, he proceeded straight ahead, turning left onto the main road and north towards the city. Tailing him was simple enough until a set of traffic lights turned against her.

"Shit!" she spat as she was forced to stop. Revving her engine, she kept a close eye on his tracks until his vehicle became a pin-prick. "Bloody brilliant! Lost him! C'mon, c'mon," she urged the lights. The second they changed to amber, she hit the accelerator, praying she could catch up. Soon enough, however, she approached a second set of lights which, to her chagrin, also changed to red. "Why? Why do they always do that when you're in a bloody rush? Swines!" As she let out a heavy sigh of defeat, she caught sight of a white car at the traffic lights, the first in the queue. It was Ian's. "Yes! Don't lose him. For God's sake, don't lose him!"

Ten minutes along Palatine Road and Wilmslow Road into Fallowfield, Ian took a left onto a side street full of Victorian terraced houses. As he approached his destination, he turned off the radio at Duffy's 'Mercy'; whistling along to it as he parked at the end of the road. After pulling his bag from the back seat, he locked his BMW and headed to the end house.

Trish tugged her hoodie tighter over her head and parked a hundred or so yards from the house on the opposite side. She grabbed her binoculars, peered into them and adjusted the focus.

It was a well-maintained, red-brick house with an equally well-kept garden, small with an array of rose bushes. The red front door boasted a shiny brass lion's head knocker and a stained-glass window above it. To the right of the door, a pair of fashionable ivory curtains hung from a tall sash window.

With a pounding heart, Trish waited, desperate to see who would answer. On the one hand, she prayed for a man to answer. On the other hand, she recalled the horror of discovering Tony in a passionate embrace with one. *No! I'd rather it be a sexy blonde than repeat that nightmare, she mused.*

However, as the door opened, Trish gasped and swallowed her words. Greeting Ian with a beaming smile and outstretched arms was a young, attractive blonde. It might have been bearable had they left it at that, but their embrace extended into a passionate kiss – all the confirmation Trish needed for her heart to plummet and her lips to quiver. Adjusting her binoculars' focus, the sickening realisation hit her: it was Fiona from line dancing. Slowly, her binoculars slipped from her fingers, dropping onto her lap, as her eyes filled with tears. The pain, almost physical, was unbearable and the word *bastard* ricocheted around in her head. Never did she anticipate this. She did not know what she expected, but never in her wildest of nightmares had she guessed he was having an affair with a friend. *Ha! Some friend! Bitch!*

Trish wondered how long this had been going on, how she could have been so blind in failing to notice, how she could live without him or ever trust another man again. She remembered their plans, how much he loved her, how keen he was for them to live together, how his interest waned when Fiona came on the scene. She recalled how Fiona always sat with them. And now Trish knew why. She retraced those line dancing evenings, trying to pinpoint tell-tale signs. There were times she could not attend and Ian assured her not to worry – he would be fine going alone. *Alone, my arse! Idiot trusting him!* After soaking her handkerchief with more tears, she took a deep, shuddering breath and hatched her plan. *Let's see if the bastard stops the night.* Rummaging deep into her handbag for her phone, she wondered if her friend Sue was free. *Sod it, phone her and find out.*

"Hiya, Sue. Are you busy?" she asked, sniffling.

"Hiya, Trish. Hang on. Let me turn the telly down." Sue was channel-hopping and glad of a friend to chat with. It had been a lonely eighteen months since her divorce and she hated spending Saturday evenings alone. "You alright, chuck? You don't sound it."

"Not really. I just found out that Ian's cheating on me," Trish sniffed, her eyes fixed up on the bedroom window.

"Aww, no, Trish! The bastard! Want us to come round?"

"You can't. I'm outside his trollop's house in Fallowfield spying on 'em. I'm gonna wait here till morning 'cos I need to know if he stops the night. I took Ryan's car so he won't spot me."

"You can't do that! It's not safe! It's not as if you're in Hale or summat," Sue said, turning off the television.

Trish wiped her eyes with the back of her hand. "I'm not going home till I know. Then I'll know we're finished. Well, we're finished anyway, but that will be the clincher. If I have to sleep here till tomorrow afternoon, I'm not budging till I know."

"I'll come and join you. It's not like I'm doing owt else," Sue said.

"You're joking? You'd do that for me?"

"Course I will, and it's for me too – it'll get me out. Gimme the address and I'll be there in about an hour. It'll be better with two of us. One of us can keep watch while the other has a kip."

"Aww, thanks a lot, Sue. I owe you one. Bring a blanket. Oh, and when you get here, could you take over keeping watch for a bit while I go home for a wee, freshen up and collect some overnight stuff?"

"Yeah, course. I'd better get a move on, then. See you in a bit."

"I'll text you the address in a minute when I know it. I need to drive back down the road to see the street sign. Oh, and remember to look out for Ryan's car – not mine. It's an old silver-grey Ford estate. Park just behind it, okay? Before you get out and get in mine, check the house – the last one on the road with the red door – to make sure you're not spotted, okay?"

After checking the street name – Bloom Street – and texting it to Sue, Trish exhaled with lifted spirits. Whilst waiting for Sue, she nodded off before snapping awake to the piercing screams of fighting cats. The sound was reminiscent of a horror movie, but the only thing Trish feared was the realisation she was losing Ian. As she kept her eyes constantly fixed on the house, she replayed their happy times together, determined that next time she would follow her head rather than her stupid heart.

Shortly after ten, the bedroom light flickered on. Fiona's slinky figure was clearly visible as she moved towards the window to close the curtains. Sliding down her seat, Trish's eyes, shooting venom, remained fixed on the window. The ivory curtains were transparent enough to allow light through, and Trish would know when the lights went out.

So that's where they're gonna be sleeping together, Trish thought as tears flowed again.

Half an hour later, Sue arrived. "Hi, chuck. You okay?" she asked, sliding into the passenger seat.

"All the better for seeing you," Trish replied, "except … "

"Except?"

"Except I just saw the trollop close the bedroom curtains," Trish said, pointing to the window. "So I suppose that's the room they'll be having it off in."

"Don't think of it. It's too upsetting. Focus on your plan. Wasn't it to go home for some things before settling here for the night?"

"Yeah, I'll go now if you don't mind holding the fort till I'm back," Trish said. "Did you bring a blanket?"

"Yeah, and some food and drinks. They're in my car. We can have a midnight feast," Sue quipped.

"Brill! You're a star. Best leave your stuff in your car in case you need them when I'm gone. I'll try not to be too long. Oh, and that's Ian's car over there." Trish pointed it out. "The white one. Keep an eye on it as well as the house, will you?"

"Yeah, course. Just get going before it gets any later. And don't be too long. I don't fancy being stuck here at night on my tod," Sue said as she bit her fingernails in mock fear before returning to her own car.

As Trish turned onto Wilmslow Road, the chatter and cheers of university students spilling out of the Friendship Inn hit her. She only wished she was a fraction as happy. She had frequented the Friendship with Ian a couple of times, and the thought crossed her mind that this would now be his and Fiona's local.

At least arriving back to an empty house was a blessing. She might break down if she had to explain to Ryan that her suspicions had been confirmed. She was sure he was out because he had taken her car. After using the bathroom and gathering her necessities, she headed back to her stake-out, returning by 11:30 p.m.

Sue vacated her car and slid into Trish's passenger seat. "Hi, hun. Thank God you're back. Mind if I open a window? It reeks of stale cigs in here."

"Sorry. Yeah, open it. I keep nagging Ryan not to smoke in the car, but I might as well talk to the wall. Seen anything?" Trish asked, looking up toward the bedroom window.

"Not a whisper. Oh, except the bedroom lights went out about ten minutes ago." Sue immediately regretted her words and hit the side of her head with her palm. "Aww, sorry, hun. That was insensitive of me."

"No, I need to know. At least I don't need to tell the kids about him now, not now I know what a cheating bastard he is. Talking of sleeping, I wonder which is comfier – back or front seat?"

"Front I suppose 'cos we can at least push the seats back and stretch our legs." Sue unzipped her holdall, pulled out her blanket and placed the holdall in the footwell. "Got yours? It's getting cold."

"Yep, I'll get it." Trish yawned as she yanked a holdall from the back seat and pulled out a woollen tartan blanket.

"Aww, you look dog tired. Why don't you have a kip first while I keep watch? I'm wide awake anyway."

"Ohh, I wouldn't say no. Ta, Sue. Can't keep my eyes open." Trish kicked off her shoes. "I owe you big time for this."

"Get away with you. You'd do the same for me, wouldn't you?"

"What makes you think that?" Trish quipped as she pulled her blanket snugly up to her chin and closed her eyes.

Being the loyal friend, Sue desperately tried to stay awake, but by 4 a.m. she felt herself nodding off. Trish was in deep slumber and Sue did not have the heart to wake her. Minutes later, they whistled a snoring duet.

The sound of birdsong and a passing car woke Trish. She felt she had not slept a wink, but must have considering the graphic nightmare that lay fresh in her mind of Ian and Fiona. They were enjoying their fairy-tale wedding, squealing with laughter as hundreds of guests threw confetti over them. Awaiting their guests in a grand château, sat a ginormous, five-tiered wedding cake. As the happy couple ate their slices, they laughed hysterically at Trish for being a loser.

Trish checked her watch. It was only 8:35 a.m. and Sue was still sleeping. She doubted the traitors would be stirring yet, let alone be up and about on a Sunday morning, so she closed her eyes and fell back to sleep. An hour later, she awoke to the tugging of her sleeve.

"Trish, wake up! They're up. She's just opened the curtains," Sue said, still half-horizontal in the passenger seat.

"Okay, I'm awake. Gimme a minute." After rubbing her eyes, she blinked furiously trying to focus on the house. "Oh yeah, they're open." She looked towards Ian's car and sighed heavily. "His car's not budged, so the bastard slept there." The devastation, etched over her face, enveloped her as she fought back her tears.

Sue reached over to place her hand on hers. "He's not worth it, hun. Think of it as a lucky escape."

"Yeah, I know, except I still love him," Trish said, wiping her tears.

"I know. Want some coffee?" Sue leaned over to the back seat for the flask and poured the hot beverage into the flask's integrated plastic cup.

Trish sniffled, accepting the coffee with a sad smile. "That's it, I'm going over!"

Sue turned to Trish, astonished. "What? To the house? You're joking, aren't you?"

"Course not. Gonna give 'em a piece of my mind," Trish replied, before taking another sip of coffee. "I'll freshen up a bit first. Least we won't need to hang around waiting to see what time he leaves. He slept over and that's all I needed to know. The bastards. They're not getting away with this that easily. I'm gonna make sure her whole street knows what a trollop she is."

"Bloody hell, Trish. Sure you want to do that?"

"Course I am. It'll make me feel better."

After draining her coffee, Trish wiped her smudged eye makeup with face wipes, and applied her eye liner, face powder and lipstick. Taking a final look into her compact mirror, she pressed her lips together and snapped the compact shut. "Right, I'm gone!" she said as she opened her door and stepped onto the pavement.

Sue, slack-jawed, gaped in disbelief at Trish's determined strides towards the house.

With a pounding heart, clammy hands and blazing eyes, Trish wondered what she should say. For her, it was usually the first thing that popped into her head. Having given three short rings of the doorbell, she stepped back and held her head high. She knew the bell was working because Ian had struck lucky with it the night before. As she was about ring again, the door swung open.

It was Fiona. "Hello, can I ..." but then the realisation hit her. She stiffened and paled before turning her back on Trish, calling loudly enough for Ian to hear, "Please leave the premises."

"Who is it, girl?" Ian called as he made his way down the narrow hallway. On spotting Trish, he froze. Stupefied and bereft of balls, all he could muster was, "Sorry."

"Bastard! Do you think I was so stupid not to notice what was going on?" Trish lied. She turned to Fiona. "And you, I can't wait for the day he does the same to you! And he will. Mark my words! Oh, and this is for your neighbours!"

Turning to face the street, Trish yelled, "Calling all ladies on Bloom Street. Watch your man before Fiona Holburn from

205

number one steals yours too! That's Fiona Holburn at number one Bloom Street, the husband snatcher. Watch your man, ladies!"

With that, Trish marched back to Ryan's Ford estate to the thrum of her angry heart.

CHAPTER 35

Zach's favourite foods awaited him for his vis-à-vis with Hannah: Matzah balls in chicken soup, goulash and challah bread followed by apple and cinnamon cake. To help soften the blow, Hannah served a fine bottle of Malbec.

After dinner, they settled in the lounge with coffee and amaretti biscuits. Zack kicked off his shoes and stretched out on the sofa while Hannah sat upright on the sofa facing him. On the wall facing Zach hung a full-length gilded mirror. Hannah used it for checking her cello-playing posture whilst seated in her button-back chair.

In the mirror, Zach caught sight of his carefree expression, albeit with an air of bemusement. As he reached for his coffee, he eyed his mother suspiciously. "Mother dear, you've gone to a helluva lot of trouble with all my favourite foods – homemade amaretti biscuits even. Is there a particular reason for all this?"

Silence.

Hannah clasped her hands together tightly to brace herself. "Actually, there is something. I was hoping to be the first to raise the subject, but since you've beaten me to it. There is something I need to tell you."

"Jeees, that sounds ominous!"

"This is incredibly difficult for me, Zach dear. Before I tell you, promise to hear me out – don't hate me and do know that regardless of what I'm about to tell you, your father loved you dearly and would have gone to hell and back for your well-being, just as I always have and always will."

"Jesus, now you *are* scaring me. What the hell is it? I thought you might have something up your sleeve, but nothing that warrants this gravitas."

"Zach, darling, there's no easy way to tell you this, so I'll just say it. Your father is of course still your dad considering how much he loved you and all he did for you, but I'm so very sorry to have to tell you that your biological father is another man – someone you don't know."

Zach paled, his mouth forming a perfect circle. The coffee cup he held remained aloft as if also in shock. After seconds that seemed like minutes, he attempted to speak, but no words came.

Hannah stood up to comfort him. "Zach, darling, speak to me."

Zach placed his cup on the coffee table and held up his palm to ward her away. He stared at her incredulously before shaking his head in disbelief. "You're saying Dad's not my father? And only now you tell me – over thirty years late!" Torment and confusion whizzed around in his head as he wrung his hands. Leaning forward, he rested his elbows on his knees and his throbbing head in his palms. "Funny I'm the only one with fair hair and blue eyes. I always wondered about that. Did he have fair hair and blue eyes?"

"Oh, Zach," Hannah said as she returned to her sofa. "Please try to understand and let me explain."

Zach raised his head and stared at her in disgust. "Did he have fair hair and blue eyes?" he spat, the veins in his neck protruding.

Startled, Hannah recoiled. "I'm sorry. Yes. Yes, he did."

Zach looked at her with contempt. He caught sight of himself in the mirror's reflection – a blue-eyed, fair-haired young man staring back at him. The scar on his forehead was visible and the worries of the world lay heavily on his shoulders. As if being physically battered by homophobes for being gay was not enough, and battered emotionally by his father for the same reason; but to be battered by his own mother with this act of betrayal was more than he could bear. She had lied to him and Saul for thirty years.

"Next you'll be telling me he wasn't Jewish. Not that it makes any difference, but was he?"

"No, he wasn't, and that's why I ended the relationship, and later met your father."

"What? If you'd ended it, how the hell did I come along?"

Hannah fought back her tears and pressed her lips together, trying not to cry. "Three weeks before the wedding he contacted me, begging me not to marry your dad."

"Jesus!" Zach said, staring at her in disbelief. "You mean I came about while you were engaged to Dad – a few weeks before your wedding?"

Hannah hung her head, fixing her gaze on her clasped hands as a tear rolled down her cheek.

"How could you? Were you ever going to tell me? So you wait until you're trapped in an earthquake before you decide? And if you hadn't survived, I would've gone through life believing the lie, bereft of my paternal family history. How could you?"

"I'm so very sorry. No words can express how sorry I am. It was never meant to happen. It was a mistake, and I'm sorry it's caused you so much pain."

"Oh, brilliant! So I was a bloody mistake as well. That makes me feel so much better. Was he bisexual – gay even?"

"I had no reason to believe he was either, and he certainly never said anything to suggest he might be. No, I'm sure he was neither."

"Yabba dabba! So my sexuality is unlikely to be nature then. Maybe I'm gay because I subconsciously suspected something was amiss – maybe being screwed up veered my sexuality from the norm?" He paused, reflecting for a while. "I'm being facetious of course. But, Jesus, I can't take this in. So I may have half siblings out there and Mimi and Sadie are only half-sisters? I'm guessing you haven't told them?"

"Of course you needed to be the first to know. I'll tell them when you're okay with it. Just say the word and I'll tell them."

"Okay with it? Okay? You think I'll ever be okay with this, ever? At least Dad didn't live to learn the truth. Is that it? Were you never going to tell me if he had lived?"

"Yes, of course I was. I'd asked Trish to tell you both if I didn't survive."

"Ahh, so you're a coward; you could only risk telling if you or Dad hadn't survived."

"That's not true. I'd decided to tell you regardless. The earthquake made me realise I couldn't take this to the grave because it wouldn't be fair on you."

"You bet it wouldn't. So who's this so-called *father* of mine? What does he do? Where does he live?"

"His name is Andrew Redmond. He's a pharmacist with his own pharmacy in Alderley Edge. We met at uni. I realise you don't care, but he happened to be a lovely, kind man."

"*Kind* man?" Zach retorted. "A kind man who sleeps with another man's fiancé?"

Silence fell as Zach attempted to take in the bombshell. His blue eyes glistened with the tears he was fighting back. Bad enough to have lost his father, to be then told his father was not his biological father after all. He brooded how he would get through this. He brooded how he would hide his pain at work. He brooded how he would ever forgive his mother. The atmosphere was tense and the pain cut deep.

Watching him discreetly, Hannah waited for the right moment to at least touch his hand. She feared he might reject her – despise her even.

"Sorry, I need to process this," Zach said, standing to leave.

Hannah followed him to the front door, desperate for the opportunity for at least a goodbye embrace.

His body language, however, remained stiff and unwelcoming. With a gentle, despairing click, he shut the door behind him with a broken heart.

Wiping her tears, Hannah laughed hysterically before her laughter turned to sobs and her stomach clenched with fear. She took a deep breath to compose herself, and stared into space. Proactive steps were needed she thought, but what those steps might be, she had no idea. After all, she had felt certain that confessing was the right thing to do, but now she was not so sure. Sleep was needed. *Yes, I'll be able to think clearly if I sleep on it. I'll worry about it tomorrow.*

The following day Zach would hopefully be in work. At least he would be safe there. During Hannah's morning break she texted, asking him to get in touch.

Maybe he's in court or with a client, she wondered after an hour had passed with no reply. At lunchtime, she texted again. Still no reply. Getting through the afternoon was hard, especially with needing to put on a cheerful face for patients.

By the time she finished work at six she was almost frantic. He was generally free to respond to her messages at this time as he finished work at five. But he remained silent. Either he was intentionally ignoring her or he was still in shock. *Or,* she considered in dread, *what if he's done something stupid?* At that, she grabbed her car keys and headed for his flat at a speed beyond her acceptance level. She pondered the likelihood of him being home. *He's always home Monday evenings after work as he does his weekly shopping Sunday, and he did his big shop before coming to me yesterday.*

Rod Stewart's 'The Killing of Georgie' came on the radio. It often brought tears to her eyes – a song about a gay man cast out by his family and later killed by a gang in New York. The timing made her blood run cold. *Please, please don't let it be an omen.*

As things stood, entering Zach's development would now be problematic. It required access through the security gates which was only possible if he accepted her call. She therefore parked her Audi around the corner and returned on foot to the gates where she waited expectantly for a familiar face.

Katy, Zach's next door but one neighbour, slowed to a halt as she approached the gates in her yellow Mini Cooper. In response to Hannah's tap on her windscreen, she opened her window. "Hi Hannah. Everything okay?"

"Hi, Katy. I'm struggling to get in. A slight issue with Zach's security code I think. Keep the gates open for a second while I get through, will you, please?"

"No problem."

Although there was neither a gate, nor path entrance to Zach's townhouse, each house was divided by pretty, well-tended garden walls. Hannah climbed three steps to his familiar black door with its large, brass knob. It was now uninviting and she shivered.

Knocking gingerly at first, her knocking soon crescendoed, as did her voice. "Zach, Zach! Open the door!"

The wait could only have been thirty seconds, but with each second, she became increasingly more anxious, having imagined every possible worst-case scenario.

She gasped as the door shot open. "Zach! Thank God you're okay! We need to – "

"Sorry, Mum, but I need to process this. I'll be in touch when I can deal, okay?"

"No, it isn't okay!" Hannah snapped. "I've been frantic worrying about you. I need to know you're okay, and I'll continue to keep in touch daily, if only with a text. If you don't respond, I'll be round quicker than you can blink. At least agree to respond to my texts."

"Okay, if you insist," he said, puffing out his cheeks. "I'll do that, but if you don't mind, please let's leave it for now. Bye, Mum." Before Hannah had the chance to reply, he gently shut the door.

CHAPTER 36

The mellow sound of a cello hummed from Hannah's lounge, persisting with determination. Her concert loomed closer and she was anxious to master Bach's 'Cello Suite No.1 in G'. She had reluctantly agreed to perform this solo and was now regretful considering the time constraints. As she pencilled in a notation, she heard a text ping into her phone.

It was Mimi: Please pick up!

Hannah returned the call immediately.

"We've heard the news," Miriam sniffed. "Zach told me everything and I've told Sadie."

Hannah gasped, taking a moment to process the news.

"Mum!"

"Yes, yes," Hannah responded in a barely audible whisper.

"We're coming round. Are you home?"

"Yes, I'm home. I'm sorry you had to hear it from Zach, but I think he wanted to be the one to tell you. Yes, come round now."

The sisters might have been harder on Hannah. However, the pitiful look on her face, coupled with her red, puffy eyes as she opened the door was enough to tell them she had suffered enough.

"It's okay, Mum," Sadie said, with a warm embrace. "Let's get coffee."

"We're not here to have a go at you," Miriam added as they made their way to the kitchen. "We're just desperate to know about Zach's blood father. Zach wasn't very forthcoming.

Whatever you can cope with telling us, we'd appreciate. No pressure."

Once coffee was made, they settled in the lounge. Looking expectantly at Hannah, the sisters placed their hot mugs on the coffee table and curled up together on the sofa, desperate for answers.

Polly jumped up, pushing herself between them. Her feline body pressed against Miriam's phone in her trouser pocket, reminding her to turn it off. In so doing, she gestured to Sadie to do likewise.

On the opposite sofa, Hannah cupped her coffee mug, as she had when she had dropped the bombshell on Zach. But this time she did not feel as anxious. This time, the recipients of the news were prepared.

Staring blankly ahead, lost in memories, Hannah recounted the time she first met Andrew, about his kindness, how much he loved her – and she him, about his twinkly blue eyes and his light brown hair, about the torturous pain in deciding to follow her head for the sake of her Jewishness and her parents' wishes, and about her last heart-breaking contact with him when she finally said goodbye. She recounted the pain and tears she thought might never end and how she had carried a part of Andrew, not merely in her heart, but physically for three decades through the blue eyes, the light brown hair, the smile and the mannerisms of her beloved son.

"So, that's about it I guess." Hannah let out a long, soulful sigh, took a final sip of her coffee and gently returned her mug to the coffee table.

The sisters blinked, slack-jawed as they processed their mother's tragic love story. Surely, they should have hated Andrew for what he had done to their father; like a stab in the heart had he lived to discover it. But they failed to even dislike him. After all, he had loved their mother dearly and had desperately wanted to marry her.

"So what now, Mum?" Sadie asked, with knitted brows. "Do you think Zach will want to meet Andrew? Do you want him to? Have you been in touch with Andrew? What…"

Hannah held up her palms in protest. "Slow down!"

"Okay. So, do you think Zach will want to meet him?"

"At this time, I think Zach would rather see him dead than meet him. I've never seen him so angry. I'm worried about him. I wonder if he'll cope with the shock. You didn't see the way he was when I told him – like he despised the ground I walked on. He refuses to talk to me. I need you to keep an eye on him; make sure he's okay. Will you do that?"

The girls threw each other a sideways glance.

"Of course we will, won't we, Mimi?"

"Yes, of course. So, have you been in touch with Andrew since?"

Hannah shifted uneasily in her seat, giving a little cough. "As I said, the last time I saw him was that night – a few weeks before your father and I married. However, I contacted him for the first time in all these years a couple of weeks ago. We've arranged to meet for lunch. Actually, on Sunday."

"Wow! Are you nervous?" Sadie asked.

"I would've been, but now I'm more concerned about Zach. Maybe I should postpone it until I'm sure he's okay? I only arranged to meet Andrew at this stage because I thought Zach would've taken it differently and might have been interested in meeting him. Ha! Fat chance!"

"Don't postpone it," Miriam urged. "You should go! So how did he take the news about him being Zach's father?"

"I haven't told him yet. All he knows is that I need to see him about an urgent matter that affects him. Naturally, he's keen to know what it is, so I'll be glad to be able to put him out of his misery. The suspense must be killing him."

"Is he married with kids?" Miriam asked, stroking Polly to feign indifference.

"He lost his wife a few years ago to cancer. He has two daughters around your age – twenty-five and twenty-eight."

Miriam and Sadie's eyes were like saucers.

"Gosh, so they'll be Zach's half-sisters!" Miriam said. "Does Zach know about them?"

"He wouldn't listen and left before I had the chance to tell him more. And now he's not talking to me so I can't tell him. If you get the chance, maybe you could."

"Yes, of course," Sadie said assuringly. "I wonder if he's changed much. I wonder if you'll still fancy each other. Where are you meeting?"

"Ha, I'm hardly going to tell you. You might spy on us," Hannah quipped. "I'll tell you after the event."

"Be sure to have some good photos of Zach on your phone to show him – photos of him growing up," Sadie suggested, before touching her chin in thought. "So, now we know why Zach's colouring is so different from ours."

"That's one thing Zach did ask," Hannah said, "whether he'd inherited Andrew's colouring. In fact Zach's resemblance to Andrew is uncanny. Aside from the hair and eye colouring, he has the same infectious smile and the same large hands with long fingers. Even some mannerisms are uncannily similar, such as his shoulder-shaking laugh and the way he always folds his arms. I wish Zach was as understanding as you two. But to be fair, it isn't your biological father who's been switched, is it?"

"I can't imagine how he must be feeling, but I'm sure he'll get over it," Sadie said. "Do you have a photo of him?"

"No. I couldn't run the risk of one being discovered – first by my parents, then by your father."

"But you can now it's out in the open. Is he on social media? He'd have a picture there," Miriam suggested.

"I tried Facebook, but nothing. Oh wait! There's a picture of him on his business website – his pharmacy. One sec, I'll show you," Hannah said, hurrying to her bedroom.

Returning with her laptop, she joined her daughters on the sofa. "Here, it won't take long. It's still switched on. Sadie, move up, please. Polly, shoo!" Hannah gently pushed the moggy further up the sofa and sat between her daughters. Positioning her laptop on her knee, she googled the key words and beamed at the quick result. "There," she said, pointing to the circular photograph of Andrew, "that's him."

"Woah, Zach does look like him, doesn't he? Especially around the eyes," Sadie said, mesmerised.

"It's no wonder you couldn't leave a photo of him lying around. It definitely would have raised suspicions," added Miriam. "Hmm, let's see," she said as she switched the laptop from Hannah's lap to her own. After typing Andrew's name into Facebook and drawing a blank, she concluded, "Yep, I think you're right, Mum. No sign of him here. She repeated the process for MySpace, again drawing a blank.

"What are you wearing?" Sadie asked.

"Oh, I don't know. Smart casual I guess."

"We'll help you," offered Miriam. "Come to mine and have a rummage through my wardrobe for something special."

Although it had pained the sisters to learn their mother had cheated on their beloved father, they loved her equally, and desperately wanted her to be happy again. If having Andrew back in her life brought her happiness, they would support it.

CHAPTER 37

When notice was given to cease trading at the garage, Ryan rang Ben, an accountant recommended by a friend.

"Have you been doing your bookkeeping and kept all your receipts?"

"Yep, my mam's been doing 'em. Mind you, the five people we hire are cash in hand, but we've noted what we've paid them."

"Hmm, that might have to change if you're hoping to expand. Drop off your files and I'll take a look at them."

Keen for the upshot, Ryan dropped off his accounts in a plastic carrier bag that afternoon.

"It looks like your business is doing well enough to afford small business premises. However, if you want a successful business, you need to do things properly. Maybe employ staff legitimately and make it a limited company to safeguard your assets."

"Assets? Are you havin' a laugh? We live in a council house and whatever we own, a junk shop would charge us to take away. Oh, hang on, we bought our council house so that's assets, init?"

"It is, but let's not worry about that for now. It's just something to consider. Once you've found suitable premises, you'll need public and employers' liability insurance and professional indemnity in relation to your finances on more complex legal matters. And of course you'll need to submit tax returns."

Ryan and Trish took Ben's advice seriously. A week after receiving notice to cease trading at the garage, they found an affordable two-roomed rental premises that permitted business use. Located in Woolington, the same area as their garage premises, there was less chance of losing local clients. It was the last shop of a row of twenty-five over an estate agent's. Its location, off the beaten track for shoppers had not been an issue for the previous business – a computer repair shop – as it was not dependent upon passing trade. The same applied to P & R Pro Cleaning. In fact, its location offered good shop frontage advertising to passing traffic, especially as it was by a pelican crossing where pedestrians crossed the road and vehicles would be stationary for long enough to notice the sign.

Trish may well have been bereft of qualifications, but her business sense made up for it. After an extensive internet search for affordable shop front signs, she found a company that made her an offer she could not refuse. Ryan argued the price was too good to be true. However, with the promise of a three-year guarantee and final payment after completion, Trish went ahead with the order, stressing the importance of it being as noticeable as possible without looking cheap. She was certainly not let down. Against a sapphire blue background shone large, bold white text: P & R PRO CLEANING | Domestic & Office Cleaning | Laundry | Ironing | Alterations & Repairs. Competitive prices. Tel: 07987 654 09 www.prprocleaning.com. Five randomly positioned stars shone above the text indicating sparkling clean results.

By Ryan's own admission, he was also impressed and thus motivated to show more effort. Working flat out, he rigged up the interior to a considerably higher standard than he had hitherto tolerated at the garage. Whatever he was unable to do, his mates helped out for a minimal fee. Woody the joiner fitted second-hand kitchen units and Baz the plumber plumbed in a kitchen sink and three refurbished washing machines. The workroom was considerably larger than the garage premises, allowing room for extra equipment. Added to this was the luxury of a WC and an office. Trish and Ryan were coming up in the world and the fact they had their own office set them apart from their staff.

"Stick this on the office door will you, love," Trish said, handing Ryan a 'Manager' brass plaque. For the first time in her life she felt important.

In the office, Ryan had replaced his former makeshift desk with a substantial corner desk and drawers with two swivel chairs – all purchased from a second-hand shop for a song. An advantage of being raised on a shoestring was learning the skills to budget wisely with an eye for bargains.

After much pressure from Ryan, the garage owner allowed a two-week extension period for the move. Much to Trish and Ryan's relief, business was unaffected; far from it since the staff had been eager to grab whatever overtime was going and had practically run the business during the interim period. Regular clients remained loyal and new ones were added to the books. This extra workload required an extra pair of hands. Any hands, however, had to be self-employed because Trish and Ryan feared being cheated by employees again. Employed staff could be difficult to fire, whereas self-employed workers could be dropped instantly.

"Once bitten, twice shy," Trish said as she struggled to thread her sewing machine needle, tutting in annoyance. "Pauline might've got away with pinching our customers and products, but I'm damned if anyone else will."

Trish and Ryan recounted first-hand experiences of staff deception – including their own during the days they were employed. Throwing sickies with dramatized, if not entirely fictional back complaints or stomach issues were familiar strategies as they were difficult to medically disprove.

"Why the hell should we pay them for doing nowt when they pull a sickie?" Trish said. "Then there's the bloody five-weeks' holiday pay! No way am I paying for people to swan off to Tenerife and Barbados when I can't afford a week in Blackpool!"

"Imagine if we called out a plumber or electrician at our gaff and paid them for doing nowt, or for them to skive on the job? It should be no different paying a cleaner for our business." Ryan said as he consulted his diary for his dental appointment. "And what about all the dental and medical appointments staff would need time for? Or invent? Not in our hours, they don't. And what happens if one of 'em gets preggers? We'd have to pay for months and months of her unpaid work while she's on maternity leave. I'd rather burn the dosh than give it to someone for having sprogs in my time."

Trish stopped sewing the hem on a skirt. "Not only that. Why should we do employees' national insurance and PAYE for nothing? It's enough we have to work like dogs running the business and doing our own tax returns without having to do unpaid work doing employees' PAYE who rob from us."

Ryan walked over to the plastic-framed wall mirror to check his tooth. "I think a bit more of my filling's come out. It's killing," he said applying pressure to his cheek with his fingers. "And what if someone's crap at their job and they took the huff if we complained? We could be done for unfair dismissal. There's nowt stopping them getting their own back and making out we treated 'em unfairly. Shit, we could …"

"Watch your language! You're not too old for a clout," Trish admonished.

"Is *bloody* okay? You say it all the time. We could go bloody bankrupt because of vindictive staff. Nope, there's no way we're gonna put ourselves and our business at risk by employing staff. We'd have to be total idiots."

The decision was therefore unanimous – they were having none of it – none of the mug's game of employing staff for doing nowt. They would not even consider zero-hours contracts because they would otherwise have to provide holiday pay and rest breaks – paying workers for doing nowt. Casual labour was therefore all Trish and Ryan were willing to consider. Sod what the accountant advised. He was obviously an idiot. The only payments they would be forking out would be for hourly work completed within the given time in the same way they pay tradesmen for carrying out jobs in their home. They therefore only accepted help from people who agreed to be self-employed; the only difference being was that P & R Pro Cleaning determined the hourly pay. At least they paid above the minimum wage in the belief they would receive a higher quality of work.

For workers who dared complain, Trish would retort, "What do you think it is – a holiday camp? You know where the door is if you don't like it. Plenty of others will be grateful for your job, and are queuing up for it."

To add insult to injury, Trish and Ryan insisted workers' mobile phones be turned off on arrival. If they needed to be contacted for emergencies, the caller was to ring the company landline with a message. Trish and Ryan had observed more times than they cared to remember the misuse of mobile phones by shop assistants, waiters and other low skilled workers during working hours.

"It's no different from stealing!" Trish argued. "Well, it ain't gonna happen at P & R Pro Cleaning! They can turn their phones off in working hours," she demanded. "In fact, let's put that in the terms and conditions, then they'll know from day one. If they don't like it, there'll be plenty more grateful for the work."

Trish and Ryan managed their business under precision timing. They had become ruthless micromanagers watching their workers' every move. Not for one minute did Trish trust workers alone in a customer's home to perform jobs to her high standards. She therefore worked with them to ensure they did.

Back at base with Ryan, other workers attended to the laundry and ironing. When Trish was not out cleaning, she focused on alterations and repairs – an extra string to her bow, as Hannah had put it.

Little did Hannah know, however, of Trish's draconian measures. Had she known, she might have had a diplomatic word with Trish whilst attempting to keep a straight face regarding the sheer irony.

CHAPTER 38

Sunday, 25 April 2009

On this bright Sunday afternoon, Didsbury's Metropolitan pub witnessed the momentous reunion of two former lovers of bygone days.

Inside, Andrew lounged on a button-backed leather Chesterfield beside a grand mahogany fireplace. He had taken extra care dressing for the occasion. He aimed to look as sexy and attractive as he had thirty years ago without showing he had made the slightest effort. A blue open-necked shirt tucked into beige cotton chinos set the tone, and a pair of brown leather brogues completed the classic style. He ran his fingers through his short fair hair; although greying at the sides, he took pride in the fact there was little sign of balding. Glancing up periodically for the first glimpse of Hannah in three decades, he scrolled through his phone, checking there were no 'running late' messages. He was three minutes early, but he always had been a stickler for time-keeping.

Five minutes later, Hannah appeared through the doorway like a mirage, looking around self-consciously. Andrew waved her over, praying she would recognise him. To his relief, she recognised him instantly, giving him a transient wave of recognition. Not wishing to reveal her elation, she gave a controlled smile, fighting back her beam of jubilance that was itching to shine through. As Andrew stood to greet her, his smile, broadening to a beam, said it all. His eyes, however, said so much more as they lovingly enveloped her. The fact he was waiting exactly where they had arranged helped Hannah recognise him instantly, but even if she had bumped into him on the other side of the world, she would have recognised him immediately – tall, handsome Andrew with his twinkly blue eyes, the corners now crinkled in an attractive, manly way, and that same infectious smile was enough to turn her knees to jelly. Even his stance was the same – with his left forearm across his waist and his right elbow leaning on it with his chin resting on his curved fingers. He took this old, familiar stance as he watched her make her way towards him.

"Hannah, it's so good to see you!" he said as he bent forward to embrace her and kiss her cheek. "You look fabulous! How are you?"

"Good to see you too, Andrew. I'm very well, thanks." A quiver of excitement ran through her as she caught a sensual whiff of his Issey Miyake.

"I've booked a table for one o'clock, but we can have a drink here first. What would you like?"

Hannah sank into the sofa next to the place he had left his orange drink. Rarely, if ever, did she drink during the day, but right now she needed some Dutch courage. "I'll have a Malbec, please."

As she observed Andrew at the bar, it seemed more like a few years than decades since they had been together – when they were deeply in love. At least this time clandestinity was not required. However, this time, she was to be the bearer of shocking news. She wondered when she should tell him – here with their drinks or over lunch. The idea of switching tables in the middle of announcing a life-changing revelation would be awkward at best. Her decision was made.

The bar was quieter than usual as customers were enjoying their drinks al fresco. Andrew therefore returned sooner than expected. "You still prefer red wine, then," he said as he handed

Hannah her wine and sat beside her. "And you're still as gorgeous as ever. You've hardly changed."

With a backward flick of her hand, Hannah said, "Oh, please, you'll have me blushing."

"Cheers!" He raised his glass to hers. "To old times!"

Hannah echoed the toast with a smile, clinking her glass against his.

"I'm obviously keen to hear why you wish to see me, but first let's catch up. How has life treated you, Hannah?"

"I was thinking the same, that it would be good to catch up first. I'll tell you why I need to see you over lunch, okay?"

"You're the one who knows what's coming so I guess you're the best judge. Sooo, what *have* you been up to these past three decades? We've ten minutes each before our meal to catch up," he laughed.

"Have you a stop watch so we can keep it fair?" Hannah said, with a chuckle.

Once the ice was broken, they relaxed, exchanging pleasantries about their family and work, and finally about the earthquake. Time flew by and before they knew it, it was 1 p.m.

After moving to their allocated table, Andrew pulled out a chair for Hannah and one for himself facing her. "Another glass?" he asked as he summoned the waiter for the menu and drinks.

"Better not – not during the day, even though I am walking."

"You live that close?" His attention switched to the waiter who was showing an air of impatience. "I'll have a J2O orange, please. Hannah?"

Hannah looked up at the waiter. "Oh yes, sorry. Hmm, a slimline tonic with ice and lemon, please. By the way, I rang yesterday to inform you I have coeliac disease. My name's Hannah Bernstein. I was told you could accommodate a gluten-free diet provided I remind you when ordering. In fact I already gave my order on the phone.

"No problem. I only take drink orders though, but I'll be sure to tell the meals waiter."

"I'm sorry you're coeliac," Andrew said, his brows drawing together into a frown. "That must be a pain, especially on top of your religious dietary restrictions."

"It's okay. I've learned to live with it. Just a bit of a pain having to ring restaurants in advance to check they can accommodate. Many have never heard of coeliac or gluten, so it takes quite a bit of explaining to assure them how simple it is to produce a gluten-free meal – I mean simple considering all whole foods are naturally gluten-free anyway. It's only processed foods that often aren't, so I simply omit anything processed when eating out. Some fob me off if they don't want the hassle, but they were very helpful here."

Shortly after the drinks and menu arrived, the food waitress appeared with a smile. "I believe you pre-ordered a gluten-free baked salmon with seasonal veg, baby potatoes, free from any sauces. Is that correct?"

"Yes, that's perfect. Thank you very much."

"Tell you what," Andrew said to the waitress, "I'll have the same. Let's make life easy, shall we?"

Once the waitress departed with the orders, Andrew moved in closer to Hannah. "Okay, drinks and food sorted, now we can get down to serious business. First, let me say again how sorry I am for your loss, Hannah. It must be hard when you also have to worry about how your kids are taking it. He seemed like a good man and I'm sure you must all be desperately missing him."

Hannah raised a questioning eyebrow. "You lost me. How would you have known Saul was a good man? You never met him."

"Hmm … look, I shall only tell you on the condition you agree not to be cross, okay?"

"If you tell me what you did, I'll tell you if I'm likely to be cross about it," she replied with a thin smile.

Andrew paused to prepare himself. "When I discovered you'd become engaged to Saul, I located his place of work and paid him a visit. I told him in no uncertain terms he'd be making a big mistake marrying you because you still loved me."

Hannah took a sharp intake of breath. "What?" she almost screeched before checking herself, remembering she was in a public place. "Did you tell him about us? About that last night we were together?"

"Good God, no. However, I told him you were only marrying him on the rebound and because he was Jewish, and I wasn't. I told him I had no doubt you would've married me in a heartbeat, rather than him, had I been Jewish."

"My God! What did he say? He never breathed a word to me in all these years."

"He asked me to leave the premises and not to show my face again. He said I was deluded. He said he had no doubt you loved him, and only him."

"I can't believe you did that, and at his place of work! Did it not occur to you that the conversation might've been overheard by colleagues and customers?" Hannah asked, shaking her head slowly.

"Of course it did. So I did the decent thing."

"Decent?"

"I chose a slack period first thing in the morning when they'd just opened. I asked the assistant if I could speak with the pharmacist. I was lucky – the very man came out. I told him it was a delicate matter and asked if I could speak with him privately. As I'd hoped, he took me into the consultation room. No doubt he must've assumed I wanted advice on erectile dysfunction or some other embarrassing issue," Andrew said with a wry smile.

"This isn't a laughing matter!" Hannah snapped. "How did you know where he worked? And how could you possibly recognise him when you'd never met him before?"

"I asked around. Besides finding out where he worked, I discovered you attended The Northern on Thursday evenings with him. It only took two of those evenings to strike lucky. I spotted you both entering in your tennis whites while I was parked strategically away from the entrance doors. Once I'd identified him, I waited outside his pharmacy the next day before opening time to be sure he was working that day. As luck would have it, he was the one to open up, followed shortly after by a couple of women."

A short silence followed before Andrew confessed, "I married Jill on the rebound too, you know. But she was special – a good woman with many qualities, so it wasn't too difficult to at least be very fond of her. But I was never in love with her. How could I be?"

"What do you mean – you married her on the rebound *too*, as if I had with Saul. Is that what you're still implying?"

"Of course. I have no doubt you married Saul on the rebound. It was far too soon after us. We loved too deeply for you to fall out of love on demand of a practicality."

Hannah took a sip of her drink, offering no reply.

"Anyway, I've been in suspense for too long. Are you going to tell me what this dilemma is that involves me?"

CHAPTER 39

Coronation Street Omnibus blared from the portable television in the kitchen as Trish prepared Iceland's battered fish and oven chips for tea. Having popped the food in the oven, she emptied the contents of canned mushy peas into a saucepan, fixing her eyes on the television as she stirred.

"Turn it down, will ya, Mam!" Ryan barked from the kitchen table. "I can't hear myself flippin' think here." With business worries now behind him, he had made a start on searching the internet for Fabio Bianchi. After forty-five minutes he was beginning to wonder if Google really was his best friend. Facebook was no longer an option ever since Fabio had blocked him, and Ryan now wanted to kick himself for failing to make a note of Fabio's restaurant when he discovered it back then. In frustration, he chewed his fingernails and cursed.

"What have I told you? Stop biting your nails!" Trish said.

"Shhh!" he hissed on realising he may have struck lucky.

As if to shout 'hooray', the cursor blinked, and there it was on the Italian Business Register's website: Fabio Roberto Bianchi, direttore di Bianchi's Pizzeria, Napoli. Checking this register had not occurred to Ryan. He merely landed on it after deciding to include Fabio's middle name in his Google search.

"Gotcha, you bastard!" he shouted, standing up to punch the air!

Trish jumped back in alarm. "Bloody hell! You scared me to death! And watch your language!"

"I found him!"

"Found who? Who've you found?"

"Father Christmas. Who else? I've found Fabio Bianchi, of course. Look!" He pointed to the jackpot text. "Not only does it give the name of his restaurant, but there's his home address and telephone number too! Can you believe it?"

"Wow! That's great, son. Bet you're dead chuffed."

"Naaa, I'm gutted. Can't you tell?" he quipped with a wry smile. "I'm gonna ring him."

"Now?"

"Why not? He needs to be told. Let me think what to say first. Oh, I need the Italian phone code too," he said as he searched Google. Having reached for a pen, he wrote the code on the Daily Mirror tabloid that lay beside his laptop.

Trish dried her hands on her apron as she peered over the laptop.

Drumming his fingers on the table, Ryan considered his options. "What've I got to lose? The worst he can do is hang up." Before Ryan had the chance to change his mind, he tapped in the long number and held his breath.

Trish crept up close, pressing her ear to the handset.

After a long wait preceding an unfamiliar ring tone, an Italian male voice answered. "Pronto!"

"Hello. I am sorry, I do not speak Italian," Ryan said, making great efforts to enunciate each word with clarity. "Do you speak English?"

"Who are you?" came the abrupt, gruff reply. The voice was too old to be Fabio's son.

Ryan covered the mouthpiece. "Shit, it's him. He knows it's me!" Before considering what to say, his words tumbled out. "This is your grandson, Ryan, from England. It is about my father – your son Tony Wilcox. He died last year in the earthquake. He came to Naples to look for you. Do not worry – I do not want money. I just need to meet – "

A loud thud resonated in Ryan's ear.

"Bastard! He hung up! I'll kill him! He can dis me all he wants but dis my dad when I've just told him he's recently passed away and I'll kill him!"

"Aww, he's not worth it, love. Don't stress over it," Trish said, rubbing Ryan's shoulder.

* * *

The following day Ryan noticed a missed call from an unknown caller. On checking it, he recognised it to be Fabio's. *Great! So he realises he was a twat hanging up and is now ready to talk. Probably realised there's a lot he wants to know.* With clammy hands, Ryan returned the call with a single tap and waited.

After the sixth ring a voice answered with the same 'Pronto!' greeting, but this time it was an elderly female voice.

"Hello. Do you speak English?" Ryan asked.

"Si, yes, little. Who you are?" she replied. Her English seemed poor compared to Fabio's; certainly inadequate for understanding the complexity of the dilemma Ryan was hoping to articulate if she was Fabio's wife.

"My name Ryan from England. I want speak Fabio. Who you are, please?"

"I Signora Bianchi."

"You Fabio's wife?"

"Si, si! I Silvana."

Jackpot! If the bastard won't hear us out, I'm sure his wife will be interested in what I've got to say. "I Fabio family. I try telephone him yesterday. Do you understand?"

"Si, yes. I have a numero from you telephone. I want capire what you want perché, ehm, because Fabio he furioso."

"Speak English problem for you? I can write email instead. Is possible? You have private email address or Facebook? Not Fabio's – only yours – private. Understand? Private," Ryan said. "It easy I explain in writing."

"Ahh, si, io capire. I have email. You have the pen? I tell the email."

"Yes, have pen. Please say email address."

Positioning his pen's tip eagerly over the paper, Ryan attempted to write each digit Silvana enunciated to him. However, two digits on, he desperately wished she knew the phonetic alphabet.

Silvana had begun with the letter 'g' which she pronounced 'j', followed by the letter 'c' which she pronounced 'ch'.

Two minutes of trying to work out the puzzle set Ryan's nerves on edge. *God, get this right! Stay calm.* He assured Silvana not to worry – they could do it. Obtaining a means of effective communication with her was paramount, if it took all day.

Another ten minutes and the mission was accomplished. It transpired that Silvana's email address was simply the first letter of each of her family members' Christian names, starting with her parents and working down to her youngest child: Giuliano, Cinzia, Fabio, Silvana, Roberto and Giulia, resulting in the email address GCFSRG@libero.it

Argh! Why didn't she say that in the first place? But it was worth the effort for the sheer satisfaction of revealing the truth to a Bianchi who was willing to listen, and hopefully take Ryan's side.

When emailing Silvana, Ryan was surprised at how quickly he recounted the story of Tony's conception in 1960 to his death in the earthquake nearly fifty years later. But then, it would be easy considering the endless times he had mentally rehearsed it in preparation for informing Fabio. To ensure Silvana understood, Ryan included an Italian translation, courtesy of Babel Fish translator.

Without a second's hesitation, he hit 'send'.

CHAPTER 40

Andrew waited with an air of patience. The suspense he felt, however, was palpable as his clammy hands clasped tightly together under the table.

Lowering her eyes, Hannah circled the rim of her glass with the tip of her finger. "So, it was at the point I thought I might not make it that I realised there was something I couldn't possibly take to the grave – something my family, Zach particularly, needed to know. But I did survive and decided they needed to know regardless. But first I had to wait for Zach to recover from losing his father. I'm afraid to say when I eventually plucked up the courage to tell him, he took it badly and has refused to talk to me ever since. Maybe I should have waited longer before telling him. After all, besides losing his father, months later he split with his partner. I guess those losses, together with the bombshell I revealed to him were all too much."

"I'm sorry, Hannah, but what are you talking about? What exactly was the news you gave Zach?"

At this crucial point, the waitress arrived with their meals. She wondered why the couple did not appear happy to see them. "You did say you *both* wanted salmon, didn't you?"

"Oh yes, that's great, thank you," Hannah replied with a smile.

"Is there anything else I can bring you?" the waitress asked, placing their hot plates before them with a flourish.

"No. This is great as it is, thanks," Andrew replied curtly, desperate for privacy.

"So? What is it you need to tell me, Hannah?" he asked, looking at Hannah searchingly.

"I was coming to it. I've thought long and hard about the best way to tell you, but there is no easy way."

He leaned in closer. "Tell me? Tell me what? Are you unwell?"

"No, I'm very well," she whispered, as her eyes looked sideways away from his stare. "You need to know because it involves you … a great deal actually. The fact is that Saul isn't Zach's father."

Andrew's eyes widened as his jaw slackened. "Yes, and?"

"You are Zach's father, Andrew."

Time stood still for Andrew as he fell mute for what seemed like minutes, although it was merely seconds. "What? Is this some kind of a joke?"

"I wish it was a joke, but unfortunately …"

"My God!" Andrew slowly shook his head in disbelief. "How could you be so sure?"

"I'm absolutely certain. Zach looks and even behaves like you. He's nothing like Saul."

"Why didn't you tell me? I had a right to know! If you'd told me this back then, I would have been ecstatic."

"I didn't know for sure until after the wedding that I was pregnant, and only when Zach's colouring – his blue eyes and fair hair – became established when he was around one did I begin to suspect. The older he got, the more certain I became. Of course I could have conducted a clandestine paternity test, but never did because I was already sure. There's nothing to stop you and Zach having one, of course. I understand it's a terrible shock for you. But it isn't as if we're expecting financial support. Zach's a grown, self-supporting man – a lawyer actually. You needed to know because when Zach finally comes around to acceptance – and I'm sure he will eventually – there's a chance he may wish to meet you and you needed to be prepared."

"Well, I always did want a son," he said, with a dazed smile. But then his smile morphed into a frown. "Aaaah!"

234

"What? What is it?"

"It's just occurred to me – it's problematic for another reason, besides the most obvious."

"What do you mean?"

"Hmm, it isn't easy for me to tell you, but when I do, I don't want you to panic, okay?"

"For goodness' sake, just tell me."

"My father developed Huntington's disease when he was sixty-two, then he became progressively worse and died eight years later. You probably know the disease is usually inherited and …"

Hannah interjected. "Oh no, please don't tell me you have it. Then Zach could too! I understand it's a cruel neurodegenerative disease that can strike at any time, can't it?"

"Yes, it can strike at any time if one carries the gene. I do know from my gene pattern that I won't develop the disorder. Unfortunately however, I can pass it on. Before Dad, we had no idea the disease was in the family. Then family members were tested – "

"Lord – and? What about your girls?"

"We had them before my dad's symptoms started – before we knew. Had we known, we might've thought twice about having kids. Harriet is clear but Phoebe has unfortunately inherited the gene. I only hope to God she lives a long life without ever suffering from it."

"I'm so sorry. So …"

Andrew read her mind. He always could. "Yes, Zach could have inherited it too."

Hannah fell mute pondering her son's fate. *I wonder how he's dealing with the idea of Andrew being his biological father? When is he going to speak with me again? Will he wish to meet Andrew? Should I give him this additional blow sooner or later?*

"What are you thinking?"

Before Hannah could reply, the waitress arrived, grimacing. "Is everything alright with your meals? You don't appear to have touched them."

Startled, they looked down at their plates.

"Oh dear, we were so deep in conversation we forgot all about them." Hannah placed the napkin on her knee and picked up her knife and fork. "Mmm, looks delicious! Thanks for the reminder."

Andrew followed suit, despite having lost his appetite. "You were about to tell me what you were thinking," he asked as he prodded the lukewarm salmon with his fork.

Hannah swallowed her first mouthful. "All sorts about Zach. When to tell him for a start."

"You already know there'll be no urgency. The best time would be when he's recovered from the first blow and is talking to you again. He needs an additional shock like he needs a hole in the head right now."

"Yes, of course you're right. I'll know when the time is right. Eat up before it freezes over!"

As they struggled with their meals, they talked some more about Zach - about his work and his interests; they talked about their other children and about their deceased spouses, about their work, their homes and interests. If only they had the courage to discuss what was paramount in their minds - whether they regretted their split.

"Hannah," Andrew said as they stood to leave, "can I see you again?"

Of course Hannah agreed. How could she not? He had been the love of her life and her feelings had not changed a jot.

Walking home, her head whizzed with concerns about Zach inheriting Huntington's disease and about the best time to tell him. Overriding those thoughts were visions of Andrew's handsome face, his sexy voice, the success of their lunch date, her relief at finally admitting the truth, the notion that their relationship could be rekindled, the fact she was now free to do whatever she pleased, and how she could barely wait to hear from him again. She wondered if he felt the same. She replayed the lunch date in her mind, searching for clues that feelings were mutual. She analysed his body language, how he looked at her and spoke to her, but most of all, his words kept buzzing around in her head:

"We loved too deeply for you to fall out of love on demand. I married Jill on the rebound too. But I was never in love with her. How could I be?"

On reaching her tree-lined road, it suddenly grew dark. Hannah looked up at the gigantic branches which formed a canopy blocking out the sky. But there was a silver lining – beautiful rays of sunlight sliced through the branches forming a mystical effect, and the sweet birdsong seemed louder than ever. She remembered the silver lining Trish referred to when they were trapped. *My silver lining is seeing Andrew again.*

A phone rang from a parked car reminding her that hers was set to silent. Her head ached from the myriad thoughts buzzing around in it. She would take a couple of paracetamol if it lingered.

Once inside, she removed the silent mode on her phone to be startled by its immediate loud ringing.

Miriam's words came fast and frantic. "Mum, thank God! It's Zach – he's been rushed to hospital! I'm here with him now. I escorted him in the ambulance."

Slowly, Hannah's knees buckled. Grabbing the back of the chair next to the hall console table, she sank into it. "My God, what happened? Is he alright?"

"I suspect he's had a breakdown. I guessed something was wrong when I called him earlier. But I'll tell you later. Just get here quick. Wythenshawe Hospital."

At the hospital, Miriam gave Hannah and Sadie the upshot. "He phoned me around six sounding very down, confused and dopey like he'd taken something. I drove round immediately and we – that's his neighbour and I – broke his window to gain access because he wasn't responding. We found him on his bed staring into space. They want him admitted for a day or two for further assessments and because they're concerned for his safety considering he lives alone."

"It's my fault. I'll never forgive myself," Hannah said before bursting into tears.

CHAPTER 41

Silvana had been oblivious to Fabio's affair. Unwilling to accept it, she demanded proof from Ryan.

Ryan pounced at the opportunity, recounting everything he knew from the time Fabio arrived in Manchester to help with his uncle's restaurant to the time he returned to Naples leaving Ryan's grandmother six weeks pregnant.

"Mio dio!" Silvana stared at the screen, gasped and let out wailing sobs. Desperate to disprove it, she questioned Ryan in Italian on her tear-splashed keyboard. "What did he look like? How tall was he? Could it have been a mistake – someone else? What was his uncle called? What was the name of the restaurant? It can't be!"

Satisfied, albeit devastated at Ryan's consistently correct answers, Silvana's trust in him strengthened and she opened up even more.

Ryan learned that Fabio and Silvana were practising Catholics. They had two children – Roberto aged forty-nine and Giulia, forty-five, and an eighteen-year-old grandson from Giulia's marriage. Comparing Roberto and Giulia's birth dates to his father's, Ryan ascertained that Fabio cheated on Silvana while she was heavily pregnant with Roberto.

Bastard! So when his missus needed him there for the birth of their first kid, he was busy getting my gran knocked up. Ryan laughed out loud. *Ha! Calls himself a Catholic. Bleeding hypocrite!*

"I'm coming to Naples to see Fabio. Please tell him, whether he likes it or not, I'll see him," he told Silvana.

Silvana, still numb with shock, agreed without question.

He's gonna lie through his teeth, the bastard, and there's no way I'm letting him get away with that. I'd have to be a frigging saint to turn a blind eye to what he did to my dad, not to mention my gran. Twat. How the hell can I look him in the eye without wanting to beat the crap out of him? But you have to, you prick. How else will you get the information out of him to answer my dad's questions? But Dad's dead. Yeah, course I know that, but you never know about the spirit world and beyond. Ryan tilted his head to one side in contemplation. *But if there's a spirit world and Dad can look down on us, he'll probably have worked everything out for himself anyway. Whatever, I wanna see his bastard father brick it for what he's done and nowt's gonna stop that mission. What if he denies it? Take all the proof you've got. What proof? I don't know – make a list. You've got to prepare yourself for the worst case scenario. Think of what he might do that'd really piss me off. He could be smug about getting my gran preggers. He might show not to give a shite about Dad. Then what? How do I react? Kill the bastard!*

Silvana also pondered how she should confront Fabio. Quiz him to test his response? Ask him outright if he has ever cheated? Pounce, telling him she knows everything? Or simply show him the evidence?

The decision made, she printed copies of Ryan's emails. She considered herself a good Catholic who believed in forgiveness. She did not have a vindictive bone in her body and did not seek revenge. All she wanted was the truth. She wanted to observe Fabio's expression as he read Ryan's accusations. Would it reveal guilt or would he adopt a convincing poker face? She hoped she knew him well enough to read the signs.

Fabio gulped, taking his time to read the printed emails. He then looked anywhere to avoid Silvana's glare, his mind in overdrive as he cooked up a lie. An impressive show of feigned bemusement then followed. With a look of astonishment, his arms flailed in protest. "Who is this madman?" he asked. "You believe a madman who tells you these lies? Are you crazy too? He must be after money and you fall for it. I'll sue him for slander. Never in my life have I been unfaithful to you. You know that. Where would I have found the time when I was busy helping Uncle Paulo – when we were so busy with a new restaurant? We have a good marriage. Why would I go with another woman when I have a good wife I love? I take offence that you think so low of me to believe this poison."

That night Fabio slept on the sofa in feigned disgust at being 'falsely' accused. It was little loss to him considering their sex lives had been non-existent for years.

At breakfast, the row continued over cappuccino and croissants. More lies and denials followed with further insults – Silvana was obviously insane to have believed Ryan the madman, Fabio argued.

Nevertheless, Silvana chipped away with her interrogation, bit by bit. She was not giving up that easily.

The chip, chip, chipping away took its toll on Fabio's head. By day three it had a miraculous effect on his memory. "Did you say the woman's name was Rosemary?" he asked, scratching his head.

"You know very well I did," Silvana retorted as she sorted the warm socks she had pulled out of the tumble dryer.

"Ahhh, I remember now!" he exclaimed, raising his finger. "There was a woman – Rosemary – she used to eat at the restaurant. She had a reputation for sleeping around. Yes, I see now. She must have fallen pregnant and had no idea who the father was, so decided to blame me. Who better to blame but an Italian who returns to Italy and becomes untraceable?"

Silvana folded her arms. "How would she have known you had returned to Italy if you hardly knew her?"

"She was a customer. Uncle Paulo would have told her," Fabio asserted with shifty eye contact. "Maybe she mentioned she had not seen me in a while and he told her."

Silvana folded Fabio's blue shirt into the ironing basket. "Perhaps you would like to explain that to Ryan when he comes to Naples to see you. Explain that his grandmother was a whore."

"I'm not meeting him. Why would I want to meet a lying madman whose grandmother tried to destroy me?"

"You have no choice. He will find you if you don't agree to meet. I really think you should meet him to clear up the misunderstanding. Surely you'd want to do that, wouldn't you? Clear up a misunderstanding … if you are innocent? Anyway, you don't have a choice. He is coming."

"Okay, okay, okay! Stop nagging. I will meet the lunatic if you insist, just to tell him I will take legal action if he doesn't stop harassing us." Fabio reached for the landline telephone and dialled a familiar number.

"Who are you phoning?"

"Roberto. We need to warn him and Giulia about this madman and … ah, Roberto, pronto!"

CHAPTER 42

As the chicken roasted in the wall oven, a ratatouille bubbled on the induction hob. On the worktop, salad ingredients awaited French dressing, and a long baguette, fresh from M&S, peeped out of its brown paper bag.

This was far from the challah bread Zach was accustomed to eating, but he no longer cared. He had rejected his Jewish faith when his father rejected his sexuality. *How could I possibly love a God who disapproves of the sexuality He himself created for me?* Zach had agonised over this conundrum for months to finally conclude he did not wish to know such a God. However, up to the fall-out with his mother, he continued to enjoy Friday evening family Shabbat dinners with her, and at home continued with kosher food. Certain aspects of Judaism were as instinctive as breathing.

Classic FM was one aspect of his former life he had no problem abandoning, despite his love of classical music. He was far too discerning about classical music to tolerate anything thrown at him. Smooth FM was his preference. But he was in a particularly discerning mood this evening, preferring to listen to his MP3s. 'Yellow', one of his favourite Coldplay tracks was playing, which he cheerily sang along to. It was Friday evening and he wanted to make an effort for Robin's arrival home from work.

When Robin had learned from Hannah about Zach's breakdown, he had been Zach's rock. Hannah had informed Robin with the hope it might rekindle his and Zach's relationship.

And she was right. When Robin arrived at the hospital, it was as if the couple had never parted. Robin had even offered to care for Basil and Sybil despite his immense dislike of cats. Mercifully, Miriam had already offered. There had been no question as to who should take Zach home on discharge. Thereafter the status of their relationship was confirmed.

It had been a fortnight since Zach's discharge. He had wondered which had been the most effective antidepressant – Duloxetine or having Robin back in his life. The latter he thought, but doctors and loved ones stressed the importance of continuing with the pills until advised otherwise. He had decided the dry mouth side effect a welcome trade-off compared to the mental torment when sick. The dread of his mental illness returning did not bear thinking about. It was hard enough coping with the homophobia he sometimes faced; and forming lasting relationships was an additional challenge, but to then lose his father, and later the split with Robin was more than his mental health could bear. To be finally told his beloved father was not his biological father was the final straw. Mothers are supposed to be loving, yet his had committed such an uncaring act against himself and his father. It was no wonder he went under.

Why can't they believe I hadn't intentionally overdosed? I just wanted sleep – sleep I'd wake up from. So I dulled my senses with drink. Was it such a crime? Okay, I was in a very dark place and yes, I wanted to be dead, but I'd never have gone that far. Misjudging the dosage of pills is easily done when you're plastered and distraught. So why don't they believe me?

He ran his wrists under cold water to prevent watery eyes from chopping onions – a tip he had learned from Hannah.

My pills! They were due at three and it's nearly six. He took two Duloxetin from the kitchen drawer and washed them down with a glass of water. *Robin's my best anti-depressant though. Thank God he came back. God knows how I would've got through this without him. He's so good for me. He completes me. Wonder if it's mutual?*

He says it is, but he has to, doesn't he? Wish I could read his mind. He'll be here soon. Better get a move on.

Minutes later came the sound of a key turning in the front door followed by Robin's approaching footsteps. "Home, babe! Where are you?"

"Kitchen! Come and get me," Zach called.

Robin entered the kitchen, removed his brown leather bag from his shoulder and hung it over the back of a chair.

"Had a good day?" Zach asked, as they kissed and embraced. "Been kind to your candidates?"

"Kinder than some deserved. One distinction, two merits, two passes and two fails. Really didn't have a choice with the fails – they were pretty dire."

"Oh dear. Poor kids," Zach replied, with a chuckle. "No students tonight, are there? You would've said, wouldn't you?"

"Not until Monday – two half-hour lessons seven till eight." Robin lifted the pan lid to peer inside. "Mmm, smells good. Ratatouille?"

"Yep and chicken in the oven. Thought we'd eat early tonight so we can do something later."

"Whatever you fancy, hun. Your call. How was your day? Anything eventful?"

"So, so. A couple of calls from clients, including the rape victim I told you about. Looks like she might be backing out of appearing in court. Terrified of seeing her rapist, the poor woman. Be glad to be back at work next week to catch up with the backlog. Oh yes, Sadie phoned."

"Oh? Glean any more about your biological father?" Robin asked, popping a baby tomato into his mouth.

"No, she just wanted to know if I'd checked his pharmacy website link. She was keen to know if I'd seen his photo. I told her I had and agreed I could see the similarities. She thinks I'm his double. Ha, I wouldn't go that far. She reminded me that I have two half-sisters I should meet."

"Woah! Hard to believe. I wonder if they look like you? It'd be great to meet them, don't you think?"

"Maybe. One step at a time though. Haven't decided if I want to meet him yet," Zach said, stirring the ratatouille.

Basil, curled up with Sybil in their bed, elongated himself with a dramatic stretch before jumping onto the worktop next to the oven. The smell of chicken had been impossible to resist.

"Down! Down! Sodding cats!" Robin spat, swatting him with a tea-towel.

Zach opened the oven door, pulled the tray out to find his perfectly browned, piping hot chicken tempting its drooling onlookers. "Looking good. I'll leave it to rest a while."

"Looks great! I'm starving. Let me help. What can I do?"

"Maybe the salad," Zach replied, pointing to the ingredients on the worktop.

Placing the lettuce into a salad bowl, Robin returned to the Andrew matter. "You're being harsh about your blood father, you know. He couldn't help loving your mum, and can you blame him for fighting for her? After all, he was first on the scene and was only trying to convince your mum she should follow her heart rather than her parents' wishes?"

"Let's talk about it another time, Robbie. Fancy going out after dinner? Could do with getting out after being cooped up all week."

"Yeah, sure. Where do you fancy?" Robin asked as he poured French dressing over the salad.

"Hmm, quite fancy Didsbury. Not been in a while. Fancy the Woodstock?"

"Sure. Whatever your heart desires, babe."

The Woodstock Arms on Barlow Moor Road was a favourite of theirs ever since seeing it featured in *Cold Feet* comedy-drama television series.

* * *

At the Woodstock, they climbed the grand mahogany staircase and chose a small table on the first floor. As they were about to enjoy a peaceful drink together, Zach spotted a familiar face.

"Shit, there's a friend of my mother's!" Zach switched his gaze toward his feet, hiding his face with a mock forehead massage. "Don't look up!" he said through ventriloquist's lips.

But it was too late – Margot made her way over. "Is that you, Zach dear?" she asked, with her cut glass voice. "Ah yes, of course it is! Hello, dear. How are you? And the family?"

Zach coughed, embarrassed she had noticed him trying to avoid her. Rearranging his face into a beaming smile, as if her presence had only just registered, he replied enthusiastically, "Oh hi, Margot! Good to see you! We're all fine, thanks. And yourself? Still playing clarinet in the orchestra?"

"I certainly am. In fact there's a concert coming up soon. It would be good to see you there. I'm sure your mother will give you the details. Are you going to introduce me to your friend?"

"I think you and Robin have already had the pleasure, haven't you? Remember, Robin's the saxophonist who played at RNCM when you came with Mum. Oh wait, sorry, you wouldn't have met him because he was on stage. Silly me!" Zach rolled his eyes to the ceiling in faux self-ridicule.

"Ahh yes, I remember the evening now," Margot said, turning to Robin. "Zach is quite right, Robin. We didn't meet because you stayed back stage during the interval."

For what seemed like an age, Margot wittered on, until, to Zach and Robin's relief, her husband beckoned her over. A waitress stood beside him tapping her pen against her notebook in anticipation of Margot's order.

"Okay, mister!" Robin playfully poked Zach's shoulder. "I think that could be a cue for you making peace with your mother, don't you?"

"Can't say it's top of my agenda," Zach said, before sipping his red house wine.

"Oh, c'mon, hun. It's so wrong you're not talking. She's a good mother and doesn't deserve this. Who hasn't made at least one whopping cock-up in their life? Besides, which parent accepted your coming out without question?" Robin thought to add that Zach's father never did, but thought better of it. "Forgive her. I miss her and I miss her Shabbat dinners. I'm sure you do too. I wish my mother was as understanding."

Zach offered no response.

"What are you thinking?" Robin asked.

"I'm wondering when you're gonna give up. Besides, I talked to her when she visited me in hospital."

"You had no choice. Let's invite her round for dinner and arrange to meet your biological father, if only out of curiosity. Surely you must be curious? The suspense is killing me!"

A reply was unnecessary. Zach's icy expression said it all.

"Okay, forget him for now, but at least call your mother. Please. If not for you or for her, but for me?"

"It's not as simple as that. What would I say?"

"Maybe you could start with telling her you've seen Margot who sends her regards. Assess her mood and if welcoming, tell her that maybe you'd been a bit harsh on her. Then ask her to join us for dinner. Unless you'd prefer to see her alone? I mean, you have so much you want to ask. All the questions you mentioned to me: Has she been seeing him again? Did she mention you're gay? What was his response? Does she still have feelings for him? Please call her. Now."

"Now? With all this noise. It'd be off-putting. Besides, it's Friday."

"So? Since when has your mother followed Shabbat rigidly since your father passed?" Robin looked around for a quiet corner. "Let's sit over there where it's more private." He picked up their wine glasses and changed tables to the far corner of the room. "Ring her before you change your mind."

Zach complied while thinking *please God, don't answer.*

God, however, failed to comply.

"Hello, it's me," Zach whispered reluctantly, hoping she would not hear.

"Zach! Is that you?" Hannah said in joyful disbelief.

"Yep, it's me."

Robin poked Zach in the arm and gave him a *behave* stare.

"Yes, it's me," Zach reiterated in a more congenial tone. "How are you?"

"Oh, Zach darling, how lovely to hear from you! How are you? Are you feeling better? How's work?"

"I'm very well, thanks. Work's good too," he replied in an even warmer tone for Robin's benefit who continued to glare. However, he could not bring himself to call her Mum. "I'm in the Woodstock and have just seen your friend Margot. She was asking after you."

"Ah yes, Margot and Max like to eat out, even on Friday evenings since they're not at all religious. But never mind Margot. I can see her any time. How are you and Robin?"

"We're well, thanks. It's great to be back together. Robin was wondering if …"

Robin gave Zach another glare which worked like magic.

"I mean Robin and I wondered if you'd like to join us for dinner one evening."

For a moment, Hannah was rendered speechless. To compensate for her delayed response, and to ensure Zach had no time to change his mind, she spurted, "Ohh, I would love that! When?"

"Sunday evening okay?"

"Yes, Sunday evening would be perfect. I'll look forward to seeing you both."

CHAPTER 43

16 – 17 May 2009

The flight to Naples was turbulent, but not as turbulent as Ryan's stomach. He was anxious about meeting the man he loathed. He wished he had brought a spare top as the vomit he spewed over the one he was wearing left an after-smell, despite washing it with soap and water in the WC.

From the airport, a shuttle bus took him to his hotel two miles from the Bianchi's. He had arranged to meet them the following morning at 11 a.m. They had stressed the venue needed to be as far from their home as possible. They were not prepared to run the risk of being overheard by people they might know. They therefore opted for Squisito, a café six miles from their home.

Squisito was quiet for the time of day. Ryan chose the smaller and most private of its two rooms at the rear. Drumming his fingertips on the square wooden tabletop, he cast a glance towards the entrance door for the umpteenth time before taking another sip of his cappuccino. His first coffee had not been enough to fill an eggcup, which he returned to the bar with pursed lips and a 'too little' thumb and forefinger pinch gesture. He glanced up at the eclectic mix of framed pictures hanging randomly on the whitewashed walls. Most depicted local scenes: the bay of Naples with Vesuvius, Castel Nuovo, and Piazza Plebiscito; others were random portraits of Italian women, one of Sophia Lauren.

I wonder what'd be harder – hearing Bianchi admit how he deserted Gran when she was expecting his kid, or hear the bastard tell a pack of lies denying everything. After some consideration, he concluded that to be lied to would be far worse. He hoped Fabio would own up and show some remorse for the pain he had caused. He hoped Fabio would regret missing the opportunity of meeting his son Tony. *Yeah, and pigs fly!* But Ryan had to be positive in time for their arrival. He wanted them to see his charming side – a side more likely to elicit the truth from Fabio. *Smile and stay calm. For Christ's sake, don't lose it,* he thought, chewing his fingernails.

On the word 'lose', his eyes widened. *Shit, did I pack them?* In a flurry, he rummaged deep into his backpack and exhaled in relief on finding them in a manila document wallet. He pulled them halfway out before changing his mind. *No, this isn't the time. Later, but don't forget!*

He spotted them immediately – an elderly Italian couple looking around nervously. The man, short with a Roman nose, deep brown eyes, grey hair and sallow skin appeared apprehensive and fidgety. Although he had a full head of hair for his age, the throbbing veins in his temples were visible, showing his anger at having to be there. The woman, with short silver-grey hair, seemed older than Fabio going by her heavily wrinkled skin.

Ryan smiled and beckoned them over.

"Ah, Ciao, Ryan!" Silvana called as they approached.

Fabio remained stubbornly silent, his face saying he would rather be in a sewer than with Ryan. Silvana discreetly nudged him, and between her clenched teeth demanded he smile. Pretending not to notice, Ryan gestured to the seats. Fabio hastily chose one furthest away from Ryan on the opposite side.

"Let me get you a drink. What would you like?" Ryan asked.

To Silvana's alarm, Fabio shot up, holding his palm towards Ryan. "No! I get our drink," he said pointedly.

Silvana, looking flushed, asked Ryan if he would like a coffee.

"No, thank you, Silvana. I have one here," Ryan replied with a forced smile.

Exhaling deeply, Fabio edged his way to the bar, relieved to have escaped the tense atmosphere. Turning to Silvana, he mouthed he was going to the toilet. Before Silvana had the chance to show her annoyance, he turned away from her glare and scurried off.

By the time Fabio returned with two espressos, Ryan was clutching on to his last thread of patience. *Breathe. Stay calm. Breathe. Stay calm. Bastard!*

Silvana glowered at Fabio.

Fabio knew Silvana well enough to recognise when he had pushed the boundaries. Forcing a smile in the direction of Ryan, albeit a twisted thin one, he returned to his seat, asking Ryan if he was sure he would not like a coffee.

"So," Ryan began, without any preamble, "I am here because I want to prove to you that my father Tony was your son – that I am your grandson. Remember I told you this on the telephone? I told you he came to Naples to see you last April, but then was tragically killed in the earthquake? Remember you put the phone down on me? I hope you can show more sensitivity and respect this time. Can you?"

"I put phone down?" Fabio questioned, playing for time.

"You know you did," Ryan barked.

"I sensitive man – a good, honest man. I need you show me respect. You not show me respect when you lie – say I do something I not do."

"Are you saying you did not know my grandmother Rosemary?"

"She was customer. That is all."

Silvana shifted uncomfortably in her chair. She prayed Fabio would not refer to Ryan's grandmother again as a woman who slept around. She had warned him not to even hint at such an insult, and Fabio promised he would not. Under the table, she kicked his foot as a reminder.

"Okay," Ryan continued, "if you didn't know each other well, how could she have known so much about you? She knew you had a younger brother called Giorgio. How could she have known that?"

Fabio shot Silvana a glance in the hope of support.

But Silvana hungered for the truth as much as Ryan.

"Is that true, Silvana?" Ryan asked. "Is Fabio's younger brother called Giorgio?"

"Si, yes. Is true."

"My grandmother also knew that your mother was ill with tuberculosis. Is that true, Fabio?"

Silvana turned to look at Fabio quizzically. She had no knowledge of this fact. "Allora?"

"Many people sick with tuberculosis in that day."

Ryan's voice rose in volume and pitch as he snapped, "Did your mother have it?"

"Yes. So?"

"So? Are you serious?" Ryan said, his anger palpable as he clenched and unclenched his fists under the table. "How could she have known such private details about your mother unless you had a relationship? Christ, not even Silvana knew."

Fabio looked away, rolled his eyes and exhaled ostentatiously.

"Okay, if you refuse to admit the truth, I have some evidence for you," Ryan said, pulling his backpack onto the table.

Fabio's body stiffened as he took a sharp intake of breath, his eyes focusing on the backpack Ryan pulled open.

From it came the manila document wallet. Ryan took his sweet time for the sheer pleasure of watching Fabio sweat. From the wallet, he slowly extracted a batch of photographs.

The look of horror on Fabio's paled face spoke volumes. He gulped again. Game over.

Silvana glared at Fabio, but he was too focused on the photographic evidence emerging to notice.

But where was it? Fabio saw no sign of any evidence – no images of himself or Rosemary. With a grin, he slumped back into his chair in relief.

On the table, Ryan had positioned snapshots of Tony at various stages of his life: as a new-born, a toddler, his first day at school, his first communion, his wedding day, and one of him during each decade thereafter. The photos may well have lacked conclusive evidence but Fabio and Silvana's eyes nevertheless widened. The stark resemblance between Fabio and Tony was unmistakable.

"My dad looks just like you, don't you think?" said Ryan.

But Fabio being Fabio made one last stab at deceit. "So what if he look a little like me. So do many people. So what?"

"A little? You must be joking!" Ryan said. "You could be twins! C'mon, Fabio, you know you can't keep this up. We all know you're the father. Just bloody admit it, will you, and let's move on."

Silvana turned to Fabio, placed her hand on his and gently pleaded with him to come clean.

A long silence followed as Fabio's head hung low.

Ryan and Silvana fixed their eyes on him as they waited with bated breath. Just as they were about to lose hope, Fabio lifted his head with a faraway look in his eyes.

"Is possible he is my son. So? We all make mistake. But I different man now. Then I a boy. Stupido. Now I good, honest man."

Ryan and Silvana shot each other a glance and exhaled deeply.

As Fabio continued staring into space, Silvana squeezed his hand and whispered, "Grazie."

Ryan stood to make his way to the bar, allowing the couple a private moment. "I'll get some more coffee, okay?" Before doing so, he paid a visit to the toilet to allow them the time they needed.

Returning with their espressos, he was pleased to see the couple chatting amicably. *Thank God she's not ripped his knob off.*

When he approached, however, their conversation stopped short as Silvana shifted uncomfortably in her seat.

"There you go." Ryan placed their espressos on the table before returning to the bar for his cappuccino.

When he returned, Fabio asked, "What you want? Money?"

"What? I already told you I don't want a penny. I just wanted the truth for my dad's dying wish. I also want to know my roots. That's all. Nothing else."

"Va bene. Good," Fabio replied.

"But there is one last thing I would like."

"Ah! I knew there is something – something to trick me."

"No, no! It is not a trick. All I ask is to meet your children – my father's half brother and sister. It is what my father wanted." It was what Ryan desperately wanted too. He wanted to embrace whatever remained of his father, and he wanted his father to be acknowledged and respected by his Italian kin. Had Ryan anticipated Fabio's response, he might have tested the waters first.

Trembling with rage, Fabio pushed himself out of his seat and lunged towards Ryan. "You crazy bastardo! You want destroy my life, do you? I never allow they know. You not meet them. Never!" he yelled before striding out of Squisito.

Silvana, aghast, grabbed her handbag and scurried after him in tears.

CHAPTER 44

Sunday, 17 May 2009

Zach and Robin had planned to serve baked Mediterranean sea bass with couscous and seasonal vegetables, followed by crème brûlée and fresh berries. Planning the meal was a welcome simplicity for the foodies. The complexity would be avoiding another family conflict. Strategic planning was called for. Robin was to excuse himself shortly after dinner to attend to an urgent task, and until that point, conversation was to be kept strictly light.

All went to plan, especially as Hannah had the foresight to set boundaries on arrival, after noticing a hint of unease in the air. "Relax, boys, I promise to be on my best behaviour – nothing too intense – especially not politics, unless you've converted to conservatism since I last saw you," she said, laughing at the ludicrous notion of staunch socialists even dreaming of such a thing.

Appreciating the joke, Zach and Robin joined in the laughter.

This reminded Zach of the time he took revenge against his father's homophobia by making an ostentatious show of socialism. Zach's laughter morphed into a frown at the memory. After all, his father meant well, despite his ignorance.

As planned, dinner conversation remained light, about work and about Sadie's miraculous turn around with her studies, about Hannah's orchestra and her book club, and about the duets Zach and Robin had recently mastered.

At the first opportunity after dessert, Robin drained his wine and leaned back in his chair. "I'm sorry, but as much as I hate to miss out, I'm going to have to love you and leave you. I have a mega backlog of marking to finish for tomorrow morning. If it's not finished tonight, I'm gonna have to be up two hours earlier than normal, and getting up at seven is bad enough."

"Ha, yes, don't we know it!" Zach quipped, with a chuckle to Hannah. "Did you know, he sets two alarm clocks to wake up in the morning, and then has the gall to use me as his third!"

Amidst the laughter, Robin left his seat and with outstretched arms made his way towards Hannah who stood to receive a goodnight embrace.

"It's been lovely seeing you, Robin. Don't work too hard and try getting to bed before it's time to wake up!"

Zach exhaled in relief at the accomplished mission. At the same time, he felt uneasy about the one-to-one with Hannah. Despite tension from the unspoken words hanging in the air, their small talk continued.

"Look, I realise you're keen for us to discuss *the issue*, so shall we just get it over with?" Zach said.

Hannah blinked. "Oh, if you're sure you're okay with it, absolutely. And thank you for bringing it up. I wanted to, but was worried about upsetting you again."

"Don't worry. The worst part was the initial shock. I'm prepared for it this time. Besides, Mimi and Sadie have already filled me in with quite a bit about him."

"That's good, dear. What have they told you so far?"

"I know he has two daughters, that he lost his wife to cancer a few years ago, and that he's a pharmacist who lives and works in Alderley Edge. Actually, I've seen his profile photo on his website."

"Could you see the resemblance to yourself?"

Zach shifted uneasily in his seat, reluctant to admit the truth. "A little, I guess."

"Your sisters saw it immediately. And it's a compliment of course since he's a very handsome man." As soon as the words slipped out, she regretted them. She filled their wine glasses, stalling conversation to think. "Zach dear, please tell me if I say anything that may upset you in any way, won't you? Maybe I shouldn't have mentioned that Andrew is handsome. I don't want you to think for one second that I would ever compare him with your father. Of course your father was very handsome and had many qualities that made him the wonderful man he was. If I mention any of Andrew's qualities, I do so merely for your benefit considering you may have inherited those genes."

"Don't worry about it. I get what you mean," Zach replied, taking a sip of his wine.

"If there's anything more you'd like to know about him, about his work, his daughters, his health, I'm here to answer any questions, show you photos, anything. Just ask."

"Yes, I will. Thanks," Zach said, getting up to leave the table. "Excuse me. Need the loo. Be right back." He was torn. One part of him desperately wanted to be loyal to his father and have nothing whatsoever to do with Andrew – the loathsome cheat who attempted to steal his father's fiancé from him, impregnated her weeks before the wedding, causing her huge anguish when she realised she was pregnant with his child – this man who caused Zach's identity crisis. On the other hand, Zach was curious to meet the man whose DNA sculptured his looks, his character traits, and his very being. He was curious to know as much about him as possible because to know him would help him understand more about himself and also his mother – help him understand why she succumbed to that deplorable temptation. Knowing Andrew would help Zach fit pieces of the jigsaw puzzle together. Zach was a lawyer after all – a lawyer with a questioning mind.

When Zach returned, he found Hannah had moved the wine and glasses to the coffee table and was sitting in the armchair facing the sofa.

"As I was saying," she said, after Zach settled himself on the sofa, "I'm always happy to answer any questions about Andrew. One thing you don't know is what he's like as a person and whether you two would get along. You can't know until you've actually met him. I would love you two to meet and get to know each other."

"I'd be lying if I said I wasn't curious, but I can't say I'm ready to meet him. Not yet anyway."

"Andrew asked after you every day when you were in hospital, and before that when I told him you'd taken the news badly. He was genuinely concerned about you. He'd dearly love to meet you, Zach."

"So you've been seeing him, then?" Zach asked, reaching for the wine bottle and pointing the bottle top towards her. "More?"

She held up her palm. "No thanks. I'm driving." She hoped he would forget the question he had asked, but he continued looking at her expectantly.

"We've seen each other a few times," she said, "though most contact has been text messages and phone calls about you." Hannah was not one for lying, but apt at being economical with the truth when needing to protect someone's feelings. "I had to make that first contact, you see, in order to break the news to him about you. You may have wanted to meet him sooner or later and he needed to be forewarned, obviously."

"So how did he take it?"

"Surprisingly well, actually. He wasn't as shocked as I'd expected him to be. It was more a case of him being unhappy about me keeping it from him. He felt he had the right to know he had a son. He said he would've wanted to be fully involved in your upbringing and is very disappointed he was deprived the opportunity. He was upset at how you reacted and desperate to be able to help in any way he could. He was genuinely concerned for you, Zach."

Zach pushed himself up from the sofa and headed for the kitchen. "Coffee?"

JULIET AYRES

"Yes please. I'll help."

"Thanks, but no. Won't be long." He needed time to think.

Hannah hoped the coffee was not an avoidance strategy, not now it was going so well. However, she needn't have worried as he returned sooner than expected.

"There you go," he said, placing her mug on the coffee table. "Still take it black, I assume."

"Yes, lovely. Thank you, dear."

Zach took a sip of his coffee, and asked, "Okay, when would you like me to meet him?"

Hannah glanced at him before blinking a double take, hardly believing her ears. Outwardly, she kept her cool considering the delicate nature of the agreement. "That's fantastic. Thank you, darling. I appreciate it. I'm sure you're making the right decision, and Andrew will be thrilled to be meeting you."

"So when?" Zach asked.

"I'll text him later and let you know. I'm sure he'd love to meet you at the first opportunity."

In her car, she pulled out her phone eagerly and tapped in Andrew's number.

"That's marvellous news, Hannah! Such a relief. So shall we leave it to Zach to choose the venue? A pub, restaurant or my house with the girls out of the way. What do you think?"

"Up to him I guess. I'll give him the options and take it from there. I'll tell him about the Huntington's too before he meets you, okay?"

"Good idea. That'd help a lot. It'll give us more things to talk about if Zach feels uncomfortable. Hope he takes it okay."

"Don't worry. If he can cope with discovering you're his biological father, he can cope with anything!"

CHAPTER 45

18 May 2009

How Silvana managed to persuade Fabio to agree to a family gathering, Ryan would never know. He was only thankful she had. She had telephoned Ryan the evening after the showdown at Squisito's explaining that she and Fabio had rowed about it for hours. After sleeping on it, Fabio finally agreed, albeit reluctantly. Once the decision was made, they informed Roberto and Giulia.

Silvana had hoped to make a special dinner for Ryan's visit. Fabio, however, fiercely opposed, insisting he could only stomach Ryan's visit for a minimal period. She should be thankful, he said, that he had agreed to have him in his house in the first place. And so, they planned for Ryan to drop by for coffee and cake for the purpose of a brief meeting with Roberto and Giulia.

Ryan took a taxi to their apartment, which was situated in a gardened tree-lined complex surrounded by grey metallic fencing. In keeping with local style, its exterior was painted apricot with the central façade in a darker tone of brick red. White concrete balconies and a large white entrance porch provided contrast whilst emphasising its need for refurbishment with its visibly evident flaking paintwork.

"Shit! What's their number?" Searching the bell buttons, he mercifully spotted 'Bianchi' next to number 22. After giving the button two short presses he waited nervously, conscious that he was as welcome as a police raid at a cannabis farm as far as Fabio

Bianchi was concerned. *Let's only hope he hasn't poisoned Roberto and Giulia's minds against me as well as his own. At least Silvana's on my side.*

To his relief, Silvana's high-pitched cheery voice welcomed him.

"Ciao, Ryan! Come, come. I wait the top."

The click of the heavy communal door followed, inviting him to enter. On the left of the foyer stood a narrow lift door and further along the foyer a stone staircase. After contemplating his choices, he opted for the lift, which he soon regretted considering the time it took to arrive, setting his nerves further on edge. It was not as if it was a high-rise flat; it was merely a four-story block. Once inside, he was surprised to find the lift even smaller than he imagined. At least its size briefly took his mind off his troubles as he pondered how on earth people managed to fit inside with their shopping bags or luggage. Presently, the steel door opened and Silvana appeared with a welcoming smile.

"Ryan! Benvenuto! Come, come!"

After beckoning Ryan to her front door a couple of yards from the lift, she ushered him into a narrow hallway in which an array of coats hung from brass wall pegs. A strong aroma of coffee and freshly baked almond cake greeted him.

Nice she's made the effort, Ryan thought.

The sound, however, of ominous whispering dampened his optimism.

"Come," Silvana said as she led him into an open-plan lounge and dining room.

Amongst a variety of framed family pictures on the lounge wall hung a luminous plaster cast crucifix, a print of the Madonna holding baby Jesus, and a photograph of Pope Benedict XVI.

Fabio was slumped on a brown faux leather sofa in the lounge. His eyes were fixed on a large television screen, despite its volume being almost inaudible. Making no attempt to acknowledge Ryan's arrival, he continued to stare at the screen. Giulia and Roberto were seated on either side of him. They turned to look at Ryan and stood to greet him, Giulia being the first to step forward, offering a warm welcome.

Unsure whether a handshake or hug was fitting, Ryan shifted uneasily waiting for a cue. To his relief, Giulia approached him with open arms and he gratefully reciprocated an embrace. Warmth radiated from her smile and he liked her immediately. *To think she's my auntie and Roberto my uncle. Christ, all these new relatives I never knew existed!*

"Ryan, I happy to meet you. Welcome to our 'ome. You come at a good time. Now it rain and you inside dry." Giulia pointed to the raindrops on the balcony French door windows.

Ryan was relieved he had at least broken the ice with Giulia. He was not so sure about Roberto, however, who gave a strained smile with a limp handshake.

"Hello," Roberto said flatly, avoiding eye contact.

Silvana beckoned Ryan to an armchair. "Sit, sit, Ryan. I make a coffee and get a biscotti and torta, erm a cake."

"No, lo farò!" Fabio said, pushing himself out of the sofa and heading for the kitchen.

Silvana shot him a disapproving glance before sitting on the arm of the sofa and smoothing down her floral printed apron.

Ryan placed his backpack on the tiled floor and gave a nervous cough. "I hope me coming here does not cause trouble. I just wanted to follow my father's dying wish – to meet his Italian family. I am sorry if it was a shock for you. But it is better you know the truth."

"Don't worry. We understand. Is okay," Giulia said.

Silvana had her eye on Ryan's bag. "Ryan, you have fotografie?"

"Sorry? Ah, photographs! Yes, I brought them," Ryan replied, reaching for his bag.

"Aspettare. Hmm, wait. I get fotografie also," Silvana said.

"That would be great. Thanks," Ryan said.

"Prego," Silvana replied as she headed for the hall.

"Giulia, Roberto, would you like to see my photographs?" Ryan asked.

"Si, va bene. We love to see," Giulia replied expectantly.

Ryan pulled out the pack and a wave of sadness enveloped him as he looked at the image of his father's smiling face.

The siblings leaned forward, wide-eyed.

"This is my father Tony – your half-brother. It was taken the day before the earthquake – the day before he died. That was the reason he came to Naples – to meet you and his father, your father. It was his dream to meet you all. I think he looks like you, don't you?"

A lump in Giulia's throat delayed her response. "Si, he does," she whispered. "The nose and eyes a lot."

Roberto nodded, remaining silent.

Ryan placed the photo at the back of the pile and pulled out the next. "And this is when he was a bit younger." He paused to look around. "Hang on. Can I use your coffee table to lay them out?"

"Si, of course." Roberto held the palm of his hand out towards the glass-top table.

Ryan laid them out in chronological order – the baby photo first and the most recent last.

One particular photo of Tony gaffa-taped to a lamppost drew Giulia's attention. She laughed as she pointed it out. "What he do here?"

"It was his stag do. I brought it to show you what a great sense of humour he had."

"Stag do?" Roberto repeated slowly. "What is the stag do?"

"Oh sorry, I forgot you wouldn't know." Ryan tilted his head in contemplation. "Hmm, it's when a man who is about to get married celebrates with his friends before the wedding."

Roberto's eyes lit up. "Ahh, si! We have here – l'addio al celibato – farewell to celibacy."

"Farewell to celibacy?" Ryan repeated with a loud guffaw. "Are you serious?"

"Si, yes. Is true," said Giulia, joining the laughter.

"Ace!" Ryan said. "He's wearing the Liverpool football kit. The joke is that Manchester football fans support either Manchester United or Manchester City. They *hate* Liverpool! Liverpool are Man United and Man City rivals, so it took guts to do that."

"Guts?" Giulia asked, looking bemused.

"Courage."

"Ahh, so he love the Manchester United?"

"Actually no, and this is funny too – he hated football! His friends were Man United supporters and they persuaded him to do it."

This time all three burst into a loud guffaw.

"Is very funny your papà not like the football and he do that!" Giulia added, wiping the tears from an eye with her index finger.

"Si, very funny. Ooh! Aah! Cantona," Roberto added, still laughing.

However, the loud slamming of the kitchen door wiped the laughter from their faces in a flash.

Fabio appeared, arms flailing and veins protruding from his neck. "You dare to laugh! What you laugh?" he shouted as he rushed toward the photographs.

"Nothing. I was just showing them photos of my dad. What's wrong with you?" Ryan snorted in disgust.

Fabio lowered his eyes towards the photographs. "Swine! You think is funny? You try poison my family mind from me! We see about that. Basto!" he screamed as he swiped the photos off the table, sending them scattering over the tiled floor.

"Papa, no, no!" Giulia cried aghast as she attempted to stop him.

Enraged, Ryan's eyes blazed as he lunged towards Fabio. "I'm the one who should be livid. If it wasn't for you, my dad would still be alive now, you bastard!"

CHAPTER 46

Along the rain-pelted streets, an ambulance sped by, sirens blaring. Vehicles pulled over, allowing it to pass.

There had been an emergency call from the Bianchi's. Silvana had cried hysterically that her husband was dying. Unable to console her, Roberto took over the call to give the address and a description of Fabio's condition. Fabio was barely responsive and the family feared for his life. Creating a duet of clicking rosary beads, Giulia and Silvana prayed more than they had prayed in years.

* * *

Ryan had hailed a taxi, returning to his hotel before the ambulance arrived. His heart still pumped double speed when he reached his room. Slowly, he lowered himself onto the edge of his freshly-made bed, distressed things had turned out as they had. Above all was a sense of remorse for letting his father down. Flopping back onto the bed, he sobbed, "Sorry, Dad. So sorry."

* * *

In the Bianchi car park, Roberto paced up and down, willing the ambulance to arrive.

Indoors, Giulia flitted from her father's side, to the window, and to the bedroom to pack a hospital bag. Keeping busy helped keep her mind off the dread of losing him. Despite her activity, punctuated by her rosary recital, the waiting felt like an eternity.

She prayed her father would make it, prayed for the ambulance, prayed Roberto would not take the law into his own hands against Ryan, and prayed her mother would find the strength to get through this, whatever the outcome.

Silvana found it the hardest. At least Giulia had her own family, and Roberto his computer programming business – his baby. Fabio was all Silvana had and the stakes were too high to leave his side. She feared it would be tempting fate to turn her back, for even a second. As for his sin of adultery, it no longer mattered. All that mattered was his life. As he lay splayed on the cold tiled floor, she clung to his limp body as she thumbed her rosary beads.

They desperately wished they had at least learned basic first aid. They had seen CPR on television, but had not taken sufficient notice to know how to apply it correctly, if indeed it was the treatment required.

After an agonising wait, Giulia spotted the blue flashing lights and whispered, "Grazie Dio!" Glancing back to check her father, she heard her mother assuring him he was going to be okay. Giulia was not so sure, but smiled at Silvana encouragingly.

At least they had a plan. Silvana and Giulia were to accompany Fabio in the ambulance while Roberto followed in his Fiat Punto. Giulia was to take charge of the hospital bag and message relatives, allowing her mother to focus on Fabio. God forbid, it could well be their final moments together and she did not wish to deprive them of that. They thanked God the hospital was less than five miles away and the roads were traffic free.

Seven minutes later they arrived at the hospital. At great speed, medics whisked Fabio away on a gurney along light green corridors, leaving Silvana and Giulia scurrying after them. Family were not allowed in the emergency treatment room and the wait to be given the upshot was agonising.

Minutes later Roberto arrived. As he waited, he felt a dire need to vent his rage on Ryan. He would have preferred a face-to-face, but there would be time for that later. Considering his calls to

Ryan went straight to voicemail, for now he had to settle with text.

You put my father in the hospital. You happy now? I see you for this!

At this time, however, Roberto's parents were his priority. Silvana seemed to have aged ten years since Fabio's collapse. If Roberto and Giulia had not kept an eye on her, Roberto feared she would have been laid up in hospital next to Fabio. Roberto was too young to be orphaned, he thought. He wanted to kill Ryan, but was too good a Catholic. He looked at his mother and Giulia seated on the green vinyl-covered corridor bench – his mother staring into space through red, puffy eyes and Giulia giving her concerned sideways glances. He was about to suggest bringing them coffees when an elderly male doctor's voice enquired if they were the Bianchi family.

Silvana and Giulia eagerly shot up. "Si, si!" they said, studying the doctor's face for clues.

The snail-paced speed at which the doctor geared himself up to speak was unbearable.

Too fearful for words, the Bianchis begged with pleading eyes.

Interlinking his long fingers, the doctor gave the upshot in slow, deliberated speech about Fabio's condition. Now that Fabio was more comfortable, they could see him briefly one at a time, though a response from him was unlikely due to him being heavily sedated.

A nurse led Silvana to Fabio's bedside. From the emergency treatment room, Fabio had been transferred to a single-room ward in preparation for the following day's surgery.

The machines to which he was wired caused Silvana to gasp. She should have been warned. *But he is alive. That is the main thing. Thank Madonna he is alive.* A cauldron of emotions swept over her, of gratitude, of love, of relief and of fear – fear of the possibility he might not make it. The overpowering smells of antiseptic and rubber tubing reminded her of the hospital where she had lost both her parents to cancer. *Forget that,* she told herself. *Be positive and think of Fabio getting better.* She positioned a chair close to Fabio's bedside where she seated herself quietly. As she took hold of his left hand, she rubbed his gold wedding ring. They had been blissfully happy on their wedding day. She vowed he would be the only man in her life, and she meant every word. She said his name as cheerfully as she could muster, waiting for a response.

There was not even a flicker.

She called his name louder, begging him to wake up. Through her tear-filled eyes, she scrutinised his eyelids for a hint of movement. The tiniest flicker would do – anything to raise her hopes. She waited and squeezed his hand harder, begging, pleading for him to arouse. Watching ever so closely, she dared not blink, frightened of missing a crucial nanosecond of eye movement.

But nothing.

As she began to lose hope and drift off to sleep, her hope was restored when she noticed a miniscule flicker of his eyelids. She stiffened and watched intently as they rose, if only momentarily. She waited, squeezing his hand as she recited the Hail Mary under her breath, punctuated by the call of his name.

Again, his eyelids flickered, this time more noticeably. Then his brown eyes opened.

She gasped, called his name, told him she was there for him and that everything was going to be alright. He might be unable to turn his head to her, she thought. She leaned over the bed into a position that allowed their faces to meet. By the time she had done this, his eyes closed again. She called his name out loud, urging him to stay awake, telling him she loved him and needed him.

Slowly, his eyes re-opened and remained open, staring at her.

She imagined it was an apologetic look, but she told herself not to be silly: he was unaware of the present, let alone the past.

She told him he had no choice but to get better because without him her life would be worthless. She gently scolded him for getting worked up over Ryan's photographs. She reminded him how his heart could not take such stress, and that a bigger heart attack was inevitable if he continued upsetting himself. But bringing this up could be adding to his stress and a feeling of guilt swept over her. Smiling, she shifted the blame onto his eating too much pasta and rum babà. She assured him that his heart would as good as new after the surgery, and then he could have all the pasta and rum babà his heart desires to celebrate.

And he smiled.

* * *

Ryan slid into his hotel bed to read Roberto's texts. An additional wave of guilt engulfed him. He may well have hated Fabio's guts, but he never meant him harm. He blamed his temper. He always had a quick fuse. If he had counted to ten, as Trish often advised, this might never have happened. *At least I didn't punch the crap out of him as I'd liked to have done. I didn't lay a bloody finger on him, so they can't put the blame on me. And he did provoke me. I was only showing them the frigging photos, for Christ's sake.* Still, Ryan's conscience got the better of him and after much deliberation, he texted Roberto.

> Roberto, I am truly sorry your dad is ill in hospital. If I had known he had a bad heart I would never have yelled at him. Please tell him I'm very sorry for upsetting him. Wishing him a full and quick recovery. Ryan.

His text to Roberto was sincere, but the one to Silvana was a far greater outpour of remorse and warmth. After all, she had always been good to him – she believed him – and he owed her for that at least. He hoped she, of all people, would forgive him.

CHAPTER 47

Early June 2009

Manchester had two crown courts: Minshull Street, which was a stone's throw from Zach's home; and Crown Square, slightly further away. Generally, Zach would walk to Minshull Street or cycle to Crown Square.

On the morning of his Crown Square hearing, however, he took his Volvo due to heavy rain. It also happened to be the day he was to meet his biological father for the first time. Additional stress was the last thing he needed.

During long drives, he tended to listen to audio books, the radio or his MP3s, but this was a short drive and he needed to give some thought to the case he was defending. It was the type of mundane case he least enjoyed – driving without due care and attention whilst disqualified. How ironic, he thought: he was also struggling to keep his attention on the road and could well be in the same boat if he failed to take more care. Mentally revising court cases whilst driving was his default setting, but worrying about personal problems was all-consuming and emotionally draining. Regardless of his efforts, his mind kept switching from the road, to his court case, to the upcoming meeting with Andrew that evening.

Oh Dad, I hope you understand I'm only doing this to make sense of my identity and to please Mum. You know she won't give up till I agree. Then there's the Huntington's disease I need to discuss with him considering it's hereditary. I don't want you to think that I'll ever see him as a father-figure or forgive him for what he did to you. I'll only ever have one dad, and that's you. You know that. I'm completely on your side, one hundred percent. I'd hate for you to think I was betraying you. You were a better father to me than most biological fathers and I'll never forget ..."

A loud blare of a car horn startled him and he jerked to attention.

"Where's your learner plate, dickhead?" shouted a young male driver, giving Zach the finger.

"Sorry!" Zach mouthed, holding his hand up in placation. *Shit! Concentrate,* he berated himself, staring at the road ahead with wide, saucer eyes.

However, at the next set of red lights, his thoughts drifted off again. *Why did I agree to see him? Why? It's too soon. I'll be a bag of nerves and it's going to be awkward. What the hell am I supposed to call him? It'll never be Dad – ever! What the hell will we talk about? At least I can ask about Huntington's. I wonder if he knows I'm gay. I'll ask Mum after the hearing. Better get things right. At least he seems decent enough, going by Mum's account and from his website. And he seems to care about my well-being.* He tilted his head to the side to reconsider. *Wait. What are you talking about? How can he possibly be decent after what he did to Dad? Bastard! If Dad had known, it would've killed him. It would have killed Grandma and Grandad too. It would've destroyed the whole family. At least none of them are here to know the truth. Oh God, what am I to do? I wish you could tell me what you'd like me to do, Dad. I'd want to do what makes you happiest. If it upsets you for me to meet him, I'd rather not go. Wish you could give me a sign.*

Unfortunately, no sign was forthcoming except a 'No Entry' on a road he was about to turn into.

"Christ!" Turning his wheel to a full lock, he managed to get back on track and arrive at the court car park unscathed.

* * *

Prior to leaving for Andrew's that evening, Zach checked Google Earth to get a feel of Andrew's house in Alderley Edge. At least this gave a sense of familiarity as he walked down Andrew's path. He pondered whether the doorbell or knocker would give the quickest response. He did not relish the idea of waiting too long because the longer he waited, the louder his heart would thump. He wanted speed – speed in entering, speed in the formalities and speed in leaving. *The bell might not work,* he thought. And so, he knocked hard to the rhythm of rat-a-tat-tat and politely stepped back. The door was painted a racing green and the house Victorian like his mother's. *They must have similar taste. Even the door colour's similar to Mum's back door.*

A ceiling light in the hallway lit up and footsteps approached. Zach's heart hammered and he felt the urge to turn on his heels and run. But it was too late. The door opened and there stood a tall man who Zach not merely recognised from his website photo, but recognised in himself: the same height, eyes and smile – like a mirror reflection – except older. Had Andrew not turned grey, his hair would have also been the same colour as Zach's.

A lump came to Zach's throat and he gulped. "Hello. I'm Zach." He could not think of another word – he who was so articulate was lost for words.

"Ahh, Zach! How marvellous to meet you at last. Come in. Come in." Feeling emotional, Andrew gestured to hug him.

Zach, however, responded with a limp hand-shake and Andrew smiled broadly to conceal his disappointment. A sense of awkwardness cut through the atmosphere.

"I can't tell you how pleased I am to finally meet you, Zach. You are even more handsome than in your photos."

"Pleased to meet you too, though I can't say this is going to be easy."

"I know, but nothing a cup of tea won't fix. Or do you prefer coffee? Or something stronger?"

"A coffee would be great, thanks."

Andrew ushered Zach down a long hallway. A Moroccan runner rug lay over polished floorboards and two large impressionist paintings graced the walls. At the end of the hallway, an open kitchen door awaited them. It was a large room boasting a Shaker butcher's block island with an oiled oak top and pale teal sides matching the kitchen units. Over the island hung a large stainless steel rack from which hung stainless steel pans, sieves and colanders. At the far end of the kitchen stood a refurbished Victorian pine table with six chairs, all of which were painted a similar colour to the kitchen units, apart from the table top that was stripped and oiled.

"Take a seat, Zach. Make yourself at home." Andrew added a spoonful of instant coffee to Moroccan hand-painted mugs. "Instant okay? We're out of fresh, I'm afraid."

"Instant's fine, thanks. Nice kitchen."

"Thanks. I can't take credit though. My daughters were mostly responsible for the design and colour scheme. I do like it though."

"Your daughters obviously have good taste. My mum would love it too. It's exactly her taste."

"Yes, I believe so. She drooled over it when she visited," Andrew chuckled, stirring the coffees before making his way to join Zach. "Oh, just a sec. I've biscuits as well," he said, turning on his heels to the worktop where he had left a plateful of ginger nuts, chocolate digestives and custard creams. "There you go. My favourites. Hope you like at least one type," he said, placing them next to Zach's coffee cup.

"Thank you. I'm partial to them all actually." He took a chocolate digestive, biting into it, hoping Andrew would initiate conversation.

The conversation began light-heartedly for some minutes until Andrew interlocked his fingers on the tabletop. "Zach, I hope you know that you can ask me anything. I could fire away with the history of how you came about, but I'm not sure you want that and I don't want to risk making you feel uncomfortable. Sorry if I'm getting it wrong. I'm happy to chat about this situation in any way you choose. Is there anything you'd like to ask? I'm happy to answer any questions you might have."

"I hadn't expected an offer of a Q and A, otherwise I would've made a list. Sorry, I'm not being facetious – I do happen to be a list person. I admit questions have buzzed around in my head since Mum's revelation. Okay, this one for instance," he said, cupping his chin between his thumb and forefinger. "Why did you pressurise Mum into seeing you when you knew she was soon to be married? Did you not consider the fact her fiancé – my father – wouldn't have been too pleased? You seem like a decent enough guy, but what you did conflicts with decency."

"I'm truly sorry, Zach, and I have to admit I'm not proud of it. I contacted your mum because I missed her desperately. I was deeply in love with her and knew without doubt that she still loved me. You can't turn love off like a switch just to please parents. I'm sure she loved your dad too, of course she did, but I do know the only reason she felt she couldn't marry me – when I asked both times – was because it would have devastated her parents, and she cared about them too much. So she married your dad instead to make life easy."

Zach slowly shook his head. "If the earthquake hadn't killed my dad, discovering what you did would've torn him apart. He adored my mum and my mum loved him. It would've broken my grandparents' hearts too if they'd been alive to see it."

"I'm so sorry for the pain it's caused you, Zach. At the time I wasn't thinking straight because I was too traumatised about my loss. I simply couldn't accept there was no hope. I guess I should've listened to my head as well as my heart. Having said that, I'm still very happy and proud to know you're my son, despite realising that feelings are far from mutual. I'm a stranger to you and I appreciate that as far as you're concerned, you only had one dad. I completely understand and respect that."

"My father was one in a million."

"I'm very happy to know you were raised by such a good father, Zach. And you have done your parents proud. I'm very proud of you too."

"I believe you told your daughters as soon as you found out," Zach said. "How did they take it?"

"Obviously they were shocked and upset initially, but they soon got used to it and have since been very keen to meet you. In fact they're now happy at the idea of having you as their half-brother. Of course there's no pressure. Any meeting with them is entirely up to you. Of course, I'd love you to meet them, but this is about you since you've been the most traumatised by the revelation. Let me get the photo album. I'd like you to at least see pictures of them. Two ticks," Andrew said before leaving the room.

Zach helped himself to a custard cream whilst checking his phone for messages. There was one from Robin asking how it was going. Zach's quick 'OK' was all he had time for.

A minute later Andrew returned with two large photo albums – a new one and another that looked decades old. "I'm afraid I'm still a dinosaur. My daughters keep on at me about digitalising this lot but I actually prefer to view them from albums like this. I have some on my phone but they're far too small to see properly. Maybe I should get one of those smart phones with improved visibility. Anyway, here they are," he said as he opened the newer album at the last page, pointing to the most recent pictures of his daughters. "Here they are at their friend's wedding last year. They look like you, don't you think? Phoebe especially. She's a solicitor like you too. Spooky, don't you think?"

"They look lovely. You must be proud of them." *For God's sake, don't show me all your holiday snaps.*

"I certainly am, and I'm proud of you too, if you don't mind me saying."

"Of course not. Thanks. Seeing Phoebe has reminded me about the Huntington's. Mum told me. I'm sorry to hear you both carry the gene, though I understand you won't develop the disease, which is something I guess. Hopefully Phoebe won't develop it either. I did want to ask you about it, although I've already done a fair bit of research. I understand I might also have a chance of carrying the gene. My partner Robin is adamant I should be tested, but I'm not so sure. Not sure I want to know, to be honest. I need time to process it and maybe in a couple of weeks or so I'll have a better idea of what I want to do about it, if anything."

"I totally understand where you're coming from, Zach, and respect your decision, whatever it may be. It's your life. The plus side is that there is just as much chance you won't carry the gene, as was the case with Harriet." From his back trouser pocket, Andrew pulled out a business card. Flipping it over, he scribbled his home number on the back. "Here's my numbers – home and business. If you remember anything else you wish to know about the disease, about your roots, about anything for that matter, please call me anytime – day or night." In fact I'm very much hoping we can meet up again. Soon. But that's entirely up to you, of course. Absolutely no pressure."

Zach accepted the card and placed it in his wallet. "Thanks. I'll certainly think about it."

"Do you mind if I ask you a question, Zach? I really don't want to put you on the spot, so please say if you'd rather I didn't."

"Sure. What is it?"

"Did you ever suspect your dad wasn't your biological father?"

Zach reflected for a moment. "Actually, I did sometimes wonder about my hair and eye colouring considering both by parents are dark-haired with brown eyes. I asked Mum once when I was in my teens and she said she had an aunt with similar colouring. I guess I chose to believe it because people believe what they want to believe, don't they? Maybe deep down I suspected something, but chose not to rock the boat."

"I hope you know that I would have, without question, supported you and your mother had I known. I would have urged your mother to marry me instead … well I did before knowing about you, but she refused both times. Even if she had told me after her marriage, I would've insisted on supporting you in every way possible."

Zach pondered momentarily. "It would've destroyed their relationship if she'd come clean, not only with my father but with her parents. Mind if I ask one more thing?"

"Course you can. You can ask me anything under the sun. Interrogate me if you wish."

After a smile of appreciation, Zach asked, "Do you still have feelings for Mum? I mean, do you still love her?"

Andrew took his time replying, staring ahead as if into the past. "My late wife Jill was a wonderful woman – a devoted wife and mother, and I did love her. Of course I did – I married her, but truth be told – I never stopped loving your mother. She was the love of my life and I never quite got over her." His eyes lit up as he remembered the photograph album. "Which reminds me – this other album has pictures of your mum. She refused to keep any photos of us together for fear of her parents discovering them, but she had no objections to me keeping any."

"What about your late wife – was she okay about you keeping photos of your former girlfriend?"

"She was absolutely fine. She did the same with her previous boyfriends, reasoning they were part of our history and it would be wrong to hide them away as if they never happened. Jill was a very agreeable and understanding woman." Andrew thumbed through the album until he reached the photos he was looking for. "Ahh, here they are. This was taken in the Lake District. Whenever we had time together, your mum preferred we went away for the day. Less chance of being spotted by anyone who might know her parents." Andrew turned a few pages. "This one was taken in Chester and this in North Wales. I remember those days like they were just a few years ago. See how happy we look?"

"You do look very happy, yes." Zach was struck by how much in love they appeared – holding hands in every picture and in others, gazing into each other's eyes. He struggled to recall a single photo of his parents, even on their wedding day, looking as happy and as much in love. Added to that, the resemblance between himself and young Andrew was so remarkable that Zach's mouth dropped open. *Maybe I have been a tad harsh on him.*

CHAPTER 48

July 2009

Hannah considered the number of times she and Andrew had been in touch since their reunion. *Mmm, let me see. Six face-to-face, numerous phone calls and emails, and endless texts. Surely, if he felt the same about me, he would've made a move by now?* Granted, the reasons for contact were invariably about Zach: initially to inform Andrew he was Zach's father; then to discuss strategies for dealing with Zach's reluctance to meet Andrew; and when the meeting was achieved, an exchange of notes on how it had worked out. There was also the possibility of Zach carrying the Huntington's gene. Zach's reluctance to be tested then became another topic of concern and exchanges. Although the Hannah-Andrew contact had always been about Zach, it had given them the opportunity to catch up with past decades and assess rekindling potential. Hannah desperately hoped their relationship could be rekindled, but she was too proud and old-fashioned to make any first moves.

"Keep your dignity and never throw yourself at a man," came the advice from her mother, and the rule had stuck.

Little did Hannah know that Andrew had bided his time for an opportunity to ask her on an official date. As luck would have it, a spare concert ticket became available, providing the perfect opportunity. He had purchased two of the tickets in May for himself and Harriet to see Elbow perform with the Hallé

Orchestra at the Bridgewater Hall. Harriet was an Elbow fan and although Andrew appreciated them, he preferred the Hallé.

Harriet was excited about the concert, especially as it received huge media coverage. However, she had since received an unexpected twenty-first party invitation from her friend Laura for the same evening – Thursday the 9th July. The party was originally set for the following Saturday at a local hotel, but was cancelled due to flood damage. Although Harriet was disappointed at having to miss the concert, she could not possibly miss Laura's twenty-first. She dreaded telling Andrew, especially as she had pressurised him into purchasing the tickets in the first place. "I hope you don't mind too much, Dad. Hope you find someone else to go with," she said on the phone.

On realising his opportunity to invite Hannah, Andrew's eyes lit up as his voice feigned disappointment. "Oh dear, what a shame, but of course you have to attend Laura's party, sweetheart. Don't worry about me. I'm sure I'll find someone to join me." After hanging up, he immediately rang Hannah.

"Elbow? What an odd name. Who are they?" Hannah asked, trying to sound nonchalant.

"A Manchester guitar band. Last year's Mercury Prize winners for their fourth album actually. Harriet's a big fan. Playing with the Halle will be a first for them and I believe a first for the Halle to be collaborating with a local guitar band, so it's naturally drawing massive media attention. Harriet's disappointed about having to drop out, but she could hardly miss her friend's twenty-first, could she? I believe tickets were sold out in record time, so we're very lucky to have them."

Hannah's eyes lit up. "I love the Halle and the Bridgwater Hall, and I'm sure I'll be free on the ninth as I rarely go out Thursday evenings. I'm intrigued about Elbow too. Anyone with a name like that must be interesting!" she chuckled. "So thank you. I'd love to come." On hanging up, she smiled from ear to ear, incandescent with joy.

* * *

With the help of Miriam's makeup and guidance, Hannah looked stunning on the night. She had also been given free rein of Miriam's wardrobe from which she chose, with gentle persuasion, a royal-blue sleeveless, knee-length, fitted dress with a co-ordinating chiffon shawl wrap and navy T-bar high heels. Initially, she protested, but the longer she admired herself in Miriam's full-length mirror, the more her protests waned.

Miriam held up her navy sequined clutch bag. "Look, I'm leaving the lipstick and face powder in here. Be sure to touch up during the interval. Makeup doesn't last all night, you know."

"Thank you, darling. I appreciate it," Hannah said with a smile. "Right, I'd better get home in time for him to collect me," and with that, Hannah headed for her Audi, a little wobbly in her unfamiliar heels. *Must practise walking in these before he arrives.*

When the doorbell rang, Hannah's heart did somersaults. That old familiar butterflies feeling she never thought she would experience again felt so good.

At the front door, Andrew let out a long whistle. "Wow, you look amazing!" He had arrived in good time, allowing thirty minutes for a pre-concert drink.

His contingency plan paid off considering the bar was heaving and it was near impossible to find a seat. After drinking up, they made their way to the concert-hall. It was early, but at least they would have seats.

By 7:30 p.m., the dimly lit auditorium was packed to the rafters. Over two thousand people created a hubbub of excited chatter whilst studying programmes and pointing out items of interest.

Taking centre stage on the conductor's podium stood Joe Duddell. A shiny, grand piano stood to his immediate left, an upright piano faced him and an impressive concert harp sat to his immediate right. Guy Garvey, Elbow's lead singer and lyricist, took centre right stage with his singers. Surrounding them like a pair of embracing arms sat the Hallé Orchestra. Above the stage stood the Hallé Youth Choir, females in red tops, males behind them in black. At a higher level on the right, a large two-way screen enabled the concert to be relayed live to the Castlefield Arena for those who missed the opportunity to purchase tickets. Behind the choir and screen, covering the entire rear wall, shone the spectacular £1.2 million pipe organ in all its glory.

Although Elbow songs were new to Hannah, she found herself clapping along to some, along with the audience, in particular 'Grounds for Divorce'.

Andrew was keen to hear Hannah's opinion after each song but the attempt to be heard over the thunderous applause was futile. "Never mind. Later!" he mouthed.

The performance closed with the audience on their feet, waving their arms and singing along to 'One Day Like This', almost drowning out the orchestra and band. Along with this euphoria, came the town hall bells projected onto the stage screen, ringing out for almost thirty minutes.

"Wow! That was quite something!" Hannah said as they were leaving the auditorium.

"It certainly was. Let's exchange notes about it over drinks, shall we?

Andrew had given much thought to planning the evening. Besides wishing for it to be special – and the concert certainly was that – he wanted the evening to end on a high. The option of inviting Hannah back to his place after the concert was not grabbing him due to the chance, albeit unlikely, of Harriet arriving home earlier than expected. He therefore checked Yahoo Maps for bars and pubs within walking distance of the Bridgewater. That's when he was reminded of the perfect venue a mere stone's throw from it – the iconic Midland Hotel, a Grade II listed Edwardian building which had attracted noteworthy VIPs over the decades, including Queen Elizabeth and Winston Churchill. Attempting to impress was not his intention as there was no need with Hannah – they were soulmates. He simply wanted a venue special and beautiful enough for their first official date in thirty years.

"Ooh lovely, the Midland will be the icing on the cake," Hannah said in response to Andrew's suggestion.

Having entered its magnificent lobby, they made their way to the Midland Bar where they found two quiet seats in a dimly lit corner. Andrew persuaded Hannah into trying a cocktail.

"Hmm, a Mai Tai I think since it's the only one I've heard of."

"Good choice. I'm going to have alcohol-free Paloma Tequila since I'll be driving."

In terms of helping the relationship progress romantically, it was fortunate the concert's atmosphere had been so electric in lifting their spirits to an intoxicated state.

"We were lucky to get the tickets." Andrew beamed.

"If you hadn't been so lucky, we could've always joined the audience at Castlefield Arena," Hannah said, stirring her Mai Tai with its cocktail stick. "The two-way screens were such a good idea, weren't they?"

"Absolutely! And it was decent of whoever initiated it to allow five thousand people to watch it free of charge."

"Yes, very charitable when they could've made a huge profit from it. I also liked the way the lead singer … what's his name?"

"Guy Garvey."

"Yes, Garvey. I liked the way he bantered with the Castlefield crowd on screen. Made them feel equally included."

"Yes, that was nice of him. It's a shame there were only two performances. I'm sure this could've run for weeks and still would've sold out."

"You're probably right." Hannah nibbled the tip of her cocktail mint leaf. "The band integrated so perfectly with the orchestra too, didn't they?"

"Yep, which is pretty impressive considering they don't read music."

"Really? That makes it an even greater achievement. Good for them! The audience couldn't get enough, could they? I enjoyed the clapping participation to that catchy song about divorce."

"Ah, good song – 'Grounds for Divorce'," Andrew said, recalling the endless times he had heard it from Harriet's sound system.

"I like his eclectic style too. The concert certainly deserved the standing ovation."

"So, you enjoyed it, then?" Andrew asked, laughing through his nose.

"No," she replied, shaking her head in mock disappointment before laughing. "I loved it!"

"I know you did. You looked totally captivated. You also looked beautiful," he said, reaching for her hand.

Hannah squeezed his hand and met his eyes, but he had a faraway look.

"What are you thinking?" she asked.

"Nothing." Andrew shook his head as if to toss away his thoughts.

"It must be something, going by the expression on your face," she said, giving his hand another squeeze.

"Okay, I can see you're going to prise it out of me," he said with a grin. "I was thinking I don't want this evening to end. It isn't as if we can have a nightcap at my place to extend it, is it?"

"I know. I wish it could last longer too. You could come back to mine for coffee if you like."

"I was also thinking, but didn't dare suggest it for fear of you jumping to the wrong conclusion, that ..." he paused for the right words.

A look of expectancy crossed Hannah's face. "That?"

"I was thinking what better place to extend our wonderful evening than right here. I was wondering if they happen to have a room, but wouldn't dream of suggesting such a thing in case you thought I'd orchestrated it, but I swear the thought hadn't entered my head till just now. I merely thought this place would be perfect for drinks with it being close to the Bridgewater and …"

"Inquire about a room if you wish," Hannah interposed, eyes bashfully looking anywhere but at Andrew.

Andrew complied exuberantly, and their blissful evening extended into morning.

CHAPTER 49

August 2009

The blaring phone broke the anomalous silence; intentional silence due to Trish's concern about missing the call. She had been sitting at her kitchen table for fifteen minutes with an instant coffee and her list. The list was much-needed to ensure she remembered everything she planned to tell Hannah. Because contact between them was so infrequent, there was much catching up to do. Had it not been for Trish's suggestion in email, this arranged call might never have happened. But Hannah was caught off guard without an excuse to lean on. At least Hannah had good news about reuniting with Andrew, which she felt sure would interest Trish.

After exchanging preliminary greetings, however, Trish burst into a flurry of her own news. "Guess what? Me and Ryan started a cleaning business like you suggested and it's doing really well," she said before crossing the point off her list. "We've got smashing premises in Woolington for it – on the main road with a big workroom and an office."

"That's wonderful news! I'm very happy for you," Hannah replied with genuine delight. "Are you employing staff?"

"Oh, yeah, we have a few part-timers. It's doing really, really well. We do all sorts, just as you advised – cleaning, laundry, ironing and even alterations." Trish's pen hovered under her next reminder. "Oh, and Ryan's depression got better soon after starting the business. It's given him summat to get up for – all thanks to you. He's been playing his guitar as well."

"Marvellous! That must be a huge weight off your mind. I remember how depressed he was about being unemployed and splitting with his girlfriend. I'm so glad he's fought off his depression. Even after the loss of his father?"

"Oh, course he got worse after losing his dad, then we started the business and that's when he started to get better, thank God. Thanks to you," Trish said, stroking Rambo who had come to sit by her side. "Oh yeah, and Ryan finally met Tony's father in Naples. They had a big bust-up, but at least he's met him and his family now, so that's more good news." By this stage, Trish's reliance on her list had evaporated as her points began to flow freely. "It's not all good news though," she added, her smile morphing into a frown.

"Oh dear. What's the bad news?"

"Remember the fella I was seeing – Ian? The fella I hoped to settle down with after leaving Tony?"

"Yes, of course. How is he?"

"How is he? He's a bastard! That's how he is. The swine ran off with another woman. Funny 'cos when I wasn't free, he was desperate to live with me, then as soon as I was free, he lost interest. To be fair, at first it was me putting him off 'cos it didn't seem right living with him too soon after Tony's death. But when I wanted to a year later he wasn't as fussed."

"I'm very sorry to hear that. How did you find out?"

"I got suspicious and followed him one night. Turns out he'd slept at this trollop's house – someone we knew from line dancing – a bimbo called Fiona. The cow! Me and my friend waited in Ryan's car overnight for proof he'd slept there. And he did. I knocked at their door in the morning and gave them a right mouthful. You should've seen their faces when they came to the door! Haha! They looked like they'd seen a ghost. I let her neighbours know what a trollop she is too. I yelled it at the top of my voice with them both stood at her front door. Least it made me feel better."

Hannah gave a slight cough. "What a dreadful experience for you. I'm so sorry. But better to have learned this before, than after moving in together."

"Yeah, dead right. Anyway, what about you?"

Forget it, Hannah mused. Her intention of sharing her good news about Andrew evaporated. *It would be like rubbing salt into a wound.*

Besides, she and Trish had hardly established a friendship. After the rescue, they had merely exchanged a few brief emails, and contact soon dwindled. Considering they had been trapped for a week in an earthquake-damaged building, struggled shoulder to shoulder fighting for their lives; considering they both carried skeletons in their closets which they revealed only to each other before anyone else; considering they both had men in their lives who happened to be gay and neither men were raised by their biological fathers; considering their greatest family concerns when trapped was for their youngest child; considering these women vowed to become friends (at least Trish had) after the rescue; considering all this, it was strange they never became acquaintances, let alone good friends; strange their terrifying tribulation counted for nothing in terms of developing a bond.

Or was it so strange? After all, every fibre of their existence was as different as chalk and cheese. Take food alone for instance, kosher aside. Hannah's groceries consisted of a vast array of quality, wholesome foods, many of which Trish had never heard of. Trish's, on the other hand, consisted predominantly of ultra-processed foods that would make a nutritionist wince. For Hannah, cooking was time-consuming by choice – a labour of love, whereas the priority for Trish's 'cooking' was to get it over with as quickly as possible. Better still, throw a ready-meal in the oven or have a chippy tea. Hannah insisted her family ate together and woe betide anyone who turned their nose up at any food served to them, or dared use the unacceptable 'I don't like it' phrase. They ate what they were given. Trish, on the other hand, held no qualms about her family eating in front of the television at different times from each other and demanding different meals to what was on offer, like it was a hotel.

It was not so much cultural differences, however, that divided the women. It was their differing values – neither right, nor wrong – just so vastly different.

CHAPTER 50

18 September 2009

Hannah contemplated the table settings and finishing touches for her Rosh Hashanah (Jewish New Year) dinner party, which also happened to have fallen on Shabbat. She also planned to take the opportunity to make a special announcement.

The fragrance of furniture polish lingered in the air and from the kitchen came the appetising waft of roast chicken. Happy at least with the aromas, she studied her twelve-seater dining table and wondered about guest numbers. She enumerated expected guests on her fingers: "Andrew, Miriam, Yosef, Sadie, Zach, Robin, Harriet, Phoebe and me. Nine." *Oh, what about Sadie's new young man? Hmm, she might invite him, in which case it'd be ten.*

Sadie had returned to Lancaster University the week before, to then have to return home for the event. She was vague about the man she had been seeing for the past few months and equally vague about where she was going prior to the dinner party. Her plan, she said, was to catch up with friends, get ready at their house and arrive home in time for dinner.

I'll set another place in case she brings him. Hope there's enough challah. At least it's a large one. At each end of the table, she arranged dishes of sliced and whole red apples, and two pots of honey with dippers. Traditionally, sweet foods are eaten at Rosh Hashanah to secure a sweet new year – apple and honey being practically synonymous with the celebration. Pomegranate is another favourite because it is seasonal and because its abundance of seeds symbolises a new year full of good deeds. Challah loaves also feature at Rosh Hashanah and Shabbat. For the former, they are traditionally circular to symbolize the cycle of the year. Hannah placed the loaf in the centre of the table in between a pair of crystal glass candlesticks holding tall white candles.

In former years, serving challah for Shabbat dinners presented the additional challenge of having to bake a gluten-free one due to Hannah's coeliac disease. Much to her delight, however, her local Jewish bakers introduced a gluten-free option. Hannah pounced at the opportunity and never looked back. Until then, she would bake herself a mini gluten-free challah. However, the risk of cross-contamination from the primary challah was too great and her family insisted on gluten-free Shabbat dinners for all. Much to Hannah's relief, this tradition stuck.

Although Hannah abandoned many Jewish laws after Saul's death, some traditions were so ingrained in her lifestyle, such as keeping kosher, that they stuck, especially for Shabbat dinners: the lighting of candles, sharing challah at the start of the meal, and saving unnecessary work for other days. A lifetime of adherence to Shabbat laws had trained her to be meticulous in her planning, as she had been for this dinner. Following Rosh Hashanah tradition, the meal would begin with sharing the challah which would be dipped in honey and eaten with sliced apples. Hannah planned a main course of roast chicken, turnips, pomegranate sauce, roasted sweet potatoes and smoked paprika-honey butter. This was to be followed by a number of desserts including salted caramel apple pie.

A prominent aspect of Rosh Hashanah is giving to charity – one aspect Hannah was not prepared to compromise. Traditionally, she made ten small apple honey cakes for the elderly who lived alone. She would deliver nine to synagogue members and the tenth to Jack, an eighty-six-year-old non-Jewish widower who lived a few doors away. She appreciated him keeping an eye on their home when they were away. The cake was the very least she could offer as a token of her appreciation. During the first two years after his wife's death, Hannah invited him to join them for Rosh Hashanah. However, he declined both invitations due to his shyness in mistakenly believing he would not fit in. Having a sweet tooth, however, he could never resist Hannah's apple honey cake.

"Oh, go on then. You've twisted my arm," he would say, chuckling with a twinkle in his eye.

"The shofar!" Hannah hurried to fetch it from a drawer in the lounge. A shofar is similar to a trumpet, typically made from a ram's horn. It is blown during morning synagogue services on Rosh Hashanah, or at home for those unable to attend a service. The reasons for blowing them are varied, but generally it is thought to be a call to examine one's behaviour and prepare oneself for the upcoming new year. Hannah and Saul's was a polished ram's horn, medium-sized about sixteen inches in length. Saul had learned to blow it, a skill which came in useful whenever family members were unable to attend synagogue to hear it. An exception to blowing the shofar at Rosh Hashanah is when it falls on Shabbat, which was the case on this occasion. Nevertheless, Hannah gave it a prime position on the window sill close to the dining table, if only as a reminder of its significance to Rosh Hashanah.

By seven o'clock, guests began trickling in bearing Rosh Hashanah greetings and embraces. Zach and Robin arrived first, followed minutes later by Andrew, Harriet and Phoebe, and finally Miriam and Sadie at quarter past seven.

"Shanah Tovah!" Miriam called to each arrival.

All reciprocated with gusto, apart from Harriet and Phoebe, who whispered self-conscious responses.

"It means good year," Zach explained.

They thanked him and repeated with greater clarity. "Shanah Tovah!"

With each meeting, the bonds between Zach, Andrew and his daughters strengthened, which brought enormous relief to Hannah. It was more than she had ever hoped. Zach was fond of both his half-sisters, though Phoebe was the one he most connected with due to them being fellow lawyers. Zach could discuss law till he was hoarse.

As Sadie hung up her black leather bomber jacket, Hannah said, "Sadie, darling, didn't I say you're more than welcome to invite your young man? What's his name again? William? Is he coming?"

"He's called Will. He's a bit shy. Next time maybe."

"That *is* a shame. Oh well, do be sure to invite him next time, won't you?"

Half an hour after pre-dinner drinks, guests settled at the dining table. At the head of it, Hannah lit the candles, reciting, "Shanah Tovah!" to which everyone echoed before enjoying their celebratory meal.

During after-dinner coffee, Andrew stood, cleared his throat and gently tapped his glass with a teaspoon. "Attention everyone, please!"

Immediately, the room fell silent as eager recipients to the announcement listened attentively.

"I have an announcement to make about our wedding. Good news, you'll be pleased to hear. We've set the date for Sunday, seventeenth of October."

After gasps of delight, a cheer erupted, followed by beaming smiles and congratulatory comments.

Andrew waited for the excitement to subdue before continuing. "We realise it's short notice. And no," he laughed, "it's not what you're thinking! The venue we really wanted – Didsbury House Hotel on Didsbury Park – was booked for at least six months. But then they rang us a week later with a cancelation. Naturally we pounced. It caters for both the ceremony and the reception, so we'll have it to ourselves all afternoon into the evening. It's a perfect venue – tasteful and the perfect size for a small, intimate wedding, which is what we want – just close family and one or two close friends. That's the bride and groom's friends – not yours," he laughed.

"Spoilsport!" Zach quipped, laughing. "But seriously, wonderful news, you two! Really pleased for you both!"

"Where will you be living?" Sadie asked, concerned about losing her family home.

"Don't worry, darling," Hannah said, "Andrew and I have decided that our house, rather than his, will accommodate both families better, and Andrew does love Didsbury."

"Phew, that's a relief! Nothing against Alderley Edge, Andrew. It's lovely. I just don't fancy being uprooted."

After a flurry of congratulatory hugs, kisses and handshakes, Andrew uncorked the champagne and the evening ended with excited wedding plans chatter.

CHAPTER 51

12 October 2009

Jane dispensed a supply of digoxin into a plastic pill bottle. After attaching the prescription label, she signed the tear-off section and called Andrew for his double-check signature. He was seated at the computer keyboard close to her, but gave no response.

"Planet earth to Andrew Redmond," she quipped.

"What?" Andrew replied as his fingers hovered over the keyboard.

Waving a black biro at him, Jane gesticulated for him to sign. "Lanoxin, 125 mcg for Pricilla Dankworth. We're low on them. Have you re-ordered, or shall I?"

Andrew stopped his feigned typing to sign the label. "Have you not checked the system? To be honest, I can't remember. Just check it," he said in a brusque tone, which he immediately regretted.

"I would if you stop hogging the computer!" Jane retorted.

Something weighed heavily on Andrew's mind – something he wanted to discuss with Hannah – something he needed to confess. But he was unsure how, or whether he should. He considered the possibility of taking his secret to the grave, but thought better of it. *No, we have to be honest with each other – start as we mean to go on. She'll be finishing work soon. I'll phone her – go round and test the waters before coming totally clean. Yes, easy does it,* he assured himself as he called her number. "Darling, I know we'd planned to meet Wednesday, but can it be sooner? Tonight? I need to see you about something."

Customers waiting for prescriptions stood within earshot. Hannah edged her way into the dispensing room for privacy. "Sure. Is there a problem?" she asked with a furrowed brow.

"Nothing to worry about, but I'd rather discuss it when we're together. I'll be round about eight if that's okay. Give you time to eat and freshen up. Unless you'd prefer we eat together?"

"I'd planned a Russian potato salad – not a favourite of yours, so maybe you'd prefer to eat before coming?"

Having agreed on eight, Hannah grabbed her belongings and dashed to her Audi. She would need to be quick to make time for preparing her meal, eating and freshening up. *Okay, change of plan – forget the potatoes. Stick with eggs, which will be quicker, and there's chicken left over from yesterday,* she mused, planning the best time-management strategy. *While the eggs are boiling, slice the chicken, butter some bread and prepare a salad.*

Arriving home, Hannah followed her plan to a T despite her concerns. Although Andrew said there was nothing to worry about, she did worry because the phrase *nothing to worry about* usually meant the opposite. *Oh, Lord, what if he wants out? What will I do?*

She sniffed. The smell of a burning pan brought her back to reality. "Argh, the eggs!" she screeched, sprinting to the hob to turn off the gas. It was not so much the burned eggs that peeved her, but the stench that would need airing out for hours. Time was tight. As she flung open the window and wafted the back door to and fro, she pondered what to have instead of eggs. There was coleslaw in the fridge. While soaking the burned pan in cold water, binning the eggs and preparing her salad, her niggling concern returned. *What does he need to tell me that's so urgent? He seemed a bit icy.* She placed her unappetising meal on her oak island top, but her appetite had evaporated. She forced down a morsel of chicken, prodding the rest with her fork before deciding to scrape it into the food recycle bin.

Having given the back door another wafting, she headed upstairs to shower, a much-needed one to warm up from the cold kitchen and wash away the stench of burned eggs. *Just enough time if I'm quick enough.*

Andrew, however, anxious to face the music, arrived earlier at 7:45 p.m. Ever since he and Hannah had become an item, he carried his own set of keys and let himself in. "Hi, Darling! Where are you?" Receiving no response, he popped his head around the door of each room before heading upstairs, calling her name again.

As Hannah stepped out of the shower, she finally heard him. "In the shower! Won't be long. Make yourself a coffee while you're waiting. Oh, and excuse the smell. I burned the eggs."

Having flicked the kettle on, Andrew returned upstairs. "Kettle's on. Let's have coffee when we go down."

Whether Hannah's insecurities had prompted her to make an extra effort, it was hard to say considering even Hannah was unaware of the effort she had made. But the effort showed. Instead of her usual old jeans, she chose a pair of brown Aztec print wide-leg silky trousers with a co-ordinating beige jumper – both inherited from Miriam.

"You look lovely."

"Thank you." Hannah looked down at her attire in surprise.

"Decided to come a bit earlier."

"Good, I'm keen to know what you need to see me about," she replied, slipping her feet into beige slip-on slippers. So? What is it?" she asked as she sat on the edge of her king-sized bed.

"It can wait till we're downstairs. Just wanted to know if you want a coffee. Do you?"

"Coffee can wait. I need to know what's on your mind. Must be important considering you brought our date forward two days."

"But you're done up here now. So let's go down. Then I'll tell you."

Hannah's heart thumped. *He's procrastinating because he hasn't the courage to tell me.*

Making his way to the sofa, he sat and patted the cushion next to him.

Grateful for small mercies, she sat close to him and slipped her hand into his. *Could be the last time. Better make the most of it.*

Andrew made a throat-clearing cough. "First off, can I ask you a question?"

"Please, just spit it out. I'm anxious to know what this is about."

"Yes, I will, but first tell me this – are you okay about me being Zach's father? Or do you still regret it?"

Hannah opened her mouth to speak before hesitating to find the right words. "Well, obviously life would have been a lot easier if you weren't. But the situation is so much different now, isn't it?"

"Are you saying you're now happy about it? No regrets?"

"Obviously, I would have preferred my children had the same father. I would've preferred not to have traumatised Zach with the revelation that his father was someone he didn't know. But what's done is done and there's no point being negative about what we can't change, is there? At least you being Zach's father has positive elements for us, doesn't it?"

This was not entirely the answer Andrew was hoping for. "Okay, fair enough." He looked around the room for a distraction. "I see you've been writing out the wedding place names. How are you getting on with them?"

"Is that relevant to what you want to tell me?"

"It could be depending on how you take what I'm about to tell you," Andrew said, holding her hand tighter.

"What is that supposed to mean?" *My God, am I going to be dumped?*

"I'm concerned about how you'll react. It's not easy, but I have to be honest – have to start how we mean to go on."

Hannah exhaled. *Mean to go on. Thank God, so we have a future together.* "Okay, go on, then."

Andrew looked down at their interlinked fingers, avoiding eye contact. "Look, darling, I'm so sorry and extremely ashamed to have to tell you this, but the reason we conceived with Zach, despite the condom, is because I pricked a hole in it. Well, that's not entirely true. I pricked a few holes in it."

Hannah's mouth dropped open as she attempted to process what she had heard. Realising from his straight face that it was no joke, she yanked her hand out of his. Motionless, she sat wide-eyed and mute. When she eventually found the words to speak, she could only muster a whisper. "What?"

"Please don't make me have to repeat that, unless you actually didn't hear me."

When Hannah managed to speak, it exploded into a high-pitched shriek of disbelief. "Tell me you're bloody joking. You are joking, aren't you?"

"Let me explain."

"Wait! Ah, yes! I remember now. I had wondered why you weren't that surprised when I told you Zach was your son. It's because you half expected it, isn't it? Why in God's name did you do such an idiotic thing? What would be the point? As soon as I discovered I was pregnant, I would naturally have assumed the baby was Saul's because you used a condom. So what was the point? Insanity obviously! My God, I'm about to marry a lunatic!"

"Let me explain, please. Calm down and let me get a word in, okay?"

"How can you possibly justify that with anything other than insanity?"

"Okay, I admit I was young and insane. I was out of my mind at the thought of losing you. It was my last hope of you coming back to me once you realised the baby was mine – and I was hoping if you did fall pregnant with my child, you'd know by its colouring. I realise it was a tall order and to be honest, I didn't really think I'd be lucky enough to pull it off." Andrew's eyes widened at his unintentional choice of words. "No pun intended, of course!" he said holding both hands up in innocence.

A crease between her eyebrows formed as she wrinkled her nose. "What pun?"

"When I said I didn't think I'd be lucky enough to *pull it off* – you know, like pull the condom off. It was a poor choice of words. Sorry."

"Hadn't noticed. You were saying?"

"I had thought if there was a chance in a million, it was worth it – that you and Saul might split over it and you'd return to me. C'mon, you can't blame me for trying to fight for the love of my life, can you? And hey, isn't your concealing my son from me for over three decades worse? C'mon, Hannah, let's say we're equal now, shall we? Please."

"So that's it? It was just to confess you'd pin-pricked holes in the condom?"

"Of course, because I felt bad about it and wanted to be honest with you."

Hannah fell silent as she processed the absurdity of his confession.

Desperate for her response, he watched her closely.

Slowly, a hint of a smile crossed her face, followed by a chuckle that morphed into a burst of raucous laughter, the type that becomes uncontrollable when the person sharing the joke joins in.

Andrew did join in, and they guffawed together uncontrollably.

"Oh, my side hurts. Stop!" Hannah begged.

"Erm, you started it!"

"Excuse me?" she said, owl-eyed in mock surprise. "And who was it who pin-pricked the condom?" She arranged her face into a mock scorn. "Dear, dear, I'm about to marry a lunatic," and once again they doubled up into fits of laughter as Hannah repeated, "Lucky enough to *pull it off!* Why bother when you can pin-prick it? Oh my!"

* * *

A sore subject had also arisen at Piccadilly Waterside. Zach and Robin had been playing duets in the lounge – Zach at the cello and Robin the piano. Puccini was a favourite from which they had created a duet 'Your Tiny Hand is Frozen' from *La Bohème*. The subject matter of a dying lover brought Robin's thoughts back to Zach's Huntington's gene test. He wanted to support Zach to the best of his abilities if and when the time arose, and was anxious to know if Zach was likely to develop the disease. Conversely, he did not want to be worrying about something that might never happen. He was anxious to know because the unknown worried him more than knowing the worst. He had seen how his eldest sister, after giving birth to a sick baby boy, had been terrified of the chance of him having Down's syndrome. It was not so much the confirmation that he had Down's that they feared, but the waiting – the not knowing. Once the blood test returned positive, although the shock was profound, they soon learned to accept and became remarkably sanguine about it. Robin felt sure it would be the same regarding Zach's gene test, should it be positive.

They had argued about the matter the previous day when Zach made a conscious decision not to have the test. Robin, however, was not giving up that easily. He would broach the subject again, after playing a more upbeat piece of music. He selected Pachelbel's 'Canon in D', another one of their favourites. After playing it several times, the final time to perfection, they beamed, proud of their performance.

"Put it there!" Robin held up his palm for a high five. "We should include it in our charity repertoire."

"Absolutely!" Zach replied enthusiastically as he placed the sheet into his repertoire ring-binder file.

Robin considered how to raise the sore subject again, conscious that Zach would not relish a repetition of their previous disagreement about it. *Sod it! I'll just tell him straight.*

"Fancy Coldplay's 'Viva La Vida'?" Zach studied the music sheet. "Haven't played it in a while."

"Sure, you know I love Coldplay. Listen hun, I've been thinking," Robin said, swivelling round on his piano stool. "You're going to hate me for this, but I just can't let it go, not without one last try. I really want you to have the test. Please do it, if not for you, at least for me."

"Jeeez, not that again!" Zach snorted disapprovingly as he thumbed through the music pile. "How many times do I have to tell you? I don't want to know. If it's positive, I'd be a nervous wreck for the rest of my life wondering when it might hit me. And you'd hate the person I'd turn into."

"Oh, so you can mind-read now, can you? And how many times do I have to tell you if it's negative, we can forget about it and relax. You'll no longer have the dread hanging over you. Imagine how great that would be? If the test's positive, we'll deal with it – together. Nothing is ever as bad as one imagines when there's someone to share the load."

"Thanks. That's sweet of you, but have you seen some of the case histories? It might put you off me if it's positive – knowing you'd be lumbered with a disabled person for the rest of your life. Of course I doubt you'd react that way, but you can never be sure how you'll react until you've actually been there. Remember Jay? Remember Gary swearing he'd stand by him when he discovered Jay was HIV positive? Remember what Gary actually did? He walked out when Jay's symptoms took hold. Everyone convinced Gary would've stood by him. Remember how staggered everyone was when he walked out? You just don't know how you'll react."

"I'm not Gary and I take offence that you're comparing me to him. I'm nothing like him. Do you actually think I'd be that fickle?"

"Nobody thought Gary would be. To be fair on Gary – it's not about fickleness – it's about emotional maturity. Some people simply can't deal with traumas. It's impossible to know how you'll handle it until you live it. Besides, I really don't want to know. Ignorance is bliss. What you don't know can't hurt."

"Yeah, yeah. Ignorance is bliss for the ignorant, but knowledge is euphoric for the wise, and you're wise, babe – very wise. It's only because you're scared, and I can understand that, but you have me by your side. I love you no matter what. End of. Please. Do it for me, if not yourself." He looked up with pleading eyes.

"What is it you don't understand about no? Watch my lips – No!" Zach mouthed with exaggerated rounded lips.

Robin fell silent, crestfallen.

"I'm sorry, darling, but I can't help it if I'm scared shitless. Let's drop it, okay? Coffee?"

Robin hung his head low in silence.

Zach headed for the kitchen to make coffee. He took his time to consider the possible implications of denying Robin his wish. *He might resent me. It could lead to another split. Jesus, I couldn't stand that again.* He opened the nibbles cupboard, thinking how he needed more than coffee to butter Robin up. There he saw Robin's favourite Battenberg cake. After slicing and arranging the pink and yellow chequered slices onto a side plate, he presented them on a musical notes serving tray with two mugs of coffee.

"There you go, darling," he said, placing the tray on the coffee table.

Although Robin was now slumped on the sofa, he remained mute.

"It's your favourite. You can have it all if you like. Just leave me a crumb. That's how much I love you."

The silence remained deafening.

Zach joined Robin on the sofa. He stroked Robin's hair, hoping for at least a flicker of response, but nothing. With each failed attempt, Zach's panic intensified. In defeat, he held up his palms. "Okay, okaaaaay! You win."

Robin slowly raised his head. "What? Seriously?"

"Seriously."

"You're absolutely sure you want to?"

"Of course I'm not sure, but I don't have much choice, do I? Not unless I want to put up with you looking like someone died, or run the risk of losing you. I don't want to lose you again, Robbie."

"Come here," Robin said, enveloping Zach into a tight embrace. "Thank you so much. You won't regret it. It'll be good whatever the result. Trust me, hun."

* * *

On the morning the results arrived, Zach thrust the envelope into Robin's hand. "I daren't look. You open it."

Without hesitation, Robin tore it open, read its contents, smiled broadly and flung his arms around Zach. "You're clear, hun. You're clear!"

CHAPTER 52

17 October 2009

Sentimentality and fuss was not Hannah's style. All she wanted was to be Andrew's wife, as she should have been decades ago. Until he placed the wedding ring on her finger she could not relax, ever fearful something might go wrong.

She need not have worried. Andrew was equally keen to make the commitment. His old friend Jonathan was to be his best man, whom Hannah also knew from their university days. With the aim of keeping numbers down, Andrew limited his guests to family: his daughters Harriet and Phoebe, his brother and sister, two cousins, and his eighty-year-old Aunt Jane. She was the only close relative from his parents' generation still alive.

Hannah especially needed to limit her numbers as the insistence of a small, intimate wedding had been entirely hers. She therefore allowed herself only two friends – Margot and her book club friend Diane. A few of her relatives disapproved of the marriage which they considered too soon after Saul's death. The fact Andrew was not Jewish added to their disapproval.

"At least that'll help keep the numbers down," Hannah said facetiously.

And so, from Hannah's side there was Zach and Robin, Sadie, Miriam with her husband, Hannah's sister with her husband and three offspring, and two of their cousins.

As a mark of embracing her Jewishness and keeping her children's surname, as well as a mark of respect to Saul, Hannah retained the name Bernstein. She assured Andrew she would not do this if it caused him the slightest concern; she would revert to her maiden name Cohen if he preferred. But Andrew, being the sweet, agreeable person he was, would not hear of it, and so Bernstein she remained.

Although Hannah wished to retain certain aspects of her Jewishness, she kept many Jewish wedding traditions out of her itinerary. "A Jewish wedding wouldn't seem right considering you're an atheist non-Jew and I'm practically a non-believer," she told Andrew. A synagogue or church wedding was therefore out of the question, as was a register office because Hannah considered them cheap conveyer belts.

And so, they chose Didsbury House Hotel for its beautiful Victorian gothic charm and for the exclusive use of the premises throughout the day into the evening – the perfect intimate house-party effect they desired. The fact it was local was a bonus.

Despite relishing the idea of a tasteful venue, Hannah wanted as little fuss as possible – no bridesmaids, no veil and no professional photographers considering there were ample amateur photographers amongst the guests. Miriam and Sadie, however, insisted on taking charge of Hannah's bridal attire and makeup. After disputes and frayed tempers, they eventually reached a compromise: the bride wore a long sleeved, calf-length ivory lace dress with a low back; ivory, peep-toe heels; a small posy of white roses with lily of the valley and gypsophila; and a spray of gypsophila pinned to the side of her hair added to the finishing touches.

Going by the 'oohs' and 'aahs' as Hannah made her entrance on Zach's arm into the Blue Lounge, the make-over paid off, and Andrew considered himself the luckiest man alive. Despite his efforts to look understated in his three-piece, grey suit, to Hannah he looked as handsome as the day he first wooed her three decades earlier. Hannah was not the only one to notice.

Zach studied Andrew's face – his features and colouring so like his own – and he wondered if he would be as good looking at Andrew's age. He had finally warmed to Andrew and was delighted to be supporting the wedding.

He and Robin offered to perform a repertoire of their duets, but Hannah would not hear of it, insisting they enjoy every second of the wedding celebrations. As a compromise, she gratefully accepted their offer of creating a compilation of hers and Andrew's favourite tracks on an iPod for the special day. An eclectic mix of classical, contemporary jazz and blues accommodated everyone's taste, and carefully planned playlists were created for easy access. Hotel staff played tracks for the bride's entrance and the couple's exit, while Zach and Robin managed music for other highlights of the wedding – for the photo shoots, the reception entrance, the first dance, the buffet, and the cake-cutting ceremony. Two particular tracks stood out: Elton John's 'Your Song' for the couple's first dance and 'Hava Nagila', an Israeli folk song, for the hora dance.

Hannah did not relish the thought of being hurled up on a chair at her age, but wanted to include all other aspects of the hora, including the waving of handkerchiefs whilst being encircled by dancing guests. She was Jewish after all!

CHAPTER 53

March 2011

Hannah and Andrew's Friday evening Shabbat dinner was about to begin – in earnest as it was a particularly special one. Aside from celebrating the Sabbath, it was also in celebration of a family member's conversion to Judaism. Although Hannah had practically abandoned strict adherence to Shabbat laws since Saul's passing, she made greater efforts on this occasion for the benefit of the newly converted. Because of her extra workload, Miriam and Sadie had insisted on helping, and together they produced a Shabbat dinner to remember.

Taking centre stage, the elegantly-dressed Victorian dining table stood proudly, surrounded by twelve matching mahogany balloon back dining chairs. Despite diners having made the extra effort to dress for the occasion, the table display outshone their personal efforts. Draped over it lay a snow-white damask tablecloth adorned with silverware, cut-glass crystal jugs and wine glasses and a bone china dinner service. Two silver candlesticks, each holding tall, ivory candles stood like majestic king chess pieces at the head of the table. Next to them sat a silver wine chalice filled with red wine. A deep plum velvet challah cover, finished with fringes interwoven with gold thread, draped over two braided challah loaves in preparation for the blessings. Unlike the Rosh Hashanah challah that was circular to symbolise the cycle of the year, these were plaited and rectangular.

In accordance with Shabbat law, lighting the candles needed to be done twenty minutes before sunset to usher in Shabbat. And so, Hannah lit them shortly before 6 p.m. As if to invite the candlelight to her face, she waved her arms three times over the flames. As the smoke's subtle fragrance enhanced the ceremony's serene mood, she smiled contentedly.

Seated in his high chair, one-year-old Jacob was even more content, cooing with delight at the flickering flames and at his father's arrival from synagogue prayer. His father was the newly converted, keen to follow his new religion to the letter.

"Shalom Aleichem!" (peace be upon you) he called.

"Aleichem shalom!" came a unison reply.

He then broke into the 'Shalom Aleichem' hymn that welcomed angels into the home.

There is generally an order to which Shabbat rituals occur. Blessing the children came next, for which Jacob's parents placed their hands on his head and recited:

"May you be like Ephraim and Menashe.

May God bless you and guard you.

May God show you favour and be gracious to you.

May God show you kindness and grant you peace."

"Amen!" all said in unison.

Immediately after, Hannah half-filled each wine glass with red wine and passed them around. Holding her own, she gave thanks for the Shabbat by reciting the Kiddush in Hebrew. Guests concluded with 'Amen' before taking a sip of wine. Instead of wine, little Jacob was given grape juice in his trainer cup, half of which dribbled down his chin.

When Jacob's father first experienced a Shabbat dinner, he had been bemused at diners leaving the dining room for the kitchen immediately before dinner. Were they, he wondered, wishing to help with the serving? But no – their trip to the kitchen was for the hand-washing ritual.

And so, on this special celebratory conversion evening, he adhered to the law, as he had every Friday evening for over a year.

This entailed filling a cup with water, pouring it over the back and palm of the right hand three times and repeating this for the left hand. Following the hand-washing came adherence to silence until eating commenced.

Hannah was one of the first to return to the dinner table where she waited in silence for others to join her. When all were seated, she removed the ornate cover from the challahs, raised each one with five fingers as she recited the blessing. Again, this was followed by the unison recital of "Amen". Having ripped equal pieces off the first loaf, she passed the pieces around for diners to eat before the food arrived.

"Shabbat Shalom!" guests concluded in unison.

"Shabbat Shalom! And now for the food," Hannah announced.

Mindful that Miriam and Sadie had already contributed a great deal of help, she turned to Zach. "Zach, give me a hand with the food, will you, dear?"

Presently, Zach wheeled in the food trolley filled with aromatic dishes of matzo ball soup; mujaddara – a rice dish with lentils and onions; salmon salad on a bed of lettuce; and olive tapenade.

Wiping her hands on a tea towel, Hannah asked, "Would someone be kind enough to serve the bread, please?"

Andrew, being the closest to the loaves, skirted around the table with them, waiting for diners to tear off their share. Whilst relishing the first course, diners settled into animated conversation exchanging their news.

"More soup, anyone?" Hannah ladled an extra serving to Robin. "There's plenty more food to follow, so do leave room, won't you?" She offered this information discreetly for the benefit of non-Jewish newbies: Andrew's daughters Harriet and Phoebe; and Margaret, an elderly neighbour who had recently lost her husband to a stroke. Hannah, being the charitable sort, had insisted she joined them.

After first course dishes had been cleared, Hannah wheeled in the main course of honey and orange-glazed baked chicken; apple cider beef stew; string beans; and rosemary scalloped potatoes.

Margaret took an ostentatious whiff. "Mmm, it looks and smells delicious!"

"There's a variety of desserts to follow, so do remember to leave room for them," Hannah reminded them as she served the food.

Most guests paid little heed and made pigs of themselves, yet easily found room for desserts when they arrived: zesty lemon cake, hamantaschen (a three cornered pastry filled with poppy seeds and jelly), jelly doughnuts, and a fresh fruit salad. The intention of serving a variety was to provide options, but for most guests, the temptation was too great to stop at one.

Margaret leaned over to examine the temptations as she tapped her chin in concentration. She turned towards Hannah. "I'm lactose intolerant. I suppose I'll need to stick with the fruit salad, huh?"

"I'm glad you asked, Margaret, otherwise you might've missed out. All my desserts happen to be dairy-free," Hannah replied as she waved her serving spoon.

"Really?" Margaret said, wide-eyed.

"Yes, absolutely because milk is prohibited when consumed at the same meal as meat."

"Ooh, I'm not going to be able to resist any now, am I?" And so, this special Shabbat dinner turned out to be particularly enjoyable for Margaret.

Moreover, it was an especially happy occasion for the newly converted Jew. On the piano next to the dinner table were two unopened congratulations greeting cards. One depicted a gold Star of David; the other, a five-arm brass Shabbat candelabra holding five candles. Both read: "Congratulations on your conversion to Judaism".

With a beaming smile, Sadie presented the envelopes to the newly converted.

"For me?" he said in mock surprise. "Aww, thanks, love. Do you want me to read the messages aloud?"

"Yes, please. That would be lovely."

After looking around at smiling anticipatory faces, he pulled the first card from its envelope and read the message imprinted on the inside.

> To my darling Ryan,
> May your new life rich in traditions bring you peace, joy and fulfilment. I am so proud of you. Mazal tov!
> From your loving wife, Sadie. xxxx

Reaching over to Sadie, Ryan kissed her cheek. "Thanks, babe. It's ace." On pulling the second card from its envelope, he spotted Hannah and Andrew's signatures. He gave them a sideways smiling glance before reading their warm, congratulatory message.

A ripple of applause erupted, accompanied by a hubbub of 'Mazal tov!' and 'Well done!' overlapping like a round of 'Frère Jacques'.

As Trish wrapped Ryan in a hug, tears glistened in her eyes. "I'm dead proud of you, son."

CHAPTER 54

Pre-March 2011

Fool! Hannah remonstrated herself. *If I hadn't mentioned Jazz Fusion to Trish, Sadie and Ryan might never have met.*

Although Trish remembered the club's name, she could not remember where she had heard about it when she had suggested it to Ryan.

Ryan had turned up over a year later, not so much to lift his spirits – his business venture had already achieved that. He had taken up guitar again and wondered if he could match the open mic talent. As he entered, he caught sight of a beautiful vocalist spotlighted on stage with long dark hair bouffanted high on her head. The song she was singing hit a nerve and his steps towards the bar slowed to a halt.

> "Daddy's gone, gone, gone
> Earthquake took him
> Our hearts forever mourn
> Crumbled walls, hearts forlorn
> Daddy's gone, gone, gone."

As he listened intently, he studied her lips in an attempt to lip read. *Must be bloody hearing things. Daddy's gone. Earthquake took him.* He stood rigid, taking in every word. The connection he felt for the singer was instant and an overwhelming rush of emotions enveloped him: sadness from the lyrics that moved him to the core; astonishment that they reflected his personal experience; a feeling of admiration for the singer's talent and beauty – how she reminded him so much of Amy Winehouse whose looks and music he greatly admired.

Thirty minutes of singing was thirsty work. After her performance, Sadie headed for the bar, exchanging smiles and pleasantries with punters complimenting her performance. Four tall vacant stools stood side by side at the bar. She climbed onto the middle one, wriggling herself into position and tugging down the short hemline of her pencil-tight, halter-neck red dress.

Ryan watched her every move, waiting for an opportune moment to strike up a conversation. If she remained alone at the bar, this was it and he was not going to blow it. Inching his way toward the bar as inconspicuously as possible, he slid in beside her as she surveyed the stage. She had taken a fancy to the dreadlocked singer of the four-piece band setting up their instruments. Ryan remained standing. He did not wish to appear presumptuous. *For God's sake, don't blow it!* Holding her in his peripheral vision, he watched her long, red fingernails rummage in her handbag for her purse, and the scent of her heady, floral perfume intoxicated him. Not wishing to startle her, he waited for her to turn towards him before speaking. "Great gig! I loved your earthquake song. Did you write it?"

"Thanks very much. Yes, all my own work – the lyrics and the music."

"It was beautiful and really moving. Amy Winehouse, eat your heart out!" he said, laughing through his nose.

"Ha, I wish. I love her."

"Me too. You could be her twin."

"Don't think I've seen you here before. Is it your first time?" she asked, keeping her eye on the barman as she held up her hand to grab his attention.

"Yeah, first time, but hang on, let me get that – a token of my appreciation for that amazing song. What are you drinking?"

"Okay, thanks, a white house wine, please. So you liked it *that* much?"

Their conversation was interrupted by the barman requesting their order.

"A pint of Stella and a white house wine please, mate," Ryan said, before returning his attention to Sadie. "Yeah, I like the song a lot, especially the lyrics. So you write all your own, then?"

"Most of them, especially when I have strong feelings I want to express. I then make the music match the mood of the lyrics."

"You're obviously multi-talented. Self-taught or did you have lessons?"

"I had piano lessons for years, but taught myself guitar. And the lyrics – they just come from my emotions."

"Well, you definitely express them with loads of emotion. The song about the deceased father made the hairs on my arms stand on end and when I tell you why, you probably won't believe me." Ryan pulled a ten pound note from his fleece jacket pocket as he waited for her response.

Sadie returned her purse into her red clutch bag. "Try me," she said with a twinkle in her eye.

When the drinks arrived, Ryan ordered the barman to keep the change. Something he rarely did. *First impressions count*, he thought. Slipping onto the stool next to Sadie, he slid her drink towards her and took hold of his pint of lager. "I'm guessing the lyrics about the earthquake were metaphorical, right? I mean, I lost my dad in an earthquake last year in Naples," he said, observing her response closely, "and it'd be a chance in a billion if you had too."

Sadie turned slowly to face him, her lips parting as she stared at him in disbelief. She returned her wine glass to the bar. "You lost your dad in an earthquake? In Naples? I'm so very sorry to hear that, but are you serious?"

"Yeah, I'm sorry to say. Last year. Him and my mam were trapped in a hotel – the Palazzo Napoli. At least my mam survived, thank God. You must ….." Sadie's stunned expression caused Ryan concern. "Are you okay?"

She shook her head sharply as if to tune back in. "I'm fine, thanks," she whispered.

Ryan frowned. "You don't look it. Sure you're okay?"

"Jesus, I don't believe it. My father died in that very hotel and my mother survived too. My God, it's the same earthquake, isn't it?"

Ryan fell silent as he considered the revelation. "God, it must be. Christ. Are you okay? Not sure I am. Maybe you should knock that back and I'll get you another for the shock," he said, before taking a couple of long swigs of his lager.

Sadie downed half of her wine, keeping hold of her glass with the intention of draining it all.

"I'm fine, or at least I will be. Just need to take it in. I can't believe it. I mean, what are the chances of such a coincidence happening? Were you there during the rescue?"

"Yeah, I flew over as soon as I heard. I arrived just as they were taking her to the ambulance, so I was able to travel with her to the hospital."

Again, Sadie's mouth fell open, too stunned for words.

"What?" Ryan asked.

"Same here. My mother was pulled from the wreckage and my brother, sister and I had arrived in time to accompany her in the ambulance."

"We were probably taken to the same hospital. Saint Leucius," said Ryan.

"Unbelievable! We went to that one too. Ospedale di San Leucius."

A wave of realisation hit Ryan. "Christ, you must be the daughter of the woman my mam was trapped in the bogs with. Is it you? I think the woman was called Anna. She was Jewish."

"My God! This is surreal. My mother's called Hannah and she was trapped with a woman called Trish. Jeeez! What's your mum's name?"

"Christ! Her name's Trish!"

Speechless, they sat dazed, processing the revelation.

Presently, Ryan said, "I didn't wish them a safe journey and a happy holiday before they left. I didn't even see them before they left. I'll never forgive myself for that."

"Gaawd, it gets spookier by the minute. It was the same with me and my parents – worse. I'd had words with Mum the day before their flight and we'd not made up. I didn't even say goodbye. I felt so bad about that more than anything."

By the end of the evening, Ryan and Sadie felt they had known each other for years to the extent that it did not appear too personal when he complimented her on the gap between her front teeth.

"Another reason you look like Amy Winehouse," he said.

Before they knew it, it was past closing time and they were the only two punters remaining. So much to say. So many thoughts to share. Of course they exchanged numbers. That was a given.

CHAPTER 55

Sadie had been two months pregnant at the time of Hannah and Andrew's wedding. Neither Hannah nor Trish had an inkling Sadie was even seeing Ryan, let alone carrying his child. The deception was simple enough to pull off as Ryan had moved to his own flat in Rusholme – a safe distance from both mothers' prying eyes.

Sadie had no doubt Hannah would disapprove, especially if she knew Ryan was Trish's son. Although Sadie had never heard Hannah say a bad word about Trish, she sensed the disapproval in Hannah's tone. Likewise, Ryan kept it from Trish, knowing she would spring it on Hannah quicker than a crocodile snaps its prey if she knew.

When Hannah suspected Sadie was seeing someone, she started asking questions. The most Sadie gave was Ryan's invented nickname 'Will' and his age. At the time, Sadie had no intention of spoiling her mother's wedding with the revelation. She and Ryan had planned to wait for an opportune moment after the honeymoon to break the news. However, Sadie let Ryan's name slip. It may well have been after the honeymoon, but the moment was ill-timed. Hannah and Andrew had arrived home from their honeymoon in the Dordogne only the day before. Sadie was helping unpack a huge delivery of online supermarket shopping while Andrew was at work.

As Hannah lugged a Sainsbury's carrier bag onto the worktop, she said, "I thought you said his name was Will? You just called him Ryan!"

Sadie coughed. "Did I? Will's his nickname." Slowly, she placed six eggs into the fridge as she considered how to get out of this one.

"Where does it come from? I mean people's nicknames often come from their surnames. What his?"

Sadie stood mute, still holding the fridge door open.

"So what's his surname?"

"Hmm, not sure," Sadie lied, closing the fridge door and reaching for a can of tomatoes.

"Oh, come on – you must know his surname after all these months. What are you hiding, Sadie?"

Sadie gulped, praying Hannah did not know Trish's surname. But of course that was wishful thinking.

"Wilcox," Sadie replied under her breath as she placed the can in a head-height cupboard.

Hannah's head tilted quizzically to the side. "Sorry, what was that?"

"Wilcox," Sadie repeated louder in defeat, slamming the cupboard door.

Hannah's eyes grew rounder and her words crescendoed. "Ryan Wilcox!"

Sadie looked away from Hannah's glare, speechless.

"Why didn't you tell me?" She pulled out a stool from under the kitchen island. "Sit down. We need to talk."

"I'm sorry." Sadie took a seat next to Hannah. "I didn't tell you because I knew you wouldn't approve."

"You're absolutely right there! What on earth can you possibly have in common? You're worlds apart!"

"We have lots in common. We're in love, our fathers died in the same earthquake, we appreciate the same music, we play guitar and write songs, and we're both spiritual."

"Spiritual? You mean you're both fond of alcohol?"

"Don't be facetious!"

"What you also need to take into account are the negatives. He's an illegal drug user and will be an extremely bad influence on you!"

"Oh, come on, Mum. So was Amy Winehouse. I'm a huge fan, but I wouldn't dream of following her drug-taking habits, would I? Besides, he only takes weed."

"Only?" Hannah screeched. "Only? You say it like it's coffee! Have you forgotten the damage cannabis does to the brain? Have you forgotten the study I told you about? Persistent cannabis use by people in their teens resulted in a neuropsychological decline, losing an average of eight IQ points, and those lost mental abilities are lost forever, despite quitting as adults."

* * *

Of course Sadie took no notice and continued seeing Ryan. When she announced their engagement a week later, Hannah raised volcanic eruptions.

In a voice an octave higher than usual, she screamed, "Have you taken leave of your senses?"

Sadie was quick to retort. "Andrew isn't Jewish and your relationship works, so you can't use that one!"

"You know as well as I that it has nothing whatsoever to do with Ryan being non-Jewish. I'm sorry to say this, Sadie, but Ryan is the last person on earth I'd wish to see you with – someone who does drugs, despite being raised to say no to them, someone who smokes like a trooper and drinks like a fish. For the love of God! This is all first-hand from his own mother, don't forget – from the person who knows him best. Mixed marriages, whether interracial or interfaith are challenging enough, but interclass marriages rarely work. During the honeymoon period, his low standards – the drugs, the excessive drinking and smoking, not to mention his expletives and poor grammar won't bother you, but in a few years' time, especially at your children's parents' evenings and sports days, you'll think differently."

"My God, can you hear yourself? You're such a snob! Anyway, I don't care what you say, we're getting married, whether you like it or not. I love him and he's a good guy. He'll do anything for me – even convert to Judaism and be circumcised."

"A good guy? Sadie, darling, he's an illegal drug user. He could be arrested and you'd go down with him – at least socially. You've always said you'd never date anyone who smokes nicotine let alone pot, weed, whatever you call it. And now you're telling me you want to marry someone who does both!"

"Everyone does cannabis. It's no big deal."

"What?" Hannah shrieked. "How dare you! Already he's brainwashed you into believing that utter garbage. Remember, we Jews, of all people, know that if a lie is told repeatedly, people will eventually believe it. Or have you forgotten Hitler's Nazi propaganda too? Before Ryan, we hardly knew a soul who smoked cigarettes, let alone did drugs, and now you're telling me everyone does. Please God, don't tell me he's already brainwashed you into trying …"

"Of course not! What he does is his business. You know I've never been into nicotine, let alone weed. Besides, he hardly smokes it now he's with me."

"Look, I know you think it's snobbery with me, but it's not that at all. It's about standards. I'm merely being a realist. It will never work. Yes, you can turn a blind eye to the tattoos and the piercings now because they may be gone one day, but his addictions to cannabis, to alcohol and to nicotine, not to mention his bad language, poor diction and grammar will be harder to remedy. He would be a poor role-model for your children."

"Good God, can you hear yourself? You're being totally discriminatory!"

"I'm being a realist, darling. If I don't spell out the truth, who will? Forget political correctness when it's about your future – your life. Let's talk common sense. Look at statistics and see for yourself. Such marriages rarely, if ever, work."

Everything, however, Hannah desperately tried to get into her daughter's obstinate head, fell upon deaf ears. Instead, it caused Sadie and Ryan to dig their heels in deeper, announce the pregnancy and rush into marriage.

Trish, on the other hand, was ecstatically happy. Her son marrying into such a decent, well-educated and wealthy family was like winning the lottery. *Sadie will be a great influence on Ryan. Hopefully, he might kick the weed into touch if he doesn't influence Sadie into taking it.*

* * *

Sadie had assured Ryan that a traditional Jewish wedding was unnecessary. However, enthusiastic about his conversion, he was keen for the real McCoy, especially after seeing traditional Jewish weddings on YouTube. Once he gained Rabbi Rosen's approval to have his personal chuppah erected in the synagogue, Ryan had delighted in creating it. For the posts, he stood four bamboo poles into soil-filled plant-pots. For the canopy he used white voile which he also twisted decoratively around the posts. Artificial garlands provided the finishing touches. Sadie chose the flowers to create a romantic effect which matched her bouquet and the button-holes: eucalyptus and lemon leaves, hydrangeas and gypsophila.

And so, following tradition came the breaking of plates by the happy couple's mothers, and the breaking of glass underfoot by the groom. Wearing a long white satin dress, Sadie looked stunning, and Ryan looked as handsomely Jewish as any other with his white kippah clipped to his dark hair.

Ryan had taken a particular liking to the hora. "It'll be a right laugh," he said, and he was right after almost falling off the chair he was lifted on in fits of laughter.

Sadie, pregnant with Jacob, could only stand by roaring with laughter at the hilarity of the situation, along with everyone else;

everyone except Hannah who was still in recovery from the shock of the poor marriage match.

Once married, Hannah had little choice but give her blessing. To do otherwise would have risked losing her daughter. She now needed to focus on the positives: at least Sadie would continue to embrace her Jewishness and Ryan was happy to convert. It could be a lot worse.

However, the conflicts continued. Baby names were the next bone of contention.

"If it's a boy, I was thinking of calling him Tyler."

"Good grief, you can't call him that!"

"Why on earth not? Not that I've decided on the name, but why not?"

"Because a name like that will brand him the second his teachers spot it in the register. Teachers' high expectations are with the Jeremys, the Timothys and the Julians. They'll look for low attainment with a Tyler, and may well find it. The child may well be a genius, but you of all people as a psychologist should understand the power of the self-fulfilling prophecy – children are likely to behave in ways that confirm teachers' expectations."

"That's it! I've had it with you!" Sadie barked as she stomped to the door, slamming it behind her. At least this time she could blame her fluctuating pregnancy hormones.

* * *

When Ryan had learned he was to be the father of a Jewish baby (since the inheritance of Jewishness is passed down through the mother), he had, with the influence of Sadie, become enthusiastic about converting to Judaism. Although he had abandoned the Catholic faith that had been drummed into him throughout his childhood, he never quite lost his belief in God. He also believed in the benefits of raising children within a religion. He believed his religious upbringing had contributed to making him the morally upstanding person he was. He had disregarded his illegal drug use as an immorality due to his firm belief, influenced by the company he kept, that cannabis was no worse than cigarettes or alcohol. He seemed to have overlooked the probability that his long-term cannabis use had hitherto stifled his motivation to get out of bed in the mornings or make the effort to find employment. Disregarding the evils of illegal drug use, Ryan wanted a similar moral grounding for Jacob – anything but Catholicism. And so, the decision was made – the religion in which to raise Jacob would be Judaism.

Before Jacob's birth, however, Ryan had developed twinges of doubt about converting. He had heard that conversion to Judaism is often discouraged by Jews. Had it not been for Sadie's assurance of the invalidity of this argument, he might have pulled out.

"Let me tell you – you'll be a better Jew than some born into Judaism who don't embrace their Jewishness. They had no choice but to be Jewish, whereas you, despite the risk of antisemitism to yourself and your children, and the intense training you had to undergo to get there, not to mention the circumcision – despite all that, you still chose to convert. That deserves respect and I assure you, you will get it from many Jews – certainly from my friends and family."

Jacob had arrived six weeks early, spending the first month of his life in the neonatal intensive care unit. At least he had a well-established head of hair – a thick black mop of it that stood on end like a frightened cat. The greatest fears, however, were Sadie and Ryan's: fears he might not make it, and if he did, that he might be disabled in some way; and a fear there might be a repetition with future babies. At least there was a silver lining: the experience helped turn their lives around. So devoted were they to little Jacob, they vowed to remove all negativity from his life – the cannabis, the smoking, the excess drinking, and expletives in his presence.

Once Jacob arrived, Ryan's twinges of doubt about converting to Judaism evaporated. During the time he had been with Sadie embracing her Jewish lifestyle, he had developed an even greater admiration for it, benefitting from its spirituality and warmth. It was decided – this was the religion he wanted for his son.

The preparation for Ryan's conversion took over a year. This entailed studying Jewish beliefs, rituals and practices; observing the Torah commandments; learning some Hebrew; and living as full a Jewish life as possible. The final commitments of circumcision, immersion in a mikveh (ritual bath) and appearing before a Bet Din (Jewish court) for their approval had finally taken place.

Ryan's sense of pride in his achievement and the love for his new family was palpable, as it was for Sadie. Displayed prominently on their bookshelves was an assortment of family photographs. One depicted Grandma Hannah and Nana Trish at Ryan's conversion ceremony, smiling broadly as they each held one of baby Jacob's hands. A larger family photo, taken in Naples, depicted Sadie and Ryan tenderly embracing baby Jacob. Behind them stood Fabio, Silvana, Giulia and newlyweds Roberto and Trish gazing lovingly into each other's eyes.

By Trish's own admission, she had always been a sucker for handsome Italian men.

Dear Reader,

I hope you enjoyed reading *A Glimmer Through the Breach* as much as I enjoyed writing it. If so, I hope you'll consider giving a quick review at Amazon or the retailer where you purchased it.

Thank you and happy reading!

JULIET AYRES

ACKNOWLEDGEMENTS

Writing *A Glimmer Through the Breach* has been a labour of love and I wish to thank the following for their contributions in bringing it to fruition.

Heartfelt thanks to my husband for his invaluable comments and suggestions in response to reading my numerous drafts; for assisting with the cover; and for his unwavering patience and encouragement.

Huge thanks to Ram and Martin for their much-appreciated constructive feedback in response to reading an early draft.

Many thanks to Val and to Louise for their helpful comments after reading a later draft.

Thanks to Meghan for assistance with title suggestions and to family and friends for helping me decide (finally!) on the one.

Grateful thanks also to Rabbi C for checking over all things Jewish. As for all things Catholic, I thank my personal memories.

Last, but by no means least, sincere thanks to my readers for taking the time to read this book.

ABOUT THE AUTHOR

Juliet Ayres is an author of contemporary adult fiction. Before penning her first work in 2018 with novelette *Caught on the Web,* she had been an English tutor for over twenty years. After graduating with a PGCE, she taught Basic Literacy in Further & Adult Education and continues to tutor English privately.

Daughter of an Italian mother and English father, Ms Ayres was born and bred in Manchester, UK where she continues to live with her husband and Burmese cat within close proximately to her three adult children, one of whom has Down's syndrome.

Printed in Great Britain
by Amazon

26436517R00185